A Meadowlark Calling

By
Patricia Martin

Copyright © 2003 by Patricia G. Martin

ISBN 0-7414-1242-X

First Published as an Original Paperback, 1981

Second Revised Edition
Published by:
INFINITY
PUBLISHING.COM

519 West Lancaster Avenue
Haverford, PA 19041-1413
Info@buybooksontheweb.com
www.buybooksontheweb.com
Toll-free (877) BUY BOOK
Local Phone (610) 520-2500
Fax (610) 519-0261

Printed in the United States of America

Printed on Recycled Paper

Published March, 2003

Dedicated to the one who lived it –

Mary Streifus Hamilton

1877 - 1968

Chapter 1

The train rolled westward with the steady drone of steel upon steel. For the first few hours Amber did nothing but watch the Ohio countryside flash past the window. The rolling, wooded hills were fresh with renewed life, and her senses delighted in the strange new sights. A whole new world unfolded before her eyes – a world she had only heard about, for all of her ten years had been spent in the town of Massilon, until now. Until the accident. She sighed, determined to enjoy this new experience and to forget the circumstances which had brought it about. "After all, I'm going out West!" she said to herself, the words creating a certain excitement within her. "Out West! Out West! Out West!" she repeated in rhythm with the clack-clack, clack-clack, clack-clack of the train wheels. Still, it was strange. Here was a train, taking her to a new life in a place called Kansas, and it had been a train which had taken her Papa's life.

Like a bad dream, the effects of which still lingered, the somberness of that awful day of the funeral still haunted her. Maybe it was the rain which had made things so dreary. Viewed through her tears and the misting rain, the funeral would be etched in Amber's memory forever as a blur of black – black horses pulling a black hearse, the black coffin, the big, black umbrellas under which huddled the small crowd of shivering mourners. Amber had not been able to bring herself to look at the wooden coffin, shiny and wet with rain, nor to think of the still form within. She must remember Papa as he had been – his gentle nature, his faith in God, his acceptance of the hardships of life. This was the legacy he had left – riches of the spirit, not riches of the world.

"You can be very proud of your Papa," Mama told Amber and her five little brothers and sisters after the accident. "A flat-car broke loose and one of Papa's fellow workmen on the section gang was about to be run over. Papa pushed him out of the way. He died to save another man's life," she said, then paused to contemplate the words, drawing from them the desperately needed consolation that there was a reason behind her loss.

Like the seasons, life, Amber knew, was continually ending and beginning again. She glanced up at her Uncle John and his new bride, Grizelda, who shared the seat facing her. Man and wife, they would start their life together on a Kansas homestead. The newlyweds were engrossed in each other just then, and Amber took the opportunity to study her new guardians.

Aunt Grizelda sat very erect, her corset tightly cinched to define a tiny waist and high bosom. Maybe that's why she never smiles, Amber thought. I'm glad I don't have to wear one of those things! The yards and yards of dark green velvet in Grizelda's dress modestly covered her from chin to ankle, and the long, fitted sleeves left only her slender hands exposed. She had dark eyes and handsome features, but her black hair was parted down the middle and drawn into a bun at the back of her neck, making her look much too severe. Amber tried to imagine her hair hanging softly about her shoulders and decided it would be a great improvement.

The fragrance of gardenia perfume surrounded Grizelda, heavy and sickeningly sweet. The aroma made Amber remember the first day she had met her, the day of Papa's funeral. "Uncle John has come back to claim his bride," Mama had said, and later with tears in her eyes she told Amber, "John and Grizelda have offered to take you to Kansas with them. With Papa gone, it's going to be hard for all of us...so very hard. At least you won't go hungry there. You know how it breaks my heart to send you off to school with no lunch half the time. Perhaps, if things get better here, I can send for you. Just remember what your Papa always said, 'You can do anything you set your mind to.' "

The memory of her mother brought a lump to Amber's throat and she felt hot tears sting her eyes. She turned abruptly towards the train window, blinked away the tears and studied her reflection in the glass. Before she'd left home, Mama had dressed her in her Sunday best, a dark blue Mother Hubbard, and then brushed and brushed her long brown hair for her, taking more time than usual, at last pulling it back on the sides and fastening it with a single clip in back. Then she turned Amber around, looked deeply into her eyes and hugged her close for a long time, perhaps wondering to herself if it might be for the last time. Amber would cherish the poignancy of that moment forever, aware even now that Aunt Grizelda could never take the place of her mother.

Amber wondered why a woman like Grizelda, who was obviously used to a life of comfort, would give up everything she had known and follow her man to an uncertain future out West. Probably the same thing that had prompted her Papa to trail her Mama halfway around the world, when she had come to America with her family years ago. Amber had always loved to hear Papa tell that story.

But, she couldn't see why Uncle John would choose someone like Grizelda to be his wife – she was so different from him! He was such a jovial, good-natured fellow. Even his eyes showed his good nature, for little wrinkles at the corners lent him an appearance of perpetual gaiety. Amber had always been intrigued with his eyes. They were a deep blue, with pinpoints of other colors dotting the irises. Too pretty for a man to have, she thought. He probably didn't even know how pretty they were. The thing he was proudest of was his mustache. Papa had been proud of his, too, she remembered. All men seemed to be, although for the life of her, Amber couldn't see why. Grownups were sure difficult to understand!

When she tired of staring out the window, Amber pulled a brown paper sack out from under the seat and opened it up. There wasn't much in it besides her other dress, but it was everything she owned. She rummaged around searching for her book. Instead, her fingers closed upon a small square box. She withdrew it slowly from the bag and opened it carefully. There, on a square of white cotton, lay a round brass medal suspended from a blue ribbon, inscribed with the words "First Prize." She had earned it for being the best speller in Miss Lewis's fourth grade class. Amber wished Papa could have shared this small triumph with her. He would have been so proud! Feeling a new flood of tears welling up inside her, she hastily closed the little box and slipped it back inside the sack.

She found her book and opened the cover. Inside was inscribed:

Amber Lockhardt
Her Book
Feb. 18, 1888

Amber sighed as she recalled the day she had penned these words in her very best hand. Could it really have been three whole months ago? "Tenth birthdays are special," Papa had said as he handed her the book and kissed her on the forehead. Amber knew how hard money was to come by, so she didn't care if the book was old and worn with use. It was a gift from Papa, the only book she had ever owned. She would treasure it forever.

Thoughtfully she studied the title page. *Introduction to the English Reader: or, A Selection of Pieces, In Prose and Poetry; Calculated to Improve the Younger Classes of Learners in*

Reading and To Imbue Their Minds With the Love of Virtue. Amber wasn't sure what all that meant, but she liked the stories the book contained.

Through habit, she turned to her favorite tale which was entitled simply, "The Horse." Accompanying it was a picture of an Arab astride his fiery white stallion. Many were the times Amber had studied that exciting picture and dreamed of such a horse. She had memorized every detail – the delicate head with its flashing eyes and flared nostrils, the proudly arched neck, the slender legs, the flowing mane and tail. It symbolized for her all that was beautiful and proud and strong.

Noticing her entranced interest in the picture, Uncle John leaned forward and looked at it, nodding his mutual appreciation. He sat back, gazed at Amber for a moment, then said, "You like horses, don't you?"

Amber looked up at him. "Oh, yes!" she replied. "I just love horses. I always wished that Papa had one, but. . ."

"Well, all I have now is a team of work horses, but if we ever get a little bit ahead, maybe you can have a riding horse. Would you like that?"

Amber's brown eyes widened. "Oh, yes, Uncle John! I really would!"

"The idea!" Aunt Grizelda broke in. "Young ladies are supposed to be interested in homemaking. Horses are for men and boys!"

"That's all right," replied Uncle John with a smile. "There's plenty of time for that. Right now she can be interested in both. We'll just have to see how things work out." Then he slapped his knee and asked, "How about some lunch?"

While Aunt Grizelda pulled the basket of food from beneath the seat, Amber leaned back and stared out the window, her mind whirling with new thoughts. A real horse of her own! Maybe Kansas wouldn't be so bad after all, she decided, little suspecting the trials and heartaches that lay ahead.

After the initial excitement wore off, the trip became monotonous and tiring. Only the scenery changed. The wooded hills gradually fell off behind them, giving way to green undulating prairies, traversed by wandering streams, which swept westward all the way to the Mississippi. Amber heard the whistle blow as they crossed the river late the second day, the sound floating back to her on streams of black smoke. The setting sun turned the surface of the water into a burnished sheet of gold, and on it she watched the distorted reflection of the moving train.

Farther on, the rolling prairie was broken occasionally by low rounded hills, but as they neared their destination, the land stretched before them perfectly flat and treeless.

On the afternoon of the third day, with the screech of brakes and the hiss of steam, the train pulled into Great Bend. "Is this Kansas?" asked Amber, unable to conceal her disappointment.

"This is Kansas!" replied Uncle John.

As the trio stepped down, they were met by a huge whirlwind of dust which swirled the length of the platform, snatching hats and billowing skirts. "That," said Uncle John, "was a dust devil! You'll have to get used to them here."

Amber cleared the dust from her eyes, and as soon as Aunt Grizelda was looking the other way, she spat to get rid of the grit in her mouth. Uncle John caught her out of the corner of his eye, but he only winked and said nothing. He left them then, with Grizelda's trunks stacked on the station platform, and hurried off to get the team and wagon he had left at the livery stable.

As she stood in the hot sun, Amber surveyed her new surroundings. The depot was bustling with noisy activity, a reenactment of the scene they had witnessed in the dozens of towns they had passed through in the last three days. She saw people of every description hurrying here and there with assorted bags and baggage. Everyone, it seemed, was headed West, and the fastest way to get there was by train. She was relieved when at last she spied Uncle John making his way through the crowd with his wagon.

"Sorry this isn't a fancy buggy for you ladies," he said as he drew up beside them, "but out here a lumber wagon is much more practical." Bowing with mock gallantry, he helped them aboard, Amber in back with the baggage, and Grizelda on the seat beside him. Then he clucked to his team of big bay horses and headed them out of town.

"How far is it to your farm?" asked Amber.

"About fifteen miles," Uncle John replied. "It'll take us about three hours."

"Don't we have to watch out for wild Indians?"

"No," chuckled Uncle John, "there haven't been any Indians around this part for a long time. Leastways not any *wild* Indians. There used to be lots of them though, before the white man came. The ones that are left are mostly all on reservations, where they won't bother anybody."

"Why is Kansas so flat? And why aren't there any trees?" Amber wanted to know.

"Well now, I don't know why it's so flat – only God could answer that! But they say the reason there aren't any trees is because of the buffalo. Millions of them used to roam over these plains, and they ate the little green shoots before they could grow into big trees."

Amber found it difficult to imagine millions of buffalo when all she was used to was one old milk cow.

There were no roads once they were out of town, and no fences, so Uncle John headed cross-country. "As the crow flies," he called it. Amber wondered how he could possibly find his way. Most of the time there was nothing to be seen in any direction except the waving grass and the cloudless sky. Now she knew why her uncle often referred to the plains as the "big sky country." The blue dome above them, stretching unhindered from horizon to horizon, was overpowering in its dominance of the flat landscape. Only occasionally did they pass within sight of a homestead, which was always surrounded by a grove of young trees, like a tiny island of security in a vast and lonely sea of grass.

The gusty winds seemed to be trying to push them faster, ever faster, but the horses would not be hurried. They plodded on at a steady pace, their hooves thudding almost soundlessly upon the prairie sod.

Amber could still feel the swaying sensation of the train within her head, and the sight of the tall grass blowing and rippling in the wind made her dizzy. She jumped down from the wagon to walk for awhile. Not used to idleness, her muscles were cramped from the long train trip, and it felt good to be able to exercise them. With her long hair tossing in the wind, she skipped here and there, picking the wildflowers that dotted their route. Every so often she would flush a quail or meadowlark from its grassy hiding place. It would rise into the air, struggling against the force of the wind, and failing, would glide with it instead.

"Don't step on any rattlesnakes!" Uncle John called back to her. The wind quickly snatched the words from his mouth and threw them at her with alarming impact.

Rattlesnakes! She remembered reading a story of a man who was bitten by a rattlesnake and died a horrible death. "I think I'll ride awhile," she said as she climbed onto the tailgate of the wagon. "I am getting kind of tired." She felt relieved to pull her feet off the ground. She sat there studying the bouquet she had gathered but didn't recognize any except the golden yellow sunflower which Uncle

John had pointed out to her earlier from the train. She would ask him about the others when they arrived at the farm.

But to Amber's dismay, the flowers were badly wilted long before Uncle John called back to tell her they were almost there. Shielding her eyes from the setting sun, she looked ahead and saw a windmill and several buildings outlined against the sky. They seemed terribly bleak and lonely, for there was nothing else to be seen in any direction.

As they drew nearer, signs of life became more evident. There were crops coming up in the fields, and row upon row of young cottonwood trees were planted around the house, with many more to the west. Pigeons had already taken up residence in the barn, and a flock of White Leghorns strutted about the chicken yard. Above all, the windmill was turning frantically in the strong breeze.

"My cattle and hogs, what few I have, are over at the Mitchells'," explained Uncle John. "That's the farm I pointed out to you over yonder." He gestured to the northeast. "They looked after things for me while I was gone. They're real fine folks. Don't know what I'd have done without 'em! You can go over with me tomorrow and get acquainted."

"Do they have any children?" asked Amber hopefully.

"Six," replied Uncle John. "Four boys and two girls." He pulled the team up at the back porch of the little house. The two horses heaved weary sighs and stretched their necks to slacken the reins. "Well, here we are." Uncle John jumped down from the wagon and reached up with both hands. "May I help you down, Mrs. Hagen?" he said to his new bride, with a twinkle in his eye. He lifted her lightly to the ground. "As you can see, the house isn't very big, but with no trees around, lumber's expensive. There's just the kitchen and one bedroom. I figured we could always build on later if we need to."

Amber was glad to see that it wasn't a soddy, the sort of house so many of the other homesteaders lived in. Uncle John had told them stories of how the soddies harbored mice and insects in their dirt walls and even collapsed sometimes during hard thunderstorms. At least they didn't have that to worry about!

"Take your things up to the attic, Amber," Uncle John told her. "You can sleep there. There's no bed, 'cause I didn't know you were coming back with us, but I'll build you one tomorrow."

Amber jumped down from the wagon. She could feel fatigue stealing over her and she was glad they had reached the end of their long journey. Well, she told herself, you're home. But the ache in her heart said she was not.

Chapter 2

The relentless wind tore at the pages of Amber's book. *Like other birds, the meadowlark claims its territory with a song. So remember, whenever you hear a meadowlark calling, it is a song of joy, a sign of belonging.* It was no use trying to read. Sick at heart and blinded by tears, she gave up and put the book on the ground beside her. She lay on the thick buffalo grass and buried her face in the crook of one arm. Once again, as it had done so often in the past weeks, homesickness swept over her in never-ending waves, engulfing her in misery.

"Oh, Mama! Oh, Papa! I miss you so much," she cried. "Why did I have to come out here? I hate this lonely, awful place! I hate herding these cows! Uncle John has no time for me, and Aunt Grizelda hates me. Oh, Papa! Why did you have to die?" For a long time her frail body shook with bitter sobs.

After a while, she rolled over onto her back and stretched out on the grass, wiping away the tears which still clung to her dark lashes. As if to mock her, the melodious call of a meadowlark sounded above the wind. "You may belong here, but I don't!" she yelled at it. Startled, the bird darted into the sky with a flash of yellow breast feathers.

She lay for a long time, watching the fluffy white clouds being whisked across the Kansas sky. Why does the wind always blow here? she wondered. It's never still. I wonder where it comes from and where it's going? I guess God knows. Maybe He knows where I'm going, too. She sighed with resignation and squinted into the depths of the blue sky. Papa was up there – somewhere – in heaven with God. She remembered, when she was tiny, asking Papa what God looked like, and he had answered simply, "God is love. What does love look like?" Then he had taken her upon his lap and told her, "I like to think of God as a huge, shining mirror, reflecting love, and beauty, and goodness. And we are each like a tiny piece of that mirror that God broke off and sent into the world. If our lives reflect God's love and purity, we'll return to Him someday and once again be a part of Him." It was wise and yet so simple, his way of explaining things. Papa was good at that.

Suddenly Amber remembered the cattle. "Oh, no!" she exclaimed, when she saw how far they had wandered. She jumped up, dashed after the way-ward animals and herded them back to graze on the unfenced pasture land where they belonged.

She returned to her place at the edge of an old buffalo wallow, determined to watch the cows more closely. If she let them get into the corn field, she'd really be in for it! And she sure didn't need to get in trouble again! It seemed as though she'd been in trouble ever since she got here. She let out a long ragged breath. Even though she tried her best, she just couldn't seem to do anything to please Aunt Grizelda. Why was she so hard to get along with?

Only yesterday Aunt Grizelda had whipped her with the leather quirt again, this time for climbing after young pigeons in the rafters of the barn. Before that, it had been for helping Uncle John deliver a new calf. And another time, she had tried to grab a runaway piglet around the neck and been dragged through the mud. Amber didn't see anything wrong in those things, and apparently neither did Uncle John. He would just laugh and shake his head. But it was not Aunt Grizelda's nature to take things so lightly. Each time, Amber had been rebuked for her impulsiveness and given a long lecture on how to act more lady-like. The leather quirt which hung on the wall behind the cookstove was a constant reminder of the punishment which awaited her for any infraction of the rules.

As the summer passed, Amber's homesickness, as well as her bitterness, faded. She came to the conclusion that she must accept her situation, so she set her mind to making the best of it. In time, she would even come to love the unique character and beauty of the prairie, with its ever-changing moods and eternal winds. Alone herding the cattle, she could give full rein to her imagination, which was as vast and limitless as the prairie itself. Through her half-closed eyes, the bounding brown tumbleweeds became herds of stampeding buffalo galloping wildly over the plain; the prairie dogs appeared as stout little castle guards, protecting the ramparts of their homes, all the while barking endless orders to unseen subordinates within; the dust devils were ghosts which stole silently across the land, through fences or over gullies, vanishing as suddenly and mysteriously as the wind itself.

Besides herding the cattle, Amber helped wherever else she was needed, often working side by side with Uncle John and Aunt Grizelda. There were new fields to plow and plant, fences to build, and cottonwood trees to be started and nurtured along from slips. Toiling from sunup to sundown, Grizelda no longer smelled of gardenias; now the odor of sweat accompanied her, and her once-soft hands were stained and calloused by the hard, dirty work. Before long, she began to complain of not feeling well, and her enlarging waistline soon told Amber the reason.

Little Kris was born in February of 1889, just a week after Amber's eleventh birthday. He was followed in rapid succession by Lucy in November of the same year, and then by Hilda the following August. Although this meant added work and responsibility for Amber, she welcomed the arrival of each little cousin, for they helped ease her lonliness for her own brothers and sisters.

She also hoped Aunt Grizelda's disposition might be improved with children of her own, but she discovered that the strain of pregnancy and motherhood, along with the hardships of homesteading on the windblown prairie, only made matters worse. Aunt Grizelda became increasingly irritable and short-tempered, creating an atmosphere so unlike the warmth and love Amber had always known. Although here she never went hungry, Amber wondered if perhaps love was not more important, the kind of love Mama and Papa had shared.

She often tried to picture her mother as she remembered her, but the image always became blurred with Aunt Grizelda's harsh features. Many times she would experience a nostalgic longing to feel the soft touch of her mother's loving hands, instead of the angry blows received from Aunt Grizelda's whip. And she longed to hear her mother's sweet voice, instead of the shrill insults and incriminations hurled her way, which flew like knives through the air, finding their mark in her heart.

In October of 1890, Indian summer was upon the land, as nature took one last fling before the suspended animation of winter. The young cotton-wood trees surrounded the house like burning torches, and the inflamed willow bushes along the Arkansas now edged the river with gold. Other evidence of the transition of seasons showed more subtly on the barren prairie. It was noticeable in the fuzzy, velvety look of the animals' coats as they initiated new growth, in the purple haze in the distance, in the sharp, crisp tang of the air.

Amber stood looking out the back door of the house, savoring the coolness of the morning air, which contrasted sharply with the cookstove's warmth filling the room behind her. If only I had a horse, she thought, I'd gallop off across that prairie and never come back!

"See that you take good care of Kris and Lucy while we're gone," Grizelda told her as she went about making last minute preparations for a trip to town after supplies. "And don't forget all the things I told you to do."

Amber was still watching out the door, lost in thought.

"Are you listening to me?" snapped Grizelda.

"Yes," answered Amber, whirling around to face her aunt. "I heard everything you said." She began counting each item off on her fingers. "Churn the butter, bake the bread as soon as it rises, clean and fill the lamps and trim the wicks, rip those flour sacks apart at the seams and wash them."

"And don't forget to keep the fire going in the smokehouse. One more day and that meat should be finished curing." Aunt Grizelda began wrapping little Hilda in a blanket. "And for heaven sakes, don't put cow chips on the smokehouse fire this time!"

"I won't," replied Amber, trying to keep her exasperation from showing. She guessed Aunt Grizelda would never let her forget the greenhorn mistake she had made that first fall. They had used "prairie coal," as it was called, as fuel for cooking, washing clothes, and making soap; it had never occurred to her that it was not acceptable for smoking meat.

"Are you ready, 'Zelda?" John called from the farmyard. "We need to get going. I told Josh we'd pick them up by eight."

Amber followed her aunt outside as Grizelda rattled off several more instructions. Uncle John then helped her onto the wagon seat. Amber watched the trio start out for the Mitchell farm, Uncle John walking alongside the horse until their neighbor's animal could be added. Sharing horses and wagons for trips into town was another one of the ways neighbors helped each other in this lonely country.

"Maybe there'll be a letter in town from your mother," Uncle John called back to Amber.

"I hope so," she answered. "I wrote her not long ago." She stood on the porch holding little Lucy on one hip, while Kris hung onto her skirts and wailed loudly after his departing parents. As she watched the creaking wagon roll across that vast expanse of treeless country, a feeling of loneliness and despair descended upon her, more intense than any she had experienced since those first miserable weeks.

As usual when she felt depressed, her thoughts instinctively turned to her family back in Ohio. Always smoldering within her was the same hope that someday she would return to them. But so far Mama's letters didn't sound too optimistic. Taking in washing barely provided her with enough to keep the small family together.

Amber wondered if Mama would even know her now. No longer was she the frail little waif who had left Ohio more than two years before. Encouraged by the hard work, regular meals, fresh air and sunshine, her lithe young body had filled out and she looked, as well as felt, strong and healthy.

Disturbed by Kris's crying, Lucy squirmed and began to cry also, bringing Amber's attention quickly back to the present. It was time for the baby's morning nap, so Amber carried her inside, took a dry flour-sack diaper off the line behind the stove, and changed her. After laying Lucy in her cradle, she quietly closed the bedroom door, leaving her to fuss a bit, as usual, before she drifted off to sleep.

She hung up the wet diaper to dry, glad to see that little Kris had already forgotten his troubles and was playing happily on the floor. Strange, she thought, that two children should be so different. Kris was a cute, chubby little tow-head, who luckily had inherited his father's good nature. But Lucy's cranky, unpleasant disposition made caring for her a trial. It bothered Amber that the baby never seemed happy or satisfied. She wondered if Lucy would ever be content with life.

Amber busied herself all morning with the various chores Aunt Grizelda had specified. By dinner time she found that her spirits had lightened, and she set about preparing something for the three of them to eat. Lucy was already crying for her food, so Amber set her in the wooden high chair Uncle John had made, tied up some bread and sugar in a clean rag, dipped it in milk and gave it to the baby to suck. Then she made a small fire in the cookstove, cut up some potatoes and made soup, stirring in an egg at the last moment the way Aunt Grizelda always did.

After they had eaten and Amber had put the two children down for their afternoon nap, she slipped quietly out of the house. She crossed the farmyard to check the smokehouse and then walked to the corral. The big workhorse, Archie, was dozing peacefully in the warm afternoon sun with one back hoof resting on its toe, lazily swishing his tail at several flies, the last of summer's buzzing horde.

"Hi fella," Amber said to Archie, as she patted his velvety brown neck through the board fence, relishing his warm, horsey smell and the softness of his coat. Archie opened one eye, shifted his weight to the other hind foot, and resumed his nap.

Suddenly Amber got an idea. She walked into the barn and peered through the random shafts of sunlight which penetrated the cool, dim interior. She drank in the pungent aroma of hay and horses and stood for a moment listening to the murmuring chuckle of the pigeons in the loft while her eyes adjusted to the light.

Archie wasn't a riding horse, but he would do. Several times Amber had seen Uncle John jump on him and ride to and from the field where they were working. Once, he had even let her ride him back from the field. She thought she'd better not try it bareback, however. In one corner she found Uncle John's old saddle. It was dusty from disuse, for he had sold his riding horse when he bought the team to work the homestead.

She brushed it off and lugged it out to the corral. Archie eyed her warily, obviously displeased with this intrusion on his nap. Amber knotted a rope through his halter ring and tied him to the fence. Then, after much pushing and struggling, she finally settled the heavy saddle into position on his broad back, high above her. She pulled the cinch up as tight as she could and led the horse into the yard. After standing on the edge of the water trough to mount, she settled herself into the saddle and ordered, "Get up, Archie!" The big horse reluctantly plodded away from the corral.

How she wished she had a horse of her own! Then she could ride like this every day. But Uncle John had apparently forgotten his offer to get her one. Riding was more fun than anything! Yet, she could just imagine the scolding Aunt Grizelda would give her if she ever found out she was riding. And astride! Ladies never rode astride!

Amber knew she had to stay close because of the children, so after going a short way, she turned Archie around. Headed back toward the barn, he quickened his pace and Amber decided to let him run. She kicked him into a rough, lumbering lope, the long stirrups flopping uselessly below her feet. What a glorious feeling, riding along in the bright sunshine, her hair tossing in the wind behind her. "Oh, if I only had a horse of my own!" she shouted to the wind.

Suddenly she felt it! The saddle began to turn, and as she instinctively gripped tighter with her legs, Archie took it as a signal to run faster. Then, as the horse felt the saddle slip further around to his side, he panicked and started to buck. Amber clung desperately to the saddle, but the second jarring lurch loosened her hold and she felt herself hit the ground beneath Archie's pounding hooves with a terrible jolt. One anvil-like hoof hit her a sharp blow in the back as the big horse jumped over her. She lay there stunned, gasping for breath, but her concern for the horse brought her to her feet. She saw Archie standing quietly by the barn, his head turned quizzically to the saddle hanging under his belly. Amber stumbled up to him and, to her great relief, horse and saddle were both all right. Still shaking, she put Archie back into the corral and returned the saddle to the barn, wincing at the stabbing pain in her back.

She made her way to the house and, rather than climb the stairs to her own bed, she collapsed on the one downstairs, just as a wave of nausea swept over her. Her breath came in short, shallow puffs and cold sweat formed on her forehead. She could feel the nervous excitement coursing through her body until it made even her fingers tingle. She wondered vaguely if this was what it was like to die. In the cool, dim stillness of the bedroom the sensation gradually subsided and the queasiness in her stomach disappeared. Just about the time she decided she wasn't going to die after all, Kris awoke and crawled off the bed. His happy jabbering woke his baby sister and she began to cry.

Amber got up stiffly. When she picked Lucy up, the pain in her back was excruciating. "There, there now, don't cry," she said to the baby, ignoring the throbbing pain. It would be hard to conceal her injury from her aunt and uncle, but she knew what would happen if Aunt Grizelda ever found out about her escapade. It was not long before she heard the wagon rattle into the farmyard. Amber drew a deep breath and started out to greet them. "They must never find out," she told herself with determination.

Chapter 3

Amber watched as Uncle John's plow turned the sandy rich sod back over the potato eyes she had dropped into the last open furrow. Glancing up at the sound of hoofbeats, she said, "Someone's coming!"

Uncle John halted his team of oxen and followed her gaze across the windy prairie stretching flat and warm in the March sunshine. "Riding fast too," he said. "Must be trouble!" They both knew that no one would run his horse that hard without a good reason. He left the oxen and started walking to the edge of the plowed field. Amber followed, trying to match strides with her uncle over the rough furrows, her heart beating faster with excitement. Who could it be?

The horse and rider headed straight for them, and as the figures came closer, Uncle John stopped short and his worried expression changed to one of happy surprise. "It's Karl!" he exclaimed.

The big buckskin was pulled to a sliding stop in front of them and the rider jumped off, all in one smooth motion. The man, wearing a big hat, tight pants, and a fringed leather shirt, resembled John except that he was somewhat bigger and had a wiry bristle of rust-colored beard.

"Howdy, Brother!" he thundered, stretching out his hand to John.

John grabbed it in both of his and pumped it up and down vigorously. "Karl, you ol' rascal! By golly, it's good to see you again!" Their happy back-slapping thumped in Amber's ears as she stood first on one foot and then the other, wondering when Karl would notice her.

"I guess it has been a spell, hasn't it?" replied Karl.

"Almost four years!" exclaimed John, holding up four fingers for emphasis.

"Say, who's this pretty little gal?" asked Karl, turning to Amber and removing his battered, broad-brimmed hat.

"This is Amber," said Uncle John, putting his arm around her shoulders. "You remember, Catherine's oldest girl."

As Karl surveyed her from head to foot, Amber was captivated by her uncle's eyes. Warm and gray, they had Uncle John's same happy wrinkles at the corners.

"Well now, when I left Ohio, you weren't as big as a bug's ear! And look at you now – pretty as a picture! Takes after her Ma, don't she, John?" he said with a wink. "By the way, how are your folks?"

"Papa died three years ago," said Amber. She was surprised at how easy it was to talk about that now. "I've been living here with Uncle John ever since."

Karl paused a moment and looked down at the hat in his hands. "Well now, I'm right sorry to hear that. Your Pa was a good man. Yessir," he said quietly, "a good man."

"Say," said John, pulling out his pocket watch. "It's almost noon. I'll bet the wife has dinner ready. Come on, let's go eat! We're finished planting these potatoes anyhow. I can mulch them later." He went back and unhitched his team of oxen from the plow and started them toward the house.

Karl turned to Amber. "Little gal, how would you like to ride ol' Buck? He's been carryin' me for four hundred miles and he's probably tired o' me by now. I need to walk a spell anyhow."

Before she could answer, he lifted her lightly into the saddle, setting her on sideways. Then he laid the reins over his arm and the horse followed as he and John walked toward the house. Amber crooked her right knee over the saddle horn and tried to arrange her skirts over her bare feet. She loved Buck's sweaty horse smell mingled with the aroma of saddle leather, and she was intrigued by all the gear Uncle Karl carried.

An old army canteen hanging from the pommel was pressing against her left knee, and she could hear the water sloshing around inside. Inquisitively she ran her fingers over the braided rawhide rope coiled on the right side of the saddle, then felt the smooth, polished stock of the long rifle strapped under the right stirrup leather. Twisting around to look behind the saddle, she saw a bedroll neatly tied on top of a pair of bulging saddle bags. Uncle Karl sure didn't look like a Kansas dirt farmer!

"You've done a good job with the farms, John," Karl was saying. "Your wheat's comin' up real good, yessir, real good. And I see you've planted some more cottonwoods for me."

"Are you back to stay?" asked Uncle John hopefully.

"Well now, there's a lot of country I want to see yet and I ain't gettin' any younger," Karl answered, rubbing his stubby beard.

"But two farms are a lot for one man to take care of," replied John. "When are you going to come back to farm this timber claim of yours instead of just planting trees on it?"

"Well now, we can talk about that later. Tell me about you and your family and what's happened since I left you."

Amber listened as Uncle John quickly recounted his further efforts at homesteading, the death of Amber's father, and his marriage to Grizelda, ending with, "Wait 'til you see our three little ones. And we've got another one due in May."

As they neared the house, the big dog, Shep, started barking and Amber saw Aunt Grizelda step out the door to see who was there. Heavy with child, she walked awkwardly, wiping her hands on the flour-sack apron which hung from her neck. Little Kris and Lucy followed along behind, clinging shyly to her skirts.

"Grizelda, this is my brother Karl, the one who helped me start this homestead."

"Why hello!" she said with a warm smile. "I've heard a lot about you."

"Howdy, ma'am," said Karl, doffing his hat. "Well now, ain't you a pretty one! Ol' John did

28

right well for himself, I'd say. He didn't tell me he'd married the prettiest gal in Ohio! Yessir, nothin' like a pretty woman to make a man think twice about settlin' down, I'll tell you for sure!"

Grizelda was suddenly quite self-conscious of her bulbous figure, her bare feet, her hair stringing loose at the sides. Shuffling her feet back out of sight and attempting to smooth back her hair, she finally stammered, "Oh Karl, how you do go on!"

"And this is my boy, Kris, and our oldest little girl, Lucy," John said, nodding towards the little faces peering from behind their mother.

"And little Hilda is inside. She's the baby," added Grizelda.

"Well now, if this boy ain't a chip off the ol' block!" exclaimed Karl, grinning at Kris. "Quite a boy! Yessir, sure makes a man think twice about gettin' married and startin' a family of his own."

"Come on!" John broke in, slapping Karl on the back. "Let's get washed up so we can eat!"

After dinner Karl put his horse in the barn and brought his gear in. Amber showed him where to put it in the attic. She had given up her bed, with its straw-filled mattress, to Uncle Karl. This courtesy to her elder was expected of her, and she willingly obliged. Hoping to see what interesting things he carried with him, she lingered to watch him unpack his belongings and found herself fascinated when he unrolled his bedroll. "Is this a buffalo robe?" she asked, wide-eyed, stroking the dark shaggy fur.

"You bet your boots it is, little gal," replied her uncle. "Shot that critter myself when I first came out West. An Indian squaw tanned it for me. Same one that made me this here shirt." He paused for a moment and a far-away look came into his eyes. "Those were the days, let me tell you! Buffalo were everywhere on the plains, thick as hair on a dog's back! Now they're gone. All gone. And a whole way of life has gone with them." He shook his head sadly.

"I wish I could have seen them," Amber said wistfully. "It must have been terribly exciting."

"That it was, little gal, that it was." He continued unpacking. "But the West is gettin' civilized and tame these days. It's gettin' harder and harder to find the adventure we had in the old days." Karl abruptly changed his focus. "Bet you've never seen gold dust, have you?"

"Gold?" asked Amber. "Real gold?"

"Take a look at this." He tossed a small leather pouch onto the bed. Amber picked it up, carefully opened the drawstring and peered into the little bag.

"Here, let me show you," said Uncle Karl. He took it and poured a yellowish powder into the palm of one hand. "That, little gal, is real gold dust."

Amber was a bit disappointed. It wasn't as bright and golden as she had imagined.

"Yessir, I was all set to get rich quick, but it took me one whole summer in the Rocky Mountains to pan that little bit." He chuckled. "It ain't worth much, so I'm just sorta keepin' it for a souvenir."

He poured the gold dust back into the leather pouch and returned it to his saddle bags.

"You ready, Karl?" came Uncle John's voice from downstairs.

"Be right with you!" And then to Amber Uncle Karl said, "How would you like to use this here buffalo robe to sleep on tonight?"

"Oh yes!" exclaimed Amber. "Thank you!"

Then Karl and John were off to look over the farms, while Amber helped Aunt Grizelda prepare for the evening meal. It would have to be something special, so they killed and plucked a fat hen for stewing with noodles and dumplings and made a cobbler with dried apples. There would also be bread, warm from the oven, spread with freshly-churned butter.

Besides the good food, supper that evening was most enjoyable, with Uncle Karl's humorous slang and infectious laughter generating a warmth and easiness that reminded Amber of her home. Even the children, ordinarily shy with strangers, were put at ease and responded to his gentle teasing, giggling with happy embarrassment.

Uncle John finally voiced Amber's own thoughts. "Karl, I always said that with your gift of gab you could convince a rattlesnake it was downright lovable if you had a mind to." This evoked a guffaw from Karl that set them all to laughing.

Afterwards, Amber cleared the table while Grizelda took the children into the other room to prepare them for bed. The two men leaned their chairs back against the wall and relaxed. Uncle Karl produced a deer bone toothpick from his shirt pocket and casually began putting it to use.

"Where all have you been these past four years, Karl?" asked John, lighting up his pipe. Amber began to wash the dishes in the pan of hot water on the cookstove, being as quiet as she could so as not to miss a word.

"Oh, Colorado and Wyoming mostly. Beautiful country up that way. Yessir, beautiful country. You ought to see those Rocky Mountains! Why, they're so tall you can't see the tops of 'em for the clouds half the time. And the snow never melts on top, even in the summer! They're a beautiful sight, let me tell you. And gold! Why those mountains were just full of gold! Every time it rained the streams used to run yellow with the stuff, but most of it was gone by the time Wenz and Phil and me got there."

Amber could not even remember her uncles' other two brothers, Wenzel and Phil.

"But. . .where's there's gold and silver, there's people. That's why I left. . .too many folks. This whole country is gettin' too civilized to suit me," he went on. "Why, I used to be able to ride for days without comin' across a livin' soul, 'cept maybe an Indian now and then."

He turned to John. " 'Member how you and me used to shoot deer right from the door of our shack here? Bet you never even see deer around these parts any more, do you? That's because of people! Every place I go there's more and more of 'em! It's gettin' so's a man can't breathe free no more. That's

32

why I have a hankerin' to see Texas. They say there's lots of open country down there yet, and it's one place I've never been."

John said nothing, just puffed slowly and thoughtfully on his pipe.

Amber finished and hung the dish towel on the line behind the stove, then came over and sat on the floor near Uncle Karl. She pulled up her knees and rested her chin on them, her eyes riveted on her uncle in rapt attention. Aunt Grizelda quietly closed the door to the bedroom and joined them, bringing along her perpetual pile of mending. She sat down heavily. Resting her arms on her protruding abdomen, she began sewing as she listened to the men talk.

As Uncle Karl narrated tales of his various exploits, Amber felt the same elation she experienced when she read the adventure stories in her book. This was life, full and exciting! But at the same time, she was aware of a feeling of frustration because it was life as she herself would never know it.

"I was sure hoping you'd stay for good this time," John was saying. He took several slow deliberate puffs on his pipe. "I've got big plans for the farms, but I need your help to carry them out."

Grizelda spoke up. "I agree, Karl. You really ought to find yourself a wife and settle down on this claim of yours. I know a widow at church. . ."

"Well now, 'Zelda, I've always had itchy feet. You don't know how hard it was for me to stay here and prove up on my place for those two years.

There's just too much I want to see and do before I get tied down on one piece of ground." He paused and Amber saw him throw John a quick wink before continuing. "When I do decide to settle down, I might bring me back a squaw. I hear they make good wives – wait on you hand and foot and never give you no back talk neither."

Aunt Grizelda sat bolt upright in her chair, a startled expression on her face. "Karl, you wouldn't! I mean, not an Indian squaw for heaven sakes!"

"Well now, some of my best friends are Indians," he said with obvious sincerity. "I'd trust them a lot farther than some white men I know, too." He grew sober and reflected a moment. "Yessir, they were a proud, dignified, independent people. And if they are somethin' else now, it's because of us. And that's nothin' to be proud of on our part, let me tell you.

"I was just joshin' you about the squaw though. They do make good wives on the frontier, but they wouldn't be content on a Kansas farm – not enough work to do!" He watched for Grizelda's reaction out of the corner of his eye and, slapping his leg, laughed loudly when she rose to the bait and started to take issue with him.

Uncle John laughed too. He seemed to know when Karl was kidding, but Aunt Grizelda sure didn't. She had never come across anyone quite like this brother-in-law, and she didn't know just how to take him. She obviously did not like being the butt of a joke, however slight. In an effort to divert the attention focused on her for the moment, she looked down at Amber and snapped, "It's your bedtime, Amber!"

"Yes, ma'am," Amber answered dejectedly. "Good night."

"Good night, little gal. See you in the mornin'," answered Uncle Karl.

She climbed the stairs to the attic and found the buffalo robe spread on the floor for her behind the curtain Aunt Grizelda had hung. She lay down on the hide and absently stroked the soft, dense fur. Sleep was the furthest thing from her mind.

"How long do you plan to stay with us?" she heard Uncle John ask Karl.

"Well now, I reckon I'll be movin' on come mornin'. Time's awastin', and I'm not gettin' any younger! And the way I figure, the sooner I get gone, the sooner I'll be back, once I see what all Texas has to offer. Might go through Oklahoma Territory, too, and look up Wenzel and Phil. When we split up in Colorado, they were headed down that way to try for some of that free Indian land they're givin' away down there."

Amber lay awake listening to the drone of voices which were punctuated frequently by Uncle Karl's booming laughter. Why did he have to leave so soon? She found herself quite drawn to this carefree, bewhiskered gent with the same laughing eyes as her Uncle John, and she was eager to talk with him more about his many adventures. Here was someone she felt she could confide in and who would understand. Would he really come back and take up farming, as he said? Somehow she just couldn't picture Uncle Karl behind a plow!

Before long, she heard Uncle Karl say, "There's one favor I'd like to ask of you folks. Do you mind if I take a bath tonight? It's one of the niceties of life I don't get around to very often, travelin' like I do, and it's been a spell."

"Sure," replied Uncle John, and Amber heard him take the wash tub from off its peg out on the porch.

"You folks just get on to bed now and I'll manage the rest myself," said Karl.

Amber could hear him puttering around then, heating the water on the old four-hole stove and pouring it into the tub. It took him longer to prepare than it did for bathing, and she soon heard him emptying the water outside. Then he blew out the coal oil lamp, and she could hear him feel his way quietly up the stairs and lie down on the bed. The only sound then was the wind and the steady rasp of Uncle John's snoring from down below.

"Uncle Karl?" Amber spoke softly through the curtain that separated them.

"You still awake, little gal? You should'a been asleep a long time ago," he said in a croaking whisper.

"Uncle Karl, take me with you!"

There was a short pause as Karl weighed the sincerity of Amber's request. But there was no mistaking her earnestness, even in the dark. "Can't be did, little gal, just can't be did," he said at last. "If you were a boy, it'd be different, but you ain't, and my kind of life is no good for a girl. Heck, your Ma would wring my neck if I was to take you away from here. She wants you to grow up to be a fine lady, with manners, and pretty clothes, and beaus comin' courtin' – not a good-for-nothin' rover like me."

"But I don't care about any of those things, really I don't," Amber pleaded. "There's nothing exciting about that kind of life. I'd lots rather do the sort of things you do."

"Well now, there's lots of things about the way I live that ain't no fun. Never knowin' where your next meal will come from, sleepin' out in all kinds of weather, ridin' for days at a time. It's not all excitin', I'll tell you for sure."

"I wouldn't mind any of that! It sure couldn't be as bad as staying here. And I just love horses – I know I'd never get tired of riding. When we first came out here Uncle John told me he might buy me a horse someday, but he never has. I guess he's forgotten all about it by now," Amber said, disappointment evident in her voice. Then she decided to tell Uncle Karl about her wild ride on Archie that fall day six months ago. "But that doesn't mean I can't ride!" she hastened to add, when she had finished. "I'd have done fine if that saddle hadn't turned."

"Well now, I'm sure you would have," responded Uncle Karl kindly. "Ol' Archie blew up on you, that's what he did."

"What do you mean?"

"He sucked in air and made his belly bigger as you were cinching him up. Then when he let the air out, the cinch wasn't tight."

"So that's it! I just knew I had it tight. I'm going to remember that."

"I'll bet you will! You're a spunky little gal, and I'd like to take you with me, but I hope you understand why I can't. I'm sorry."

Amber heaved a heavy sigh. Of course Uncle Karl was right, but she had hoped there was some way. Soon Uncle Karl was snoring peacefully. But Amber slept fitfully, her head filled with a mad melee of stampeding buffalo, wild Indians, and galloping horses.

Chapter 4

The rooster crowed and the sun cast its first golden rays over the wooden shingles on the little house as Uncle Karl led the big buckskin up to the porch. "Just smell that sagebrush!" he exclaimed, as he tied his saddle bags back on his saddle. Amber then handed him the buffalo robe she had carefully rolled up. "Well now, I guess that's all," he said, after it was in place. He emphasized the point by slapping Buck on the rear with one hand, raising a small cloud of dust which was quickly swirled away by the wind. "Thanks for everything, John. Take good care of my claim for me."

John shook his hand and seemed reluctant to let it go. "Good luck, Karl. Don't stay away so long this time. And let us hear from you once in awhile, do you hear?"

"Glad to have met you, 'Zelda. Your cookin' was really a treat, let me tell you, after the grub I've been used to. Yessir, John's sure a lucky man!"

"Thank you, Karl. Come back and see us any time," said Grizelda, brushing the windblown strands of hair from her face.

Uncle Karl nodded toward the house. "Tell the little ones goodbye for me," he said.

"Say, if this new baby is a boy, we'll name him after you," offered John.

"I'd like that fine," replied Karl. He walked over to Amber and placed his hands on her shoulders. "Goodbye, little gal. You be good now. And one of these days a good lookin' feller will come along and sweep you right off your feet. You'll see." Seeing the tears starting to fill her eyes, he added, "Tell you what – I'll send you something from Texas when I get there. How would you like that?"

Amber tried hard to smile, but she just nodded her head.

"You best leave that Archie horse alone, too. You're no bronco-buster!" Karl said over his shoulder as he mounted Buck. " 'Bye now." He waved his hand and was gone in a dusty clatter of hoofbeats, never suspecting the repercussions of his innocent remark.

"Amber, what did you do, try to ride Archie?" her uncle asked quietly.

"Yes," she admitted hesitantly, "and I hurt my back . . ."

"So! Thought you could get away with it, did you?" interrupted Aunt Grizelda angrily. "I'll teach you!" She grabbed Amber's arm and pulled her roughly into the house. And once more Amber felt the lash of the all too familiar leather quirt.

The rest of the day was as miserable as its beginning. The baby had the colic and cried most of the time; Lucy was even more quarrelsome than usual; and besides getting into the fly paper, Kris pulled the bucket of drinking water off the shelf and doused himself twice. And as though mocking them all, the March wind howled around the corners of the house, blowing dirt inside and across the bare floors, honing everyone's nerves to a fine edge.

"Set the table for supper," ordered Aunt Grizelda.

Amber dutifully obeyed, thankful the day was almost over. Nothing had gone right. And to make things worse, she had cut the palm of her hand on a nail as she carried a small barrel of flour to the cellar. Aunt Grizelda had been in no mood to offer sympathy, but she did help her tie a clean rag around the wound. What next? thought Amber, as she picked up the tin can of silverware to set on the table. All of a sudden, it slipped from her painfully awkward grasp and crashed to the floor, scattering the utensils in every direction.

Grizelda let out a shriek and flew at her in a rage. Amber felt herself fall backwards to the floor, and before she could get up, Grizelda kicked her viciously in the side. She was then jerked roughly to her feet. "Now pick those up and get that table set!" growled her aunt. "And don't you breathe a word of this to your uncle, or you'll be sorry!"

At that moment Amber felt determination begin to grow within her – she resolved that this would be the last time she'd be the victim of Aunt Grizelda's wrath.

Late that night, when she was sure her aunt and uncle were sound asleep, Amber crept down the stairs and quietly out the back door, her bare feet making no sound as she walked. She spoke softly to Shep, who was asleep on the porch, so he would recognize her and not sound an alarm. He started to follow, but she sent him back, commanding him to stay.

She stood in the darkened farmyard for a moment and gathered her shawl more closely around her shoulders with her good right hand. The cut on her left one was throbbing with pain. She took a deep breath and winced again at the pain in her ribs. Just bruised, she thought, as she gingerly fingered her side through her flimsy cotton dress. She turned to her left, walked past the granary, and headed south, in the same direction Uncle Karl had gone earlier that day. She wondered how far it was to Texas. Well, no matter. She would just keep walking 'til she got there. Once she found Uncle Karl, he would have to let her stay, for awhile at least. Maybe in that time she could convince him that she would be better off there with him. Anyplace but here!

There was a full moon in the velvety black sky, making the prairie silver and softly beautiful. The strong winds had died down to a breeze which carried the smell of the river, of the rich earth, and of wildflowers blooming amidst the prairie grasses. Amber felt a comforting oneness with nature, as though she was a part of it all – the earth, the sky, the moon and stars. She was reminded of something from her book: *Behold how rich and beautiful are the works of nature! What a beautiful provision is made for our wants and pleasures.*

As she walked, she could hear the mournful cry of a coyote and the sudden rustling of grass as night creatures scurried out of her way. The only things she feared were rattlesnakes, and a shudder ran the length of her spine at the thought of stepping barefooted on one of the horrible creatures. For once she wished she had some shoes on, but the only pair she owned were too small and hurt her feet, although Aunt Grizelda insisted she still wear them to church.

Suddenly she noticed a dark form on the horizon and a thrill of fear went through her. Then she realized it was just the grove of trees around the homestead of their nearest neighbor. She skirted it carefully, not wishing to excite the family's dog. She knew every homesteader had a dog, and sometimes two or three.

As the night wore on, Amber found it difficult to keep her bearings, and she was getting increaseingly tired and sleepy. Reluctantly, she decided to stop and rest before going farther. She lay down in the thick buffalo grass, pulled her shawl tightly around her, and was asleep before she knew it.

She awoke with a start to find the warm sun upon her and two small faces staring at her in amazement.

"Go get Pa!" said one boy, and the other darted off.

"No!" cried Amber. "Don't!" But it was too late.

"We thought you was dead," said the little boy, looking at her quizzically. "Are you lost?"

"No!" retorted Amber, angry with herself for falling asleep and allowing herself to be discovered. Why hadn't she seen that farm house so near?

A man in tattered overalls soon came puffing up, close on the heels of his young son. Amber stood up quickly and tried to appear as calm as possible. She must not let them know she had run away! She would have to bluff her way through.

"Are you lost, missy?" queried the man.

"Oh no, I'm not lost," she answered

"What's your name?" he asked.

"Amber. Amber Lockhardt," she said. Surely he wouldn't connect that name with John Hagen.

"Well, where you headed?"

"To Texas. My folks died and I'm going to live with an uncle there."

The farmer looked a bit incredulous at this, but he continued, "Well, it's a long ways to Texas and I'll just bet you haven't had breakfast. Why don't you come on to the house and let's see what we can find you to eat. No sense starting a long trip on an empty stomach." He took Amber by the arm and herded her in the direction of the house, unmindful of her attempted protests.

They were met at the door of the house by a large woman with a face as wrinkled and worn as the calico dress she wore. She was a pleasant, motherly sort, however, and Amber took an immediate liking to her. She somehow reminded Amber of her own mother, and she felt a sudden stirring of old memories.

"Sarah, this is Amber and she's on her way to Texas," said the man, giving his wife a knowing look. "How about finding her something for breakfast while I. . .uh. . .get back to my work."

"Sure now, and what would you like, missy? Scrambled eggs all right?" she asked kindly, escorting Amber inside.

"Yes, ma'am, anything will be fine." Amber sat down at the table and glanced about her. The little kitchen was neat and clean, with colorful pictures on the wall, and red-and-white-checked gingham curtains matching the tablecloth. There was an air of cheerfulness and hominess about it that put Amber at ease and almost caused her to forget her reason for being there. She couldn't help thinking how different things might have been had she lived here, rather than under the stern domination of Aunt Grizelda.

Sarah carried on a continuous conversation with her. as she prepared the meal, being overly careful not to pry, for which Amber was thankful. The talk was mostly idle chatter about one thing and another, as though the woman was grateful for someone to visit with. The aroma of the food cooking made Amber realize just how hungry she was, and she soon forgot everything except the plate of eggs and cold biscuits set before her.

Sarah poured herself a cup of tea and sat down opposite Amber, holding the delicate, white china cup between toil-roughened hands. Still maintaining a steady flow of talk, she paused only occasionally to study the young girl before her. "I never had no girls," she was saying. "Five children and all boys! How do you like that? You'd think I could've got a girl in there someplace, but the Good Lord didn't see fit to give me none, and it ain't for us to question Him now, is it?"

Amber looked up and smiled and nodded "yes" or "no" accordingly as the woman rambled on. When she broke open a biscuit, Sarah was quick to notice the injured hand.

"What on earth did you do to your hand, child?"

Amber dropped it back to her lap. "Oh, I cut it on a nail. It's not deep, but it sure does hurt."

"Of course it does," replied Sarah kindly, "and I've got just the thing for you." She hurried over to the cupboard and brought out an apothecary jar. "Here we are! These balsam leaves will take the soreness out and help heal your hand right up. As soon as you're finished eating, I'll wrap some over the cut for you. You could use a clean bandage on there anyhow."

Amber hated to take the time, for she felt a sense of urgency to be on her way, but she knew Sarah wouldn't take no for an answer. "All right," she agreed, and in no time her hand was doctored and freshly wrapped with a piece of soft pink flannel.

Sarah explained about the scrap of pink cloth. "I was really hopin' for a girl the last time, but. . ."

Amber was afraid she'd never get away if Sarah got to rambling on about her family again. "Thank you for everything," she said sincerely. "You've been so nice to me. But I really must be going now." Sarah did her best to delay her longer, but Amber gradually eased her way toward the door, thanked the woman again for her hospitality, and headed south across the prairie once more.

She hadn't gone but a few miles when she heard a wagon coming up behind her. Without looking around, she quickened her steps and pretended not to hear. It was almost upon her when she heard a familiar voice call out, "Amber!"

Her heart fell. She stopped but didn't turn around.

"Amber, come on. Let's go home," Uncle John said quietly.

Shoulders sagging and eyes downcast, she turned reluctantly and walked to the wagon. She climbed up and sat in silence as Uncle John turned the team in a wide circle and headed back. Neither said a word for quite awhile, although Uncle John glanced her way occasionally, as though expecting her to speak. Finally he broke the long silence, speaking quietly, with no evidence of anger in his tone. "Why did you do it, Amber? Why did you run away?"

Staring straight ahead, she replied flatly, "Because Aunt Grizelda hates me, that's why!"

"What makes you think that?" Uncle John asked with honest surprise.

"She whips me all the time. I can't do anything to please her."

"When she punishes you, it's because you did wrong, not because she hates you," her uncle replied.

Amber said nothing, so he continued. "I don't think you understand how it feels to be responsible for bringing up a child, especially someone else's child. Grizelda is taking the place of your mother. She and I are both responsible to her for the way you're brought up. If you need to be punished, you'll have to be punished. I've always left the discipline up to Grizelda and if she thinks it's necessary, that's all that matters.

Amber wanted to tell him about the many injustices she had suffered without his knowledge, but she was afraid of what Aunt Grizelda might do if she found out. Besides, she knew she couldn't expect him to see her side of it; after all, Grizelda was his wife.

Uncle John leaned against the back of the wagon seat and propped one foot up in front of him as the team plodded on. "This kind of life is hard on a woman, with all the wind, and the dirt, and the loneliness. Things were so much easier for 'Zelda back East. Maybe I never should have brought her out here," he said, staring out across the barren, wind-blown prairie, "but when you're in love, everything seems possible. Anyway, we're here and we've all got to make the best of it."

Amber had never heard him talk like this before, and she turned to look at him now. For the first time she was seeing him not as her uncle, but as a husband and father, struggling against the insecure-ities and responsibilities of the life he had chosen. She began to feel a sense of guilt and shame for her childish actions. "I'm sorry, Uncle John," she said, "for all the trouble I caused you, having to come after me and all."

"Well, just so it doesn't happen again." He paused and studied Amber for a moment, then looked away. "I guess you aren't very happy here. But I think you're better off than you would be back in Ohio. At least you're not working ten or twelve hours a day in some dingy factory. Lots of children your age do, you know. I know all about it – from experience. It's a rotten way to grow up." He paused. "If there was anything I could do to make you happier here with us, I would, but I don't know what it would be," he said, looking at Amber once more.

Suddenly Amber brightened, and she turned toward him as best she could on the narrow wagon seat. "Oh, Uncle John, if only I could have a horse of my own!" she pleaded. "That day on the train you said you might get me one, remember?"

"By golly, I did say that, didn't I? All right, I'll tell you what," he said, suddenly sitting erect. "If the wheat is good this year, and it looks like it will be, I'll get you a horse. But you'll have to promise me one thing – that you'll never, ever run away again."

"I promise," Amber said solemnly, shaking her head up and down.

"All right, it's a deal!"

Chapter 5

Amber awoke with a thrill of excitement. Already it was the end of June, and today they would begin the harvest. Every day for the past week, Uncle John had gone into the fields and picked one head of wheat, crushing it in the palm of his hand. On the day the grain fell free and the hulls blew away, he had announced it was ready. And for the first time, he had given Amber the responsibility of driving one of the two header boxes, a decision which irritated Aunt Grizelda.

As Amber lay there in the early morning darkness, she recalled the scene at the supper table the night before. "With four babies to look after, I want Amber here," Aunt Grizelda had said in a firm voice. "It's only been a month since little Karl was born and I still don't have my strength back. Besides, Amber's only a child!"

But Uncle John had replied just as firmly, "With all the other wives here to help fix the dinner, you'll have all the help you need. We're short-handed in the field this year, with Josh laid up, and I need Amber's help."

Grizelda's chair had grated roughly on the floor as she rose brusquely and began washing the dishes in the pan of heated water on the stove.

Uncle John had ignored her icy silence and relaxed in his chair, lighting his favorite pipe.

"Amber will do fine," he said then, as he thumbed through the pages of his well-worn *Farmer's Almanac*. "She can drive a team as good as any man. She'll do just fine."

Aunt Grizelda's opposition only gave Amber added determination to justify her uncle's faith in her. "I *will* do a good job, Uncle John," she had told him. At that moment she had been hit in the back of the head by the wet wash cloth Grizelda had thrown at her. "Get those kids washed and ready for bed," her aunt had commanded.

Now, at Uncle John's first call, Amber jumped out of bed, dressed hurriedly, grabbed her sun-bonnet, and rushed downstairs for breakfast.

"Perfect day for the harvest – just perfect!" exclaimed Uncle John, greeting the neighbors who had come to help. He beamed like a small boy as he scanned the cloudless sky. The neighbor men all agreed as they shook hands all around and began planning the day's work ahead.

Amber had always thought the golden fields of grain waving in the wind were a glorious sight, but they seemed even more so, now that her dream depended upon it. Ever since Uncle John had made his promise, she had daydreamed of racing the wind on a beautiful white horse, like the one in her book. Filled with a youngster's anticipation for a new experience, Amber was eager to get to work.

She found out that she was to drive the header box, pulled by Archie and Charley. A wagon with very tall sides, it was driven alongside the header, which a span of four horses pushed in front of them, to receive the wheat as it was cut. Uncle John stood in the back of her header box and quickly stacked the long stalks of wheat in neat bundles as they came to him. When the box was full, the second header box took its place while the grain from Amber's was stacked on the ground in rows to await the coming of the threshing crew later in the week.

By mid-morning, Amber found her initial enthusiasm wilted by the stifling heat, the annoying wheat bugs, and the fine layer of dust which settled over her, although she would rather have died than admit her discomfort to anyone. She was grimy, hot, and tired, but she did her part well and without complaint. The men responded by treating her as an equal and this pleased her. She was, after all, doing a man's work. That night she fell into bed, her whole body aching with weariness, and slept as she had never slept before.

The second day of the harvest dawned unusually still, and for an unexplained reason, Amber felt uneasy. Occasionally she squinted up at the cloudless sky as she worked, and she found herself wishing for the familiar cooling winds. The sun beat down unmercifully, and for once, she was glad Aunt Grizelda had insisted that she wear her hated sunbonnet. She was glad when one of the women came out from the house to tell them dinner was ready. The men called a halt, tended to the tired workhorses, and trudged to the house, wiping the dripping sweat from their faces as they walked. They took turns washing up at the well and then entered the kitchen, which was steaming from the combination of warmth from the cookstove and the heat of the day. Taking their tin plates of food, they all hastened back outside, seeking the meager shade afforded by the house and the young cottonwood trees in the yard.

Amber followed the procession of men and found a place next to her Uncle John on the north side of the house. She wasn't as hungry as she thought she would be – she guessed it was the heat – but she cleaned her plate and leaned back against the wall of the house.

What would a person do without neighbors? Amber wondered. She studied the folks around her, people drawn together by the loneliness of the empty land they shared. She closed her eyes momentarily to rest them, and fanned herself with her sunbonnet as her thoughts rambled on. Neighbors are always around when you need them, ready to help you harvest your crops, nurse your sick, bury your dead. It seems no favor is too great to ask. But then, she decided, they know that we will be ready to help them, too, when they ask us.

"Well, back to work!" announced Uncle John, all too soon. Amber got stiffly to her feet and headed for the fields once more. She was tired, but she had only to think of the horse she was going to get and that made all the hard work worthwhile.

The afternoon passed quickly with the busy routine of the harvest, although the hot sun continued to torture man and beast, and there was even less wind than earlier. Amber glanced skyward to determine by the sun what time it might be. As she did so, she thought she saw a cloud bank building up on the horizon to the southwest, but she couldn't be sure. She knew the shimmering heat waves had a way of distorting objects in the distance. You're seeing things, she told herself.

The next time she happened to look that way, she knew it was no trick of the eye. The clouds were there all right, and they were building fast into towering white thunderheads. She turned to her uncle behind her in the header box. "Uncle John, look!" she cried, pointing at the sky.

He gazed toward the southwest, all the while continuing to stack the wheat as it came from the header. Amber saw each of the others cast a worried look in that direction also, as word passed among them. "I don't think we have anything to worry about," said Uncle John. "It's pretty far away. Probably peter out before it gets this far. Hope so anyway," he added, giving Amber the feeling that he was more hopeful than sure.

Amber continued to keep an eye on the gathering storm for the next hour, and she was amazed at its rapid development. Already the tops of the thunderheads were streaming out to one side in the familiar anvil shape, obliterating the sun entirely, as lightning played continually through the darkened lower portions. The men felt a compelling urgency to hurry, and even the horses stepped up their pace, their ears now flicking back and forth nervously as they sensed the first rumbles of the distant thunder.

"Well, boys," said John, "we'd better quit for the day, so you can get home before the storm hits. Let's hope this blows on over," he added, knowing there was much grain yet to be cut – not only his, but some of his neighbors' as well.

As the men unharnessed their own animals and trotted off in every direction, Uncle John shouted to Amber above the rising, dust-laden wind, "I'll take care of the team. You go down by the river and bring the cows back. Tell Frankie Mitchell he'd better head for home with his, too, if he hasn't already."

Amber jumped down from the header box and dashed off toward the river where the neighbor boy had been herding both families' cows. Great volleys of thunder shook the air and large raindrops began to thud to the ground as she neared the river. Frankie and his cows were nowhere in sight, but she had no trouble finding Uncle John's cows, which were already heading homeward and needed little prodding. A quick count of the herd told Amber that one cow was missing. Must be ol' Belle, she thought. She *would* have to pick a time like this to have her calf! Amber gave a quick look around. I feel sorry for her, but I sure can't go looking for her now! she decided.

By this time, Amber was drenched by the increasing downpour. Her wet skirts clung to her legs uncomfortably as she hurried the cows along. Suddenly she noticed one hailstone and then another bounce to the ground from the leaden skies. "Oh no!" she cried aloud. "Not hail!" Soon they were at the mercy of the raging storm. Amber could see small welts being raised on the cattle by the pounding ice. Instinct now told the animals to stop and turn tail to the onslaught of the storm, and it was all Amber could do to keep them moving.

It seemed an eternity before they reached the shelter of the cowshed. Amber's strength was nearly exhausted. She paused a moment to catch her breath and then dashed across the farmyard to the back door of the house. Once inside, she warmed herself beside the cookstove while Uncle John watched the fury raging outside the window. Amber knew the anguish he felt as they witnessed the hail batter the remaining wheat crop into the ground. He drew a deep breath and turned to his wife as she sat in the rocking chair nursing the new baby. "Well, the Lord was good enough to let us get part of the wheat cut," he said. "I guess we can be thankful for that."

Amber went to the window and looked out. Now she knew she would never get her horse. It would always be something. . .hail, grasshoppers, drought. Bitter tears began to sting her eyelids, and she kept her face turned away so no one would see.

Although the roily, dark clouds still indicated great turbulence, the hail suddenly ceased its pounding and an ominous silence ensued. Nothing outside moved. Suddenly, Amber's heart quickened, and she stared awestruck at the sight she witnessed. A sinister-looking, black funnel had dipped down from the darkest mass of clouds and was snaking its way across the prairie directly towards them. "Uncle John! Is that – ? Is that a – ?"

"Cyclone!" answered John, fear visible on his face in the eerie half-light.

"Oh, John!" gasped Grizelda, clutching the baby closer to her.

"Quick!" John shouted, "Everybody into the cellar!" He swept Hilda up from her cradle and grabbed the coal oil lamp, leading the way out onto the porch. Amber caught up Lucy and Kris, who by now were whimpering with fear, and hurried them outside and down the narrow stairs into the dark, musty cellar.

"Hurry! Hurry! Hurry!" shouted Aunt Grizelda, but her words were all but drowned out by little Karl's howling over his interrupted supper.

Amber's heart was pounding in her ears as Uncle John set the lamp down and cleared places for them to sit on the floor. Once they were settled, the children became quiet. The air in the cellar was strong with the odor of the earthen walls and the onions and other vegetables stored there, and the stillness, together with the warm glow of the lamp, engendered a false sense of calm, making the situation outside seem unreal and far away.

Amber sat and silently contemplated the menace bearing down upon them. It's not happening! she told herself over and over. It will disappear and nothing will happen! Her efforts at complacency were overcome by a tremendous roar, almost deafening in its intensity. Huddled on the floor against the dirt wall, Amber embraced her two little cousins tightly and closed her eyes, certain that the house above them would be lifted into the air at any moment.

Then abruptly, the thunderous noise ceased and the only sound to be heard was the children sobbing again. Amber opened her eyes, fully expecting to see daylight above them. "It's still here!" she cried jubilantly. "The house is still here!"

Uncle John retrieved the lamp and led the way up the stairs. The house was untouched, but evidence of the twister's capricious fury lay scattered about the farmyard in the weird, premature twilight. They found the two workhorses standing safe and sound at their manger where Uncle John had tied them, but the barn that had enclosed them was strewn about the landscape like giant toothpicks. The chicken house, too, had been smashed as though by a giant fist. Dead chickens lay everywhere, curiously stripped of their feathers; yet, oddly enough, not one feather was to be seen upon the ground.

"My poor chickens!" exclaimed Aunt Grizelda in horror and disbelief. "Are they all dead?"

The answer was a frantic squawk, followed by several more, as the half-dozen surviving fowl struggled from beneath the splintered remnants of the chicken house, minus most of their feathers. The pitiful creatures seemed totally unaware of their loss of plumage, and began to cluck and strut around, though still somewhat dazed by their ordeal.

"Well, all in all, I'd say we got by pretty darn lucky," surmised Uncle John, "considering what could have happened." He hugged Hilda closer to him and tousled Kris's blond hair. "At least we're all right. 'Zelda, you and Amber take the kids back in. I'm going to ride over to the Mitchells' and see how they made out. They may need help."

Not until days later did they learn the full extent of the tornado's havoc. It had hopscotched across the prairie for five miles, leaving some farms, like the Mitchells', unscathed, only to vent its wrath upon others. Luckily, the only fatalities counted were among the livestock, although many buildings in the path of the storm would have to be rebuilt, and half of the area's wheat crop was totally lost, a sad and devastating blow to the already hard-scrabble existence of the homesteaders.

Chapter 6

Two days after the storm, Belle was still unaccounted for. Amber set out early that warm June morning with strict orders from her aunt to find the missing cow and bring her home, her supply of fresh milk needed for hungry children. "Don't waste time now," Aunt Grizelda admonished, above Lucy's loud wailing. "I want you back here to make a batch of soap – we're almost out."

Amber had little doubt where she would find Belle. She knew a cow ready to calve would seek the security of the willow bushes along the river, which afforded the only natural protection around. As she neared the banks of the river, she heard the faint but frantic bawling of a young calf, punctuated frequently by the deeper bellowing of its mother. Amber stopped short to listen and then broke into a run, heading for the sounds of trouble. As she made her way hurriedly through the thick growth of willow bushes, the moist sand at the river's edge was pleasantly cool beneath her bare feet, and the damp smell of muddy water hung heavy on the warm summer air.

When she brushed aside the last branch and the open river bed lay before her, she realized her quest was over and a harder task awaited her, for there was the new calf, mired in quicksand up to its back, calling plaintively to its mother. Belle stood on a nearby sandbar, pacing helplessly and mooing motherly encouragement to her offspring. The little brindle calf was exhausted from its efforts to extricate itself and had ceased to struggle against the sucking ooze which enveloped it, its pleas for help growing more and more feeble.

Amber knew she would have to act fast to save the little creature from a slow and terrible death. There was nothing to do but go in after it. "Well," she told herself aloud, "you can do anything you set your mind to!" Quickly she skirted the quicksand and came up on the sandbar beside Belle. "Take it easy, old girl, we'll get your baby out," she said, patting the animal's bony back. Then Amber carefully place one foot and then the other onto the deceptive surface of the quicksand. She was thankful the calf was not too far out, for she was aware she must stay as close as possible to the firmer footing of the sandbar.

The tired calf offered no resistance as Amber reached around it and began tugging against the force of the treacherous quicksand. Gradually it began to relinquish its hold, although, at the same time, Amber felt herself sinking deeper. She really began to worry when she felt it reach her knees. "Remember," she repeated, as she struggled with the calf, "you can do anything you set your mind to!"

Suddenly the tiny calf was free! As Amber slowly turned back toward the sandbar, she was startled to see a pair of fringed Indian moccasins, and as her eyes traveled up the tall, dark-skinned figure towering over her, her insides froze and shattered and her pulse quickened. Two long black braids hanging from beneath the flat-brimmed black hat framed the ugliest face Amber had ever seen. She gasped when she looked up at that scarred countenance, obviously disfigured by some long-ago accident into a permanent, grotesque sneer. But when she met his gaze, she was surprised to find that his dark eyes were warm and friendly, and she thought at once how out of place they seemed amid such forbidding features.

The mysterious stranger immediately extended two huge, gnarled and bronzed hands, motioning to Amber to give him the calf. She did so gratefully and without hesitation. He took the animal and laid it down, then offered his hand to Amber and helped her onto the sandbar without a word. After assisting the calf to its feet and returning it to its worried mother for some needed nourishment, he said simply, "You both safe now. I go."

Amber was still shaking, but tried not to show it, as she found her voice at last. "Yes, and thank you. Thank you for your help!" she called after the lanky figure as he disappeared, silent as a shadow, into the willows on the far side of the river. Amber stood there for a moment wondering about this ugly but kind stranger who had befriended her. Who was he? Where did he come from? What was he doing here?

Suddenly, she remembered Grizelda's warning not to waste time. Quickly, she washed the sand from her legs and brushed the sand from her wet dress. The little calf, seemingly none the worse for its ordeal, had regained some of its strength by now, so Amber gathered it up, carried it up the river bank and started Belle and her calf toward home. It was a long walk in the hot sun. Why had she forgotten to wear her sunbonnet? If she got a sunburn, Aunt Grizelda would never let her hear the end of it!

When they finally reached the farmyard, she put the cow and calf in the corral, and as she walked to the house, she heard Uncle John laughing and whooping. Peering through the screen door, she was astonished to find him dancing Aunt Grizelda around the room. As Amber stepped inside, he quickly caught her up by the waist also and gave her a twirl. "What's going on?" Amber exclaimed.

Uncle John blurted out excitedly, "A lumber man from the Dakotas bought the team of oxen for fifty dollars!"

"Oh, Uncle John! That's wonderful!" she cried, catching his excitement.

"He was on the Santa Fe Trail," John explained, "looking for oxen for his lumber operations, and he heard about Raeph and Rube from old man Myers in Pawnee Rock. You should have seen his face when he laid eyes on that team of mine! Fifty dollars! Fifty dollars cash money! Look at it!"

"Now I can get a new stove!" declared Aunt Grizelda.

"Hold on now. You forget we have a barn and a chicken house to rebuild," John reminded her. "Your stove may have to wait."

"But this one is so small. You just don't know what I go through trying to cook for seven people on such a little stove," she whined.

And the spell of their merriment was broken.

Amber said quietly, "I'll go out and start the fire for the soap."

Making soap was one chore she didn't mind, although it wouldn't be too pleasant on such a warm day, so she sought the shade of the largest tree. It was intriguing to her to watch the white, crystalline lye turn such curious ingredients as cracklings and old grease into a smooth, useful, cream-colored soap. Cut into bars, it was this strong soap which they used for bathing and for washing clothes, dishes, and even their hair.

Amber built a fire under the big iron kettle in the yard and slowly stirred the mixture as it began to bubble. She stood as far back as possible to avoid the heat and the acrid smell of smoke and hot fat, while her thoughts kept returning to her experience at the river earlier that morning. She had decided to keep the incident to herself, for she knew how Aunt Grizelda felt about Indians, and there was no use setting her off on another one of her endless tirades.

When the soap was done several hours later, Amber wiped her face on her apron and set the kettle aside to cool. As she was putting the fire out, the thudding sound of galloping hooves caused her to look up. Loping toward the farm across the open, uncultivated land to the north was a rider leading a string of four horses tied one to the other. The man sat his spotted horse with the relaxed ease of a born rider, and Amber recognized him at once as the tall, ugly Indian who had helped her out of the quicksand.

The string of horses moved easily along behind, except for a scrubby, steel gray mustang on the end. Reluctance evident in his every move, he followed unwillingly at a stiff-legged trot, his neck and head stretched out against the pull of the halter rope. "Uncle John!" shouted Amber, as she ran to the granary to find him. "Someone's coming! It's an Indian!"

The stranger rode into the farmyard, scattering the chickens in every direction, and dismounted easily as Amber and Uncle John approached him. "Hello," he said to Amber.

But John answered instead, "Hello, what can we do for you?"

"You need horses maybe?" the Indian replied in halting English. "I sell."

"Well, I don't know. The girl here has been wanting a pony, but the storm hit us pretty hard," explained John, gesturing toward the stack of splintered lumber he had gathered. "I'm afraid she'll just have to wait until we can better afford it."

Amber was eyeing the gray mustang, who snorted the dust from his nostrils and stamped one foot on the ground as though in defiance. The color of an angry storm cloud, he was small and scraggy, with a rough coat that Amber was sure had never felt a curry comb or brush. Nor had his thick mane, part of which fell to the left and part to the right of his scrawny neck, with the rest standing up in the middle in complete indecision.

Amber walked over to him and began scratching him behind the ears, to the pony's obvious enjoyment. He then proceeded to rub his forehead vigorously on the front of her dress, pushing so hard that Amber almost lost her balance.

At that moment, she heard Aunt Grizelda yelling to her from the house, "Amber! Get in here and help me get dinner!"

Amber hated to leave the pony, but she knew better than to keep Aunt Grizelda waiting. She gave him one last pat on the nose and ran into the house.

"Tell your aunt we have company for dinner," Uncle John hollered after her.

Glancing over her shoulder as she jumped onto the porch, Amber saw the mustang still looking her way, head up and ears pricked forward.

Everyone knew that pioneer hospitality dictated that no visitor should be turned away at mealtime. But as Amber set a place for the Indian, Aunt Grizelda complained angrily under her breath. "The idea! Having to invite a savage into my home and eat at the same table with him! It's disgusting!"

I don't think so, Amber said to herself. I think it'll be interesting!

As soon as dinner was ready, she opened the screen door and shooed off the flies. "Uncle John – dinner!" she called. He and the horsetrader were squatting in the shade of the granary, talking and gesturing back and forth.

As the two men sauntered to the house, Amber saw Shep come into the yard, panting hard from his favorite past-time of chasing rabbits. The big dog's tongue lolled from his mouth and he walked on three legs, carrying a foreleg. Uncle John passed on by, ignoring his plight, for stickers in Shep's feet were not unusual. But the lanky Indian spoke softly to the dog in his native language as he knelt down, took the paw, and carefully extracted the painful thorn. Shep licked his hand gratefully and headed for a drink at the water trough and a nap in its cool, damp shade.

During the meal, their guest ate in silence, while Amber stole furtive glances in his direction as she fed the two children on either side of her. How she wished she were allowed to talk with him! Aunt Grizelda was polite, but maintained a dour aloofness, grimacing in disgust at the stranger's complete lack of manners. First of all, he failed to remove his hat, even at the table. Then he mixed everything on his plate into one unidentifiable heap, and grasping his fork tightly in his left fist, proceeded to shovel it rapidly into his mouth. Unlike the family, who were all accustomed to shooing the flies away from their food as they ate, the Indian made no effort to do likewise, and the creatures crawled at will over his plate.

He finished before the rest, sopping the last bit of gravy from his plate with a crust of bread. Then he licked his fingers noisily and wiped them on the front of the greasy leather vest he wore. Leaning back comfortably, he patted his stomach with both hands and grunted at Grizelda with satisfaction.

When the Indian rose without a word and followed John back outside, Amber again noticed his moccasins, which were decorated with beautiful beadwork and had tiny metal cones on the fringes. She listened to the soft click of the metal tips as they swished against the wooden floor with each step he took.

As soon as the men were out of earshot, Grizelda began muttering sarcastically, but Amber had learned to ignore her incessant prattle. She wanted to finish her work quickly so she could join them, but Aunt Grizelda kept thinking up additional chores for her, in an obvious attempt to prevent her doing so.

She knows I want to go out there, Amber thought resentfully. She was scrubbing the oilcloth cover on the table when she heard the Indian leaving with his string of horses. She paused and listened to the hoofbeats fade in the distance, then slowly resumed her work.

"Thank goodness he's gone!" Aunt Grizelda said scornfully.

"Amber! Come here," Uncle John called from outside.

She stepped into the hot sunshine of the farmyard and stared in disbelief. Uncle John was standing beside the gray mustang. "He's yours," he said, handing her the lead rope.

"Oh, Uncle John," she said incredulously. "Is he really mine?"

"Yes. The Indian said the pony was holding him up, so he let me have him for five dollars, since he was going to belong to you. I think that half-breed kind of took a liking to you," he added, with a twinkle in his eye. "He told me about your little adventure this morning down by his camp on the river."

Amber threw both arms around the mustang's neck. "Oh, I love him! I love him!" she cried. Then she hugged Uncle John. "I'm so happy! Thank you so much!" she said, as tears of joy rolled down her cheeks.

"What are you going to name him?" asked her uncle.

"I don't know yet," replied Amber thoughtfully, as she stroked the pony's neck.

"The half-breed called him something in Kickapoo that means 'One-that-is-not-wanted,' but I can't remember how he said it."

"Kickapoo?" asked Amber. "What's that?"

"That's the tribe his mother came from. He told me his father was a white man, but he was raised with his mother's people. He's not a real Indian, just a half-breed Kickapoo."

"Kickapoo," repeated Amber. She liked the way the strange word clicked off of her tongue. "Kickapoo. That's what I'll call him!"

"Well, why don't you take Kickapoo to the corral and find a brush to use on him? His coat's sure been neglected, looks like," observed John. "I'll tell 'Zelda you'll be busy for awhile."

Amber spent the rest of the afternoon with her pony, grooming his coat, feeding him handfuls of ground corn, and confiding to him the secrets of her heart. She couldn't have loved him more if he had been the fiery white charger of her dreams. She felt a rare comradeship with the little mustang, and he seemed to sense her friendship. "No one wants me either," she told him, "but now we have each other, and we're going to be the best of friends, aren't we?"

"Amber! Get in here now! You've wasted enough time out there!" screamed Aunt Grizelda from the door.

Amber could tell from the exasperation in her aunt's voice that she was headed for a hard time, and she was right. From the moment she entered the house, she found herself the target of Grizelda's sharp tongue.

"The idea! That man must be out of his mind buying you a horse!" she fumed. "You don't earn your keep around here as it is, and now with that animal taking up your time, you sure won't! Just wait 'til that uncle of yours comes back in! I'll set him straight!" She lighted a fire in the cookstove and slammed the lid down on the burner with a loud clank, ignoring the two whimpering toddlers tugging at her skirts. "I can't have a new stove, no! But you – you can have a horse! Sure you can! A stove isn't important, but a horse is!"

Amber could hold her tongue no longer. "But Kickapoo will be a big help, especially herding the cows," Amber countered. "And I can go after things in Pawnee Rock for you, or go after the midwife when you need her. And he only cost five dollars. You can't buy a stove for five – "

"That's enough out of you, young lady!" snapped Aunt Grizelda. "I can do without any back talk. You just mind your own business and take care of these kids. I'll take this matter up with your uncle."

Amber went to bed that night as her aunt's shrill voice resounded throughout the house in a heated argument with Uncle John. He withstood the verbal barrage hurled at him by his wife, then Amber heard him put up the same argument as she herself had used in favor of the pony. At this, Grizelda burst into tears. "No one listens to me around here! No one cares about me!" she cried, and Amber heard her stomping from the room.

There was sudden darkness as Uncle John blew out the lamp. Amber heard him follow his wife into their bedroom and quietly close the door.

Amber thought she had only dozed off for a moment when she gradually awoke to the same piercing sounds of discord from downstairs. But the rooster was crowing, and she suddenly realized that the darkness was fading and a new day had begun.

"I knew it! I knew it!" Aunt Grizelda was saying. "I knew that savage wasn't to be trusted! But no one pays any attention to me around here!" Her raucous voice was beginning to wake the children.

"Now, 'Zelda, don't get all upset again. We don't know for sure that the Indian took it. But it does kind of look that way," John admitted, "him being here yesterday and all."

By this time Amber had come down to see what was going on. "What happened?" she asked, rubbing the sleep from her eyes.

"Someone stole some meat from the storeroom last night," explained Uncle John. "The door was standing wide open this morning when I got up. Whoever it was, they didn't take much, but anytime somebody steals food from poor folks like us, it's serious."

"What do you mean 'whoever it was'?" interrupted Aunt Grizelda. "We all know who it was! It was that horrible-looking Indian! You never should have invited him in!"

"Well, I don't think he did it," Amber announced boldly. Her aunt glared at her. "He . . . he seemed nice to me," she said. "I just don't think he's a thief."

And no one could convince her differently. Twice she had seen compassion on that craggy face. Of course, she supposed there were compassionate thieves, but she just couldn't bring herself to believe that her Indian friend would steal from them. He was on her mind all that day, and she was still worrying over the incident as she went to bed that night.

Amber lay in the darkness, wide awake and alert, and tried to discover what had awakened her. It was as though a voice had suddenly called her, or a hand had shaken her shoulder. But there was no sound from the other members of the family. All she could hear was the whisper of the wind.

Then she heard something and sat up in bed to listen. There it was again! She caught her breath and held it as she suddenly recognized the familiar sound. Someone had tripped the latch on the door of the storeroom! Could it be the half-breed? She sat in the darkness with fearful excitement surging inside her. Could Aunt Grizelda be right after all? Maybe he did take the meat! Still, she could not bring herself to accept this, even now. I have to find out, she told herself, I have to know for sure! Quietly she slipped out of bed and crept down the stairs. She was afraid the whole family would awaken from the sound of her pounding heart.

The night was warm, and both doors had been left open to allow for more air. Amber could see the door of the storeroom on the porch standing ajar. She hesitated, not knowing just how close she wanted to get. I've got to know, she kept telling herself, I've got to know if it's him! She hoped she could not be seen inside the darkened house as she made her way stealthily to the doorway and waited.

There was no sound from the little room where the meat was hung. Maybe he's already gone, she told herself, but suddenly her thoughts were interrupted by a thud and then a subdued click, click, click as soft footsteps came her way from

74

inside the storeroom. Amber stifled a gasp with her hand as she recalled in a flash that the same sound had been made by the half-breed's moccasins when he had left the kitchen. She was more disappointed than afraid now as she peered into the darkness for the tall, slender form of her Indian friend.

But the dark, hulking shape that came slowly through the door was not the Indian, nor any man. Amber's first startled thought was bear! But at the same time she knew better – there were no bears in Kansas. Yet it must be an animal of some sort. Only when the creature had fully emerged and stood silhouetted against the moonlit farmyard did she recognize the big dog, Shep.

Oblivious to her presence, he was occupied with dragging off the large piece of meat he had stolen, his long toenails clicking on the wooden porch with each step. Amber breathed a sigh of relief and leaned against the doorway. So! It was Shep and not the half-breed! Tears came to her eyes. She was glad her friend was not guilty, glad and thankful. Wiping the tears from her face, she peeked around the doorway once more before going back to bed. She saw the dog on the far side of the farmyard, burying his ill-gotten goods for enjoyment another day.

Chapter 7

Now that she had Kickapoo, Amber was the happiest she had been since coming to Kansas. All her spare time was spent with him, combing the snares from his mane and tail, and brushing his gray coat until it shone in the sun like a bright tin pan. She talked to him constantly in tender, quiet tones, and each night before she left him, she would squeeze his neck lovingly and kiss his soft nose.

With no bridle for Kickapoo, Amber made do with a length of twine tied around his lower jaw. And, since Uncle John no longer had his old saddle, she rode bareback, sitting the mustang sideways with nothing but a rope around his middle for a handhold. Amber knew ladies were never supposed to sit astride, but she applied this rule only when someone might see her; otherwise, after a cautious look around, she would throw her right leg on over and ride the sensible way – astride.

Either way, she rode with the agile grace of an Indian. Moving together as one, the pair would fly like the wind over the prairie, racing tumbleweeds, rabbits, and even the large, harmless bullsnakes which abounded on the plains. Kickapoo not only let her escape physically from Aunt Grizelda and all she represented, but he carried her into a wondrous new world of make-believe: she was Joan of Arc leading her armies into battle; she was an Indian brave hunting buffalo; she was a mountain man exploring the vast, unknown country of the West. It was great fun!

Kickapoo's many scars spoke of past cruelties, but like Amber, his spirit was unbroken. From his wild ancestors the little mustang had inherited a proud dignity that endeared him all the more to Amber. But others saw it only as an ingrained stubborness, a fault to be overcome by the whip.

All summer, Uncle John attempted to work Kickapoo in harness, for without the oxen, he needed another work animal. But each time, the little mustang steadfastly refused, while Amber stood by and watched in helpless misery. First, Kickapoo would balk, and no amount of coaxing or use of force could induce him to move. As tempers flared, Kickapoo reared; he kicked the wagon and lunged over the traces. If Uncle John was not convinced by then, the mustang would simply lie down and refuse to budge.

Amber suffered along with Kickapoo through each encounter, feeling a strange mixture of anger, pity, and at the same time, admiration for his unconquerable spirit. But she shuddered to think of the battered wagons, snapped harness, and broken traces abandoned in his wake. She was sure her uncle knew how much the mustang meant to her, but at night she had recurring nightmares of Uncle John disappearing behind the barn with Kickapoo, as he had with Shep the day he had found the dog sucking eggs. Then the thunderous roar of his shotgun would awaken her, and she would lie there, praying that the bad dream never came true.

One morning late in August came the final battle in the contest of wills. "I'm going to try harnessing Kickapoo to the plow between Archie and Charlie," announced Uncle John at breakfast. "With a big horse on either side of him, he won't be able to do much acting up. Maybe he'll settle down and behave himself. That horse has got to learn to work – only rich people keep horses just for riding."

Nervously, Amber helped him hitch the three horses to the plow. Kickapoo, many inches shorter than the big workhorses, looked even smaller standing between them. "Please be good, Kickapoo, and do what Uncle John wants you to," Amber pleaded with him. But already Kickapoo's ears were back and his neck was stiffly erect.

"Okay, Archie, Charlie, let's show him how it's done," said Uncle John, as he gathered up the reins and clucked to his team. The two bays started off, with John walking behind. Kickapoo hung back, bracing himself stiff-legged. Archie and Charlie hesitated, but on Uncle John's command, leaned into their collars and forced Kickapoo to move. He took several reluctant steps, then reared up and wildly tried to lunge over Archie's back, unsettling both Archie and Charlie.

Uncle John stopped and calmed them all down. His jaw was set with determination, and Amber could tell that his patience was wearing thin. Please be good, Kickapoo, please be good! she prayed.

When they started forward once again, Kickapoo threw himself on the ground, but instead of halting, Uncle John urged the other horses on, and they dragged Kickapoo between them. "Get up, Kickapoo! Get up!" cried Amber, as she followed along, tears brimming in her eyes. "Oh, please move, Kickapoo!" But he would not.

"Whoa!" commanded Uncle John finally. "I give up!" he said to Amber in disgust, as he wiped the sweat from his brow. "That cussed horse will never learn. I'm going to quit fooling with him. Looks like you've got yourself a riding horse after all!"

From that day on, much to Amber's relief, Kickapoo was all hers.

In the fall of 1891, Amber's brother, Lonnie, came to live with them in Kansas. He had arrived by train, all alone, with nothing but a note pinned to his jacket instructing people along the way as to his destination. Amber found that he hadn't changed much – still slight of build, with shaggy brown hair that was always in his eyes. He had a habit of jerking his head abruptly to flip it aside. Little things about him, like the way he walked, reminded her of Papa. It was good to see someone from home. Amber questioned him endlessly about their family and friends back in Ohio, and in the attic at night they lay in their beds and whispered back and forth, laughing over past incidents.

"Remember when we used to try and see who could swallow the biggest rock?" asked Amber, giggling.

"Yeah!" Lonnie snickered. "And I remember that time the doctor came to vaccinate us against smallpox. You hid under the porch and no one could find you for the longest time."

Amber had forgotten this little episode from their childhood and chuckled at the recollection, muffling the sounds in her pillow. She was too late to avoid a sharp reprimand from Aunt Grizelda. "You two shut up and get to sleep!" she yelled up the stairway. "Or I'm going to take the whip to the both of you!"

Lonnie was getting a quick initiation into their aunt's harsh discipline.

Although Amber had the Mitchell children to socialize with, visits were few and far between, with everyone always busy working the farms. So she was glad for the daily companionship of someone nearer her own age; however, Lonnie's arrival made her doubt for the first time that she would ever return to Ohio. She was somewhat surprised to realize how little it mattered now, but at thirteen, she was beginning to feel a growing independence. Going back home just didn't seem so important any more. Besides, now she had Kickapoo!

It was a warm, dry fall that year, and one beautiful day followed another. Amber would never forget the second Sunday in October. That was the day church services were held in town, and it was such a beautiful day that Aunt Grizelda decided to go along and take all the children. Amber was surprised by her decision for, although such things were never mentioned, she knew her aunt was going to have another baby.

By the time they had picked up the six Mitchell children, Uncle John had a wagonload, but the trip was pleasant for the boys and girls riding on the pile of blankets in the back of the wagon. Amber always enjoyed these occasions, for it was one of her few opportunities to get away from the farm and have fun visiting with her best friend, Katie.

They had been on their way for an hour when the left rear wheel began to squeak. "I knew there was something I forgot to do!" Uncle John complained. "I meant to grease those blamed axles before we left home!" The noise gradually became a piercing screech which caused the smaller children to clasp their hands over their ears in protest.

"We've got to do something about that!" said Uncle John. He pulled the team to a stop and jumped out of the wagon. Amber leaned over the side as he inspected the troublesome wheel. "If we go any farther without some grease on that axle, the wheel will be ruined for sure," he said with a perplexed look. He took off his hat and scratched his head thoughtfully.

"Uncle John, what about butter?" suggested Amber. "That's grease, isn't it? I put lots of it on our bread for lunch."

"You know, that just might work, if we could scrape enough off," he answered. "Get out the lunch, 'Zelda, and let's give it a try!"

For the rest of the way into town, the wheel was quiet and the two hours passed quickly in the happy congeniality of friends. The church bell was ringing as they crossed the bridge into town and Uncle John urged the horses into a trot. Amber, Aunt Grizelda, and the two Mitchell girls, Katie and Sarah, hurriedly traded sunbonnets for flowered church hats and pinched their cheeks to make them rosy. "Everybody sit up straight!" commanded Grizelda. "Let's show people we're as good as anybody!"

Later, as Amber sat in church trying to concentrate on the sermon, she found herself studying the people around her. Many were local farmers like themselves, dressed in drab, homemade clothing which was patched and worn. It wasn't hard to distinguish the townspeople in the congregation; their clothes were nicer and not so plain. Life in town must be easier than living on a farm, Amber decided. She was wondering what it would be like to live in town, when Lucy began creating a disturbance and Aunt Grizelda motioned for Amber to take the toddler outside.

The autumn sunshine was blinding after the subdued light that filtered through the stained-glass windows inside the church. Amber sat on the steps holding Lucy and gazed with interest at the buildings that lined the main street of Great Bend. She imagined what fun it would be to wander up and down that street, visiting the many different stores, and she wished she could go on one of Grizelda's shopping trips sometime, instead of always having to stay home with the children.

Since today was Sunday, the town wasn't as busy as the first time she had seen it over three years ago, but it had grown some, sprawling in every direction upon the surrrounding prairie.

It was almost noon. Amber was beginning to feel hunger pangs. "That's what's wrong with you too, isn't it?" she said to Lucy, who was still fussing and chewing on one chubby little fist. "We'll get something to eat before long."

Then, with a sudden opening of the double doors, the mass of people began to stream out of the church.

As soon as they were loaded up and Uncle John's wagon had crossed the Arkansas, hats were again exchanged, lunch pails were opened, and the group passed around hard-boiled eggs and the butterless bread. Katie and her sister had also brought along enough dried apples for everyone. Any kind of fruit was always a real treat and Amber ate hers slowly, savoring the tartness and trying to make it last as long as she could.

After lunch, with the warm sun upon them, one by one the smaller children curled up and went to sleep. The other youngsters' friendly chatter gradually quieted, and Amber herself dozed.

She awoke suddenly and was surprised to find that she was shivering. A chilling wind assailed them from the north. She turned quickly and looked behind them. The northern sky was a mass of slate gray clouds, rolling low over the prairie like thick, billowing smoke. Its menacing appearance sent added shivers through her. How could this have come up so suddenly? There had been no hint of it when they had left town. Uncle John and Aunt Grizelda kept glancing over their shoulders to watch the rapidly-approaching storm, and Amber could see that they were becoming increasingly concerned.

"You kids better get under those blankets!" Uncle John called back to them, as he got an old coat from under the seat for himself and wrapped a thick comforter around Grizelda and little Karl. "It's probably going to get a lot colder, and you'll have to try to keep each other warm." He cast another worried look to the north. "I think we can get home before it catches us – we're over halfway."

But within the next hour, the blizzard was upon them with a vicious shriek, engulfing the slow-moving wagon in its swirling, icy wrath. The blinding onslaught pelted them with half-snow and half-dust and the stinging particles pierced their eyes and nostrils like needles. The blankets provided little protection for the shivering boys and girls huddled beneath them. It was all the children could do to keep them from being whipped off altogether by the howling winds.

Amber soon heard Uncle John shout something to Grizelda, and she peeked out from under the blankets to try and catch his words. All she could make out was ". . . lost! . . . giving the horses their heads!" She ducked quickly back under the covers to relay to the others what she had heard. Enveloped in the smothering snow, Uncle John had evidently lost all sense of direction. He was going to have to rely on the horses' instincts to guide them home through the storm. Amber was scared. Could they do it? She'd heard that horses were able to find their way home no matter what, but these had never had to before. What if they wandered around and pulled the wagon off into the river? She shivered and snuggled down closer to Kris, Lucy, and Hilda, trying to cover them as much as she could with her own body. Where was Lonnie? she wondered. He should be helping her keep the little ones warm!

Before long, she felt the wagon stop. They couldn't be home – not this soon! What was the matter? Were they hopelessly lost? Then she heard Uncle John yell out, "I'm going to check on the kids!" When he reached the back of the wagon, he shouted with alarm. "Hey, you kids! Put Lonnie up there in the middle of you all and warm him up! He was out from under the covers! He's almost frozen!"

The group of youngsters stiffly changed positions to make room for Lonnie who was already drowsy with cold, and Uncle John rearranged the blankets over them as best he could before continuing on. Amber was worried about her brother, but there was nothing she could do for him with the three babies to take care of.

After an eternity of traveling through the snow, wind, and cold, the team hesitated and then stopped. Amber stole a glance from under the covers. Barely, she could make out the shape of a building, but what was it? A barn? Yes! They were in the Mitchell's farmyard! She felt like rushing to the two horses and hugging them, she was so relieved.

"Frankie! Katie! All you Mitchells come on! You're home!" Uncle John called out. He handed the reins to Grizelda and climbed down to help the children unload. "Frankie! Help me unhitch your horse." Working blindly and with fingers numb from the cold, the two released the horse from the wagon.

The dark form of Josh Mitchell suddenly appeared beside them in the wind-whipped whiteness of the blizzard. Taking the horse from John, he cupped both hands around his mouth and shouted above the roar of the storm. "You folks better stay here with us 'til this is over!"

"It's not far now! We can make it!" John hollered back. "Liz will have her hands full enough as it is! We'd best go on!"

John heaved himself back up to the wagon seat and took the reins of his impatient horse, who was about to jerk them from Grizelda's grasp. Although tired and now pulling alone, Archie was anxious to get home and he needed no urging. It wasn't long before they drew up in their own farmyard.

While Uncle John tended to the stock, Amber helped Aunt Grizelda bundle Lonnie and the children into one bed and build a fire in the cookstove in an attempt to heat the cold house. Soon the sides of the stove glowed a cherry red, but the heat had little effect, for the icy winds penetrated every invisible crack. Tiny particles of snow were driven through the cracks and piled around the floor in small drifts. The calendar hanging at an outward angle from the wall and the ice in the water bucket bore mute testimony to the frigid force of the raging storm. Human breath and steam from the bubbling coffee pot and the simmering kettle of beans on the stove turned to frost on the window panes, creating exquisite designs on the glass.

Accompanied by a sudden blast of wind and snow, Uncle John stomped into the house. "Whew!" he exclaimed. "That's some weather we've got out there!" He spread his hands over the stove to absorb the warmth of the fire. "I piled a bunch of corn cobs outside the window, to burn when we run out," he said, inspecting the diminishing supply in the wood box. "All we'll have to do is reach out the window and get them. Is everybody all right? How's Lonnie?" he asked, glancing over his shoulder toward the bed crowded with the five children.

"He'll survive," Aunt Grizelda declared flatly, pulling a shawl around her shoulders. "If any of us do."

How can she be that way? thought Amber, as she briskly rubbed Lonnie's hands to warm them. Doesn't she care that he almost died? He could have rolled off the wagon and we'd never have known it.

Later that night she helped Lonnie up to bed and tucked the covers under his chin. "Let me know if you need more covers," she said, brushing the hair back out of his eyes. "I'll give you one of mine." Lonnie smiled and nodded, but she knew he'd never ask her for one, no matter how cold he got.

Sometime in the night the wind died to a fitful moan, and snow stopped sifting through the roof onto Amber's patchwork quilt. Only then did she finally fall asleep, though she was still restless with cold.

The crowing of the rooster heralded a cold and bright new day. The sparkling white landscape lay unblemished beneath a brilliant blue sky, with snow swirled and piled in great drifts on the south side of the buildings, while other patches of ground were swept almost clear.

Uncle John was unable to get either door open, due to the snow blown against them. "I guess I'll have to crawl out the window," he said as he buttoned up his heavy coat. "The stock needs tending."

"Uncle John, may I go out with you?" Amber asked. "I'd like to see how Kickapoo is."

"You stay here!" Aunt Grizelda said sharply. "Your uncle can take care of the animals. Someone's got to entertain these children and see that they stay off the floor. They could catch their death of cold down there."

Amber shrugged and turned her attention to the restless, squirming children on the bed. They played tic-tac-toe on Lonnie's slate; then she read to them from her book, and the Bible, from the *Farmer's Almanac* and back issues of the *Kansas City Star*. Even the youngest seemed to enjoy listening to her, whether or not they understood what she was reading.

Amber thought of Uncle John's favorite saying, "If you don't like the weather in Kansas, just wait five minutes and it will change!" For the next day the plains lived up to this reputation. Mild fall weather returned and the snow disappeared almost as quickly as it had come. Amber had learned long ago that the only thing constant was the wind – and Aunt Grizelda's temper.

On a Saturday afternoon in November, the package Uncle Karl had promised Amber arrived. "Hey!" yelled Josh Mitchell from the yard. "I've been to town and picked up your mail. There's a parcel here for Amber, too."

"Much obliged," said John as he took the mail. Josh waved and clucked to his team.

Amber's hands were shaking with excitement as she set the small box on the table. She carefully untied the string from the brown paper wrapping on which her name had been printed in black ink. As Grizelda snatched up the usable twine, Amber lifted off the top and began discarding wads of tissue paper.

"Oh," she murmured softly. Packed in the center was a small bottle, flat and oval-shaped, with a gracefully pointed glass stopper in the neck. On the front was a label with a picture of a beautiful lady and the words *Eau de Cologne* written in elegant, flowing letters.

Beneath the cologne she found a large silk scarf that was as blue as a cloudless prairie sky. "Oh," she murmured again, as she unfolded it and held it up for all to see. "Isn't it beautiful? I've never had anything so nice. Wasn't that sweet of Uncle Karl to send me two gifts!"

"One must be for me," said Aunt Grizelda with sudden interest.

"Did he write a note?" asked Uncle John.

Amber began looking through the box. "Here's one!" she said, holding up a small, folded sheet of paper. She opened it and began to read aloud as Uncle John looked over her shoulder. The graceful, prosaic hand on the paper seemed odd, not at all like Uncle Karl's easy-going manner.

Dear Brother & Family,

I hope this here letter finds you all in the best of good health. Buck & me finely made it to Texas & it is quite a place! I miss the Colo. mts. & dry climit up north however. I been working at odd jobs here & there & moving on when I feel like it. I was cooking for a cow outfit, but they went broke. I been here in San Antonio for 2 mos. now. You see a lot of Mex. style things here – clothes, food, saddles & the like. A lot of the white people speak Mex. real good, too. I even lerned a few words myself!

I hope the little gal likes the scarf & cologne I am sending her. I'll bet she is prettier than ever!

As always,
Your Brother Karl

"Well, Karl never was one for writing long letters," said Uncle John, as Amber carefully refolded the piece of paper along the original creases. "I'm surprised he wrote as much as he did."

Aunt Grizelda stormed off and did not mention the gifts again, so Amber said nothing.

The next day John and Grizelda went to the Mitchell's for a brief visit, and Amber decided to take advantage of her aunt's absence to inspect her gifts more closely. As soon as the children were napping, she tiptoed upstairs and took the box from its hiding place under her bed. After carefully breaking the seal on the bottle of cologne, she daubed the golden liquid on her neck, delighting in the wonderful fragrance which enveloped her.

Then she laid the large square of blue silk on her bed and folded it diagonally. Tying it about her head, she peered into the irregular piece of looking-glass hanging on the wall above her trunk. She experimented by tying it on different ways, each time scrutinizing the attractive young girl reflecting back to her.

I wish I were beautiful like the lady on the bottle, she sighed to herself, and the shadow of a frown flashed between her dark brows. Still, I guess I'm not ugly, she admitted. She leaned forward and inspected her appearance close up: her reddish-brown hair with just a hint of natural curl; her complexion, as flawless and smooth as a cameo; her full lips ending in graceful upward curves at the corners of her mouth. No, she wasn't ugly. But she did wish she had eyes like Uncle John's, with all those pretty colors sparkling in them. Brown eyes were so. . .so uninteresting.

Outside, the wind whistled softly as it fingered the eaves of the little house. Then a sudden gust shook it to its foundation, rattling windows and causing the boards to creak in protest. Briefly startled, Amber jerked her head toward the attic window, but the panes were too dusty to see through. Silly! she told herself. It's only the wind!

Her sudden movement caused the scarf to slip down around her neck and she liked the effect it created. She loosened the knot and draped the scarf around her shoulders, at the same time envisioning herself in a full-length gown of soft, filmy blue. She was humming and twirling around in an imaginary waltz when she came face to face with Aunt Grizelda.

"Oh!" Amber exclaimed. "You're home! I didn't hear you come back. I was just. . .just seeing how I looked," she said, motioning toward the mirror. "Would you like to try some of my cologne?" she said, offering the bottle to Grizelda.

"Don't you know that vanity is a sin?" exploded Grizelda, angrily grabbing the bottle of cologne from Amber's hand.

"No! No!" cried Amber, but it was too late. Aunt Grizelda dashed it to the floor, smashing to bits all but the little glass stopper. Tears glistened in Amber's eyes as she helplessly watched the precious fluid soak into the rough boards of the floor. "You had no right to do that!" she cried. "That was mine and you had no right – "

"Why, you impudent little brat! Don't you tell me what I can or can't do! Now get that scarf off and clean up this mess! We've got no time for such foolishness!" Grizelda stomped down the stairs.

Tearfully, Amber picked up the pieces of glass and tossed them back into the cardboard box. Then, on impulse, she retrieved the glass stopper and carefully hid it away in her treasure box with her spelling medal from school.

Chapter 8

"Amber! Amber!" Someone was calling through the mists of her dreams. "Wake up, Amber!"

"Hmm?" she answered, responding now to the hand shaking her shoulder.

"We need you to go for the midwife," Uncle John whispered.

Amber opened her eyes. "Oh!" she said, sitting up and rubbing the sleep away. "I didn't think the baby was due so soon."

"It's coming early. 'Zelda thinks it won't be long, so I'd better stay with her just in case. Hurry now!" The tone of his voice matched the worried expression on his face, giving Amber the impression he hadn't even been to bed.

A chill fingered its way up Amber's backbone. "What time is it?" she asked.

Uncle John pulled out his pocket watch and held it towards the glow of the coal oil lamp in his other hand. "It's four-thirty," he whispered. "It'll be light before too long. Hurry! And you'd better dress as warm as you can – that wind's pretty cold." He set the lamp down on the wooden crate that served as a nightstand and headed for the stairs. "I'll go get Kickapoo ready for you."

When Amber slid out of bed, her face felt hot. She peered through the dim light at her reflection in the mirror and noticed her cheeks seemed flushed but forgot to wonder about it in her haste to get dressed. Quickly she donned her knit chemise, several petticoats, and the long black stockings she always seemed to have trouble keeping up. She shivered as she slipped into her faded blue dress and felt the cold fabric touch her skin.

As she fastened her high-buttoned shoes, she heard Lonnie roll over and yawn. "What's going on?" her brother mumbled from the other side of the curtain that separated them.

"Aunt Grizelda is having her baby. I've got to ride to Pawnee Rock after the midwife." Hurriedly she brushed her hair, ignoring the sudden chills it brought to her head.

"Let me go instead," begged Lonnie, peering around the end of the curtain. "I could find it – I know I could!"

"How could you when you've never been there?" Amber snapped. "Besides, you couldn't handle Kickapoo." She could see the intense disappointment on her brother's face and she scolded herself for being so short with him. Her voice softened. "Why don't you get dressed and see what you can do to help Uncle John? We'll be needing lots of hot water, so make sure the wood box is filled, and – "

Lonnie brightened. "Yeah! Maybe I won't have to go to school today!"

"Probably not," muttered Amber, as she grabbed her coat and shawl off the hook on the wall, picked up the lamp, and hurried downstairs. Lonnie's attitude toward school irked her. He only went three months out of the year, but he considered even that too much. He's a typical boy, thought Amber. The authorities make sure Uncle John sends him to school and he doesn't even appreciate it. I wish someone would ask me if I wanted to go! Boys have all the luck! Why is it no one seems to think schooling is important for girls?

In all the years since Amber had come to Kansas to homestead with her aunt and uncle, this was the first time she had been called upon to help when a baby was born. The other four had arrived without complications. This time there must be problems, bad problems. But Amber felt little sympathy for her grouchy, ill-natured aunt. Aunt Grizelda was a witch and it served her right, she decided.

She felt sorry for Uncle John though – he seemed so worried and upset. Amber thought the world of her uncle and would do anything he asked, even this. As she rode Kickapoo bareback through the early morning darkness, she thought about Uncle John's parting words: "I hate to ask you to take the shortcut, with the river up like it is, but I'm real worried about 'Zelda. She's...it's never been like this before and I don't know what to do for her. We need Mrs. Tyneson just as fast as you can get her here."

Amber wasn't worried about crossing the river. She had done it lots of times and knew the best place. However, the darkness dictated the need to be more cautious.

Kickapoo snorted occasionally in the cold February air, his breath coming out in great white puffs visible even in the dark. Amber was glad to be able to ride astride, for the little mustang spooked at every tumbleweed or clump of soapweed they passed. He sensed the anxiety through her tension and jogged along in a half-walk, half-trot, tossing his head and grinding his teeth, impatient to run.

They had to hurry, but Amber knew she shouldn't run a horse blindly over the prairie at night. There were too many prairie dog and badger holes. She remembered all too well the day she and Kickapoo were racing a jackrabbit and how the little mustang had stepped in a hole and somersaulted head over heels with her on his back. She recalled how scared she had been that he might have broken a leg and didn't want to risk that again – not at a time like this!

As they approached the river, Amber could hear the sound of rushing water which had been fed by the melting snows and recent rains farther upstream. The river was up all right, as high as she had ever seen it. Kickapoo's ears were pricked forward and he was giving all his attention to the water, blowing through his nostrils in nervous apprehension.

Amber patted his neck. "It's all right, Kickapoo. Don't balk now. We don't have time to go by way of the bridge."

It took all her riding skill and much coaxing to get the reluctant horse into the swift current, and as the cold water swirled higher and higher about his legs, Kickapoo suddenly reared up and tried to turn back.

"No, Kickapoo! We've got to cross here! We've got to!" Amber cried, as she pulled him back around. She urged him on through the shoulder-deep water, kneeling on his back to keep from getting wet. When Kickapoo clambered up the opposite bank, he braced his legs and shook the water from his coat, nearly losing Amber in the process. She shivered as she gripped his cold, wet sides with her legs and felt the water soak through her stockings.

The darkness was fading from the eastern sky as they reached the edge of Pawnee Rock. Kickapoo's hoofbeats echoing down the deserted streets of the slumbering settlement attracted several yipping dogs to his heels, causing him to react by flattening his ears and tossing his head.

Following Uncle John's directions, Amber had no trouble locating the midwife's house, a neat little place with a white picket fence. Mrs. Tyneson answered her urgent knock wearing a pink flannel nightgown, her steel-gray hair done in one loose braid over her right shoulder.

"My aunt – Mrs. Hagen – she's having her baby!" blurted Amber breathlessly.

"Oh! I'll be right out. Can you harness my horse up? She's in the shed out back."

Amber nodded and dashed to the little barn behind the house. Quickly she harnessed the old sorrel mare to the buggy which had been purchased by the grateful people helped by Mrs. Tyneson over the years. By the time Amber led the horse out to the street, the diminutive lady appeared in a navy blue dress and cape, her hair sleeked into a bun held by bone hairpins.

Mrs. Tyneson laid her carpetbag on the seat, climbed into the buggy, and pulled up her hood against the blustery north wind. "Come along," she said to Amber.

"No ma'am, you go on," replied Amber, wrapping her wool scarf more tightly about her head and neck. "You have to go by way of the bridge, and I can save three miles cutting 'cross country. I need to get back as soon as I can." As she jumped onto Kickapoo's back, she felt a strange dizziness and grabbed a handful of mane to steady herself.

"Very well, young lady," said Mrs. Tyneson, frowning slightly, "but be careful at the river – it's running high, you know." She flopped the reins on the sorrel's fat rump and the mare took the buggy down the dusty street at a brisk trot.

Amber turned Kickapoo around and headed him back the way they had come. The biting wind was at their backs now, and it was light enough to see where they were going, so she let the mustang out at an easy lope.

The sun rose colorlessly behind gray clouds. As Amber rode across the prairie, she sought some clue, some hint that spring was not far off, but the bleak, brown landscape yielded nothing. The plains were like that. Here, she had discovered, the seasons did not give in graciously to one another. When spring did come, it would not come shyly, but all at once.

Spring had always been her favorite time of year, and she delighted in each one that came along. Except for the year Papa had died. It would be four years, come spring. She had lived with Aunt Grizelda's harsh discipline for four long years. Four years and four babies, she complained to herself.

And now, there would be another child. Another place at the table, more wet diapers hanging behind the stove, another little one to tote around on one hip and have hanging onto her skirts. Why did Aunt Grizelda keep having babies all the time? "Here I am fourteen and I feel like I've been married all my life!" she grumbled aloud to Kickapoo. The pony's ears flicked back to catch her words. The little mustang had settled down into a fast walk, ignoring the same tumbleweeds and clumps of soapweed which previously had made him skittish. All he wanted now was to get home.

As they approached the river again, Amber sensed Kickapoo's hesitancy and uneasiness. "Oh, come on," she said, aware of a growing exasperation. "You did it once, you can do it again." She was tired and didn't feel well and she was eager to get home. "It's all right. Come on!"

After several false starts, Kickapoo finally stepped into the swirling, muddy current. Once again, as the roily water came higher, Amber gathered up her skirts and doubled her legs up under her.

"So far, so good," she said, when they were halfway across. She gave Kickapoo his head. "Go on, boy."

Suddenly, in one terrible moment, there was no footing beneath the horse and he disappeared for an instant beneath the surface, plunging Amber into the icy water. She went under, then came up, gasping and sputtering, just in time to grab Kickapoo's tail. She held on with all her strength and let the horse pull her until she felt the sandy river bottom beneath her feet. She let go and waded awkwardly to the bank.

Kickapoo lunged up the river bank and stood dripping, his sides heaving. He shook himself vigorously, blew the water from his nostrils, and warily eyed the sodden figure coming up behind him. "Easy, boy, easy," said Amber, trying to keep her teeth from chattering. She stretched out one hand toward him. Just as she was almost close enough to grab the cord dangling from his lower jaw, a tumbleweed, caught up by the wind, blew against his legs. The mustang wheeled and, with a toss of his head, galloped for home.

"You come back here!" cried Amber. "You hear me? You come back here, you rotten, good-for-nothing mustang! You – ! You – !" Further insults were stifled by her chattering teeth and the shivering which convulsed her body. There was nothing to do but walk the mile to the farm.

As she walked, the wind cut through her wet clothes like a sharp blade of ice, and when she removed the soggy shawl from her head, she touched miniature icicles that were forming in her hair. Her legs were becoming numb, but she could still feel the cold water squishing out of her shoes with each step.

"I'll never make it," she told herself aloud, her lungs aching from inhaling the cold air. Once again her father's words came back to her, and she repeated them over and over. "You can do anything you set your mind to. . .anything you set your mind to. . .anything." Amber gritted her teeth and plodded on.

She was almost to the house. Only a little farther. Already she could feel the warmth from the stove reaching out, encompassing her.

But the fire was within her, a fervid, searing wildfire spreading throughout her exhausted body, causing her to swelter in its heat. The illness which had been stalking her now pounced upon her with a savage fury. Suddenly, the ground began to reel beneath her feet. She tried to call to the house for help, but the cry died in her throat. No one heard it, and no one inside the house saw the figure in the farmyard slowly crumple to the ground.

Amber heard the moan of the wind. Or was it someone crying? It grew louder, sharper, and became a piercing scream. In her fevered mind the sounds took shape and became visible images; they swirled and eddied like the river itself. Surrendering herself to the current, she swayed and floated, content to drift and to be carried along.

Then a shrill voice momentarily intruded. "It's coming! It's coming!" The words conjured up new illusions. . .she was lying helpless in the farmyard, cold and wet, her belly swollen, distended. . .she was having a baby. . .through the pain she could hear herself breathing hard, gasping for breath, her own sobs an echo of those from somewhere below.

Little by little, jagged pieces of reality penetrated her delirium. Gradually, through the fog which shrouded her mind, she comprehended the ordeal taking place downstairs, and for a few agonizing moments, Aunt Grizelda's suffering became overwhelmingly real. Listening to her aunt's cries of anguish brought tears to her eyes, for Grizelda's pain became Amber's pain and her screams Amber's own muffled sobs finding greater expression. My God! she thought. The pain. . .it must be terrible! Poor Aunt Grizelda! Please, God, she prayed, let it pass.

Suddenly she was falling. . .drowning . . . struggling. . .crying out for help. But there was no one. . .no one. She was all alone . . .sobbing.

"Amber? You're all right, Amber. Amber? Can you hear me? It's all right, you're safe now."

She opened her eyes to the familiar pattern of boards making up the attic roof above her, but it was not until she felt a hand on her forehead that she was able to make out the face of her Uncle John leaning over her bed. "Uncle John," Amber whispered. "I heard Aunt Grizelda. . .she had the baby. . .is she all right?"

"She's fine, just fine."

"Thank God," murmured Amber, surprised at her own sincerity.

"But now we got you to worry about."

"What happened?" she asked through dry, cracked lips. She was tired, so very tired. "I can't seem to remember. . ."

"It's all right now. You took a spill in the river, and I reckon you've got the fever. It's all my fault, too. I never should have asked you to take the shortcut. But you did good – you fetched Mrs. Tyneson here just in time," said Uncle John, squeezing her hand. "She made it just in time to deliver twins!"

"Twins!" whispered Amber, with a weak smile. Inwardly, she sensed that something, some imperceptible attitude had changed. In some strange way, she had shared Aunt Grizelda's ordeal, and momentarily at least, she felt that the sharing had forged a common bond of femininity between them. She sighed heavily and closed her eyes, aware of a contented feeling of accomplishment.

Amber awoke and stared vaguely at the pattern of shingles and parallel rafters above her, not realizing for the moment where she was. She tried to sit up, but fell back weakly upon her pillow. This was still her room upstairs, and the wind was still blowing, and the sun was still shining through the cracks in the low attic roof.

She tried to remember what had happened. As in the recollection of an unreal and forgotten dream, she slowly relived her early morning ride to Pawnee Rock. She could almost feel Kickapoo's feet go out from under him in the middle of that rushing river, and once again she experienced that agonizing sensation of helplessness. She remembered starting toward the farm, but from there on, her memory was hazy. And she was tired – so tired. She was about to go over everything again and try to unravel the mystery when she heard footsteps on the stairs and Lonnie appeared.

"Well, hi!" he said. "How do you feel?"

"Not too good," replied Amber, her voice scarcely more than a whisper. "What. . .what happened after I fell in the river? I can't seem to remember. . ."

Lonnie sat down on the edge of the bed. "I guess you got as far as the farmyard and collapsed from the fever. We wondered why you didn't come back. Finally decided you were takin' the long way around with Mrs. Tyneson. She's the one who found you layin' there half froze. Uncle John figured right off what had happened. He carried you in and then went to look for Kickapoo. Found him over behind the granary tryin' to get at the corn. What did he do – get balky and throw you off?"

"No," said Amber. She found it a tremendous effort to talk. "You know how that river is. Kickapoo was crossing just fine, when he must have hit a hole. Anyway, he went down. I was in the water before I knew it." She paused for a moment and moistened her lips. "When we got on across, something spooked him and he hightailed it for home as fast as he could go. I was so mad at him! But there was nothing I could do but start walking."

She took a deep breath. "From then on, I don't remember much."

"I guess not!" replied Lonnie, tossing his straight brown hair out of his eyes with a quick jerk of his head. "You were burnin' up with the fever, and you've been out of your head for two days now, moanin' and mumblin' crazy things. I thought you were dyin'."

"Two days?" said Amber. "You mean I've been here. . .in bed. . .for two days?"

Lonnie nodded.

"Oh, I've got to get up! Aunt Grizelda. . . the twins. . ."

"No you don't, not yet," Lonnie said firmly, pushing her back down onto her pillow. "You just rest awhile longer. You still look kinda feverish to me. Maybe you'll feel better tomorrow."

But Amber didn't feel better the next day, or the day after that. She alternated between consciousness and spells of feverish delirium during which she knew nothing. Days passed. Gradually her fever subsided, but the illness had so weakened her that the slightest effort tired her greatly. Most of the time she just lay there and listened to the whistling of the wind outside and the sounds of the family downstairs – the different footsteps and voices, the clatter of dishes, the clank of the stove lids. One or another of the children was always crying, and it was usually little Lucy.

By the end of the second week, Amber knew the exact number of boards making up the roof above her and was familiar with every knothole within view. She could even estimate the time of day by the position of the sun shining through the cracks.

Adding to her misery was the usual rash of boils that plagued them all in the spring, and the painful, festering sores seemed worse than ever this year. Today she counted no less than fourteen on one arm. Am I ever going to get well? she complained to herself, as she tried to cool the potato soup Lonnie had brought up for her supper. Her mouth was also full of blisters, and drinking the hot soup was extremely painful. She gave up and set the cup aside.

Oh well, what's the use? she told herself, flopping back onto her pillow. Maybe it would be better if I did die! No one would care. No one cares about me – not even Mama. Seldom had Amber allowed herself to entertain thoughts of self-pity, but now she was overcome with a sense of hopelessness and despair that was more than she could bear. Her eyes filled with tears. She turned her face to the pillow and cried for a long time.

Afterwards she lay quietly, emotionally spent. Soon she heard Lonnie's quick footsteps on the stairs as he came up to bed. "Hi!" he said brightly.

Amber envied his lightheartedness. "Hi," she returned. She was glad it was too dark for him to see her tear-streaked face.

"Mrs. Tyneson has to leave tomorrow," Lonnie said, as he began to undress for bed. "The Miller baby is due in the next week or so, and she wants to go home for a spell before she has to go over there."

"How are the twins?" asked Amber.

"Oh, they're doin' just fine. Uncle John was kinda worried about 'em 'cause they were so small at first, but they're gainin' weight and lookin' better. I can finally tell 'em apart – the boy is bigger. Who'd have ever thought Aunt Grizelda would have twins," he mused. "I guess that's the reason she had so much trouble. I've never seen Uncle John so worried. He was sure glad to see Mrs. Tyneson show up!

"Now he's worried about you. He doesn't say much, but I can tell. I went with him that day to Pawnee Rock to talk to the doctor. He was in Doc's office an awful long time. That's when Doc Carter gave him that bottle of medicine for you."

"He never talks like he's worried when he comes up to see me," Amber replied, somewhat bitterly.

"He's just trying to cheer you up. It wouldn't do any good for him to come up here and moan and groan along with you!"

Amber had to smile at Lonnie's frankness. "I guess I have been a problem, haven't I?"

Lonnie paused. "Just get well, Amber," he said earnestly.

And, although she was still weak, Amber decided then and there that she would go down for breakfast the next day. When she did, Aunt Grizelda's eyes followed her coldly as she slowly took her place at the table.

"My, but you look pale, Amber," remarked Mrs. Tyneson, as she set a plate of eggs and a bowl of gravy on the table.

"Oh, she's just putting on!" said Grizelda, taking her place opposite John. "She thinks she'll get out of a little work around here, that's all."

Mrs. Tyneson stared at Grizelda in puzzlement. The little woman started to speak, but evidently thought better of it and turned back to the stove, while Amber, her hands shaking, began to fill her tin cup from the crock of milk on the table. She caught her breath as the dipper missed the cup and milk splattered onto the oilcloth. Mrs. Tyneson hurried over to wipe it up. "That's all right, child, don't worry about it. I think you're just too weak to be up yet," she said kindly, putting an arm around Amber's shoulders. "You get back up to bed and I'll bring your breakfast up to you."

"She's all right!" declared Aunt Grizelda. "She hasn't been through half what I have. She can either eat her breakfast here or do without."

"What's the matter, Amber?" asked Lonnie one warm June day as the two of them brought the cows in from grazing along the lush river bottom. "Ever since you were sick, you just don't seem the same somehow." Amber walked on and appeared not to be listening, but her brother continued. "You're so quiet all the time, and you never laugh any more. Are you still sick?"

He saw a troubled look cloud the dark depths of Amber's eyes. "No," she replied. "I'm all right."

Something in her tone told Lonnie not to pursue the matter further. He shrugged and trotted back to prod one of the cows which had stopped to eat a particularly tempting bunch of grass.

But her brother was right. Amber knew she was not the same. She seemed possessed by a mood of depression and an attitude of defeat that smothered her inner spark and drive. It was reflected in her brown eyes which no longer sparkled with an exuberance for life, by the passive, rarely changing expression on her face, and by the submissive silence into which she had retreated.

She was aware, too, that her usual interest in life had been replaced by a general disinterest in everything. Not even Kickapoo could bring her out of her profound despondency. Amber still had not quite forgiven him for running off and leaving her at the river, and she had not ridden him since that day in February, although Uncle John had tried several times to revive her interest in the little mustang. He, too, had noticed the change in Amber and she knew that he was worried that perhaps her recovery from the strange, debilitating illness she had experienced was not complete.

The summer passed. When the willows and cottonwoods were tinged by the first touches of autumn gold, and there was no change in Amber's solemn mood, Uncle John tried once again to bring her out of it.

"Amber," he said one crisp morning, as she hung the washing on the line to dry. "I sold three of our steers to the butcher in Great Bend. He's sending a fellow out to get them today sometime. You know how those critters are when they haven't been driven much. He'll need help driving them as far as the river, but he figures he can handle them alone once he gets them in the river bed. It's dry now and he can follow it clear to town."

Amber finished her job and turned to face her uncle. His blue eyes were direct and unwavering.

"I want you to help him," John continued. 'Zelda's been keeping you so busy you don't have any free time any more, and Kickapoo's gettin' fat and sassy from no riding."

"But, Uncle John – "

"No buts now! You've been moping around here for six months. You need to get away for awhile, and a ride on a nice day like this will do you good. And don't worry about 'Zelda. I'll tell her what you're going to do."

Three hours later, the cowboy, Clint Tackett, galloped up in a cloud of dust. He was just in time for dinner, and Amber figured he'd planned it that way. He was wiry and well-built, with ruddy, angular features, and a thatch of unruly blond hair. Amber took an instant dislike to him when he swaggered into the house with Uncle John a few minutes later. "Boy! That smells good!" he said with confident enthusiasm. "I sure am hungry!" He promptly pulled out a chair from the table and sat down, tossing his dusty, black hat onto the children's bed.

The brash young man pretended to know a little bit about everything and, as they ate, he carried on a breezy conversation with John about the price of beef, the weather, and happenings in town. Amber could feel his gray eyes almost constantly upon her, but she was preoccupied with feeding the children and rarely looked up. When she did, their eyes met, causing her to glance quickly away. The stranger made her feel uncomfortable, and she was relieved when the meal was over.

"Amber here is going to help you with the steers as far as the river," explained John, as they got up from the table and started outdoors.

"Good!" replied Clint.

Amber, however, was not the least bit enthusiastic. As she led Kickapoo from the corral, she wondered how the pony would act, since he had not been ridden for so long. It would be embarrassing if he bucked and threw her off.

"Here, let me help you up," offered the cowboy, as Amber finished tying the rope around Kickapoo's middle. Before she could refuse, two strong hands were placed around her waist and she was lifted easily onto the mustang's back. She was glad to find that Kickapoo planned to behave, for she couldn't ride astride with someone along. Clint Tackett grabbed his saddle horn and swung lightly to the saddle without using the stirrup. He then spurred his horse, an ugly black one, into the corral and drove the three brindle steers out.

"Watch 'em close now, Amber," warned Uncle John, as he closed the corral gate. "They're pretty rank. They probably won't want to go."

Amber soon found that the steers were willing to go, just not all in the same direction! At first, she and the cowboy had trouble keeping them bunched and moving. But Kickapoo was alert to their movements, and Amber was able to turn them back each time they tried to dart her way.

After a while she was aware once more of the young man's eyes upon her, but she pretended not to notice as she again turned back a headstrong steer. Clint Tackett whistled in amazement. "You sure can ride, little lady!" he said, his smile revealing crooked yellow teeth. Amber ignored his remark, keeping her attention on the cattle.

"What's the matter, good lookin', cat got your tongue?" he said, reining his horse in alongside Kickapoo. The little mustang flattened his ears and made a quick pass with his teeth at the black horse. Amber felt the same distaste for the pair, but tried not to be so obvious.

"You better get over there and watch those steers," she said, motioning him away. "If they scatter – "

"Aw, they're plumb doe-cile now. All you gotta do is show 'em who's boss. Just like with women. Show 'em who's boss and they won't give you no trouble. Ain't that right?"

"I'm sure I wouldn't know," retorted Amber coolly.

"Well! You don't have to get all huffy! I just wanted to see if I could get a rise out of you. You're cute when you're mad, you know that? Fact is, you're about the cutest thing I've seen in a long time."

Amber felt her cheeks burn. She looked straight ahead and continued to ignore him.

"What's the matter with you anyway?" he asked. "You act like you don't even like me." He pushed back his black hat at a cocky angle. "I'm not such a bad guy, you know. Why don't we stop awhile and let these steers eat grass while you and me get acquainted?"

"No!" replied Amber firmly. "I've got to get back." She reined Kickapoo to get away from Clint, but the cowboy returned to her side. He was so close that his knee was pressing into Kickapoo's right side, and Amber was aware of an unwashed smell of sweat and stale tobacco.

"Aw, come on now," he said, grabbing Amber's arm. "I ain't used to bein' turned down."

"Let go of me!" cried Amber angrily. "Let go!" For a moment she was afraid she would be pulled off her horse. Then, in one swift instant, she raised her arm and bit down hard on the hand encircling it, at the same time throwing her right leg over Kickapoo's back. Free of the cowboy's grasp, she wheeled the mustang to the left and dug her heels into his sides.

"Ow! You little wildcat! You come back here!" Clint Tackett yelled after her, nursing his injured hand.

"Please don't buck, Kickapoo! Please don't buck!" Amber prayed, as the ground began to fly beneath the mustang's pounding hooves. Seeming to sense the urgency of this flight, Kickapoo ran as he had never run before, the wind whipping his long mane back into Amber's face and bringing tears to her eyes. She wiped them away on the sleeve of her dress, along with the salty grit in her mouth.

As soon as she dared, she peered back over her shoulder and saw that she was not being followed, for her sudden actions had spooked the steers and they had bolted in three different directions, leaving Clint Tackett in quite a predicament. Serves him right! Amber thought to herself. Then she patted her galloping pony's neck gratefully. "I love you, I love you, I love you!" she shouted into his ears.

Her momentary fears past, Amber surrendered herself to the sheer joy of racing her pony across the wind-swept prairie. She had forgotten how gloriously exhilarating it could be, riding wild and free with the sun and the wind in her face. She felt her spirits begin to rise, and then soar to the very heights of the vivid blue sky.

On impulse, she decided not to return home just now and guided Kickapoo instead toward a favorite spot up river, slowing him to a walk as they approached the rough sand dunes near the bank. Once into the willows, she slid off, took the rope off his lower jaw and tied it around his neck. "We won't have to worry about that smart-alec Clint Tackett here," she told Kickapoo, as she tied him to a stout willow. "He'll be heading the opposite way, once he gets those steers rounded up. I wonder how he'll ever get them all the way to town!" She laughed out loud for the first time in months. Giving the winded mustang a loving pat on his gray nose, she made her way through the shimmering golden willows and sat down on the bank of the dry river bed.

This was a curiously beautiful place on a bend of the Arkansas which directed the wind in such a way that the sand was swept in ever-changing contours and designs, never the same way twice. Once the level of the wind-blown sand might be high on the trunks of the willows, and the next time she came, their roots would be bared. Amber liked to think of it as the hand of God at play. She had always felt close to Him here, and the natural beauty of her surroundings, created by such an awesome, unseen force, imparted a tremendous feeling of spiritual renewal within her.

All of a sudden, Amber felt as though she had been living in a shroud of fog and had just now broken free into the bright sunshine. It suddenly occurred to her that she would not stay here on the Hagen farm forever. One day she would leave and find a life of her own. With the limitless time but limited vision of childhood, she had never really contemplated her future; now, she found herself wondering what lay ahead.

Would there be a young man for her? And marriage? She knew men found her attractive. If she had not been sure of it before, today's experience had left little doubt. But would she find someone who truly wanted her for the person she was? Still, at the thought of any marriage, something within her rebelled. Right now, marriage seemed to mean only hardship, constant irritability, and a brood of hungry, crying youngsters forever tugging at your skirts.

Was that all there was to look forward to? No! There must be more to life than that! There had to be. She felt her future beginning to beckon, and she was determined to meet it at least halfway. Like the meadowlark she heard singing in the prairie grass, she was determined to someday find her own place of belonging.

As she mounted Kickapoo and headed for home at last, a sense of lightness she had not known for months was upon her, and new hope and courage possessed her heart.

Chapter 9

The year 1893 started out like most other years, but things soon began to go wrong. The spring rains failed to come, and drought stalked the land. Crops withered and died in the fields. As the hot breath of summer scorched everything a uniform brown, the homesteaders were plagued with the accompanying menace of dust storms and prairie fires. Coyotes and chicken hawks, deprived of natural prey, increased their daring raids on poultry yards. With water and finances both in short supply, worry became the constant companion of the weary, hard-pressed homesteaders.

It was hot in the house after supper and even hotter in the attic. Amber took pencil and paper and slipped out to the grove of trees north of the house. It would be shady and quiet there – a good place to sit and write a letter while she let Kickapoo graze among the trees.

July 31, 1893

Dear Mama,

Here it is the last day of July and still no rain. I can't even remember the last good one we had, it's been so long. We did get a thunderstorm night before last, but it was all thunder and lightning, with just enough of a shower to settle the dust.

Remember the little calf I wrote you about, the half-starved orphan Uncle John gave me to raise? He was struck and killed by lightning during the storm. I sure hated for that to happen! He was coming along so well. Like Uncle John says, everything seems against us this year.

At least we have good well water and lots of it. We have one well by the corral and one right outside the back door. I wish I had a nickel for every bucket of water I've pumped and carried out to the vegetable garden this summer! Lonnie and the other children help, too. The ones too little to carry water help by scaring away the crows.

It's a lucky thing we had an extra good wheat crop last year. Most of this year's has either burned up or blown out of the ground. But Uncle John says, as long as we have water for the stock and the garden, we'll make it. He reminds me of Papa, the way he always looks at the good side of things. He keeps repeating that things could be worse, and I guess he's right. Some folks have had to pack up and leave.

I always used to look forward to summer because it meant get-togethers, like barn dances and spelling bees, but we sure haven't had many this year. No one is in the mood for such things. They're too busy trying to get enough food put up to see them through the winter. I have been helping Aunt Grizelda can vegetables from the garden and store them away in the cellar. Next month the corn will be ready to pick and then dry in the sun.

It's sad to see the prairie so parched and brown. The lack of grass is beginning to tell on the animals. We only got to cut one crop of hay along the river, because some neighbor boys playing with matches started a wildfire that burned up the rest. So there won't be much for the cattle. Uncle John is going to sell off most of them so we don't have to feed them through the winter.

Kickapoo is getting thin, too, poor thing. His ribs are showing something awful, but Uncle John says a mustang can get by where any other horse would starve to death.

Amber paused to watch Kickapoo eating grass a few feet away. He pulled a whole clump of grass out of the ground, shook the dirt from the roots, and slowly chewed it up. Then he blew the dust from his nostrils and walked on to the next bunch. Suddenly Amber was struck by an awful thought: would they have to sell Kickapoo, too? Uncle John hadn't mentioned anything about it, but could he be planning to? Maybe he had just been putting off telling her. The idea gradually became a dark worry that rolled around uncomfortably inside her and settled in the pit of her stomach like a heavy, black rock. If her horse was going to have to be sold, she wanted to know. She would ask Uncle John tonight.

She returned to her letter, but her mind was on Kickapoo and the thought of losing him. Hastily, she scribbled a few more lines about the baby Grizelda was expecting in September, and that she would try to get Lonnie to write something before she sent the letter off.

The sun had already set behind Uncle Karl's timber claim by the time she went to find Kickapoo, who by now had wandered off through the grove in search of more grass. He was reluctant to leave, but Amber finally coaxed him back to the corral to put him in for the night. She took the rope from his neck and scratched him behind the ears. Kickapoo nuzzled her arm, tugging gently at the sleeve of her dress with his lips.

"Sorry, fella, no corn for you tonight," she apologized. "We have to save it for the workhorses."

"That's all right," a voice said. "Go ahead and give him some. It looks like he needs it."

Amber turned to see Uncle John leaning on the fence behind her, smoking his pipe and quietly watching her. When she hesitated, he motioned toward the barn with his pipe. "Go ahead, it's all right."

She went into the barn, got a tin can full of ground corn and dumped it into the feed bunk. Kickapoo went after the pile of grain eagerly, keeping his ears back to warn an interested Archie and Charley to keep their distance. Amber came out of the corral, closed the gate, and stood beside Uncle John. She rested her arms along the top rail and watched Kickapoo in the fading light of dusk, as she wondered just how to ask Uncle John about what was on her mind. Maybe she ought to wait for him to bring it up. No, she decided, she'd die of suspense if she didn't find out for sure one way or another.

After a long moment, she took a deep breath and, half afraid of the answer, she asked, "Uncle John, will we have to sell Kickapoo?" She didn't look at her uncle, but stared straight ahead, waiting for his response. She must be prepared to accept his decision, whatever it might be.

Uncle John took several slow, deliberate puffs on his pipe the way he always did when he was thinking something over. Finally, he turned to Amber and said, "Aw, he don't eat much."

Amber flashed him a grateful smile, then impulsively flung both arms around his neck and gave him a quick kiss on the cheek. "Thanks, Uncle John!"

She picked up her pencil and tablet and hurried to the house to help Aunt Grizelda get the children ready for bed.

The summer dragged on, as anxious eyes watched skyward for relief that never came. For days on end, the wind blew hot and dry from the southwest, setting nerves on edge and straining tempers to the limit.

Amber glanced up from her work as Aunt Grizelda heaved a sigh and sat down heavily across the table from her. Clumsy and swollen with yet another pregnancy, she was, no doubt, every bit as uncomfortable as she looked. Strands of graying hair hung limp at her temples and fine beads of perspiration stood out on her forehead. Amber felt sorry for her. The heat was hard on all of them, and she knew it was almost unbearable for Grizelda. Eight kids, thought Amber, feeling a mixture of awe and concern. According to Uncle John, there was always room for one more, but things were getting a little crowded. The children slept three to a bed already, and when this new baby came, the last one, little Jamie, would have to give up the cradle in the bedroom and move out with the others. But none of the children seemed to mind the crowded conditions; it seemed they could adapt to any situation, however unpleasant, and they never complained much. All, that is, except the petulant little Lucy.

"Amber, play with me," the three-year-old pleaded in her annoying, high-pitched whine, flipping her golden braids back over each shoulder. Her bare feet and small, stout legs, tan with dust, were braced wide apart. In one sweaty little hand she clutched the rag doll she had received last Christmas.

Amber started to answer, but was cut short. "No!" snapped Grizelda. "Amber has to help me braid this rug." She picked through the pile of rag strips on the table. "You go on outside and play. Find Kris – he'll play with you."

Lucy began to sob. "No he won't," she cried defiantly. "I want Amber! I want Amber!" she screamed, louder and louder.

"I said no! Now be quiet or you'll wake the baby. Go on out and don't bother us, do you hear? And don't hold that screen door open – the flies are already thick in here!"

The screen door slammed. Grizelda sighed and wiped the perspiration from her forehead with the back of one hand, as Lucy's wails receded across the dusty farmyard.

Even Amber's thoughts seemed to seek relief from the heat, for she found herself thinking about last Christmas. It had been a nice holiday, one of the few she could remember when they had had snow. What she wouldn't give right now for some of the snow ice cream they had made with sugar and fresh cream from the cows. Or one of the crisp, juicy apples Uncle John had surprised them with! Or the peppermint sticks sent to them by the storekeeper in Great Bend! Her mouth watered.

Yes, it had been a nice Christmas in many ways. Their tree had been the best one ever, just a bare little branch Uncle John had cut from a cottonwood, but they had transformed it into a fairly respectable Christmas tree with the addition of cranberry and popcorn strings and paper decorations.

And, of course, there were the gifts, simple and homemade though they were. She recalled Lucy's squeal of joy when she first saw the rag doll her mother had made, and the other children's delight with their own gifts. It took so little to make them happy! Kris had received a small, wooden wagon his father had built and painted red; Hilda, a stuffed dog with long floppy ears, made from pieces of Aunt Grizelda's green velvet dress; and little Karl, a set of wooden blocks. For the twins, Mark and Martha, Aunt Grizelda had knitted matching caps. And her Home sewing machine had hummed late into the night as she made over one of her old dresses for Amber – her first full-length one, and a real surprise, compared to the hair ribbons she usually received.

Lucy's doll, made from an old sock and stuffed with sawdust, reminded Amber of the doll she once had back in Ohio – the only doll she ever owned. She remembered how she had run to Mama in tears one day when Lonnie had given it away to his little girlfriend. Mama had come to the rescue just in time.

Amber wondered what had finally become of that doll. Lisa and Amy had probably worn it out long ago. Since then, all my dolls have been real ones, she said to herself with a sigh, as she watched little Karl, Hilda, and the twins playing around on the floor with tin pans and jabbering to one another. Soon Jamie would be old enough to join them in their childish games.

Amber slipped one hand under the table and slowly eased her skirt up to her knees. Long dresses made her feel grown up for fifteen, but they sure weren't practical in hot weather!

"Pay attention!" grumbled Aunt Grizelda, as she waved away a bothersome fly. "You're not holding that tight."

"When do you think Lonnie and Uncle John will get back?" Amber wondered aloud.

"Better be shortly," replied Grizelda. "It's almost time to do chores. If they don't come before long, you'll have to start the milking."

"Digging a new well must be a big job. But with all the neighbors helping, maybe Josh can get it done today," said Amber.

"Mr. Mitchell," corrected her aunt.

"Yes, ma'am – Mr. Mitchell."

The screen door banged and Kris trudged in, grimy with dirt, from playing under the hackberry bush beside the porch. "I want a drink!" he announced, as he stood on tiptoe and plunged the tin dipper into the water bucket on the corner shelf.

"Where's Lucy?" asked his mother.

Kris paused only long enough between gulps to answer. "Don't know," he said, water dripping from his chin.

"Well, go find her and see what she's doing. I don't want her chasing those chickens again."

He returned the dipper to the bucket, wiped his mud-streaked mouth on his shirt, and went back out.

"We'd better stop for now. You get things cleared away so I can fix the mush for supper," said Aunt Grizelda, and Amber cleared the table of rag strips, needles and thread. "Now, grab a dish towel and help me shoo some of these flies out." She stationed Hilda at the door. "You hold this open for us. That's it."

Kris sauntered back through as Hilda held the door. "Can't find her," he said with boyish unconcern, as he joined them and began waving his arms to help drive the flies out.

"What do you mean, you can't find her?" demanded his mother impatiently. "Amber, you go get her."

Amber stepped out onto the porch and shaded her eyes with one hand. The farmyard was bathed in the glare of the late afternoon sun. "Lucy," she called. There was no answer. She tried again. "Luuu-ceee!" Still there was no answer. She had probably fallen asleep in the barn or some other cool place.

"Don't just stand there yelling – go look for her!" ordered Aunt Grizelda, but Amber was already off the porch.

She quickly made the rounds of the whole farmyard – the barn, the haystack, the chicken house, the pig pen, the granary, the smokehouse – once and then again, but Lucy was not to be found. "She's got to be around here someplace. She didn't just disappear!" Amber reassured herself.

The only place she had not searched yet was the corral. It did not seem a likely place, but it was worth a try. As she passed the water trough, a piercing whine caused her head to jerk around. "Lucy?" she called. It was only the the windmill's screeching complaint of metal against metal. But something bright caught her eye. Lucy's rag doll was floating face up on the surface of the water, its embroidered smile and shiny button eyes staring up at her with innocent cheerfulness. Amber picked it up. "Well, she's around here someplace," she told herself aloud.

Suddenly, fear clutched at her heart. With sickening dread, she slowly leaned over the trough and peered into the murky depths of the water. She gasped! Lucy's small, still form was sprawled face down on the bottom.

"Oh, no! No! No!" she cried, as though she could will away what she had seen. She began to sob, but fought the impulse to run screaming to the house. To panic now would not help. She must get Lucy out. Quickly she reached into the water, pulled the child to the surface and slipped both arms underneath her. Carrying the limp little body, she stumbled toward the house, sobbing uncontrollably. Tears streamed down her face and splashed onto Lucy's soaked dress, joining the dripping water to leave a dark, wet trail in the dust of the farmyard.

Aunt Grizelda's form appeared in the doorway. Amber was unable to speak, but words were not needed. With a moan of anguish, Grizelda took Lucy from her arms. "My baby! My baby!" she cried hysterically, searching the little face for signs of life. Lucy no longer looked troubled, but was peaceful now in death.

The morning sun was already scorching. Heat waves shimmered in the distance, blurring the horizon. Overhead a hawk drew slow, lazy spirals in the cloudless sky, the vee of dark feathers plainly visible on its white breast. The hot wind rustled the parched buffalo grass inside the barbed wire fence as the small crowd of neighbors entered the iron gate. *Pleasant View Cemetery*, the sign above it read. Amber wondered who had named it. The view from here was no different from anyplace else – just flat prairie stretching as far as the eye could see.

She hated graveyards. They reminded her of Papa's death. When a person was old, she reasoned, death would be acceptable, possibly even welcomed, but why was life so short for some? Would she, too, soon end up here, alone and forgotten by everyone, before she had a chance to live life to the fullest? Her musings recalled to mind the last line in the story of a great lady in her book: *And, at length, when she had greatly filled all the stations of empress, friend, wife, and mother, she bravely died without regret – regretted by all.* Life was for living; it seemed so unfair never to have the chance.

Amber scanned the rows of crude grave markers, perhaps twenty in all. Now the one Uncle John had carved for Lucy would join them in their lonely death watch. Lucy Hagen - Born Nov. 29, 1889 - Died Aug. 16, 1893 - Budded on Earth to Bloom in Heaven. Yes, Lucy's contest with life was over. Maybe in heaven she would find the contentment that had evaded her here on earth.

Amber stood holding the can of sunflowers she had cut. The water inside felt cool to her hands. She watched as Mr. Mitchell laid two leather reins, the best to be had among the neighbors present, across the oblong hole dug in the dry earth. Other neighbor men held the ends of the straps, and the little, white-washed coffin was placed on them and gently lowered into the grave.

Uncle John opened his well-worn Bible and began reading the Twenty-third Psalm. He looked haggard, for this year had etched new lines in his face. The drought was bad enough, but then had come Lucy's death. And now Aunt Grizelda was sick.

Amber was still puzzled by her aunt's strange behavior. From the moment Lucy had drowned, she seemed to retreat within herself, locking her grief inside. Although well-meaning neighbors came from miles around upon hearing of the tragedy, Grizelda refused to let anyone help her prepare her child for burial. After dressing Lucy in her best clothes, she had combed and braided her golden hair for the last time. Then she carefully laid her, with one little arm embracing her rag doll, in the small pine box lined with the blue silk scarf Amber had received from Uncle Karl. Amber didn't mind her using the scarf, but she couldn't help feeling hurt that Grizelda hadn't even asked her permission. She had simply taken it.

It wasn't long after that Grizelda had fallen ill. Amber imagined how sad it must be to lie at home in bed, unable to attend the funeral of your own child. But Uncle John was right – in her condition, the heat would have been too much for her.

At first, Amber felt her aunt was overcome by understandable grief at the loss of her child. But the more she reflected on what had happened that day, the more she wondered, was it possible Grizelda's over-wrought emotions were prompted by a feeling of guilt as well as grief?

At last, the reins were pulled back out, and two of the men picked up shovels. Amber looked away and tried to shut the scene out of her mind, but the noise of each shovelful of dirt hitting the wooden box thudded loudly in her ears. The sound chilled her, and she shivered, even in the heat.

When they were finished, she knelt down and pressed the can of sunflowers into the pile of loose soil, then rose to follow Lonnie and Uncle John to the wagon. "Goodbye, little cousin," she whispered.

It was Saturday. The women were alone with the children while Lonnie and Uncle John went to town with the Mitchells.

"Amber!" Aunt Grizelda yelled up the stairway. "Come down here!"

Amber sighed. She left her book on the bed and came to the head of the stairs.

Aunt Grizelda stood at the bottom. In one hand she held the leather quirt. "I said come down here!" she demanded. "It's time you got what's coming to you."

Amber slowly descended the stairs, bewildered by the steely anger in her aunt's words. "What do you mean?"

Grizelda's eyes narrowed. "I'll tell you what I mean!" she said, pointing with the whip. "Two of my babies are lying out there in that cemetery because of you!" She spat the words with a vehemence that stunned Amber like hammer blows.

"Because of me? Surely you don't. . . you can't blame me for what happened! Lucy's drowning was an accident. It. . .it just happened, that's all. It wasn't anybody's fault. And the doctor said you lost the last baby because you let yourself become too upset and. . ."

Grizelda stepped closer and glared into Amber's face. "It was your fault," she insisted angrily. "Watching these kids is your responsibility. You let Lucy drown, and that's why I lost the baby. You're to blame and you're going to pay for it!"

Amber was unshaken. From deep inside, anger rose within her, warm and seething like vomit. "No," she said firmly, "I won't let you."

"Why, you strong-willed little. . ."

"I'm fifteen years old now – almost a grown woman. You can't whip me any more like I was a child. I won't let you!"

Before she could raise a hand in defense, Amber felt the sharp lash of the whip across her face. Hot tears filled her eyes, but she did not cry – she would not cry. Unflinching, she kept her eyes fixed on Grizelda. All of a sudden, the anger drained from Grizelda's expression, and her mouth dropped open. The whip fell to the floor.

Amber felt something trickle down her cheek. She touched it with her fingers and saw it was blood. Pressing the back of her hand to her face, she turned without a word and ran upstairs to her room.

It was hot in the airless attic – stuffy and oppressive. Amber felt dizzy and steadied herself with both hands against the low rafters of the ceiling. When she looked into the ragged piece of mirror and saw the bloody red gash across her cheek, all her pent-up emotions of hurt and rage surged to the surface and found release in a torrent of tears. She could feel the salt in them burning the wound, just as she could feel the fury seething within her. Why did Aunt Grizelda hate her so? After a good cry, she dried her tears with a handkerchief and gently cleansed the wound, wishing she could wipe away her resentment as easily.

Then, as though guided by an unseen force, her gaze fell upon a single sentence in her book, lying open where she had left it: *Happy is the person who has sown in his breast the seeds of charity and love; he forgives the injuries of men and wipes them from his remembrance; revenge and malice have no place in his heart.*

"Happy?" Amber muttered to herself. "I've forgotten what that means! I haven't been happy since Papa died." She took a deep breath and looked into the glass again. Smoothing back her hair and squaring her shoulders, she recalled Papa's words once again: You can do anything you set your mind to.

As she stood there staring at her reflection, a new awareness came over her. It was as though the white heat of anger had at last fused her vague notions and wonderings into a firm resolve: she was going to leave. Her image mirrored this determination. Somehow, some way, she would leave.

Chapter 10

Amber's cheek healed quickly – more quickly than the wound in her heart. But rather than dwell on her troubles, she set her mind to making plans. She had everything figured out. She might have to lie about her age, but she would go into Great Bend with Uncle John one day soon and find a job – there was always some family looking for a house girl – and then she would break the news. The only one who knew of her plans was her best friend, Katie Mitchell, and she was sworn to secrecy.

"Oh, Amber, I'll miss you when you leave," Katie said, as the two of them sat alone on Amber's bed, talking. "But I can't blame you for wanting to get away from here. You know, from what you tell me, I think your aunt is touched with 'prairie madness.' If I were you, I would have left long ago."

Amber felt Katie's eyes on the scar still visible across her cheek, but it no longer bothered her. She was used to people staring, for the sunbonnet Aunt Grizelda made her wear most of the time had not hidden the mark from view completely. "But I promised Uncle John I would never run away again, after that one time, and he's been so good to me. I guess he can't help the way Aunt Grizelda is.

"This time it won't be like running away though, more like . . . like moving. I'll have a job with a family in town and live with them. I hear that house girls make as much as a dollar and twenty-five cents a week! Can you imagine actually getting paid to do the same work I do around here for nothing?" Amber paused and looked thoughtful. "Maybe I can save up enough to take the train back home to Ohio. Oh, just think how exciting it will be, having money, and being on my own, and making my own decisions. I'm old enough – after all, I'm almost sixteen!"

"Yes, and some girls even get married when they're sixteen," said Katie, excitement dancing in her blue eyes. "My cousin Ellie did. You remember her – you met her at the barn dance at the Halseys' last year."

"I don't care if I *never* get married!" replied Amber, looking away.

"Oh, Amber," Katie chided, "you'll change your mind when the right man comes along."

"Well, I don't know. Maybe. But right now, marriage is the furthest thing from my mind."

The distant boom of the old black-powder rifle jolted them out of their daydreams. "That's Lonnie," explained Amber. "He's hunting a rabbit for our dinner." She laughed and said, "I always tease him about having to shoot them – I used to sneak up on the critters when they hid in a bush and grab them! I never will forget the look on Aunt Grizelda's face the first time I brought one home!" They both giggled.

"Amber Lockhardt! You do some of the craziest things!" Katie said, laughing. Then, with mock seriousness, she added, "Don't you know that isn't lady-like?"

"Now you sound like Aunt Grizelda," said Amber dryly, as she slid off the bed. "Come on. We three are going to have the best dinner ever!" They tripped lightly down the stairs. "It isn't often we get this place to ourselves for the whole weekend. I'm sure glad you could come over."

"When will your aunt and uncle get back from Olton?"

"Sometime late Monday, I guess. It's almost 40 miles, you know, and that's a long trip. I don't envy them, with all the kids along. I'm glad they let me stay home!" She opened the lids of the cookstove and dropped in some cow chips and corn cobs.

"How come you and Lonnie didn't go along?" asked Katie, handing her several more corn cobs from the fuel box.

"Oh, Uncle John thought it would do Grizelda good to get away for awhile, so they went to Olton to see some people they used to know back in Ohio. Lonnie and I didn't know them, and Uncle John already had a wagonful, so we got to stay here and look after things." She lit the fire and clanked the lids into place. "Now, what shall we fix with our rabbit?"

"Mashed potatoes and gravy!"

"Yes, and biscuits!"

"And pickled cucumbers!"

"And peach cobbler!"

Just then, Lonnie walked proudly through the door, a jack rabbit dangling from each hand.

"Oh, good!" exclaimed Amber. "You got two! This will really be a feast!"

"I only shot one," confessed Lonnie. "I took the other one away from a hawk, and was he ever mad! What else are we having?"

"Never mind, just go back out and get those rabbits skinned so we can get them to frying."

"Okay, but fix plenty of food. I'm starved!"

"Oh, you're always starved," said Amber, giving him an affectionate nudge out the door.

Soon, tantalizing aromas vied with one another to fill the kitchen, promising the enjoyment that was to come. And no one was disappointed. Amber couldn't remember when she had enjoyed a meal more. The food was delicious, with no limit on helpings for once, and with no children to tend, it was a real holiday of leisure.

"Ohhhh, I'm stuffed," moaned Amber at last, as she leaned back in her chair. "I couldn't hold another bite."

"Me neither," agreed Katie. "Everything was just great. We're pretty good cooks, aren't we, Amber?"

"Yes, even if we do say so ourselves." Amber threw a sideways glance at Lonnie.

"Huh? Oh, yeah, it was real good," he said, yawning lazily and stretching. "Well, guess I better go clean the gun." He ambled out.

"And we'd better get these dishes washed, so we can go for a ride in that new cart of yours," Amber told Katie. "I've never ridden in a two-wheeler."

They were laughing and talking girl talk as they worked. Suddenly they heard the rifle explode with a deafening roar, followed instantly by the sound of shot splattering against the side of the house.

"Lonnie!" screamed Amber as she dashed outside, her friend at her heels.

They rounded the corner of the house, and Amber was relieved to see Lonnie on his feet. His back was to them, and in one fist he clenched the gun's iron ramrod. But Amber could not believe her eyes. One end was bent back almost double! "Lonnie! Oh, Lonnie! What happened?" she cried.

As she rushed up to him, Lonnie dropped the ramrod and put both hands up to his face. He staggered dazedly and slowly turned around to face her. Blood oozed from between his fingers, running in red rivulets down his arms. Katie gasped. "Quick!" Amber told her. "Help me get him into the house!"

They led him inside and put him on the bed in one corner. Amber ran to get some water from the well and a clean rag, then gently washed away the blood. Shot had peppered his face and right hand and was embedded deeply in his flesh.

Lonnie was rolling his head from side to side and moaning. "It stuck . . . ramrod stuck in barrel . . . musta forgot to take the cap off," he mumbled. "When I pulled . . .gun went off. . .musta forgot . . ." His speech became more and more unintelligible.

"Shhh!" Amber soothed him. "Don't talk now. Just lie still." It scared her to see how pale he looked beneath all the blood.

"Oh, Amber! What shall we do? He might be dying!" cried Katie.

"Hurry and go tell your folks," said Amber. Her voice sounded strange, like it was someone else's, and her fingers trembled as she continued to wipe Lonnies's face with one hand and hold him still with the other. "Have them send someone to Pawnee Rock after the doctor. I'll just try to keep him quiet until he gets here. Hurry now!"

Katie ran out the door and jumped into her cart. Amber heard the clatter of hooves fade into the distance. Then there was only the sound of the wind blowing and the clock on the wall ticking away the minutes, slowly, so slowly, making each one seem like an hour.

One thirty. Lonnie was calmer. He seemed to be unconscious. Was that a good sign or a bad one? Oh, please God, don't let him die! Please don't take him from me! Amber prayed over and over again.

Two o'clock. Is that all? Oh, hurry, hurry, hurry! Amber went to get some fresh water from the bucket in the corner. She paused. Something was wrong – what was it? The clock, she couldn't hear the clock ticking. It had stopped. Darn! She had forgotten to wind it today. Oh well, maybe the time would go faster if she didn't have the hands to watch.

After what seemed like forever, Katie returned. "Mother came with me," she panted as she charged through the door. She was breathing hard from the rush, and her blonde hair was tangled and windblown.

Amber was glad to see Katie's mother, for Liz Mitchell was a calm, sensible person, never ruffled or perturbed. She always seemed to take everything in stride.

"Hello, Amber," she said kindly, and then studied Lonnie with concern. "How is he, child?"

"He passed out awhile back, but I think he's coming around again. Did someone go for the doctor?"

"Josh did," answered Mrs. Mitchell. "Here, let me get you some fresh water." She took the pan and went to dump it outside.

"Daddy said he'd send a wire to your aunt and uncle while he was in Pawnee Rock, too," said Katie.

Amber frowned. "Well, I suppose he had to. But after everything else that's happened, I hate to confront them with this," she said grimly.

It must have been around four-thirty when Josh Mitchell finally arrived with the doctor. As Doc Carter examined Lonnie, Amber watched his face for some indication of his findings, but his expression never changed. "He'll be all right, once we dig all that shot out," he announced finally.

Amber heaved a heavy sigh of relief. "Thank goodness."

"But one hit the pupil of his right eye dead center," added the doctor. "I'm afraid he'll be blind on that side."

Blind! The word sent a chill up Amber's spine. "Oh, no," she murmured, shaking her head slowly.

"There's no time to waste," said the doctor, taking off his coat. He opened his bag and began taking out the items he would need. "Young lady, I'll need boiling water to sterilize these instruments. And some clean rags." He began rolling up his sleeves. "Josh, lay the boy on the table here."

They all scurried about doing as Doc Carter directed. When everything was ready, the doctor poured some ether onto a rag and put it up to Lonnie's nose. "Here," he said, handing Amber the bottle of anesthetic. "Pour a few drops on the rag whenever I tell you to." As soon as he was satisfied the boy was completely under, he began the tedious job of probing for the shot, as they all stood around the table watching silently, hopefully.

One by one, Doc Carter dropped the shot into the pan of water beside Lonnie's head. Ping . . . ping . . . ping. Five, ten, fifteen. Amber lost count as the water became pinker and pinker. The sight was sickening, and she wanted to run from the room. You coward! she scolded herself. You can't run out on Lonnie now!

How much longer? Amber wondered why her chest ached so, until she discovered she was holding her breath. It was hot in the little house, and the odor of ether was strong. She felt weak and light-headed, and a fine perspiration formed on her forehead. Don't you dare faint! she admonished herself once more. Don't you dare!

"More ether," requested Doc Carter, without looking up.

Amber poured a few more drops onto the rag, then locked her eyes on the doctor's profile as he worked. He looked tired, but she had never seen him when he didn't. His salt-and-pepper hair, thinning on top, matched his neatly trimmed goatee, and he peered with a steady gaze through the spectacles perched on the bridge of his nose. He's so calm, so sure of himself, Amber thought. Did he never know fear or uncertainty?

At last he spoke. "Well, folks, that's the best I can do without disfiguring his face, and there's no need for that. It won't hurt to leave those few that are too deep." He washed his hands, rolled his sleeves back down, and gathered up his things. "Keep his eyes bandaged and make sure he stays in bed for four or five days. And tell him to take it easy! Wash his eye out twice a day with this." He produced a bottle of medicine from the depths of the black bag and handed it to Amber. "That eye won't be a pretty thing to look at, but that boy's lucky to be alive."

While Josh carried Lonnie back to bed and Liz made him comfortable, Amber walked with the doctor to his buggy. "Thank you so much, Doctor Carter."

He tipped his hat and climbed in, setting his black bag on the seat beside him. "Give my regards to your aunt and uncle," he said. "And tell John not to worry about my bill. He can pay me whenever he's able – no hurry." He swung his horse around and the bay trotted eagerly for home.

Amber felt weary. She took a deep breath and pushed the loose hair back from her face. Her apron was dirty and smeared with blood. I must look a sight! she thought. As she turned to go back inside, she remembered the gun still out in the yard. She'd better not leave it there.

She found it still propped in the fork of one of the cottonwoods. Apparently Lonnie had put the gun there to hold it while he tried to pull the ramrod out. The rifle must have moved just enough to trip the hammer and explode the cap. If only he had remembered to remove that first!

Carefully, she lifted the heavy firearm from the fork of the tree, then picked up the strangely bent ramrod lying where Lonnie had dropped it. She stared at it in anger. This! All because this thing got stuck, Lonnie would be blind in one eye! She shuddered when she thought of the terrific force it must have taken to bend it so. Then it occurred to her that this piece of iron that had caused the accident had also saved Lonnie's life by absorbing most of the impact of the shot. How strange!

Katie rushed to the door as Amber put the gun on the porch. "Amber, come quick! Lonnie's starting to vomit!"

Amber hurried inside, grabbed the empty washpan, and ran to his bedside. She got there just in time. As Mrs. Mitchell held Lonnie's head to one side to keep him from choking, Amber and Katie looked at each other ruefully, each sharing the other's thought: Our wonderful dinner!

The coal oil lamp began to sputter as it burned lower and lower. Amber was curled up in the rocking chair beside Lonnie's bed, and Katie was a blondeheaded lump on the bed in the other corner, when Uncle John burst through the door, followed by Aunt Grizelda carrying Jamie. "Amber?" Uncle John called.

"Uncle John? Is that you?" she responded, rubbing the sleep from her eyes. "I guess I dozed off." She turned up the wick and squinted through the dim light at the clock Josh Mitchell had reset before Liz and he left. Three A.M.

"We came as soon as we could get here. Where's Lonnie? Is he. . .?"

"He's going to be all right, Uncle John, except he'll be blind in one eye."

"Thank God he isn't dead!" exclaimed John, visibly relieved. "The telegram just said, "Lonnie shot himself,' and we didn't know if he was dead or alive!"

"Neither did Mr. Mitchell, when he sent it." responded Amber.

"What on earth happened?" asked Uncle John. Then he added, "Wait! Help us get the kids out of the wagon and put to bed, then you two can tell us all about it."

During the next few days, Amber was enmeshed in the agony of indecision. Should she go ahead with her plans to leave or should she stay with

Lonnie until he was fully recovered? When the bandages came off for good, he would be able to feed and care for himself once again, but didn't her responsibility run deeper than that? She was the only real family Lonnie had close by. She felt sure that, in reality, Grizelda was just as glad as Uncle John that Lonnie hadn't killed himself, but she would probably be as hard as ever on him. She might even decide to punish him for what had happened. As though losing his eye wasn't punishment enough! They had both been whipped for a lot less.

Finally she tried putting herself in his place. Then she knew, although Lonnie might never admit it – even to himself – that he needed her. She could not run out on him now, any more than she could have during his surgery. Her hoped-for job in town would just have to wait.

Chapter 11

Spring came once again to western Kansas. No longer did the prairie lie dormant beneath the gray-brown ash of winter. Soaking rains had broken the drought, and the land was coming alive with a verdant array of living, growing things. Amber had experienced sixteen springs, but each one seemed to hold an awesome newness all its own. Her whole being joyfully participated in the renewal of the world around her: when she held in her hand the downy, yellow puff-ball that was a baby chick; when she witnessed the mosaic of color created by wildflowers blooming across the landscape, and the sudden blizzard of "cotton" produced by the friendly cottonwood trees; when she galloped her pony over the prairie in the warm spring sunshine, riding as wild and free as the wind itself. From these simple pleasures she drew new strength and courage. These were the wonders that made her life more bearable.

Ever since the first of the year, she had been giving a great deal of thought to leaving. If she was ever going to, this would be the time. February had come and gone, with her birthday passing unnoticed, as usual, by the family. It was funny, but sixteen didn't feel any different from fifteen. Somehow, she had expected to sense a new confidence, a deeper insight into life, but she could detect no magical transformation.

Maybe she wasn't as grown up as she thought she was. Maybe she shouldn't leave just yet. True, Lonnie didn't really need her any more, for he had adjusted to his loss and was getting along fine with only one eye. But Aunt Grizelda was pregnant again, and she would need help now more than ever. And then there was Kickapoo. She hated to leave the little mustang. What would become of him if she went away?

She worried about it for days. Should she put off leaving for another year, or even two? After all, she was nothing but a dumb farm girl. What if she couldn't make a go of it working in town? What would she do then – come running back here like a whipped pup, begging them to take her in again? No, she could never do that! She would never live it down. The independence that had beckoned so invitingly now loomed as bait in a trap waiting to ensnare her. Yes, maybe she had better stay awhile longer.

"We're ready, Amber," called Uncle John, as he and Lonnie finished harnessing Archie and Charley to the wagon.

Amber gave Kickapoo one last pat and hurried over to join them. "Poor Kickapoo!" she said, as the mustang began pacing the corral fence and nickering to the other two horses. "He always hates to be left behind all by himself."

"But he never wanted to go, either!" Uncle John reminded her. "Remember all those times we tried to work him in harness?"

Amber decided to change the subject. "Thanks for convincing Aunt Grizelda to let me come along with you," she said, climbing up on the wagon seat beside him.

"Does a body good to get away once in awhile," her uncle answered. He waited for Lonnie to jump in back and then clucked to the team. "You and Katie can have a nice visit while Lonnie and I sharpen all these tools and replace the rims on the wheels. It'll take us all morning."

"It's sure nice of Mr. Mitchell to let you use his blacksmith shop whenever you need to," Amber remarked.

"You couldn't ask for nicer neighbors than Josh and Liz. Don't know what we'd do without 'em," replied John.

Before long, a clanking, rattling wagon, hung with numerous pots and pans, and pulled by two stout sorrels, approached from the direction of the Mitchells'. Across the side of the wagon cover were emblazoned the words, ZAK WADDELL. GEN. MDSE. EVERYTHING FROM A TO Z. Two men occupied the wagon seat. "Howdy, folks," hollered the older one, pulling up his team. He was a big man, strong and burly, with coarse features and a ruddy complexion. He was perspiring freely, and continually wiped his face with a ragged red bandana. "I'm Zak Wadell, and this here's my son, Moe." The son, younger but even bigger, leaned forward and tipped his hat. "Need anything today?" the older man continued. "Pots, pans, needles, thread, calico, linament, medicines? Anything at all – just you name it!"

"I don't believe we do," replied John, "but tell you what. Back yonder is my homestead, and the wife might need some things. Be obliged if you'd stop by and show her what all you've got."

"Sure thing. Be happy to, be happy to," said the man, clucking to his team.

"But watch out," John warned with a grin, "she's a shrewd woman to deal with!"

Amber turned and watched the heavy wagon lumber off in the direction of the farm. When there was no wind, sounds carried great distances across the low-lying land along the river, and she could still hear Kickapoo frantically whinnying after Archie and Charley. I wish he'd be quiet, she thought to herself. Aunt Grizelda's going to get upset with him again, and then I'll really hear about it when we get back!

As they rode along in the bright spring sunshine, Amber wondered what Katie would say when she told her she had decided not to leave for another year or so. No doubt Katie would be surprised, after all the plans they had discussed together. Amber tried to reassure herself that she had made the right decision, but now, as she thought of telling her friend about it, she found herself inwardly perturbed by a haunting discontent. She had had such great plans! What had happened to them? Simple. She had gotten cold feet and taken the easy way out, and now, deep inside, she was disappointed in herself.

Maybe Katie could ease her regret. Or maybe Katie, too, would be ashamed of her, for she would know Amber for the coward she really was. Suddenly Amber wished she had not come. She wanted desperately to turn around and go back. She needed more time, more time to think. But Katie had seen them coming and was waving to her as she ran out to greet them.

All the way home, Amber pondered the value of true friendship and how fortunate she was to have the gift of Katie's loyalty. Her fears of being reproached had proven groundless, for Katie had been very understanding and sympathetic, lending full support to whatever decision Amber might make. With Katie and Kickapoo, she felt she had two valuable companions.

As they drew near the farm, Amber shaded her eyes and squinted into the late afternoon sun, watching for the little mustang pacing the corral fence, listening for his welcoming neigh. But so far there was neither. As they entered the farmyard, fear rose within her, for he was nowhere to be seen. She jumped down from the wagon before Uncle John had even brought it to a halt and ran to the corral, calling Kickapoo's name.

"Uncle John! Kickapoo's gone! Where could he be?" she cried, scanning the area in every direction.

"Well now, let's just go ask Grizelda. I'll bet she knows."

"You did what?" demanded John.

Grizelda looked smug. "I said I traded that no-good mustang for this new stove – him and the twenty dollars I had saved up."

Uncle John was as stunned as Amber was. They both stood speechless before the huge black and silver monster now occupying the kitchen.

"I needed a new stove a lot more than Amber needed that horse. He wasn't worth his salt anyway – wouldn't work a lick! And you said yourself that only rich people keep riding horses. I've done without long enough, and I decided it was high time I had a decent stove to cook on. This one has a warming oven and a hot water reservoir and everything, and it's almost brand new." Excitement colored Grizelda's words as she continued. "The peddler picked it up from some folks who pulled up stakes and left after the drought, and he was selling it cheap. It isn't every day you can get a stove like this for thirty dollars!"

Soberly, Uncle John took off his hat and scratched his head, the way he always did when he was perplexed. "Well, I wish you hadn't done it, but it's too late to do anything about it now. A deal's a deal."

Amber turned without a word and walked out the back door, letting the screen door slam behind her. She didn't care. She didn't care about anything now.

"You come back here, young lady!" shouted Aunt Grizelda, shaking her finger. "You've got work to do!"

"Let her be!" John insisted, a touch of anger in his voice. "It's your fault – you had no right to trade her pony off. He meant a lot to the girl."

Amber wandered sadly over to the empty corral, crossed her arms along the top rail of the fence, and rested her chin upon them. She discovered bits of hair from Kickapoo's mane caught in the splinters of the board. Absently, she pulled a tuft loose and held it between her fingers, watching it glint blue and silver in the sunlight.

Yes, Kickapoo had meant a lot to her. Her eyes grew moist as she thought about the two years they had shared – two years of each other's lives, both the good and the bad. Like the time he had saved her from that smart-alec cowboy, Clint Tackett. Then there was the time he got the colic and she had had to walk him in a mud puddle all night to save his feet. And she would never forget that time they fell in the river.

Nor would she ever forget the day she first saw him, how awful he looked, unwanted and so in need of a friend. That was what made their friendship so invaluable – they had needed each other. Now, like a dream, it was over, and all she had left were fond memories and these strands of Kickapoo's mane. She decided to put them in her keepsake box along with her spelling medal and the glass stopper from the bottle of perfume Uncle Karl had sent.

Suddenly she was filled with new determination. I'm through making excuses, she decided. With Kickapoo gone, there's nothing holding me in this awful place. I won't put it off any longer. Uncle John's going to town tomorrow, and I'm going with him to find a job!

The trip into Great Bend early the next morning reminded Amber of the time she had run away and Uncle John had come after her. Once again, there was a long period of silence, with her uncle occasionally glancing her way. He hadn't asked her reason for going into town, although Amber rather imagined that he knew.

The silence stretching between them made Amber uncomfortable. She tried various attempts at conversation and finally got Uncle John started talking about his plans for the addition he was going to build onto the house. The new stove took up so much room, he was going to add a room onto the kitchen area for it and a cupboard, leaving more space for the table and the children's two beds. He loved doing things with his hands and took pride in the fact that he was an excellent carpenter. It was a skill he had learned from his own father, Amber's grandfather, and Amber was glad to see that Lonnie seemed to possess the same talent. The way the West was growing, her brother would have no trouble finding a job later on, even with his handicap.

At last they crossed the bridge into town, and Uncle John pulled up in front of the courthouse. "I'll meet you back here at three o'clock sharp. Here," he said, handing her a quarter. "You'll need to buy yourself some dinner."

Amber jumped down from the wagon and watched Uncle John drive off toward the mill to sell his wagonload of wheat. She dropped the quarter into the drawstring bag she had made the night before, then smoothed her hair and brushed the wrinkles from her best dress. Well, she said to herself, what now? She decided to go up one side of the street and then down the other, asking shopkeepers if they knew of anyone looking for a house girl. At the same time it would be fun to investigate all the different stores.

She started off, trying to walk gracefully and act very grown up so people would think she had lived in town all of her life. But it was hard to keep from gawking, and last year's shoes hurt her feet.

By the time she had questioned seven store owners without any luck, her feet were really aching. Besides, it was past noon and she was hungry. It would be nice to sit awhile, eat, and rest her weary feet. She paused to scan the storefronts and signs for a suitable place to buy dinner. She could see several establishments that served food, but finally decided to try the closest one, which was directly across the street and had a large, hand-lettered sign over the door that said EAT.

She started across, picking up her skirts to spare the hems from the dust of the street. Just then, a shiny, new, maroon buggy with bright yellow wheels turned the corner and came toward her. The two matched bays trotted by smartly and in perfect unison, their eight white feet flashing in the sun. Amber couldn't take her eyes off them. They were the most beautiful horses she had ever seen, and she felt a pang of pure envy.

The young woman in the buggy giggled at her handsome escort, and Amber suddenly realized how silly she must look standing there in the middle of the street, gaping. For a moment, she thought the couple must be making fun of her, and she felt embarrassed. But as they went on by, it was obvious they were entranced with each other and hadn't even noticed her.

She hurried on across the rutted street and stepped into the little restaurant. To her surprise, there was no one inside. She hesitated for a moment, holding the door and wondering what to do. Maybe it wasn't open for business.

But then she saw moving shadows on the curtain hung in the doorway behind the counter. From the back room she could hear low, muffled voices.

"Come 'ere, sweetie, and give your ol' man a kiss," said a gruff voice.

"I told ya' before," answered a girl's voice, "don't call me sweetie! I don't like it!"

"All right! All right! But how's about a little kiss?"

Letting the rickety screen door slam behind her, Amber moved to the counter.

"Shhh!" the girl broke in. "A customer just came in."

The curtain parted and the girl stepped through the doorway. Amber was surprised to see that she was young, not much older than herself. Judging from the voices, she had expected someone older. The girl was rather pretty, but had a sallow complexion and oily brown hair.

"Hi, what'll ya' have?" she asked, tying a soiled white apron over her faded gingham dress.

"Oh, a ham sandwich and a lemonade, I guess," replied Amber, reciting the first thing printed on the menu which was tacked to the wall behind the counter. "I think I'll sit over here at a table, though, if it's all right."

"Sure," answered the girl. "Be ready in a minute."

Amber chose the table with the cleanest tablecloth, pulled out a chair and sat down heavily. If only she could take her shoes off! She must remember to eat slowly so she could rest as long as possible. If I get a job, the first thing I'm going to do is buy a new pair of shoes! she decided.

The waitress brought the sandwich and drink and set them down in front of her. "That'll be twenty cents," she said. Amber gave her the quarter and the girl brought back her change. "You're new in town, ain't ya'?"

"I live on a farm fifteen miles out," replied Amber, sipping the lemonade. It was cool and tartly sweet.

"I didn't think I'd ever seen ya' in here before."

"I'm looking for a job in town. Does your father need another waitress?" asked Amber, glancing at the curtained doorway.

"Him?" said the girl, with a toss of her head in the same direction. "He ain't my pa. He ain't anything."

Flustered, Amber didn't know what to say. "Oh," she responded feebly.

"You wouldn't want to work for him. Anyhow, you can see we don't do much business, just enough to keep us going."

The man's deep voice bellowed from the back room. "Josie! How many times I gotta tell ya' – quit gabbin' with the customers! Ya' got things to do!"

"I'm comin', I'm comin', keep your shirt on!" Josie shot back. As she moved away, she turned to Amber. "You might try Mr. Hardy – he's the druggist down on the corner. He was in for coffee this morning and I heard him say he was lookin' for a house girl to help his sick wife."

"Thanks," said Amber, as the girl disappeared between the curtains.

With this new lead on her mind, Amber quickly finished eating and went in search of the drugstore and Mr. Hardy. She found his shop with no trouble, for there was a huge make-believe bottle sitting out front with DRUGS painted vertically on two side of it. Several bearded gentlemen sitting out front eyed her curiously as she entered. Inside, a small man with a thin face and spectacles was busy waiting on a lady customer.

While Amber waited, she browsed around. It was her first time inside a drugstore, and she was surprised to find such a variety of items. A person could buy everything from Harter's Iron Tonic to Scotch Snuff. There were even displays of True-Fit Spectacles and Warner's Corset Clasps, as well as *True* and *Harper's Weekly Magazine.* She recognized the advertisement of Pink Pills for Pale People, for it was in one of these empty bottles that she had put the shot taken from Lonnie's face. But what in the world was Hamlin's Wizard Oil?

Wistfully, she studied the girl with the flowing hair on a poster advertising Harmony Hair Beautifier, but it cost one whole dollar and that was more than she'd ever had in her life. With only a nickel, she would have to settle for something less. Maybe a handkerchief. She looked around and found a nice one of white linen and began rummaging in her bag for the elusive coin.

"Now then, young lady, what can I do for you?"

Amber turned around. "Oh!" she said. "I'd like to buy this handkerchief."

"All right. Let me put it in a sack for you," said the druggist. "And will there be anything else today?"

Amber followed him over to the cash register. "Are you Mr. Hardy?"

"Yes, I'm Clement Hardy," he replied.

"I hear you're looking for a house girl."

"Why, yes, I am. My wife hasn't been well and she needs help with our two little girls and the housework. Are you interested in the job?"

Amber wanted to shout, Oh, yes! Yes! Please! If you only knew how desperate I am! But she responded with a simple "Yes."

Her silent plea, her desperation, must have shown in her eyes. Mr. Hardy gazed directly at her for a moment, then dropped his eyes to her hands nervously twisting the drawstring of her handbag. They were rough and calloused and she wished she could hide them from his view.

"You look like a good worker," he said kindly. "When can you start?"

Amber felt her heart leap for joy. "I'll have to get my things from the farm. How about next Sunday when we come in for church?"

"That's where I've seen you. At church. You're John Hagen's girl, aren't you?" he asked.

"No, he's my uncle, but I've been living with them for six years. My name is Amber Lockhardt."

"Well, Amber, you bring your things in Sunday and we'll meet after church and take you on home with us. Adele will be so pleased that I finally found someone."

"All right. Thank you so much, Mr. Hardy," she said sincerely. "I'll see you then."

Sunday couldn't come soon enough for Amber. In her impatience to leave the farm, each day seemed twice as long. However, nothing could dampen her spirits. She went about her household chores with a song in her heart and upon her lips. It was easy now to ignore Aunt Grizelda's lectures and caustic remarks. Amber wasn't going to let anyone dull this new gem of happiness for her.

"Some people don't know when they're well off," Grizelda said with a sneer, the night Amber told them her plans. "You'd better think it over before you leave here once and for all. You might find out you're not as smart as you think you are."

From then on, her aunt never missed a chance to further her attack. "You're too young to be out on your own. First thing you know, you'll find yourself in trouble. I've seen the way men look at you. It'll just lead to no good, mark my words."

It didn't even bother Amber when Grizelda said she had written to her mother. "I told her once you leave here, we're no longer responsible. I don't want her blaming me for what happens."

Amber, too, had sent a long letter to Ohio explaining everything. Mama would understand.

The sun was only a hint of pink in the eastern sky when Amber woke up on Sunday morning. She was too excited to sleep, and she lay there for awhile, thinking back over the past six years. She saw herself grow from a backward little girl of ten into a confident, independent young woman of sixteen. Experience was a strict teacher, she decided. A person was either strengthened by their hardships, or overcome by them. Her life hadn't been easy so far, but she wasn't beaten yet. She was determined that from now on, with God's help, she would plot her own course. There was a place for her somewhere in this world – she didn't know where, but when she found it, she would know it.

Quietly, she slipped out of bed, got dressed, and began packing her things into the old trunk John and Grizelda had given her as a going-away present. On the other side of the curtain, Lonnie stirred and yawned. Amber knew he was awake.

"I'll miss you, Amber," he said finally.

"I'll miss you, too." She tried to think of something more to say, but couldn't find the right words.

"Well, guess I'd better get ready for church." His voice picked up with excitement. "Joel and I are goin' huntin' down along the dunes this afternoon. We think we know where there's a coyote den. Saw it when we were herdin' the cows the other day. I'll bet it's that same pair that's been stealing our chickens."

"If it is, I hope you get them," said Amber. "The baby ducks came back from the grove yesterday without their mother."

Try as she might, Amber could not keep her mind on the church service. A thousand thoughts were running through her mind, but she felt none of the fear and uncertainty which had plagued her before. She was confident of her abilities and eager to show the Hardys what she could do.

At last, church was over and Amber and her trunk were aboard the Hardys' two-seated buggy. "We'll take good care of her," Mrs. Hardy called to them, as John helped Grizelda to the seat of the lumber wagon filled with kids.

Grizelda took Jamie on her lap. "I'm sure you will," she answered, forcing a smile.

Amber turned around and waved to all of them. "Goodbye," she called. Uncle John, Lonnie, and the children all waved and shouted farewells. Everyone but Grizelda, who made a pretense of being occupied with the baby at the moment. Uncle John turned the wagon around and headed the team back to the farm, while the children continued to wave.

They were still waving when Mr. Hardy clucked to his horse, and Amber turned her back at last and gazed down the tree-lined street ahead.

Chapter 12

Amber turned up the wick on the coal oil lamp and sat on her bed with her back against the wall, knees up, her writing pad braced against them.

May 22, 1894

Dear Mama,

I hope this finds you and the children all well. I worry about you, Mama, taking in so much washing. I wish I could send you some money, but so far I haven't been able to save any. There were so many things I needed, like shoes. I can't go barefooted here in town like we did on the farm!

I just love my new job. The Hardys are the most wonderful couple. They treat me more like a daughter than a hired girl. I told you in my last letter that he is a druggist. He brought me a real toothbrush and some tooth powder from his drug store. Wasn't that nice of him?

They own a nice house on Larkin Street and keep a horse, a cow, and a few chickens out back. I have my own room, a little cubby-hole off the kitchen. They have two little girls, Angie, 6 and Laura, 8. They are both sweet and well-mannered, and I really enjoy taking care of them. Mrs. Hardy is not in very good health, but she is the kindest woman. She is an excellent seamstress and makes the girls darling clothes. She offered to help me make some new dresses, as the two I have are both old and rather shabby. When I go to mail this letter tomorrow, I'm going to buy some calico, and Mrs. Hardy has some patterns I can use if we take them in a bit here and there.

I'll close for now. Please take care, Mama, and give my love to Lisa, Amy, Eric and David.

Your daughter,
Amber

The following day, after her morning chores, Amber walked the four blocks to town, carrying the lavender and pink parasol which Mrs. Hardy had generously insisted that she borrow for protection from the sun.

Amber noticed the parasol was even more faded than her own green dress. Through experience, she had learned that some colors faded more easily than others, even though the calico was soaked in salt water first to set the dyes. She remembered the time she had washed one dress and spread it out carefully on the grass to dry. The sun had faded the front something awful, but the back had stayed bright. There was nothing to do but go ahead and wear it that way, but after the next washing she had let the back fade on purpose. The dress wasn't very pretty after that, but at least it was the same shade all over.

She would keep these facts in mind when choosing her fabric today. A deep blue or a rich brown would be nice, she thought.

After mailing her letter to Ohio and picking up several letters for the Hardys, she hurried over to Collier's Dry Goods, where she found all the bolts of fabric stacked on one table in the corner. Calico was marked five cents a yard, with the heavier fabrics selling for twenty-five cents a yard. Amber sorted through the various bolts of the bright cloth, ignoring any pastels, and found a brown plaid, but it was a rather drab shade and not to her liking.

"Maybe you'd like some of this sateen," said the storekeeper, bringing over an armload of new bolts. "It just arrived and I haven't had time to put it out yet. It looks almost like satin, but it's just a polished cotton. It sells for twenty cents a yard."

"Thank you," said Amber, as he set the material on top of the others. She was immediately attracted to a clear, bright red. What a gorgeous color! she thought. It's so vibrant, so. . . almost daring! She had once seen a red dress pictured on the cover of *Harper's* and had secretly wished for one ever since. She closed her eyes and tried to picture herself in it. Yes, she could wear red, but could she afford to pay such an exorbitant price for it? She did some quick figuring in her head. Yes, she could manage it, but would it be practical? Who cares? answered something inside of her.

"I'll take six yards of each of these," she told the storekeeper, taking the bolt of red and the brown plaid over to the counter. "And two spools of thread to match each one. And one dozen stays. And eight of those brass buttons."

On her way back home, Amber saw the same yellow-wheeled buggy and team of flashy bays that she had been so taken with the day she was job-hunting. They were a block away, but no one could miss a rig like that. She recognized the young man, too, for he drove with the same jaunty air, one arm along the back of the seat. But it was a different girl sitting beside him this time. This one had dark hair, and the other had been a strawberry blonde. Amber decided he must be the local dandy.

"It sure is nice of you to help me make these dresses," said Amber, as she finished her basting and handed the pieces to Mrs. Hardy to sew on her machine. "My aunt can sew – she made everything, even our underwear – but she never had the time or the patience to teach me much."

The treadle machine whirred smoothly as Adele Hardy expertly guided the red material beneath the needle. Without looking up, she answered, "You're catching on quickly. The main thing to remember is not to get discouraged if it doesn't come out right the first time. Many's the time I've had to make something over again."

Carefully, Amber began to pull the two rows of threads, gathering the top of the skirt. It was exciting to watch the red dress begin to take shape. She could hardly wait until it was finished. It would certainly be eye-catching. Amber loved the style, with the tiny brass buttons down the front and the fashionable long sleeves, puffed at the shoulders and fitted at the wrists.

For some reason, she found herself thinking of the young man with the fancy yellow-wheeled buggy and the classy bay horses. Maybe Mrs. Hardy knew him. Keeping her eyes on her sewing and making her voice sound as casual as possible, she asked, "Who is the young man I see around town with the fancy rig and team of matching bays?"

"Oh, *him*," replied Mrs. Hardy, with an emphasis that made Amber wonder just what she meant. "That's Bryan Devlin." She threw Amber a quick glance. "I wouldn't set my sights on him if I were you. He's got more girls than he knows what to do with, especially since his father gave him that outfit for his twenty-first birthday."

"Oh, I'm not interested in him," Amber insisted, "but I sure do like his horses!"

Adele Hardy looked up and smiled at Amber. "Yes, his family is pretty wealthy. They own the mills here in town. You've probably noticed their house over on Walnut Street – it's the biggest one in town. I hear it has thirteen rooms!" She shook her head. "Can you imagine? All that room for only three people! His four sisters are all married and gone now. He's the only boy and the baby of the family. I don't know them personally, but they go to our church. At least Mrs. Devlin does. Bryan and the mister don't show up too often.

"There now. That's that," she said, holding up the bodice for Amber to see. "As soon as you get the stays sewn in, the top will be just about finished. I'm tired," she added, pushing back a wisp of graying hair. "I think I'll go lie down for awhile. As soon as you get the skirt gathered, I'll sew them together and we'll be almost done with this one. Then we can start on the brown one. My, but it's going to be a smart-looking dress!" She looked away and her expression softened with the glow of fond memories, giving Amber a glimpse of the girl she had been. "I had a red dress once, when I was young," she said wistfully.

She turned again to Amber. "By the way, one of the letters you picked up for us at the post office the other day was from Mr. Hardy's parents. They're going to celebrate their fiftieth wedding anniversary on the fourteenth of June, and we've decided to take the train to Wichita for the celebration. Clem's brothers and sisters are all going, and he hasn't seen some of them in years, so it will be quite a reunion.

"We'll take the girls and be gone for two whole weeks. The thing is, I hate to leave you here alone for that long. I thought maybe you'd want to go back to your aunt and uncle's and stay with them. Clem could drive you out."

"Oh, no, that's all right." answered Amber, shaking her head. "I'm not afraid to stay here by myself. Besides, you need someone to look after the animals anyway, and I'd be glad to do it. Please let me stay."

Mrs. Hardy thought for a moment. "Well, if you're certain you'll be all right. I'm sure Clem will be glad to have you look after the stock. He always hates to ask one of the neighbors to do it."

"What will you do about the drug store?" asked Amber.

"Mr. Pearson is going to take it over. He's the man who used to own it. He's a dear – I'll have you meet him before we leave. Then if you need anything, he can help you."

It was a warm, bright Saturday in June that Amber bid the Hardy family goodbye at the depot. She stood and watched the train until it was a mere speck in the distance, then returned to the buggy and untied Toby, the Hardys' skinny sorrel.

He was a pathetic creature and reminded Amber of Kickapoo when she first got him. He was lazy and dull-eyed, and even though he seemed to get plenty of hay and oats, every rib remained visible beneath his rough coat. Of course, Toby was old. That's all anyone ever called him – "Old Toby." And it was always said in a rather apologetic tone. Amber often heard Mr. Hardy mention that "Old Toby is about ready for the glue factory." Amber hated to think of such a fate for any horse.

"Wake up, Toby old boy! We've got two whole weeks to ourselves!" she exclaimed, patting his thin neck. Toby responded with a lengthy, wide-mouthed yawn.

"Wait a minute!" said Amber with surprise. She opened the horse's mouth again and briefly studied his teeth. "You're not so old! Why, I'll bet you're not over ten or twelve. You've got a lot of good years left. I think you've just been neglected. You need someone to pay more attention to you, don't you? And I think I know what your worst problem is." She put her arm around his nose and gave him a quick hug. "Toby, boy, you're my new project!"

Amber drove directly to the drug store, hopped out of the buggy, and went inside. "Hello, Mr. Pearson, remember me?" she asked the rotund little man behind the counter.

His round face lit up with recognition. "Of course! How are you today, Miss Amber? Did the Hardys get off all right?"

"Yes, they just left," she answered.

"Good! Good! And what can I do for you, young lady?"

"I need a big can of tobacco."

Mr. Pearson arched his bushy eyebrows and stared at her over the top of his spectacles, dumbfounded. "Tobacco? And what would a pretty young lady like you want with a can of tobacco?"

"Don't get me wrong," Amber said, laughing. "I'm not going to smoke it or chew it. I want to put it in the horse's feed to worm him. It's a trick I learned from my Uncle John. When a horse gets plenty to eat and still stays poor, he usually has worms. I think that's what's the matter with Toby." She nodded at the horse visible through the front window.

"Oh, so that's it," he chuckled. "Yes, I've heard of that. I've never tried it myself, but they say it works." He waddled over to the display of Polar Bear Tobacco and came back with a can.

"The only thing," Amber said with hesitation, "is that I don't have enough money to pay for it right now. Do you suppose you could tell Mr. Hardy to take it out of my pay?"

"Well, they told me to look after you and to let you have anything you might need. I'm sure they didn't have tobacco in mind, but judging from the looks of that horse out there, you need it! So don't worry about who's to pay. Clem won't mind, seeing as how it's his horse."

"Thanks a lot, Mr. Pearson," said Amber. "After this and few more tricks I know, they may not even recognize 'Old Toby' by the time they get back!"

Amber spent the rest of the afternoon working on the horse. First she trimmed his mane, then shortened his long, flaxen tail which almost touched the ground. Finally, she brushed and brushed his reddish-brown coat, but it was so rough and dry that her efforts were mostly in vain.

"Soon as we get you wormed, we'll start putting a raw egg in your feed each day. That'll slick you up in no time," she told him.

She noticed his hooves were dry, so she retrieved some bacon grease from the kitchen and smeared it on each of them. "You'll need your shoes re-set soon," she said, as she set the last foot back down and rubbed the grease on her hands into his mane. "I'll have to tell Mr. Hardy when he gets back."

Finally, she led Toby back to the shed he shared with the family cow and put him in his stall. Then she mixed a handful of tobacco with his oats and poured them into the manger. "Well, fella, that's about all we can do for you today." She ran her hand along his back and gave him an affectionate pat on the rump as she walked out.

That night, for the first time in her life, Amber knew loneliness. She had never been alone before, not really alone. There had always been children to care for and keep her busy. Now there was no one, and she wasn't used to the silence that echoed through the empty house.

She read as long as there was light, then went to bed early. She was glad tomorrow was Sunday. There would be church, and people, and things to do. She would wear her new red dress!

Amber stood back and inspected her appearance in the big looking glass on the Hardys' carved walnut dresser. Mrs. Hardy had been right – the white lace around the collar and wrists of the red dress added the finishing touch.

After brushing her hair and pinning it up, she picked up the white straw hat lying on the bed and positioned it on her head at various angles. She wasn't used to such a stylish hat, and it made her feel terribly conspicuous. Maybe I should wear a plainer one, she thought. No, Mrs. Hardy was kind enough to give me this one, and it does go with the dress. I've got to hurry, too, or I'll be late for church, she reminded herself. She tied the red streamers in a neat bow under her chin, dusted some cornstarch on her nose, pinched her cheeks, and hurried outside.

Toby was standing patiently, hitched to the buggy in the driveway. Amber congratulated herself for having him ready ahead of time. She hadn't wanted to risk soiling her new dress.

She enjoyed the short drive to the church. It was a beautiful morning – not as windy as usual – and she was pleasantly aware of heads turning her way as she passed.

The churchyard was filled with horses and carriages, so she tied Toby in the alley out back. Once inside, she scanned the parishioners for any familiar figure, but there was none within view. If Lonnie or any of the Hagens were coming, they weren't there yet.

The service began, and when the list of announcements was read from the pulpit, one in particular attracted Amber's attention. The annual parish picnic was to be held next Saturday afternoon on Walnut Creek. Wouldn't that be fun? she thought, and her mind eagerly began to toy with the prospect of going. But then she remembered there was no one to go with. The Hardys would still be gone, and Uncle John certainly wouldn't come in fifteen miles just to go to a picnic. You may as well forget it, she told herself, you can't go alone.

Throughout the rest of the service, she brooded over her predicament. The more she thought about it, the more she wished she could go. For some reason, she wanted to go to that picnic more than anything in the world.

Soon, the last hymn was sung and the service was over. Lost in thought, Amber let herself be caught up in the surge of people as they made their way outside. When she was free of the crowd, she stopped for a moment and looked around once again for Uncle John, but he wasn't there. Maybe they were still harvesting the wheat and couldn't come. She knew it wouldn't have done any good to ask him about the picnic, but at least she would have had someone to talk to for a few minutes. She sighed dejectedly.

"Miss?"

Amber turned toward the voice.

"May I take you home?"

She glanced up in surprise at the handsome, well-dressed young man standing before her. He seemed vaguely familiar, and her mind raced frantically trying to place him.

"May I take you home?" he repeated, gesturing with the hat in his hand toward the rig parked in front of the church.

Amber stared at the bright maroon buggy with yellow wheels and the team of beautiful bay horses. Of course! Now she remembered. He was *that* young man! "Well," she said, stalling to get a moment to glance quickly beyond him at her own horse and buggy. She saw Toby standing hipshot, peacefully asleep in the shade of the tree she had tied him to. "All right."

Offering Amber his arm, the young man walked her over to his buggy and helped her to the seat. Then he untied the horses and climbed in beside her. "Which way?" he asked.

Amber pointed west down the street, and the bays trotted off smartly in step. She was quite captivated by their synchronized movements and the way they arched their necks and carried their tails. "They're wonderful," she marveled aloud.

"Thanks. I like them, too," replied her escort. He glanced over at Amber. "My name's Bryan Devlin."

"Mine's Amber Lockhardt," she responded, but her eyes never left the team of horses prancing in front of them. "I've never seen any quite like them before. Are they a special breed?"

"They're Hackneys. My father had them brought from Kansas City as a birthday present for me." He turned to Amber again. "You're new around here, aren't you?"

"Not really. I just haven't been living in town long. I used to live on my uncle's farm, but now I work for Mr. and Mrs. Hardy and live with them." She was still watching the team of Hackneys. "Are they trained to prance like that, or does it come natural?"

"It mostly comes natural." Bryan paused, expecting another question. Amber just shook her head in amazement and admiration, so he went on. "You say you work for the Hardys. Is that Clem Hardy, the druggist?"

"Yes, do you know him?"

"Oh, everyone in town knows Clem. His drug store is the local hangout. I'm not sure just where he lives though. It's over on Larkin, isn't it?"

"Yes, turn here," Amber directed. "It's just a few more blocks on down."

She wished it were much farther so she could ride with Bryan Devlin longer. But they were there in a matter of minutes. "It's been nice meeting you. Thank you for bringing me home," she said, as they pulled up in front of the house. She jumped down from the buggy, and once on the ground, glanced up at Bryan to see a strange look of surprise on his face. Why? she wondered. Maybe he expected to be invited in. "I'm sorry I can't ask you in, but the Hardys are out of town," she explained.

"You should have let me help you down!" he sputtered, jumping out of the buggy and coming quickly around to her side. "You might fall and hurt yourself!"

It was Amber's turn to be surprised.

"Oh!" she said, laughing. "I'm sorry. I guess I'm just too used to doing everything for myself. I never gave it a thought. I'll try to remember next time." Now why had she said that? She bit her lip, embarrassed at her forwardness.

But Bryan Devlin seemed to think nothing about her remark. "Couldn't we sit on the porch awhile and talk? There wouldn't be anything wrong in that, would there?"

"All right," replied Amber with a quick smile. "I'd like that. It's been kind of lonesome around here with the family gone." She took off her Sunday hat as they walked over to the tree-shaded porch and sat down on the steps.

"So you're a farm girl." Bryan smiled and the look in his brown eyes was frankly appreciative. He ran his fingers through his curly brown hair. "How long have you been working for Clem and his family?"

"Since April," answered Amber. "I sure like it here, too. They're such nice folks."

"Where did you say they went?"

"To Wichita, for a family reunion. They left yesterday on the train."

"Aren't you afraid to stay here all alone?" he asked seriously.

"Afraid? Heavens no! I used to be alone out on the farm whenever my aunt and uncle went someplace, but I always had kids to take care of. My aunt had seven. I'm so used to toting a baby around on one hip, it's a wonder I'm not lopsided!" she said, laughing.

As they talked, Amber decided that Bryan, with all his money and good looks, wasn't much different from the neighbor boys she used to dance with at barn dances. Only older and more mature.

Finally Bryan pulled out his gold pocket watch and glanced at the time. "Sorry, but I've got to be going. I told Mother I'd drive her over to Mrs. Matson's tea at one."

When he stood up to leave, Amber suddenly remembered Toby. As soon as Bryan was gone, she must change her clothes and rush back to the church for him.

"Oh, by the way, are you going to the picnic next Saturday?" asked Bryan, as he turned to leave.

"No," replied Amber, staring at the ground. "I don't have anyone to go with."

He smiled and replied, "You do now."

The way he smiled caused Amber's heart to skip a beat, and for a breathless minute she couldn't think of a thing to say.

Bryan sauntered over to his buggy and gathered up the reins. "I'll see you again sometime soon, and we can make more definite plans. 'Bye now."

"Goodbye," said Amber, and she sighed happily as she watched the bays trot off down the street.

"Sometime soon" proved to be the following afternoon. Amber was just starting to work on Toby when she noticed Bryan Devlin drive up. Her first impulse was to hide her sorry-looking horse. "Oh well," she told Toby, "he'll have to see you sooner or later. I can't hide you forever!"

She pretended not to hear Bryan coming up behind her. After all, she didn't want to appear too eager. When he was almost beside her, she turned to speak.

But Bryan wasn't even looking at her. He was staring at Toby. He walked completely around the horse without saying a word. Then, faking a perplexed expression, he scratched his head and asked, "What is it?"

"Don't you pay any attention to him, Toby," Amber apologized. "Just because he happens to have the best-looking horses in town, he's forgotten what a common one looks like."

"You may as well give up on that nag. You're just wasting your time – the glue factory doesn't care about appearances," he teased. "Why, I'll bet he's old enough to vote!"

"He is not!" countered Amber. "Look at his teeth. I think he's only around ten or twelve."

Obviously skeptical, Bryan opened the sorrel's mouth and examined his teeth. "By golly, you're right!" he exclaimed, and Amber could tell that he was a little awed by her expertise.

She gave him a smug look. "He's just been neglected, that's all," she said, patting Toby's neck affectionately. "Just you wait. A few more weeks and you won't even know it's the same horse!"

Bryan positioned himself on the back porch steps and watched while Amber worked. When she was tired of brushing Toby, she joined him. She was glad for his company, and the afternoon passed quickly. It wasn't until he had left that she suddenly realized they had talked about almost everything except the picnic. "Hmmm," she mused aloud, "I guess he'll be back."

He was – every day. But Amber never knew when to expect him, and he didn't bother to let her know ahead of time. She learned that he worked for his father, keeping books at the mill, and kept no strict hours. Unpredictable as his visits were, Amber began to look forward to them more and more. She found herself paying unusual attention to her appearance, and she always tried to have some little snack fixed for the two of them to eat. She discovered that he adored fried sweet dough rolled in sugar as much as she did. The only difference was, he didn't have to worry about keeping a slim waistline!

Sometimes they went for a walk or a drive around town, but usually they just sat on the front porch swing and talked. Amber had always found it easy to talk to boys, for she shared their interest in horses, and she knew as much about them as did most boys. However, Amber soon discovered that Bryan Devlin's favorite subject was Bryan Devlin. He was a great talker though, and Amber was content to listen while he rambled on about his early life, for it had been so different from her own.

"How old are you?" he asked her one day as they were relaxing on the porch.

"Sixteen."

"Only sixteen? I thought you were eighteen at least. You're so level-headed and all. Most girls your age are all giggly and tongue-tied." He shook his head. "And I know some a lot older who still giggle too much and can't carry on an intelligent conversation." He looked at Amber and said simply, "I'm glad you're not like that."

Amber was both surprised and pleased at what he had said. She felt a little tingle in her cheeks and hoped she wasn't blushing.

"Well, I better be going." He rose to leave. "By the way, I'll pick you up around eleven tomorrow."

"Tomorrow?"

"To go to the picnic!"

"Oh!" exclaimed Amber. "I almost forgot! What shall I fix for us to eat?"

"Anything, just so there's plenty of it! And," he called back over his shoulder, "wear your red dress. I sure like it."

It was a beautiful day for a picnic, and Amber felt on top of the world as the two sleek bays pranced out of town toward Walnut Creek. "Oh, please, may I drive them?" she asked Bryan eagerly.

"You're the first girl who ever asked me that!" he exclaimed with surprise. "Sometimes I get the feeling you like my horses better than you do me!" He glanced around, then handed her the reins. "I guess it's okay, as long as no one sees us."

The team moved along easily in step. To Amber, they appeared to be walking on eggs. They had mouths of velvet, and she thrilled to their unified response to the slightest signal she sent along the lines. "They're certainly a pleasure to drive," she said, "compared to Archie and Charley, Uncle John's big ol' workhorses."

"You drive them real well. Not many girls can handle high-strung horses like these. I don't know what it is, but you certainly have a special something when it comes to horses."

Bryan leaned back with one arm along the back of the seat behind Amber's shoulders and watched her with the same curious intent she was devoting to the horses. "I sure do like that dress," he murmured, and Amber could feel his fingers gently touching the fabric of her sleeve.

As they approached the picnic area, Bryan quickly sat up. "Better let me take them from here on," he said. "I'd never live it down if any of my friends saw a girl driving me around!"

"There sure aren't many folks here yet," observed Amber, her eyes scanning the tree-lined banks of the little stream that was Walnut Creek.

"We're early. I wanted to be sure we got a good shady place."

"How about over there?" Amber pointed to a large cottonwood growing very near the creek and somewhat apart from the rest. The area beneath its sprawling branches appeared grassy and invitingly cool.

"Good! That's perfect!" said Bryan. "But I think we're supposed to leave all the horses over here so the flies won't be so bad." He guided the team up to a picket rope stretched between some of the smaller trees, where a number of carriages and saddle horses were already tied.

Amber jumped out of the buggy at the same time Bryan did.

"I thought I told you not to do that!" said Bryan, shaking his finger at her like she was a naughty child.

"Sorry!" she said lightly.

"Here!" Bryan tossed her a neatly folded blanket. "You take that for us to sit on, and I'll bring the lunch basket."

"I'll race you!" shouted Amber, and she was off like a deer through the shadows of the trees. When Bryan got to the big cottonwood, she was leaning against it, still laughing and breathing hard.

"No fair!" he cried. "I had to carry this basket, and it weighs a ton! What on earth have you got in it?"

"Rocks!" Amber retorted, as she flipped the blanket open and spread it out on the ground. "I didn't know if you liked them best baked, boiled, or fried, so I brought some of all three." She plopped on the blanket, took off her straw hat, and began fanning herself with it.

"Well, they sure do smell good, and I'm already hungry. I think I'll have me a rock right now." He opened the top of the basket, reached in and pulled out a chicken thigh. "Aha!" he said. "This looks like one of the fried ones."

After eating the thigh, a breast, and a drumstick, he finally decided he would survive until dinner. "Is that one of Clem's chickens?" he asked, wiping his mouth on a red-checked gingham napkin. "It's the biggest fryer I ever saw! Usually they're so small, there are only a few bites on each piece."

"Well, it's one of the Hardys', all right," Amber confessed, "but they didn't have any young ones of frying size. This is poor old Henrietta, the oldest one in the coop. I stewed her until she was almost done, then rolled the pieces in flour and fried them."

"Hmmm. . .aren't you the clever one!"

"But what am I going to tell the Hardys when they wonder about Henrietta?" Amber wasn't really as worried about it as she tried to sound.

"Tell them she died of old age."

"I couldn't lie to them!" said Amber.

Bryan laughed. "You wouldn't be lying. You said you chose the oldest one. So, see – she died of old age!" He shrugged. "Besides, it's only a chicken."

Amber suddenly got serious. "Only a chicken?" she exclaimed. "You wouldn't say that if you'd ever been as hard up as we were on the farm. We lived on milk and eggs and potatoes for so long, I almost forgot what meat tasted like! And by the time I left, there were ten of us, so you can imagine how far a chicken went at a meal. I never even heard of a fried chicken until I came here. They were always stewed with noodles or something so they'd go further. Why, we even ate the bones! You ought to try that sometime!"

"Hold on! Hold on! I surrender!" Bryan exclaimed, holding up both hands. "Next thing I know, you'll be telling me you really did eat rocks!"

"We did!" said Amber, laughing. "Honest! When we were little, back in Ohio, we used to see who could swallow the biggest rock!"

"You're too much!" conceded Bryan. He pulled her to her feet. "Come on, let's go see who's here."

Hand in hand, they strolled among the chattering groups of picnickers, careful to dodge the laughing, shouting children racing madly about in every direction. Amber felt proud to be with Bryan.

But at the same time, she felt a little self-conscious, out of place. She couldn't quite figure out why. Maybe it was the way people were looking at her. Then again, anyone in the company of Bryan Devlin was bound to attract attention.

"Are your parents coming?" Amber asked him finally. For some reason she was curious about them.

"No," Bryan replied. "Father's too busy at the mill, and Mother can't take the heat." He stopped abruptly. "Speaking of the heat, let's head back to our place so I can take this jacket off. I'm about to melt."

They returned to find a couple of small boys engaged in an impromptu wrestling match on their blanket. "All right, you kids! Scram!" said Bryan gruffly, as he hauled them apart by their belts. They both darted off without a word, one in hot pursuit of the other, and disappeared into the crowd. Bryan took off his coat and flung it to one side. "Kids make me nervous," he said. "I guess I'm just not used to having them around." He flopped to his knees beside Amber and eyed the picnic basket hungrily. "I'm ready to dig in!" he said.

As they pulled up in front of the Hardys' home after the picnic, Bryan startled Amber with a single command. "Now, wait!" Quickly, he jumped out of the buggy, ran around to her side, and offered her his hand. "Ah, my dear Miss Lockhardt, may I graciously assist you in alighting from your carriage?"

Amber assumed a similar regal air and answered loftily, "I'd be delighted, sir." With the empty lunch basket on one arm, she stepped down gracefully. Then, with stiff dignity, they proceeded up the walk and onto the porch, where they both burst into gales of laughter.

After a moment, Amber looked up into Bryan's face, her cheeks glowing. "Thank you for a wonderful time. I enjoyed the day very much."

"Of course you did! You were with me!" replied Bryan, taking her hand in his. There followed an awkward pause. "I'll be seeing you, probably sometime tomorrow. Goodbye."

"Goodbye," said Amber, "and thank you again."

Chapter 13

How could time go by so quickly? Amber reflected. It didn't seem possible that the Hardys had been gone two whole weeks. When they left, the time had stretched before her like an eternity; yet here she was again at the depot, watching the dark speck that was their approaching train grow larger and larger in the distance.

Gradually, she could make out the shape of the oncoming engine, its impressive diamond stack belching great puffs of black smoke. There was something thrilling and awesome about a train, even something a little frightening. When at last the cars pulled into the station, a sudden quiver – was it excitement or trepidation? – went through her as they slowly screeched to a halt and the engine heaved huge sighs of steam.

Before long, Amber spotted the Hardys emerging from the third car, and she waved to them above the crowd. As soon as she caught their attention, they waved in response and made their way toward her.

"Amber! Amber! Look what we got!" cried Angie, running ahead to show her the dainty pink parasol she was carrying.

Laura followed her little sister, but at a more sedate pace. "Grandma bought them for us," she said, happily displaying hers, too.

"Oh, aren't they fashionable!" exclaimed Amber. "Now you two will look like grown-up ladies, won't you?" The girls nodded proudly, and Amber knelt down and hugged them, an arm around each one. "It's so good to have you back. I really missed you! Did you have lots of fun at Grandma's?" She stood up then and smiled warmly as Clem and Adele Hardy reached them. "Hello! Welcome back!"

"Hello, Amber dear," answered Mrs. Hardy, a bit wearily. "How did you get along? Is everything all right? I worried about you."

"Everything's fine, just fine. Did you have a nice time?"

"Yes, we had a lovely visit. It's good to be home though. The trip was so tiring for me."

"Here, let me take those." Amber relieved her of the bags she carried in each hand, and Mrs. Hardy smiled gratefully. "The buggy's over here," said Amber, leading the way.

"I see you got the brown dress finished," Mrs. Hardy remarked to her, and Amber could feel her experienced eye inspecting it seam by seam. "It looks nice – you did a very fine job."

"Thank you. This pattern was a lot easier than the red one."

As they neared the buggy, Toby pricked up his ears, fascinated by the two small girls coming toward him with their flouncy dresses and pink parasols. He snorted softly through his nose, every muscle taut, every nerve alert. His sorrel coat glowed like burnished copper in the sunlight.

189

Clem Hardy stopped abruptly, and so did the rest of the family. All four stared in amazement. "Is that old Toby?" Clem asked.

"That's Toby!" replied Amber proudly.

"Ohhh, he's bee-utiful!" cried Angie. "Mommy! Daddy! Isn't Toby bee-utiful?"

"He certainly is!" answered her father, shaking his head incredulously. "He doesn't even look like the same horse!" Still staring at Toby, Clem put their bags in the buggy and helped his wife onto the front seat, while Amber and the girls climbed into the seat behind. Then he untied the horse, and Amber noticed him rubbing his hand alongToby's back and down his side before climbing to the driver's seat. He clucked to the horse and shook his head again as Toby moved out eagerly. "And here I thought he was ready for the glue factory! How on earth did you do it?"

Amber smiled. "Well, I didn't have much else to do, so I spent most of my time working on him. You know, he's not as old as you think, and once I got him wormed – "

"Wormed? How did you do that?" asked Clem Hardy, plainly astonished.

"I put tobacco in his feed," she said. "Once I got him wormed, he began to perk up and started putting on weight. He's still a little too thin, but a few more weeks and you shouldn't be able to see those ribs at all."

"His coat looks so nice, too," Mrs. Hardy marveled. "See how it shines in the sun."

"Worming helped that, too," answered Amber, "but I also put a raw egg in his feed each day. That gives a horse a shiny coat – that, plus lots and lots of brushing!" she admitted. "Oh, by the way, I also noticed that his hooves need to be trimmed and his shoes re-set. You might see about taking him to the blacksmith before long."

"Young lady, I have to hand it to you, you certainly have a way with horses!" said Clem Hardy with a broad smile. "And you can cook . . . and sew . . . and keep house. When you get married, some fellow will really be getting a bargain!"

Married! Who's getting married? Amber thought to herself. She turned her attention to Angie and Laura. "Now, tell me all about your trip," she said enthusiastically.

At first, Amber worried about how she was going to tell Bryan that she no longer had time for his daily visits now that the Hardys were back. Her household tasks kept her occupied, and now they would have canning to do as well, for there was an abundance of vegetables ripening in the garden. She didn't want to give Bryan the impression she was running him off, but she knew she'd be awfully busy. It presented a problem, all right. She would have to be tactful about it, she decided.

But, as the week progressed, she realized she didn't have much of a problem after all, for Bryan never showed up. The last time she had seen him was Friday, the day before the Hardys had returned.

Now here it was Wednesday and still no sign of him. I wonder if he's working hard at the mill, or too interested in his other girlfriends, Amber thought.

The kitchen where she was helping with the canning was steaming. She wiped the sweat trickling down her face with one sleeve and continued to pour the sealing wax around the edge of the metal lid. "There," she said finally. "That's sixteen pints of green beans. What shall we can next?"

"Let's do these tomatoes," said Mrs. Hardy. "They're going to spoil if we don't get them put up." Working side by side, they began washing, peeling, and cutting up the tomatoes piled in the wooden box on the table.

Amber's thoughts kept returning to Bryan. Maybe they weren't the good friends she thought they were. Maybe he had no intention of coming back. He knew she wasn't lonesome anymore, so maybe he figured he could conveniently drop out of the picture. She didn't really blame him. He'd wasted two weeks of his time with her already. She should just be grateful to him for that and let it go.

She came to a tomato too rotten to use and tossed it aside. Forget him! she told herself. He just doesn't have time for you anymore. Mrs. Hardy said he had lots of girls, rich girls, probably. Rich and educated and lots prettier than you. Oh well, who cares? she asked herself, then answered dismally, I do!

"The garden has certainly done well this year," Mrs. Hardy was saying. "I can't remember when we ever had this much. Thank goodness the corn won't be ready for a while yet! We can do that later. I was hoping to have time for some sewing." She glanced briefly at Amber. "Have you worn your new red dress yet?"

"Uh-huh. I just love it. I wore it to church once and then to the parish picnic last Saturday. By the way, we're going to start having church every other Sunday now instead of once a month, did you know that?"

"No, I didn't. That's good to hear." Without looking up, she added, "So you attended the parish picnic. . .who with? Bryan Devlin?"

"How did you know?" asked Amber in surprise.

Adele Hardy smiled knowingly. "I was talking to Mrs. Hansen across the way. She said she'd seen him over here while we were gone. . . quite a lot, in fact."

Amber thought she detected a questioning note in her voice. "Yes, he took me home from church and then came to see me every day."

Mrs. Hardy paused for a moment and looked at Amber. "I don't mean to pry, but he didn't . . . you didn't let him come in, did you?"

"Heavens, no! I'd never do anything like that! It was all very proper," Amber assured her. "We just sat on the porch and talked. Besides, we're just friends, that's all. He knew I was lonesome with you gone, and I guess he felt sorry for me. Why else would he waste his time on someone like me?" She paused. "Oh! And guess what? He even let me drive his team of Hackneys!" she exclaimed. "What a thrill that was! They are out of this world – mouths of velvet – and they handle like a dream!

Adele Hardy laughed. "You told me before that you were more interested in his horses than you were in him, and it sounds to me like you still are!"

"They're fabulous, simply fabulous." Amber sighed.

Mrs. Hardy's expression grew serious, and in the silence that followed, Amber concluded that she had more on her mind than a casual talk. What could it be?

"Amber dear," she began gently, "you know how much Clem and I – all of us – think of you. We care about you as if you were our own daughter. So please forgive me for what I'm about to tell you. I only have your welfare at heart, believe me."

Puzzled, Amber stopped, holding a half-peeled tomato in one hand and her knife in the other, and waited, her gaze intent on Mrs. Hardy. She could feel mixed emotions leap to life and begin to stir within her.

Adele Hardy didn't look up, but continued to peel the tomato in her hand with tiny, deliberate movements. "There are certain rumors around town, gossip I think you ought to know about. You see, the Devlins had a house girl working for them a year or so ago. She lived with them just as you do with us, and no one knew much about her. One day she not only quit her job there, but she also left town." She paused and her eyes probed Amber's momentarily, pleading for understanding. Then she dropped her gaze and continued. "No one really knows anything about it for certain, but there are lots of tales. Everyone has a different story. Some say she was only after the Devlins' money. Others say Bryan. . .well, you know how people talk, especially about the rich. I guess it's jealousy that makes others find fault with the wealthy."

She turned to Amber once again and said with motherly concern, "I just wouldn't want you to get involved in an affair like that. I know you're sensible and not one to. . .to lead a boy on. It's just that you're so young and trusting, and so genuinely honest yourself, I'm afraid you might believe everyone else is the same way."

Amber pondered for a moment the implications of what she had heard, trying to sift through her thoughts and feelings. Slowly she resumed her work. "I'm truly grateful for your concern," she said frankly. "Thank you for telling me. It explains a few things I've wondered about." She paused. "I supposed those rumors could be true. But what if they're not? I'd hate to let silly, jealous gossip stand in the way of a perfectly innocent friendship. All I know is that Bryan's always been a real gentleman around me, we enjoy each other's company, and we have lots of fun together." She glanced up at Adele Hardy. "Would you have any objections if I go on seeing him?"

"Of course not, dear," Mrs. Hardy said kindly.

"Anyway, you don't have to worry – as I said, we're just friends," Amber assured her, then added silently, At least I hope we still are!

Angie strolled into the kitchen, blowing on the paper pinwheel Amber had made for her. "Who is Miss Lockhardt?" she asked with a puzzled frown.

"That's me – Lockhardt is the last part of my name," Amber responded.

"Oh," Angie replied. "There's a boy at the door and he says he wants to see Miss Lockhardt."

Bryan! Amber's thoughts sang out. He's come back! Quickly, she dried her hands and untied her apron. I probably look a sight, she said to herself. Smoothing the loose hair back from her face, she hurried into the parlor.

She was crestfallen to find that the figure at the door was not Bryan. It was a boy, all right, but he couldn't have been over nine or ten. Of course, she told herself logically, Angie wouldn't have referred to Bryan as a boy – to her, someone that age would be a man.

"Yes?" Amber said, peering through the screen door.

"You Miss Lockhardt?" asked the shaggy-haired little boy.

"Yes."

"Well, I have a note here for Miss Lockhardt and I can't give it to anyone else."

"I'm Miss Lockhardt," Amber assured him. She opened the screen door and the boy handed her a small white envelope, although he still didn't seem quite convinced.

"I'm supposed to wait for an answer," he informed her. He stood impatiently on one bare foot and then the other.

"All right, just a minute," replied Amber, as she tore open the envelope and unfolded the note. Her eyes flew first to the signature – it was from Bryan – then she scanned the brief lines written in neat script:

Can you get away tomorrow night for the 4th of July celebration in the town square? I'll call for you at 7.

Bryan

Her spirits soared. "Tell him yes," she directed the messenger boy. She watched as he darted off the porch and up the street as fast as he could go. In the thrill of finding that Bryan was still interested in her, Amber had momentarily forgotten what Mrs. Hardy had said about him. Now, as thoughts of those stories crossed her mind, they left little ripples of uneasiness in their wake. A while ago she had been so sure that she wouldn't have paid any mind to the talk, but suddenly she was filled with doubt.

The rest of the day Amber found herself wondering just what the status of their relationship was. That night, as she lay in bed, she explored the various possibilities with cold logic. She finally came to three conclusions and mulled them over one by one.

The one she least wanted to consider was that Bryan simply figured her as an easy mark. But she had never given him any reason to think she was that kind of girl. No, after several weeks, he knew her well enough to know better than that.

Could he be getting serious? Surely not! He had never shown any indication that he had anything in mind except a casual friendship. After all, she hadn't even seen him in almost a week! And besides, she was only sixteen, and he was twenty-one. She felt she could firmly rule out that possibility.

That left nothing else but a simple friendship, which was all she had wanted in the first place. That's all there is to it, she decided. He's just a nice person who wants to be my friend. With this conclusion reached, she dismissed all doubts from her mind, and sleep came at last.

Amber thrilled to the excitement all around them. She had never seen anything like it – the whole town must have turned out for the celebration, for the courthouse square was thronged with people in a holiday mood. The town band was blaring away on the improvised bandstand festooned with red, white, and blue bunting, and small boys were lighting strings of firecrackers in the streets. Their report was only a faint popping barely heard above the rousing music. The din was so loud Amber could scarcely hear Bryan, unless he shouted in her ear. Like a spellbound child, she let him take her hand and lead the way through the crowd.

They passed a row of decorated booths offering refreshments and various games of chance. "Want a candy apple on a stick?" shouted Bryan.

Amber shrugged and smiled her acceptance. She didn't know what to expect, but it sounded wonderful.

Off to one side where it was a little quieter, the local photographer had set up a tent and seemed to be doing a thriving business, for there were several people waiting their turn. "Let's have our photograph made," said Bryan, and he led Amber to the end of the line.

Amber was delighted to have the opportunity for a photograph. "I hope it turns out good," she said hopefully. "I'd like to send it to Mama, so she can see what I look like."

Bryan was clearly taken aback. "You mean your mother hasn't even seen a picture of you?"

Amber shook her head no. How could she explain to someone like Bryan what it was like to be poor?

By the time it was their turn, Bryan had eaten his candy apple, but Amber wasn't finished with hers. "What shall I do with this?" she asked worriedly, as the photographer ushered them inside the tent.

"Throw it away," said Bryan, his tone unconcerned.

"No, that would be wasteful. Besides, I still want it."

"I know!" Bryan offered. "I'll hold it behind my back."

The photographer motioned to Amber. "You sit on the bench, miss. And the young man can stand around behind you. That's it. Good!" His head and shoulders disappeared beneath the black velvet draped at the back of the bulky camera, while his assistant readied the phosphorous in the little trough that he would hold up for light.

Amber hurriedly rearranged her dress and sat up straight.

"Sit still or I'll konk you on the head with this candy apple," Bryan murmured through his teeth.

Amber giggled, the powder flashed, the camera clicked.

Later in the evening, everyone sat on the lawn and listened to patriotic speeches given by local politicians and civic leaders. Their impassioned oratory was inspiring. Amber had never felt such a kinship with history, such pride in being an American. She grew solemn as she gratefully considered the miracle that had seen her born in America, rather than under the tyrannies of Europe. How strangely different her life would be now if Papa and Mama had not left the old country and come here to this land of freedom!

Bryan noticed her pensiveness and leaned toward her. "Are you all right?" he whispered.

Amber nodded and flashed him a quick smile, then joined the rest of the crowd in applauding the last speaker.

"And now, ladies and gentlemen," said the mayor, "the closing number on our program tonight will be Miss Celia Langly singing *The Star Spangled Banner*. We ask that you all please stand."

People rose, brushing themselves off, and gathering up stray children and belongings. A pretty blonde in a pink dress walked to the center of the platform and a hush settled over the gathering, disturbed only by a sleepy youngster's crying somewhere off in the crowd. Then, with the band playing softly behind her, Celia Langly's high, wavering voice intoned the well-known lines of the national anthem.

Amber's lips silently formed the words along with her. Although the name Celia Langly meant nothing to Amber, something about her seemed familiar. Was it her hair-do? They were standing quite close to the bandstand, and Amber eased up on tiptoe to get a better view of the singer over the shoulder of the man in front of her.

Celia Langly was lovely, with a face as pale and delicate as a Dresden doll, and a mass of reddish-blonde curls perfectly arranged over her left shoulder. It was only when Amber noticed Celia looking directly at Bryan that she recognized her. Celia Langly was the strawberry blonde she had seen with Bryan that day she was job hunting, the one she mistakenly thought was laughing at her. No wonder Bryan was watching her with such interest! He never once took his eyes from her.

The song ended and the crowd began melting away into the night. It had been a most enjoyable evening, and Amber was sorry it was over. Slowly, she and Bryan began walking back to the Hardys'. Once they were away from Main Street, the dark streets were practically deserted.

"I'm glad you talked me into leaving the team at Clem's," said Bryan. "All that noise and commotion would have made nervous wrecks out of them."

"It sure would. Did you see that one team when a firecracker exploded under them? They reared up and bolted down the street completely out of control. I thought that man never would get the poor things stopped." Amber shook her head. "I don't know how some children can be so cruel to animals. They have feelings, too."

Bryan made no response. He was unusually quiet for some reason. Maybe he's thinking of Celia Langly, thought Amber. Probably wishes he had taken her tonight, instead of me.

"Celia Langly is sure pretty, isn't she?" she said casually.

"Uh-huh," Bryan answered, but his tone gave no hint of his feelings.

"Can't say much for her singing, though," Amber admitted. "She was a little off-key at times. You'd think they could have found someone better for such a special evening."

"She's the banker's daughter," Bryan explained, as though that one fact settled the matter.

"What difference does that make? She still can't sing!"

Bryan laughed, shaking his head slowly. "You've got a lot to learn, little girl!"

Amber would have resented that remark if anyone else had made it, but not coming from Bryan. He offered no more information about Celia Langly, though, and Amber gathered that he didn't care to discuss her, so she let the subject drop. It was none of her business anyway.

It had been a warm, muggy evening, but there was now a slight breeze blowing out of the southeast, and they could see heat lightning illuminating the sky in that direction. "Looks like we're in for a storm," said Amber, clasping both her arms about her. She didn't know why she did it – she wasn't really cold.

Bryan edged closer and drew her into the warm curve of his arm. "Is that better?" he asked.

"Ummm," she murmured, wondering at the same time why she didn't resist. It wasn't that she actually wanted Bryan to put his arm around her. Or did she? She could have told him she wasn't really chilly, but it was nice to feel someone's arm around her, so warm and comforting. It was like when Papa used to hug her and call her "his girl." She forgot about Celia Langly, forgot to wonder why Bryan hadn't called for her in almost a week. She suddenly felt a wonderful sense of security and was very much at peace with the world.

The rest of the way home, she shared Bryan's silence, for there seemed to be nothing to talk about that fit the mood she found herself in. Never had she felt so content with life. What more could she want? She had a good job, and a nice family to live with, and a "big brother" to take her places and have fun with. As they reached the door of the darkened house, she was thinking how wonderful it would be if she could go on this way forever. But when she turned to Bryan to thank him for the lovely evening, her comfortable little world suddenly exploded, for he took her in his arms and kissed her long and hard on the lips.

Lightning split the dark sky, and Amber felt her eyes widening in startled surprise, as Bryan held the kiss for what seemed like forever. This was no neighbor boy stealing a quick kiss out behind the barn! This was something more, much more.

Then Bryan was gazing into her eyes. "I love you," he said in a husky voice.

Before Amber could utter a word or even catch her breath, he turned and left. Flashes of lightning gave her only brief glimpses of him as he hurried to his buggy and disappeared into the stormy night. The clatter of hoofbeats was echoed by a long roll of thunder which seemed to give rumbling voice to Amber's bewilderment, as her whole being spun in a whirlpool of troubled emotions.

Chapter 14

Amber awoke from a troubled night's sleep, aware of a disturbing sense of uneasiness. She lay there for a moment, waiting for something to tell her what was wrong. Then, in an instant, it all came back to her – Bryan had kissed her last night! And for the first time in her life, she had thrilled to the words, "I love you!"

But where was the excitement now, she wondered? At the moment she felt nothing, unless it was dismay. Yes, and even a touch of anger. It hurt to think Bryan merely considered her as just another girl, another conquest. Who did he think he could fool with that "I love you" line? He'd probably told that to every girl he ever courted! Here, she thought they had something special going for them, and all along, Bryan had simply wanted to add her to his growing collection of female conquests! Well, she decided, if he thought he could buffalo *her* with his sweet talk and romantic ways, she'd show him!

There was a knock on her door. "Amber?" Mr. Hardy called softly.

"Yes?"

"Adele isn't feeling well this morning, so she's going to stay in bed. She said for you to go ahead with the girls' breakfast. Don't worry about me – I'm on my way to the store – but you might take Adele a cup of tea when you get time."

Amber heard him walk away, through the house, and out the front door.

The next two weeks were hectic. Amber was so busy she hardly had time to think about Bryan, for the doctor confined Mrs. Hardy to bed, leaving Amber to handle all the household chores alone. And, although Mrs. Hardy was patient and understanding in her demands, caring for her was an extra burden nonetheless.

Amber convinced herself she didn't care what became of Bryan Devlin. His companionship had been nice while it lasted, she told herself, but now it was over. Whenever thoughts of him flitted into her mind, she dismissed them as lightly as she would a bothersome fly.

However, three times she had answered a knock at the door to find the same little messenger boy with a note from Bryan asking to see her. Each time she had returned it with her regrets scribbled across the bottom, and wished he would take a hint and stop pestering her! She had enough on her mind without worrying about him, too.

Then, one afternoon, Bryan himself was at the door. "Hi," he said. "Do you have a minute?"

"No, I'm awfully busy," Amber replied, wiping her hands on the apron tied about her waist. "Mrs. Hardy is still sick, and I'm canning vegetables from the garden."

Bryan's brown eyes were studying her intently, and Amber self-consciously dropped her gaze. She wished he'd quit staring at her that way, so direct and questioning, even a little hurt. What was the matter with him? Was she the first girl who had ever turned him down? Maybe that was it – he just couldn't take rejection. Well, she didn't care! He was the one who had betrayed their friendship.

Bryan persisted, "Then how about this evening? I'll come over about seven-thirty and we can go somewhere and talk. I. . .I have something to tell you."

"Oh, I couldn't leave," she hedged. "I have to put the girls to bed about that time."

"Okay, I'll be here at eight!"

She couldn't think up another excuse fast enough, so Amber found herself smiling and saying all right, just as though she weren't even mad at him.

It was a lovely evening, soft and warm, with choruses of cicadas droning their summer symphony from the trees. Darn! thought Amber. Why couldn't it be raining – then maybe he wouldn't come! It was bound to be an awkward situation. She would just as soon not have to go through with it, even though she had to admit, she was more than a little curious to know what it was that Bryan had to tell her.

She took her time putting Angie and Laura to bed, then changed into a fresh dress, a green and white organdy that was a hand-me-down from Mrs. Hardy. Then she spent five minutes brushing her hair and twisting it up on top of her head into what was called a "jug handle." Besides being fashionable, it was much cooler that way.

As she passed her bedroom, Amber looked in on Mrs. Hardy. "Anything I can do for you before I go out?" she asked.

"Yes, dear, would you mind lighting the lamp? It's getting too dark in here to read."

Amber lit the coal oil lamp by the bedside and adjusted the wick.

"My, just look at the way that chimney shines in the light!" exclaimed Mrs. Hardy. "You take such good care of the lamps."

Amber still couldn't get used to receiving compliments. "Thank you," she said, smiling gratefully. She walked across the room. "I'm going to lower this window a bit – you know what the doctor said about the night air being bad for you."

"Thank you, dear. You know, that dress is just right on you, Amber. You look so cool and crisp and pretty. I hope Bryan Devlin knows how lucky he is!"

Amber smiled wryly at the last remark as she viewed herself in the mirror. "Thank you for giving the dress to me. It's a beautiful one." She turned around. "Well, I guess I've kept Bryan waiting long enough," she calculated with feminine logic. "I'd better go." She walked through the house, making a mental note to beat the parlor rug tomorrow, and stepped out onto the porch where Bryan and Clem Hardy were talking politics.

"Well, here's our girl," said Mr. Hardy. He got up from the porch swing and folded his newspaper under his arm. "I'll go in and read to Adele and leave you two alone," he said with a wink. The spring on the screen door squeaked as he opened it and disappeared inside.

"Let's go for a drive," said Bryan, nodding toward his buggy which was parked in the street.

Amber stared longingly at the two sleek Hackneys champing at their bits, then forced herself to look away. "Oh, I'd rather not," she lied. "I'm too tired." She sat down on the porch swing with a convincing sigh. "What was it you wanted to talk to me about?"

Bryan remained seated on the steps. He appeared to be caught somewhat off-guard by her question, and Amber wished she hadn't been so blunt.

"Oh," he said, turning his hat around and around in his hands. "It's just that I have to go away to school in September, to St. Louis." He shrugged with resignation. "Father decided I need to study business management so I'll be ready to take over the mills before long."

"All the way to St. Louis just to go to school?" asked Amber. "How exciting! How long will you be gone?"

"Just for one term, thank goodness! I'll be back at the end of May. Will you miss me?"

Amber had to laugh at his directness. She nodded.

"Oh, just a minute, I almost forgot, I have something for you." He ran to the buggy and returned with a pretty tin box which he handed to her.

"Oooh! Chocolates!" she murmured, as her finger lightly traced the elegant script on the top of the colorful box. "I've never had these before, only hard candies. Thank you," she said, with what she hoped was a warm smile.

Bryan grinned and settled himself on the steps. "Well, aren't you even going to offer me one? ·We may as well eat them before they melt."

"Yes, of course! Help yourself!" Amber replied, opening the box. Bryan chose a piece and she did the same. It proved to be a chocolate-covered cherry, and she had never tasted anything so wonderful in her whole life. She ate it slowly, savoring the juicy tartness of the bright red cherry inside. All the while, Bryan's gaze never left her. She could feel her icy reserve beginning to melt in the warmth of his presence and the look in his eyes. Why was he being so nice to her? It sure made it hard to stay mad at him!

But what did she expect? Bryan had always been kind to her. She began to feel a little guilty, for here she was with a chip on her shoulder, as Papa would say, trying to be difficult. Well, maybe she was making a mountain out of a molehill. Okay, she would forget all about what had happened on the night of the Fourth. Maybe, when Bryan discovered that she wasn't swayed by his romantic talk, and that she wasn't going to throw herself at him, he'd forget about it and their friendship would get back to normal.

"I do want to go for a drive!" she said brightly. She could see that Bryan was surprised by her change of mind, but she felt no need to explain. While he was snatching several more chocolates from the box on the porch, she skipped out to the buggy and hopped in, without waiting for him to help her.

Bryan grabbed his hat and came running after her, mumbling his usual admonishment through a mouthful of candy.

"What did you say?" asked Amber, with pretended innocence.

"Never mind," he answered. "I thought I had broken you of that."

"Not me! I guess I'm like a mustang – Uncle John says you can't ever be sure what a mustang's going to do!"

Bryan chuckled. He signaled to his team and they moved off, their long fly-fringes tossing smartly about their legs as they pranced.

Amber was glad she had changed her mind. The day had been unbearably hot, and she found the drive refreshing in the coolness of the gathering darkness. She hadn't realized how closely she had been tied to the house the past weeks. She threw her head back and drank in the sweet, fresh air, making a quick wish for luck on the first star she saw twinkling in the heavens. "What a beautiful evening," she said. "I'm glad we came."

"Me, too," Bryan agreed.

They drove up and down the familiar streets of Great Bend, and their being together was almost like old times. Almost. For there was still some indefinable feeling that told Amber their friendship would never be quite the same. What was it? Was it the seriousness of Bryan's attitude tonight? He was the same, yet different somehow. Try as she might, she just couldn't put her finger on it. When at last they turned back down Larkin Street, Bryan grew silent, as though preoccupied with his own thoughts. This puzzled Amber even more. What was on his mind? she wondered.

When he halted the team in front of the house, Amber remembered to wait, but Bryan made no move to get out of the buggy. Instead, he turned to her and rested one hand on hers. "Thanks for letting me come to see you tonight," he said.

Amber couldn't believe her ears! This certainly didn't sound like Bryan Devlin! She sat there dumbfounded, not knowing what to say, but Bryan clasped both her hands in his and continued.

"Gosh, I thought maybe you were mad at me there for awhile." He released her hands and began fumbling nervously with the reins in his lap. "I guess maybe you had a right to be mad, after the way I acted the other night. I don't blame you one bit."

Amber was completely mystified. Just what was he talking about? Was he actually going to apologize?

"I. . .I shouldn't have run off like I did. I don't know what came over me. I. . .I've been mixed-up lately, but I've been doing a lot of thinking and I'm not confused any more." He was looking directly at her now, and Amber could feel the intensity of his gaze probing the darkness. "Amber, I meant what I said that night. I really meant it – I love you and I want you for my wife."

Amber gulped. "You mean . . . get married? But. . . but . . . you don't know what you're saying! I mean. . ."

"Yes, I do know what I'm saying, and I know that I love you." The words came tumbling out now. "I've never felt about any girl the way I do about you. I don't know how to explain it, but you're different somehow. I don't know what it is, but I love you for it. I didn't realize it myself for awhile, but ever since the Fourth of July I've thought about nothing but you. I know now that I love you. And when I thought you were mad at me – " he broke off and turned his head away, but Amber could see tears glistening in his eyes.

"Oh, Bryan," she whispered. "I. . .I don't know what to say. Except I'm sorry if I hurt you, truly sorry." She felt weak all over. Her hands were trembling, and she clasped them together to still them. "I didn't know, I just didn't know. . ."

Bryan suddenly embraced her and pulled her close to him, so close she could feel the rapid beating of his heart. She wondered if he could feel the wild pounding of hers, as they clung together for the moment cheek to cheek. Then his lips sought hers, and he kissed her even more passionately than before, leaving her limp and breathless.

"We'll be married just as quickly as possible," he told her, "just as soon as I come home from St.

Louis next spring. But we'll have to keep it a secret until then. Mother is the sort who gets all excited about these things, and I don't want her running around in a tizzy for the next ten months. When I get back, I'll take you over to the house, and I'll introduce you to Father and Mother, and I'll say, 'This is the girl I'm going to marry.' Just think! You'll soon be Mrs. Bryan Devlin! How does that sound?"

"But Bryan, what if your folks don't like me?" Amber asked him seriously. "What if – "

Bryan pressed his finger gently to her lips. "Hush now. You just leave everything to me and don't worry about it," he said. He pulled her close to him once more. "Just don't bother your pretty little head about that."

But even in the security of his embrace, Amber could not entirely push away the doubts she felt crowding in on her.

What is love? That was the question Amber would ask herself over and over again in the months following Bryan's proposal. If it could be called that. He had never really asked her if she would marry him – he just took it for granted. The possibility that she wouldn't want him apparently had never crossed his mind. After all, she'd be a fool to pass up a chance to marry the most eligible bachelor in town. Or would she?

Although Amber missed him terribly when he left for St. Louis, she wasn't at all sure she was ready to get married – to Bryan or anyone else! She had so completely dismissed the idea of marriage for the present time that she had locked it away in the furthest recesses of her mind. But now here she was, faced with something she had figured to be years in the future. Still, marrying Bryan Devlin was interesting to contemplate. For the first time in her life she would have financial security. But, even though having money would be comforting, she knew it didn't guarantee happiness. Mama and Papa hadn't had much money, yet they had seemed to possess happiness. Love, Amber decided, was the all-important ingredient.

Did she love Bryan? She knew she liked him. She enjoyed his company a lot. But she didn't think the feeling was love, for she was bothered by too many doubts, some vague and unexplainable, others a bit more tangible. For one thing, they had known each other for such a short time. A three-month friendship hardly seemed a good foundation for a lifetime together. And then there was the gulf of difference in their backgrounds, in their lives. She remembered that day at the picnic, when she had felt so out of place with everyone staring at her. Would she ever overcome that?

She wondered how Bryan could be so sure of his own emotions and convinced everything would work out all right. She hadn't even met his parents. Was he being blinded to the possible pitfalls by momentary infatuation? If so, there was the possibility that he would have second thoughts later on and perhaps change his mind about her altogether. He might even find someone else while he was away in St. Louis. Yes, she decided, a lot could happen before next spring.

Meanwhile, she had plenty to keep her busy, for even though Mrs. Hardy was eventually allowed up and around, she was not to do any of the household work. Amber did it all. She washed on Monday, ironed on Tuesday, did the mending and sewing on Wednesday, cleaned house on Thursday and Friday, and on Saturday, took care of the shopping for the week. And she still managed to bake bread every other day. Except for the cooking, she had Sundays pretty much to herself, and used the time to read books and write letters. Bryan wrote faithfully every week at first, then every other week. Amber answered each of his letters and always looked forward to the next.

As the days went by, however, she began to be plagued by disturbing moods of melancholy, followed by splitting headaches that sent her to bed for hours at a time. She had always been relatively healthy, so it was a mystery to her why she should suddenly develop these strange symptoms. She decided it must be because she missed Bryan so.

Although she wanted desperately to confide in Mrs. Hardy concerning Bryan's proposal of marriage, she was hesitant to do so for fear of reviving the old rumors concerning Bryan and the Devlins' house girl. Would Adele Hardy approve or disapprove? Would she think seventeen was too young? What if she asked Amber to leave? Worried about her reaction, Amber had decided to put off telling her friend for as long as possible.

Bryan had written that he might be home for Christmas, but changed his mind at the last minute, saying that he and his roommate had been invited to spend the holidays with friends in St. Louis. Amber was not only disappointed but a little hurt. Even the arrival of a Christmas gift from Bryan didn't do much to cheer her up. It was an elegant muff and hat set – red velvet trimmed in soft, white rabbit fur – so elegant, in fact, that she wondered where she would ever wear them. Still, it was nice to know he was thinking of her.

Amber brushed her hair and put on her warm flannel nightgown. She picked up her writing pad and glanced at the calendar on the wall.

February 18, 1895

Dear Mama,

Today is my 17th birthday, and it is snowing. Bryan will be home in 10 weeks. It seems like he has been gone forever! I guess it's because I miss him so much. He doesn't write as often as he used to, but I guess he is kept pretty busy with his studies.

Mama, I'm worried about that cough of yours, even though you say it's nothing. Lisa says you've had it for over 3 months now. I wish you would go

217

to the doctor and see what he says. Maybe there is something he can give you for it.

How are the children doing? I wish I could come back and see all of you. I just haven't been able to save up enough money. It takes so much just to live, and my $1.25 a week doesn't go very far. I guess everybody is having trouble making ends meet these days. Uncle John is even going to try to grow his own sugar cane so he won't have to buy sugar! Can you imagine sugar cane growing in Kansas?

Aunt Grizelda just had another baby girl and they named her Naomi. I think that's a pretty name, don't you? The whole family came in to church last Sunday for the baptism, and I talked to them for awhile. Lonnie seems to be doing fine. His eye looks awful but doesn't seem to bother him.

I must close now and get to bed. Do take care, Mama, and give my love to all.

Your daughter,
Amber

She blew out the lamp, knowing it must be late, but she found herself not the least bit sleepy. Wiping the frost from the tiny window next to her bed, she peered out at the snowfall. It seemed as though winter had wrapped the town in a soft, white muffler. Everything was still and beautiful.

For a long time, she sat on her bed, hugging her knees and staring out into the winter night. She was aware of a peculiar but intense longing, for what, she didn't know. Maybe this was the way it felt to be in love. For the thousandth time Amber asked herself if she loved Bryan, and for the thousandth time, the only answer was an echoing uncertainty.

She sighed. Turning back the covers, she crawled beneath the warm goosedown comforter and plumped up her pillow, determined to get a good night's sleep for a change. Like a fiendish devil who would keep her from sleep, insomnia had been torturing her with increasing frequency. At first, she had blamed it on the full moon, but it had come and waned more than once, and still she was having trouble. If only I could stop my runaway mind, she grumbled to herself, maybe I could get some sleep!

True, she was worried about her strange moods of depression and the terrible headaches she had been experiencing for the first time in her life. Could it be her troubled state of mind? she wondered.

She had to admit to a growing unease about her impending wedding. What's the matter with me, anyway? she asked herself angrily. One minute I'm excited about marrying Bryan, and the next minute, I'm running scared! I'd better make up my mind once and for all, because time is running out. Bryan will be back before long, and I'd better know what I'm going to do!

Restlessly, she turned over on her stomach, hugging her pillow beneath her. I'm going to be Mrs. Bryan Devlin, she told herself, and I'm happy! I'm happy. I'm . . .happy. Everything will be all right as soon as Bryan gets home. She decided that was her whole problem – she just longed to see Bryan, and once he returned, all would be well. So what if she wasn't sure just how much she loved him? Was anyone ever sure? Besides, she could learn to love him!

She felt a dull ache beginning behind her left eye, a subtle spark that she knew from dreadful experience would soon become a searing, burning pain. "Oh, no," she groaned, "another sleepless night!"

Chapter 15

Amber would never forget the day in May when Bryan returned from St. Louis. Never once in all his letters had he even hinted that he was growing a mustache. With that and the snappy new clothes he was wearing, Amber didn't even recognize him in the crowd of people swarming off the train. She was standing on tiptoe, still watching for him, when suddenly, there he was, embracing and kissing her. She was so startled, she forgot to kiss him back.

"Hey, babe, what's the matter?" Bryan exclaimed. "Are you mad at me or something?"

"No, certainly not," apologized Amber, flustered and breathless. "Forgive me. I – I was just so surprised by the mustache and all. You didn't tell me about that!"

"I wanted to surprise you," answered Bryan proudly. "How do you like it? Don't you think it makes me look older and wiser?" he said, with an air of dignity.

"Oh, yes, you look old and wise all right – you look just like my Uncle John!" Amber teased. She giggled and Bryan gave her another hug.

"Now, let's try that again," he said, and kissed her once again full on the lips and very hard, so hard that she found herself pulling back from him. Bryan had never kissed her like that before! It – it was almost indecent! She opened her eyes and felt her cheeks flush as she glanced around in embarrassment, hoping no one in the depot crowd was watching. Bryan himself appeared totally unconcerned.

"Gosh, it's good to be back! But it's hot standing here, and I'm so dry I could spit cotton! Would you care to join me for a cold drink at Mr. Hardy's drug store?" he asked.

"I'd love to," Amber responded quickly. She picked up the smallest of Bryan's three bags and he grabbed the other two. As they made their way through the throng of people, Amber was already anticipating the tingly coolness of one of the special concoctions Mr. Hardy called a "soda."

It was cool in the drug store and not too crowded. Bryan led the way to a small table for two over in one corner, and they had just sat down when Clem Hardy came over to shake Bryan's hand and welcome him home. "Good to see you, son, glad to have you back," he said. "What will it be? It's on the house." He raised his eyebrows at Amber, waiting for her order.

"I'll have a chocolate soda," she replied eagerly.

"Do you have Creme de Menthe?" asked Bryan.

"No, I'm afraid not," responded Mr. Hardy, taken aback somewhat by the request. "We have only chocolate, strawberry, and cherry."

"I'll have the cherry then," Bryan said, and Mr. Hardy hurried over to the soda fountain. "I should have known I couldn't get a decent soda in a one-horse town like Great Bend," he said, disgustedly drumming his fingers against the tabletop. "This place is twenty years behind the rest of the world! You should see all the swell things they have in St. Louis – things this stupid burg has never even dreamed of. I can't believe I was so dumb as to think Great Bend, Kansas, was anything! It's nothin', believe me, a big nothin' filled with a bunch of nobodies goin' no place."

Amber was shocked by his negative opinions. "I've always thought it was . . . a nice town," she said lamely. "It's sure better than living on a farm out in the middle of the prairie, I'll tell you! I wouldn't go back – "

"That's just it," interrupted Bryan. "People are so dumb! They're always satisfied where they are, until they get away once and see how the rest of the world lives. Then, if they're smart, they realize what they've been missing."

Even though Bryan was speaking to her, Amber discovered that he almost never looked directly at her. His eyes darted back and forth like a nervous animal's, and his hands fidgeted constantly. She also noticed that rough slang words had crept into his vocabulary, words she had never heard him use before, and she was astonished by his casual and frequent use of them.

"Take my roommate, Travis, the fellow I lived with in St. Louis. Now, there's a man who's been around! He didn't get along with his stepfather, so he ran away from home when he was fourteen, and he's been on his own ever since. He says there's nothing he hasn't tried, and I believe it! Yessiree, I do believe it! He can tell some stories that – "

"Oh, here are our sodas," said Amber, as Clem Hardy set the two frothy refreshments before them. "Oooh, that looks good! Thank you, Mr. Hardy."

"Anyway," Bryan continued, "Travis can tell some of the darndest stories. I nearly split a gut laughing at him! Like the time he 'made his living' killing cats for people. He explains it real serious and business-like, just as though he was ol' Rockefeller himself, and then you find out he was only eight years old at the time!" Bryan laughed.

The more he talked, the more the whole mood of his conversation disturbed Amber, and she found herself lapsing into silence except for a few polite comments now and then. This was not the Bryan she remembered.

"Then there was the time Travis stole his stepdad's expensive, store-bought cigars, smoked two in a row, and got so sick he passed out and set the barn on fire! He was lucky to get out of that little scrape alive."

Bryan chuckled again, but Amber failed to see the humor in killing cats or burning down barns. She had drunk her soda too quickly and felt all fizzy inside, and slightly sick to her stomach. "I'm sorry, but I need to get back – I promised Mrs. Hardy I'd start the spring housecleaning today. I don't look forward to beating all those rugs, but it has to be done." She stood up to leave, ignoring Bryan's protest. "You stay and finish your soda, and I'll see you sometime later on, all right?"

"You bet you will, babe." Bryan took her hand and kissed it, then looked up at her earnestly.

"You're going to be seeing a lot of me from now on."

The drug store suddenly became too warm for Amber, and she felt she couldn't stand it another second. She pulled her hand away. " 'Bye now," she said as sweetly as she could before hurrying to the door. She stood outside for a moment and took several deep breaths of fresh air to clear her head. As she started down the boardwalk, she glanced back inside the drug store long enough to see Bryan lighting up a cigar. "I wonder what else he learned from his hero Travis!" she muttered to herself.

Amber brushed her long, brown hair and piled it up on top of her head, securing it with several long tortoise-shell hair pins and the rhinestone-studded comb Bryan had brought her from St. Louis, then sat for a long time staring into her mirror. It was a somber image which gazed back at her.

She had accepted Bryan's invitation to dinner at his house this evening only because she really didn't want to spend another evening alone with him. After his first day home, she got weary of hearing him tell about Travis and their exploits in the big city, especially when he forgot half of what he had said, and she had to listen to it all over again. She could barely get a word in edgewise, but she decided it really didn't matter. All the interesting little things she had been saving up to tell Bryan suddenly seemed rather trite and ridiculous, anyway. She felt sure he wouldn't be interested in hearing how she had taught Angie to count to one hundred, or that she had been chosen to sing in the adult choir at church.

"Why can't it be like it used to be?" Amber wondered aloud to her reflection in the mirror. She and Bryan had always had such fun, laughing and joking and doing things together. But now he was always so serious, and not only serious, but cynical and disagreeable, as well. She longed for the companionship they had shared, but something told her that things would never again be the same. She didn't really understand why, but she guessed she would just have to accept the fact that things change, people change, nothing remains the same.

The whole prospect of marriage had not been her idea. It was something initiated and fostered by Bryan, and she could not shake the feeling that she was being led someplace she didn't want to go. Suddenly, in her mind's eye, she saw scenes from long ago of a rebellious, blue-gray pony at the end of a string of other horses, pulling back in stiff-legged protest, and that same pony harnessed between workhorses, lying down and being dragged along. Tears came to Amber's eyes. "Oh, God," she cried softly, "what am I going to do? I don't want to marry Bryan Devlin. You know I don't. But what am I going to do? What can I tell him? I don't want to hurt him, but I don't want to go through with this, either."

She was still drying her eyes when Mrs. Hardy knocked on the door to inform her that Bryan had arrived. He was early, so Amber took a while, trying to allow her eyes time to clear. Taking her white knitted shawl from the peg on the back of the door, she threw it loosely about her shoulders, changed her mind, and folded it over one arm instead. Stopping in front of the mirror long enough to admire the blue and white chintz dress Bryan had brought her from St. Louis, she had to admit, it was very stylish.

Bryan got to his feet as she entered the parlor. "Hi!" she said to him, as brightly as she could, hoping he wouldn't notice the redness of her eyes.

"Hi! The dress looks great! Don't I have good taste?" he bragged to the Hardys. "And just look at that fit – it couldn't be better!"

Amber smiled knowingly at Adele Hardy as she walked to the door. Neither of them told Bryan they had had to alter the dress to fit, for although it was beautifully made, it had been one size too big.

"I'm scared to death to meet your folks," Amber said with a nervous smile, as they walked out to Bryan's buggy.

"Don't be silly," he countered. "I've told you before, there's nothing to worry about. They're going to love you, once they get to know you."

Amber wondered to herself just how long that might take. She sat beside Bryan, anxiously twisting the fringe on her shawl, as the proud team of Hackneys trotted smartly across town to the Devlins'. Bryan immediately launched into another narrative about himself and Travis and their acquaintances in St. Louis, but Amber was only half-listening. She was trying to decide what she would say to Mr. and Mrs. Devlin, but nothing sounded appropriate.

"What have you told your folks?" she asked, when she could sneak a word in. "I mean, about us? Do they know – ?"

"Nah, I just said I was inviting a friend to dinner. They don't even know who it is. But just relax, babe, everything's going to be okay," he said, patting her hand.

All too soon, they pulled into the circular driveway in front of the Devlin home. The house was one of the largest in all of Great Bend, built of stone blocks, two stories high, with a large veranda across the front, and round towers jutting from the corners, all ornately Victorian and very impressive. The sight of it stirred up the butterflies fluttering in Amber's stomach, and she asked herself how on earth she would ever be able to eat. Bryan leaped out of the buggy and tied the team to the metal ring on the black iron horsehead hitching post, then helped Amber out. She thought she saw a curtain in the front window being pulled back slightly as they strolled arm in arm up the front walk.

As they approached the massive, wooden door, it swung open, and a fragile, overly-dressed woman, her gray hair slightly disheveled, smiled a welcome. "Mother," said Bryan, "I'd like you to meet Miss Amber Lockhardt."

"How do you do, my dear," said Mrs. Devlin. "We're so pleased that you could join us this evening. Let me take your wrap."

"How do you do," responded Amber with a smile. "I'm so happy to meet you." She handed over her shawl, and with bird-like, flighty movements, Mrs. Devlin dropped it into a wicker chair beside a huge potted plant.

Out of the library to their right came a rather stout gentleman, folding a newspaper under his arm. He was smoking, or rather chewing on, a short, black cigar, and although his clothes appeared to be expensive, they were rumpled and unkempt.

Mrs. Devlin motioned him over. "Jess, Sonny's back with his little friend, Amber . . . what was your last name, dear?"

"Lockhardt."

"Oh, yes! Amber Lockhardt."

"How do you do," boomed Mr. Devlin in a voice so loud that it startled Amber. He extended his hand to her, and Amber hesitated momentarily, then reached out to find his handshake as rough as his voice. "Where do you come from?" he asked. "I don't know any Lockhardts in Great Bend."

"Well, I'm originally from Ohio," replied Amber, "but right now I'm a house girl for Clem Hardy. You know, the druggist."

"Oh, sure, sure, I know Clem and Adele. I remember when they bought the drug store from old man Pearson. Clem's a good businessman. He understands how to make a profit. Pearson never did. He sold everything too cheap and gave too much credit."

"Excuse me?" A pretty, young girl wearing a white cap and a white apron had appeared in the doorway of the dining room. "Dinner is ready," she said to Mrs. Devlin.

"Thank you, Lila." The girl turned and disappeared through a swinging door into the kitchen. "Shall we go in and sit down?" invited Mrs. Devlin.

"Let's!" said Bryan. Offering Amber his arm, he led the way into the dining room and seated her at the table, then took the seat opposite.

Amber was awestruck by the beauty and elegance of the room and its lovely furnishings. The furniture was of the finest carved mahogany, and a gaslight chandelier – the first Amber had ever seen – hung over the table, which was set with sparkling china, crystal and silver. It was indeed beautiful, but Amber, even in her chic St. Louis dress, felt quite out of place amidst such opulence.

The three members of the Devlin family each began by drinking the goblet of wine set at their places. Cautiously, Amber took a sip and wrinkled her nose as a slight shudder ran through her. She found the wine not much to her liking, but she took another small taste from the delicate rim of the glass before setting it back on the table.

She was wondering where the food was, when Mrs. Devlin picked up a small brass bell. At the sound of the ringing bell, the girl in the white apron appeared, carrying a round tray with four salads. Wordlessly, she placed them one by one at each place and disappeared back through the swinging door. Amber panicked briefly when she reached for her fork. She had never seen so many pieces of silverware in her life! Not knowing what to do, she threw a quick glance across the table at Bryan to see which fork he used, then she did the same. The salad was mostly lettuce, with several greens she did not recognize, as well as slices of cucumber and radish, accented with a seasoned oil and vinegar dressing that was quite tasty. Amber was immediately aware, however, that the cucumbers and radishes were not going to sit well on her nervous stomach, but to be polite, she proceeded to eat them anyway.

"So you're from Ohio, are you?" quizzed Mr. Devlin. "What brought you to Kansas? The same thing that brought everybody? Free land?"

"Well, sort of," replied Amber. "My aunt and uncle have a homestead south of town, and I came west with them several years ago when my father died back in Ohio."

"What business was your father in?" Mr. Devlin asked, munching his salad.

"Business? replied Amber, somewhat puzzled by the question. "Well, he worked for the railroad."

"Oh, in what capacity?"

Not understanding, Amber looked at Bryan helplessly.

"He was a manager, wasn't he, Amber? he answered, nodding his head. "Yeah, a district manager."

Amber frowned at him, but said nothing. She had never felt the need to lie about Papa's job before. What difference could it possibly make?

Mrs. Devlin rang the little bell again, and the girl came to take away the empty salad plates, returning almost immediately with small bowls of onion soup. Amber was glad for the interruption, hoping the conversation would take a new turn.

"Speaking of railroads, I was just reading in the paper about the gold rush at Cripple Creek in the Colorado mountains," said Mr. Devlin. "Two competing railroads had a race to see who could get to the town first, and the whole town was wagering on which one would win. There are fortunes to be made in more ways than just by finding gold – in railroads, banks, the stock market, the retail market. Some people think you have to use brawn, but I say it's the man with the brains who's going to get ahead in this world." He glanced at his son. "If I were younger, I'd head for Cripple Creek myself and start building my own little empire in those Rocky Mountains. That's what I'd do – find a need and fill it!" He added emphasis to his statement by dropping his soup spoon into his empty bowl and shoving it away from him.

Amber still felt uneasy. She tried another sip of wine and stifled a belch with her napkin, hoping no one had noticed. But Bryan and his father had launched into a discussion of the impact of the Cripple Creek gold boom on the current economic situation, and didn't even pause when the bell was rung for the main course. Amber sat there feeling completely left out. She smiled at Bryan's mother, who hadn't uttered a word since they sat down, and tried another taste of wine. It wasn't quite as bad this time, so she sipped a little more. It felt warm going down, like the coffee she drank on cold winter mornings.

Although it was skillfully prepared, the plate of food set before her held little interest for Amber. She only picked at it, forcing each bite down and pretending to enjoy it, as she listened to Bryan's discussion with his father turn into a somewhat heated argument. Each was as hard-headed as the other, and neither would budge an inch on any issue. It was all beyond her, and very boring to listen to. Besides, their loud talk was beginning to give her a headache.

Ordinarily, Amber would have been ecstatic over something as rare as orange sherbet, but by the time dessert was served, she was in the throes of one of her severe headaches, and the cold ice cream sent even sharper pains through her throbbing head. She was suddenly seized with the overwhelming desire to run from the room, away from the glitter and polish, away from the speeches that meant nothing, away from this place where she didn't belong. Thank goodness, dinner was almost over!

While Bryan gave his opinion on how the country had narrowly averted another Panic, his father ate his own serving of sherbet in a single large mouthful. He then wiped an orange trickle from the corner of his mouth with his napkin, which he promptly wadded up and threw onto the table. "I don't know where you got your information, sonny boy, but it's wrong – dead wrong!" he said with a gruff finality that ended the conversation.

The bell was rung and the girl, Lila, began to clear the dessert dishes. In her haste, she grazed Amber's half-full wine glass, knocking it over onto the table. Amber gasped. Horrified, she watched the dark red stain quickly soak into the white damask tablecloth.

"You clumsy fool!" shouted Mr. Devlin, jumping to his feet. "Now look what you've done!"

Mrs. Devlin sat helplessly wringing her hands. Oh, dear, oh, my!" she cried.

"No, please!" Amber pleaded. "It wasn't her fault! It was mine! I should have finished – "

"Don't be ridiculous!" roared Mr. Devlin. "It was Lila's fault and no one else's. She should have been more careful." He glared at Lila, who stood rooted to the spot, frightened and undecided about what to do. "Well, don't just stand there! Get the rest of these things off of here and put this tablecloth to soak!" he ordered.

While Bryan's parents were seeing to it that the mess was cleaned up, Amber took Bryan aside. "I'm so sorry about the wine," she said, but I – "

"Don't you apologize! It was that girl's fault as plain as day," Bryan countered. "One more stunt like that and she's going to be out of a job!"

"Oh, please," Amber pleaded, "don't fire her because of me. I wouldn't want you to do that! She didn't mean to spill the wine. It was an accident, that's all, just a simple accident that could happen to any – "

"I don't care if it was an accident or not!" interrupted Bryan. "The stupid girl should have been more careful. She can't do – "

"Shhh!" cautioned Amber. "I'm sure she feels bad enough already. Don't let her hear you say that. She's just in the next room."

"So what? She's nothing but a hired girl," answered Bryan.

Amber was amazed at the total indifference with which he spoke. She stood speechless, her head reeling with the impact of his statement, while her temples continued to throb with pain. She put one hand to her forehead and closed her eyes momentarily. "I'm sorry," she said finally, "but I have a terrible headache. Will you take me home?"

Bryan's attitude changed abruptly to one of concern. "Of course, if that's what you want. I wish you wouldn't go though. The folks haven't had a chance to really get to know you. Maybe if you lie down for a few minutes, you'll be all right."

"No, please, I just want to go home."

Bryan could see the pain in her eyes and hear the insistence in her voice. He shrugged his shoulders. "Okay, but I don't know what to tell my folks. They're sure going to be disappointed."

"I am too," she said tersely.

It was a miracle! Her prayers had been answered by a miracle! Amber stood in the warm sunshine of the churchyard, hardly daring to believe Uncle Karl's letter, even as she read it for the second time.

It was almost too good to be true! Her eyes darted back to the beginning, and she scanned it once again.

May 5, 1895

Dear Amber,

Well, here we are in Oklahoma Territory, me and Phil and Wenzel. We each got us a 160-aker farm when the Indian lands were opened for settlement, and we are all working hard to prove up on them. It's good land, even better than Kansas, so it should be easy. The thing is, we need someone to keep house and cook for us, little gal, and I thot of you. If you are interested in keeping house for 3 batchlers, let us know and we will send you money for your train fare.

Respectfully,
Your Uncle Karl

"Well, what do you think? Would you want to go down there?" asked Uncle John, as he lifted the last youngster into his wagon hitched outside the church.

"Yes, I would!" replied Amber, grinning with excitement. "And to think, I almost didn't come to church this morning! I had such a terrible headache all last night, and I wasn't sure I'd be able to come. Thank goodness I did! You'll never know how important this letter is to me. Thank you for bringing it. Thank you so much, Uncle John!" She gave him a quick hug before he swung up to the wagon seat beside Grizelda and headed his team for home.

"You'd better think long and hard about that offer," Aunt Grizelda hollered back at Amber. "Oklahoma is full of rattlesnakes and wild Indians, you know. It's no place for a girl your age to go all alone."

Undaunted by her aunt's pessimism, Amber perused the letter one more time, folded it carefully, slipped it into her handbag, and made her way back to where the Hardy family stood chatting with friends. She didn't know just how she would break the news of her decision to them, but she felt sure they would not begrudge her this opportunity. While they visited, Amber began making plans. She would answer Uncle Karl's letter right away and get it off in the mail first thing in the morning. She didn't know how long it would take to hear back, but she would be ready to go the minute Uncle Karl sent the money.

Oklahoma! I'm going to Oklahoma Territory! she sang over and over to herself, oblivious to the people and the chatter around her. The very word "Oklahoma" conjured up mental images of noble redmen in feathered headdresses astride their spotted war ponies. A quick shiver of excitement shot up her spine and showered her with chills. When she shuddered visibly, Adele Hardy was quick to notice.

"What's the matter, dear?" she asked.

"Oh, nothing," replied Amber, "I was just thinking. Say, do you mind if I walk on ahead? It's such a beautiful day, I feel like taking a stroll."

"Not at all. You go ahead, dear, and we'll be along shortly," said Mrs. Hardy.

Amber hummed to herself all the way home, her step as light as her heart. She still couldn't believe the incredible good luck that had come her way. Gratitude overflowed her being, and she felt in love with the whole world. It was as though she had thrown off some heavy weight which had been pressing down upon her, and at last she was free and buoyant, like a thistle caught up by the wind.

Chapter 16

Once again, Amber found herself listening to the clickity-clack of train wheels taking her to a new life in a new place. Only this time it was no homesick ten-year-old, uprooted and transplanted against her will; the reflection she saw in the train window was that of a confident young woman, eager to experience whatever lay ahead.

Reassuringly, she touched the handkerchief-wrapped money pinned inside her chemise, the change left from the ten dollars Uncle Karl had sent for the purchase of her train ticket. It was more money than she had ever carried in her life – almost five dollars – and she worried constantly about losing it. She wished he hadn't sent quite so much. She only needed a couple of dollars for one night at the hotel and the stagecoach fare. She was told she should have the rest of it "just in case," whatever that meant.

According to Uncle Karl's instructions, she would take the train to El Reno, spend the night there at the Caddo Hotel, and catch the stage going west the next morning. It would take her to the Potter farm, and they would then drive her to her uncles' place. Amber had rehearsed it over and over, step by step in her mind, and she wasn't too concerned about getting lost. Besides, Uncle Karl had alerted everyone along the way, and they were expecting her. There was no chance of losing her way, or at least, she didn't think so.

Just then, Aunt Grizelda's admonition about "wild Indians" came back to her, and even though she knew most Indians were at peace now, she suddenly pictured herself out in the middle of nowhere, at the mercy of a horde of savages. "Oh well," she muttered to herself, "I'd rather face them than have to marry Bryan Devlin!"

Poor Bryan! He had taken it pretty hard – harder than she ever would have imagined. He just couldn't believe that she would give up everything he could offer her, to go someplace like Oklahoma Territory and keep house for three old bachelors! Maybe she *was* crazy. Only time would tell if she had made the right decision. Right now, she was sure she had.

Amber settled back in her seat as the familiar Kansas landscape fell rapidly behind. Eagerly, she watched for anything that would alert her as to when they had crossed the line into Oklahoma Territory, but so far, it still resembled Kansas – flat and monotonous. She found the book of Longfellow's poems that Bryan had given her as a going-away present, and flipped through it, reading random verses that appealed to her. It was a lovely book, and she was grateful to him for the gift until she discovered what he had written inside the cover: *I'll be waiting. Love forever, Bryan.*

So, he still wasn't going to give up! It was nice to know she could always go back if things didn't work out, but at the same time, she knew she never would, any more than she could return to Uncle

John's farm and resume living there. Life moved forever forward, and she, too, must forge ahead and never retreat.

"Pardon me, miss, is this seat taken?"

Amber looked up to find a young soldier in a rumpled uniform standing in the aisle beside her. "No, it's not," she replied, hastily removing her belongings from the vacant seat next to her. "Please sit down."

"Thank you." The soldier plopped down with a heavy sigh. "Boy, am I bushed!" he exclaimed, running one hand through his tousled blond hair.

The woman facing them in the seat opposite was preoccupied with a restless young son and a crying baby, so Amber was glad to have someone to talk with. Besides, except for a day's growth of beard, she thought the soldier was handsome. "Where have you been?" she asked. "Home on leave?"

The soldier leaned his head back and stared straight ahead. "No, I'm afraid not," he replied somberly. "I just took my buddy home to his family so they could bury him. Someone had to accompany the body, you know, and we were pals, signed up together and everything. . ."

"What happened?" asked Amber, hoping she wasn't prying.

"Cheyennes," came the reply. "Shot him right through the heart."

"But I thought the Indians were all peaceful now – I didn't know they were still going around killing people!" Amber exclaimed.

"They are peaceful, for the most part. That's why it's so ridiculous, such a waste of a life," said the soldier. "But. . .a group of young Cheyennes got drunk, and when they do, they get restless and start causing trouble. A patrol was sent out from the fort to round them up and bring them in to sober up. When we caught up with them, at Turkey Creek, somebody got trigger-happy, and the next thing we knew, bullets were flying everywhere. My friend never knew what hit him!" There were tears in the young soldier's eyes when he finished.

"I'm so sorry," said Amber, moved by his deep sense of loss. "What a shame."

"Anyway," he continued, blinking the tears away, "I'm on my way back to the fort."

"What fort?" asked Amber, slightly embarrassed at her ignorance of the territory.

"Fort Reno. It's about seven miles west of the town of El Reno."

"El Reno? That's where I get off the train!"

"Oh, really?"

"Yes, I'm going to keep house for three bachelor uncles who have homesteads northwest of there," Amber said, "and I have a feeling it's going to be quite an experience! I've never even met two of them, but the one I do know is a real character!" Amber was relating stories about Uncle Karl, when she notice the soldier's head beginning to nod.

"I'm sorry," he said sleepily, "but my buddy's family held a wake for him all night long, and I never did get any sleep. If you'll pardon me, I think I'll grab some shut-eye."

"Of course, you go right ahead."

Within seconds, he was snoring softly, his features relaxed and peaceful, with an expression that was childlike and innocent.

"Bless his heart," said the lady in the opposite seat, motioning toward the sleeping soldier. "He's been through a lot for someone so young."

The baby was no longer crying, and Amber discovered that the woman had been discreetly nursing her beneath the folds of a short purple cape. She laid the baby, satisfied and asleep, in her lap and turned to her rambunctious young son. "You've got to settle down now," she ordered, "and let Sister sleep." He sat back in the seat and stared at Amber with large, soulful eyes.

"How would you like a lemon drop?" Amber asked him brightly. He didn't reply, but shook his head up and down affirmatively. Amber reached into her drawstring bag and brought out a small white sack of lemon drops – her going-away present from Clem Hardy – and handed one to the little boy.

"Say thank you, Jody," said his mother, but Jody just sucked on the lemon drop and continued to stare at Amber.

"Anyway, thank you," the woman said. "He's always been shy with strangers. My name is Mary Hammil. We're from Missouri."

"I'm glad to know you. I'm Amber Lockhardt, and I'm from Kansas. Your son reminds me of my little cousin," she said, remembering the way Kris always hid behind his mother's skirts whenever a stranger appeared.

"Did I hear you mention you were going to El Reno? That's where we get off, too," said Mary. "My husband got some of that Indian land they gave away in '92. He wanted to make the run in '89, but Jody was being born about that time and he couldn't get away. So when we heard there was going to be another parcel of free land available, he made sure he got in on it." She sighed. "He's been there for three years proving up on it, and we're finally going to join him. He only made it back to Missouri twice in all that time." She looked lovingly at the sleeping infant on her lap. "The last time, he left me with this little gift."

"Where is your farm, do you know?" Amber inquired.

"All I know is that it's part of the Cheyenne-Arapaho lands somewhere northwest of the town of El Reno. I'm sorry I can't be more specific, but. . ."

"That's all I know, too," said Amber, laughing. "Maybe we'll be neighbors! Wouldn't that be nice?"

"Yes, it would. I can't wait to see our farm! Mary continued. "My husband says it's a real nice piece of ground. It even has a spring on it! And he's built us a house, not a soddy, mind you, but a real, wood house with three whole rooms!" Both her voice and her sparkling eyes reflected the pride she felt in her husband's accomplishments.

"How wonderful!" exclaimed Amber. "I do wish you all the best in your new home. I know you'll be very happy having your family together again."

As she chatted with Mary Hammil, Amber found herself becoming more and more envious. Here was a woman who was very much in love with her husband and who enjoyed her role as wife and mother. There was no whining complaint typical of Grizelda, no self-sacrificing martyrdom portrayed by Adele Hardy, none of the mindless dependency she had witnessed in Mrs. Devlin. Hers was a content, caring outlook on life which Amber admired very much. It made her analyze once again what she herself had given up – financial security, a loving husband, children perhaps. Was she really making the right move? Suddenly, she was no longer so sure.

Desperate for reassurance, Amber began plying her newfound friend with questions, which eventually led to her divulging the whole story about her romance with Bryan. "Anyway," she concluded, heaving a long sigh, "I just hope I'm doing the right thing, coming down here instead of marrying him. How do you know when you're in love? Is anyone ever really sure?"

"Oh, you'll know all right, you'll feel it," Mary assured her. Her brown eyes sparkled, and her rather plain face was lit with an inner beauty that fascinated Amber. Mary gazed off into space and spoke softly. "I never really tried to put it into words before, but love is. . .givingness, I would say. Yes, a total givingness, always putting the other person first. It's. . .wanting everything good for the other person, with no strings attached." She brought her eyes back to Amber and smiled. "Does any of that make sense?"

"Yes, it does," said Amber slowly. "It all sounds so beautiful and. . . unselfish. I just hope I can feel that way about someone someday. I'm afraid I have a long way to go, though!"

"Oh, you'll find the right person, and it will be beautiful – you'll see."

"I hope so," Amber replied.

"Look!" Jody was pointing excitedly out the train window at a huge prairie dog town, stretching across the prairie as far as the eye could see.

They were amazed at the color of the dirt piled around each burrow. It was a bright, rust red, and Amber had to laugh, for it had turned the prairie dogs red as well. "I wonder what makes the dirt so colorful here?" she mused aloud, as she watched a small, rust-colored whirlwind spin away from the train and swirl across the grassland.

The landscape itself was gradually changing into rolling hills dotted here and there with dark green cedar trees and scrub oak, reminding Amber somewhat of Ohio. She didn't know whether it was the unusual surroundings or the memories of her birthplace, but she had a feeling she was going to like this new territory.

Amber awoke at dawn, surprised to find the sun rising in the west. Disoriented, she couldn't remember where she was for a moment, but it all came back to her in a flash. The train had arrived in

El Reno late at night, and she had been taken to the Caddo Hotel by the Swan Bus Lines, a coach pulled by double teams of gray horses. And this morning she would take the stagecoach out to her uncles' farm! Her stomach fluttered with excitement as she donned her St. Louis dress, her Sunday hat with the pink roses and the blue bow, and went down to have breakfast. She would have to hurry – the only stage left at seven, and she didn't want to miss it.

After a delicious breakfast of hot biscuits and gravy, Amber made arrangements with the hotel to keep her trunk until her uncles could pick it up on their next excursion into town. Then she went out onto the veranda to await the stage. It was a humid June morning, and the sunshine, even this early, was already uncomfortably hot, so she strolled along the shaded veranda, trying to see as much as possible. El Reno was a town being built as you watched, for new buildings were going up everywhere. Piles of bricks were stacked in the streets, and the two wide main avenues were filled with the hustle and bustle of people rushing here and there on foot and in every conceivable conveyance, giving the whole town an air of excitement and frenzied growth.

Right on time, the stagecoach arrived, looking nothing like Amber had imagined it would, for it was simply an open surrey, with four-inch, yellow fringe around the top. And, unlike the coach that had met her at the train the previous night, it was not pulled by a team of four, but rather by what appeared to be two mustang ponies.

Eyeing them skeptically, Amber gathered up her belongings and descended the stairs. She took one look inside the surrey and went no farther. There were three men aboard, all of them smoking pipes or cigars, and one in particular she found absolutely repulsive. His graying hair was long, bushy, and matted, and there was an overpowering stench of sweat and filth about him. He leered at Amber with a crooked grin that revealed discolored and missing teeth, as he moved over to make room for her.

Impulsively, she asked the driver, "Could I ride up there with you? It's awfully crowded in there."

"I guess so, miss, if you'd rather," the young man said, clearly taken by surprise. He swung down easily from the driver's seat and loaded her bag on top with the rest. He then turned to Amber, and his hands were firm and strong around her waist as he lifted her up to the seat. "You must be the one I'm supposed to leave off at the Potter farm. You're going to work for your three uncles out by Geary, right?"

"That's right," Amber replied. "Did they tell you to watch for me?"

"Yeah, but you're a lot bigger. . .uh, older than I had in mind. The way your uncle kept calling you a 'little gal,' I thought you were about twelve!" He laughed and swung up beside her, gathering up the reins.

"That's my Uncle Karl," Amber said, laughing. Then she whispered to the driver, "I hope you don't mind, but I just couldn't ride in there with all those old men."

"Quite all right, miss. I have folks up here with me a lot of times." He paused and threw her a sideways glance. "O' course, not ladies."

Amber smiled. "No, I suppose not."

He whistled to his team and the coach lurched forward, causing Amber to grab her hat before it catapulted off her head. As they made their way through town and headed west, the horses immediately broke into a ground-eating trot, which they maintained without any urging on the part of the driver. Amber marveled at their tireless pace. "How long can they keep that up?" she asked, nodding at the little mustangs.

"They're good for fifteen miles," the driver replied, "then we change. We have fresh teams waiting at stops along the way."

As they bounced along over the crude road, Amber drank in her surroundings like a sponge. Nothing escaped her attention. Already she loved the character of this new land. There was an untraversed freshness about its gentle, grassy hills and wooded ravines that beckoned to her spirit of adventure. She thought she must be feeling the same sort of yearning that Uncle Karl had so often yielded to. They were kindred spirits, she and Karl. It would be good to see him again.

At half-past ten, they reached the first stop along the way, a farmhouse-turned-roadhouse called Ennaho, where the jaded mustangs were exchanged for a fresh team. Amber took the opportunity to stretch her legs and go out back, as did the other passengers in the coach, but she managed to avoid the unsavory-looking one.

When they were loaded once again and ready to start, a young girl about Amber's age ran out of the house with a bouquet of colorful zinnias. Shyly, she handed them up to the driver. "These are for you, Tom," she said, then eyed Amber suspiciously. "And don't you go giving them to her, either!"

"Thanks, Annalou," he mumbled self-consciously, then whistled to his team, and they were off again. As soon as they were far enough out of sight, he handed the flowers to Amber. "Here," he said, "I don't want these durn things!"

They didn't smell particularly good, and the stems were sticky in her hand, but Amber thought they were the prettiest flowers she had ever seen. There were red ones, orange ones, gold and yellow ones – all the colors of a gorgeous sunset. She promised herself she would plant some just like them all the way around the house, as soon as she got settled in.

The farther west they traveled, the more primitive the road became. Amber's Sunday hat kept bouncing around on her head at jaunty angles, and she had to straighten and re-pin it every few minutes, but, aside from that little annoyance, she thoroughly enjoyed the trip. She was even thankful for the clouds which seemed to appear just about the time she was starting to worry about the sun's effect on her complexion.

Before long, the stagecoach slowed to cross a shallow creek, then lurched up the bank of red earth on the other side. "Whoa!" called the driver, and the coach jolted to a stop. "This here's where you get off, miss," he said unceremoniously.

"What?" cried Amber in disbelief.

"This here's Lumpmouth Creek, and that's where I was told to let you off."

"But there should be a farm here!" she protested. "Where is the Potters' house? I don't see anything anywhere!"

"It's supposed to be somewhere over that hill yonder," he said pointing to the north. "I don't know just how far, but it's over there somewhere."

"But – but – "

"I'm just following the instructions your uncle gave me, miss. Now, if you'll let me help you down, I've got a schedule to keep."

The next thing Amber knew, she was standing alone on the prairie, her travel bag in one hand and a bouquet of flowers in the other, watching the stagecoach disappear into the distance. She stood there for a moment, thinking how ridiculous she must look, and then trudged off in the direction the stage driver had indicated, glancing back over her shoulder every now and then to reassure herself there was no Indian stalking her, tomahawk in hand. That soldier on the train did say the Indians were peaceful now, didn't he?

Suddenly, she heard something, and a shudder of genuine fear shot through her. Tom-toms! she thought, quickening her steps. She felt foolish when it proved to be nothing but thunder rolling down out of the gathering clouds. Still, she was almost running by the time she finally spied the Potters' homestead, a soddy built halfway into the opposite hillside. A thin curl of smoke spiraled skyward from the smokestack in the roof, and Amber's stomach growled in anticipation of a noon meal. She straightened her hat and slowed to a more leisurely pace, not wanting to give the impression she was a frightened greenhorn.

About then, the dog began barking, and Mr. and Mrs. Potter came out to greet her, for they, too, had been expecting her around that time, thanks to Uncle Karl. The couple ushered Amber inside just as the thunderstorm unleashed its brief tantrum. "Don't worry, this won't last long," said Mr. Potter. "It's just a little thunderstorm a teasin' us. It'll be over with by the time we get through eatin' and head over to your uncles' place."

On impulse, Amber presented the bouquet of zinnias to her hostess, and she in turn handed Amber an opened umbrella, for the sod roof had begun to leak giant raindrops of mud. "Welcome to Oklahoma Territory!" the woman said with a friendly grin.

Chapter 17

A hot sun was beating down on the three travelers by the time they had driven the nine miles to Amber's new home. She waved at her three uncles, who were hard at work in the fields, and they came running in to meet the Potters' wagon, as did their big white dog, which barked and bounded around in a swirl of furry excitement.

Uncle Karl was the first to greet her. "Howdy, little gal," he said exuberantly, sweeping her up in his arms and whirling her around. "My, how you've growed! Why, you're a real growed-up young lady, yessir, a real growed-up young lady!" he said, looking her over at arm's length. He turned to his brothers. "Little, gal, this here's Phil, and this here's Wenzel."

Hats in their hands, her uncles stepped forward and shook Amber's hand. "Howdy, howdy, a pleasure to meet you," said Phil. He resembled Karl quite a bit except he wore a mustache and no beard. Wenzel, who was also clean-shaven except for a thick bristle on his upper lip, just nodded and smiled shyly, then began coughing. Amber found the contrast in personalities between them and Karl as different as night and day. It was hard to believe they were related! Although they both made her feel welcome, they had very little to say and left most of the talking to Karl.

Even while they were all standing there getting acquainted, Amber decided that the first thing she was going to do was wash the filthy shirts the three of them were wearing. From the looks of the grime, she felt certain they had never been anywhere near soap and water since the day they were bought!

She was even more appalled at the condition of the little one-room house, when they ushered her inside. Soiled clothing, dirty dishes, and trash littered the room from one end to the other. Typical bachelors! Amber thought to herself, as she dropped her bag and stood there, hands on hips, surveying the mess.

Uncle Karl was quick to notice her look of consternation. "You. . .uh. . .can see why we need you," he apologized, hastily gathering up things here and there.

"I sure can!" agreed Amber. "I really have my work cut out for me, don't I?" she said, with a laugh.

They thanked the Potters and sent them on their way, her uncles went back to the fields, and Amber dug into the job before her, forgetting how many miles she had traveled since sunup and how tired she was. It was good to be physically active once again.

In the weeks that followed, Amber was happier than she had ever been. Her uncles gave her independent nature free rein, and for the first time, she was her own boss. The men moved into the cellar underneath the little house, and she arranged the main floor to suit herself. In one corner she set up her "kitchen," consisting of a small, four-hole cookstove and a wash stand, and the corner with the table and four chairs assumed the role of "dining room." A cot in another corner became her "bedroom," and her "parlor" was the corner occupied by the cupboard, a tiny stool, and a small table holding the coal oil lamp. All the room needed now was curtains to cover the bare windows, and she made a mental note to buy some fabric on the first trip into town. She also intended to buy flower seeds, but was delighted to discover that Uncle Karl already had some on hand. As soon as she got the house in shape, she planted a flower garden south of the house, weaned the baby calf so they would have milk, and set a hen in order to raise a flock of chicks.

Amber had just finished washing the breakfast dishes that beautiful summer morning, when she heard a horse going by on the road in front of the house. Her uncles had already left for the fields, so she knew it wasn't them. She stepped over to the open door and peered out just in time to see her first real Indian. He appeared to be an older man, with streaks of gray in his long braids. He was wearing a headband and plain buckskins – no feathers, no beads – and was riding a skinny paint pony that was lame in the left forefoot. The man stared straight ahead as he rode past her, a sad and empty expression on his face. Amber found the pathetic sight a far cry from the mighty image in her mind. Is this what we've done to the noble redman? she wondered, shaking her head sadly.

She watched until the Indian disappeared over the hill to the south, then opened the door wide, and began to sweep the floor, congratulating herself on the effectiveness of the broom she had constructed. She giggled to herself, remembering how she had chastised her three uncles a few days before. "What? A whole field of broomcorn out there, and you don't even have a broom?" she had scolded, with mock consternation. Now, if she could only persuade them to part with those dirty shirts long enough for her to wash them!

As she swept the floor, Amber hummed contentedly to herself, reflecting on her first weeks' accomplishments and on the incredible piece of good fortune which had brought her here to Oklahoma Territory. She felt more certain every day that she had made the right decision. It was amazing how quickly her life in Kansas was fading from the present, to be filed away in her memory like one more chapter of a book.

"Howdy," drawled a voice from behind her. Startled, Amber spun around to find a tall, lanky, young man standing in the doorway, casually leaning against the doorframe.

"Hello," Amber said in a small voice, her heart pounding.

"Heard there was a new girl in the neighborhood. Thought I'd come take a look-see. Name's Will Rainey. What's yours?"

Amber was studying his eyes, trying to determine what he was staring at up near the ceiling to the right. Her eyes quickly searched that area of the room, fearing she had overlooked some huge cobweb. When she brought her eyes back to his face, he still seemed to be looking at her. She finally realized, much to her embarrassment, that the fellow had one wayward eye! "Oh! My name is Amber . . . Amber Lockhardt," she sputtered at last.

"Well, Amber Lockhardt, I'm proud to make your acquaintance," Will Rainey said, with a shy smile. He had beautiful, white teeth and a round, boyish face, and Amber found him quite good-looking except for his eye which strayed too far to the right.

"Me and my two sisters, we're havin' a party over at our place Saturday night, and we'd sure like to have you all come."

"Why, thank you – we'd love to! What time shall we come over?" asked Amber.

A perplexed expression clouded Will Rainey's handsome face. "Well, I was planning to come after y'all around seven, but. . ."

"Oh, you don't need to come after us. My uncles and I can – "

"But. . .I'm afraid you don't understand." He seemed at a loss for words. "See, I didn't mean for your uncles to come to the party, just you!"

Amber was just as puzzled. "Oh, I'm sorry! You said 'you all' and I thought. . .that meant all of us!"

Will laughed and so did Amber. "Guess y'all will have to get onto the lingo we use in this part of the country. Where y'all from, anyway?" he asked.

"Way up north in Kansas," said Amber, making it sound like the only thing farther north was the Arctic itself. "I didn't realize folks down here talked with such a southern drawl."

"Do we?" asked Will Rainey, and they both laughed again.

"Anyway, thank you for the invitation. I'll be looking forward to it," she said, wishing she had her trunk with her other dresses in it. I guess I'll just have to make do with what I've got, she told herself.

Amber thoroughly enjoyed her status as the new girl in the neighborhood. All the young people at the party were curious about her and eager to make her acquaintance. She was introduced to Matt Pinkston, Johnny Campbell, Luke Hardesty and his sister, Marybelle, and of course, Will's two younger sisters, Ida Mae and Clara. It was quite apparent that Clara and Luke were stuck on each other, as were Marybelle and Johnny, but all of them were the best of friends, and they graciously welcomed Amber into their group.

Amber learned that Johnny's family was from Texas, and he had learned to call quadrilles, or square dances, from his father. In the absence of any music, the Rainey's parlor vibrated with their clapping, as they kept the beat while Johnny called the dances. Amber hadn't had this much fun in a long time.

We've got a new pig in the parlor,
We've got a new pig in the parlor,
We've got a new pig in the parlor,
And it is Irish, too.
Your right hand to your partner,
Your left hand to your neighbor,
Your right hand to your partner,
And all promenade.

For each dance, Amber found that she was automatically paired off with Will Rainey, and it was obvious that the other fellows considered her to be Will's girl. She would rather not have been considered the property of anyone at the moment, but there was nothing she could do about it. Why do men have to be so possessive about everything? she wondered, as Will whirled her around for the promenade. He was strong and agile and quicker on his feet than she had imagined, judging from his slow drawl and ambling walk. Wearing a fresh but faded blue workshirt that matched the blue of his eyes, he was incredibly handsome, and every time he looked at her, Amber felt her heart skip a beat. She was already getting used to the problem with his right eye, and made it a point to concentrate on his left one.

"Would y'all like to go riding with me tomorrow afternoon?" Will inquired, after the

Virginia Reel. "And I mean you, not your uncles, too!

Amber laughed. "I'd love to, but I don't have a horse," she replied, "or a saddle."

"Well, don't worry about that. My sisters have both, and they'd be glad to let y'all use 'em." He glanced at Ida and Clara for their approval, and they nodded in unison.

"In that case, I'll go! I love to ride more than anything in this world!"

Side, by side, they loped across the lush, green prairie, Amber on the fat bay mare belonging to the Rainey sisters, and Will on his rangy sorrel with the four white stockings. The mare was lazy from lack of use, but she didn't want to be left behind. Puffing and straining, she galloped beside the sorrel, taking two strides to his every one. Amber was ecstatic at being on horseback once again, although she would much rather have been riding astride than sidesaddle. Those days, she reminded herself, were gone forever.

Before long, Will pulled his horse up and she did the same. They were at the edge of a huge ravine, a blood-red gash in the earth that ran from north to south as far as they could see. Cedar trees and thickets of scrub oak clung tenaciously to the almost vertical sides of the small canyon, while dead trees, twisted and uprooted, bore evidence of the tremendous force of the deluge which had rushed through from time to time. Large chunks of earth, eroded by the rushing waters of the past, were gradually splitting away from the sides, leaving fresh new scars and ever widening the distance across.

They dismounted to allow the horses to catch their wind, and stood there on the edge of the canyon surveying the natural beauty before them, unspeaking.

"Now I understand why you wanted to bring me here," Amber said at last. "It's beautiful, simply beautiful. What carved it – water?"

"Yep. Flash floods, I reckon."

Will's hand reached out for hers, and they stood awhile longer, listening to the hushed sigh of the wind, and the birds calling from the trees below. Amber breathed deeply, savoring the pungent smell of the red earth, the cedar trees, the sweaty horses resting behind them. She experienced a feeling of total contentment, and her heart took wings, soaring like the hawk she saw in the brilliant blue sky. Never had she been so happy.

Suddenly, she realized that Will was staring at her. Embarrassed, she turned away and quickly wiped the dampness from her eyes. "Sorry to get so emotional," she apologized, "but every once in awhile. . ."

"Shall we go?" Will asked quietly. She nodded. He helped her mount, then swung easily to his saddle.

They walked the horses all the way home, chatting casually back and forth. Will Rainey was a quiet sort, not exactly talkative, and Amber found she had to carry most of the conversation. But Will patiently answered her questions, which were many, for she was always eager to learn more about the land, the Indians, the crops such as cotton, watermelons, and peanuts she saw growing for the first time – anything that would expand her knowledge of the territory. She didn't want to feel like an outsider. She wanted so much to be a part of this new land!

Tired from the long ride, they arrived back at her place late in the afternoon, and Will lifted her lightly from the saddle. They said goodbye, and Amber watched as he led the bay mare toward home. When he was a short distance away, Will turned and waved to her, flashing his beautiful white teeth in that boyish grin of his. Amber felt her heart flutter as she waved back, then she hurried inside to start supper.

And so, "the new girl" became "Will's girl." Amber didn't mind, really; there was no one else who interested her, and she did enjoy Will's company. She found his innocence and simplicity refreshing, after Bryan's worldly-wise and self-centered nature. Besides, Will made no demands upon her. In fact, even Amber had to admit before long that Will spoiled her, always letting her have her way. But he seemed content to let her make the decisions about where they would go or what they would do, and he was always agreeable, no matter what. Amber sometimes wondered what it would take to rile him or make him assert himself. She had never met anyone with such an easygoing nature, not even her beloved Uncle John. Could a person be too accommodating? she wondered.

"Uncle Karl?"

Her uncle stopped hoeing weeds in the vegetable garden and stood upright, raising his eyebrows questioningly at Amber, who stood there with both hands behind her back, looking sheepish.

"Look what happened," she said, producing from behind her back what had been one of her uncles' wool shirts. Although it was now washed clean, the man-sized shirt had shrunk to a boy-sized shirt. Uncle Karl laughed heartily at the sight. "The other ones look just like it," Amber said dejectedly. "I had no idea this would happen – you probably think I'm a real dunce!"

Uncle Karl put his arm around her. "Now don't fret, little gal, them shirts were old and about wore out anyhow. We can give 'em to the Campbell youngsters. They should fit 'em just right." He held up the shirt himself and laughed again, shaking his head.

But Amber wasn't relieved – she was still miserable. "But you each have only one other shirt, and that's not enough! What will you wear while I wash those?"

"Well now, tell you what, little gal, we'll just plan on a trip to town Saturday, how about that? We can buy some new shirts, and you can pick up some

fabric to make them there curtains you been talkin'
about." Amber brightened, and he continued.
"Yessir, we've got them two yearling calves over
there in the corral that we can take in to sell. That'll
give us some cash money to spend. Now, how does
that sound?"

"That sounds like fun," replied Amber. "I've
been dying to go to town. There are so many things
we need. I'll go in and make a list right now."

Suddenly, the white dog emitted a low growl,
while staring intently up the road to the north, both
ears pricked to catch the strange sound coming from
that direction. Amber and her uncle paused to listen.
It seemed to be a disjointed symphony of banging
noises unlike anything Amber had ever heard.

Just then, a wagon topped the hill. "Looks like
Indians," said Uncle Karl, squinting up the dusty
road. "Yep, a whole passel of 'em. Must be a whole
family. You'd best get on to the house, little gal. I
don't want no young buck gettin' any ideas."

Amber hurried into the little house and closed
the door. She stood beside the window and peered
out, hoping to catch a glimpse of the group as they
passed. Strangely enough, she had never thought
about Indian wives and children, only the warriors
pictured in books and periodicals. She wondered
what their family life was like. Surely they laughed
and cried and loved and had hopes and fears, the
same as anyone else. People were people, she felt,
no matter what culture they found themselves in.

The cacophony of sound became louder and
louder as the wagon rolled into view, pulled by a

mis-matched team consisting of a flop-eared mule and a spotted pony, and Amber finally discovered the reason for all the noise. Of the six sad-eyed children in the wagon bed, one was stationed just above each of the four wheels, armed with a good-sized club. It was their job to pound the loose, iron rims back onto the wooden wagon wheels as the wagon rolled along. An Indian man and two women, dressed in soiled and darkened buckskin clothing, sat crowded onto the wagon seat.

To Amber's surprise, the outfit came to a halt in front of Uncle Karl, and she watched as he walked over to talk with them. There was much gesturing back and forth, and then Uncle Karl disappeared in the direction of the corral, while the family waited. When he returned leading one of the yearling calves, Amber realized what was going on. She watched the Indian man climb down and count out a number of dollars, and saw Uncle Karl hand him the calf's lead rope.

As Karl turned towards the house with the money, the two Indian women leapt down from the wagon seat and immediately pulled knives from their belts. Amber was about to cry out a warning to Uncle Karl, when she discovered that their intended victim was the calf, and not her uncle.

She watched in stunned silence as they deftly slit the calf's throat and then drank its warm blood from a battered tin cup, which they passed around while waiting for the animal to weaken and topple over. It didn't take long. As soon as it fell to the ground, the women went to work with their knives, assisted by the older children. In no time at all, the calf was skinned and quartered and loaded into the wagon, wrapped in its own hide. The only trace left behind was a small area of blood-soaked earth by the edge of the road.

Amber turned to Uncle Karl, who had joined her at the window. She swallowed hard. "I've never seen anything like that in my life! They didn't leave a thing! Do they eat. . .it all?"

"Almost," replied Uncle Karl. "What they don't eat, they make use of in some way. Nothing goes to waste. We'd do well to follow their example. Whites tend to be wasteful at times. It happened with the buffalo – we slaughtered them by the thousands for their tongues alone. Tongue's a delicacy, you know. The rest was left to rot on the prairie. That's one reason these folks have been reduced to this kind of a life." He shook his head slowly.

"But where did they get the money to buy that calf?" inquired Amber

"Government allotment. They each get a certain amount for giving up their lands, but most of them get cheated out of it by crooked whites and end up with no land and no money either."

"I sure do feel sorry for them – especially the children. They look so unhappy. I never saw them smile once."

"They don't have much to smile about," said Uncle Karl, "and that's a fact."

Chapter 18

"One thing about Oklahoma," remarked Amber, as a gust of wind tried to snatch her Sunday hat from her hand, "the wind blows just as much here as it did in Kansas!"

"Yep!" agreed Uncle Karl, joining her on the wagon seat. "That's a fact! 'Cept here, there are hills and more trees to break it a little bit." He turned to Phil, who climbed in the back of the wagon. "Where's Wenzel?"

"He's bringing the calf."

Just then, Wenzel appeared from behind the barn, leading the reluctant brindle calf. "Hurry up!" Karl yelled to him. "We gotta be gettin' if we're goin' to be to town by noon."

"You just hold your horses, brother, I'm comin' as fast as I can. This here calf is just a bit on the balky side!"

"Poor thing! He must know what's going to happen to him," murmured Amber, remembering the fate of his twin.

As soon as the calf was secured to the rear of the wagon, and Wenzel had jumped aboard, Uncle Karl clucked to his team of black mules, and they were off for town. Uncle Phil pulled a harmonica out of his pocket and quietly began serenading them.

"First, we'll go by the Indian Agency at Darlington and sell the calf, and then we'll spend

267

the rest of the day in El Reno," Uncle Karl told Amber. "That should give you enough time to get all your shopping done, and we can pick up the supplies we need. And since we're going to spend the night, we'll be able to go to church tomorrow."

"Good!" said Amber. "It has been a long time."

Although it was just after dawn, a hot wind was blowing from the south, snatching up the red dust kicked up by the wagon wheels and swirling it around them in a choking cloud. Amber was glad she had chosen to wear her sunbonnet instead of her Sunday hat – she certainly didn't want to suffer the disgrace of having a tan and looking like a field hand! She would trade one hat for the other when they reached the edge of El Reno.

Excited and impatient to arrive, Amber wished she could prod the mules into a faster gait. "Uncle Karl, why do you drive mules instead of horses?" she asked inquisitively. She had no use whatsoever for the hard-mouthed beasts.

"Well now, they're better workers than horses," he explained. "They can walk a horse into the ground. Ain't near as fussy about what they eat, neither. And, the Indians aren't so crazy about eatin' them, 'cause the meat's too tough and stringy. So you don't have to worry so much about 'em bein' stole off."

"You mean the Indians eat horses?" Amber was aghast.

"Shore they do," replied Karl. "You would, too, if you were starvin' the way most of them are."

"Not me!" she said emphatically

There was a pause, then Karl, staring straight ahead, said, "Remember ol' Buck?"

Amber nodded. "You mean the Indians stole him and. . .and ate him?"

"Well now, not exactly," replied her uncle. "That is, they didn't steal him. When we made the Run, you know, to get our land. . .well, ol' Buck went lame on me. Yes sir, he just outdid himself, bowed a tendon in his front leg, and I knew he'd never be the same," he said wistfully. "Well, this here bunch of Pawnees came through, like the ones the other day, and they offered to buy him. I knew why they wanted him, but we needed the cash, and I knew no one else would offer good money for a lame horse. Besides, I took one look at those hungry little kids, and. . ." His voice trailed off, and his eyes glistened with tears.

Amber swallowed hard and blinked back tears of her own.

Uncle Karl cleared his throat and changed the subject. "Did I ever tell you about the time me and John were just settin' up our homesteads in Kansas? We were livin' in this shack – I think John still uses it for the granary – and we were all out of grub and about to starve to death. So one morning, I wake up and look out the door and, by gollies, if there ain't four deer grazin' right out there within range. The only thing was, we were plumb out of rifle shot! So I took one of them there bolts that don't have a head on 'em, put it in my ol' muzzle-loader, took dead aim on one of them critters, and fired."

He paused to lean out to the side and spit a stream of tobacco juice at the ground. "Well now, we watched four deer run away lickety-split, and I was cussin' and fumin' at our bad luck and my bad aim. But John ran out there, and I'll be durned if there wasn't a dead deer lyin' there! Apparently, one had been on the ground asleep, and when I shot one that was standing, it jumped up and ran off with the other three. Anyway, me and John ate real good for a few days." He chuckled at the memory.

"That's quite a story!" exclaimed Amber. "It's hard to believe there were deer around there then. There sure aren't many now!"

"Nope! When civilization comes, the wild animals move on. Pretty soon, there won't be no place left for 'em."

Amber pondered that sobering thought for a moment, recalling a line from her book: *Thou canst not stir a flower without troubling a star.* It had impressed upon her long ago that there was a kinship between all life – plant, animal, and man – a realization for which she was inwardly very grateful.

With casual malice, the wind continued to shower them with fine red dust, which stung their eyes and adhered to the perspiration on their faces. After wiping her brow a few times, Amber's white handkerchief became so stained with the rust-colored dirt, she was afraid it would never come clean. Thank goodness, she had chosen to wear her brown dress instead of the lighter colored one. The dirt might not show quite as badly on this one. She had finally adjusted to the fact that her hems would never be clean, her only consolation being the fact that everyone else's looked the same!

The dust caused Wenzel to have another one of his coughing attacks that Amber had grown used to hearing, rising up from the cellar at night. Uncle Karl turned to him. "You better go see Doc and get some more of that there medicine he gave you last time. You sound worse every day." Wenzel continued hacking and said nothing.

No wonder he's so grumpy and disagreeable, thought Amber. He couldn't sound that bad and feel well. She turned and glanced his way sympathetically.

"Stubborn cuss!" muttered Karl, under his breath.

They had been traveling more or less parallel to the North Canadian River, and around eleven o'clock, several red brick buildings came into view ahead, on the opposite side of the river. "That there's Darlington Agency," Uncle Karl explained. "That's where the Cheyenne and the Arapaho go to get their government issue of food, clothing, and blankets."

"Do they live there?" asked Amber.

"Indians don't like to live in houses. Most of 'em just pitch their tepees nearby. See? There's a bunch of 'em over there," he said, pointing out the encampment in the cottonwood trees along the river.

The sight of the twenty or more tepees sent a shiver of excitement through Amber. There were ponies and wagons in among them, as well as children and dogs running in and out. It was a whole colorful tableau come to life right before her eyes, and she drank in every vivid detail.

"We have to go a ways north of here to sell the calf," Uncle Karl was saying. "That's where the issue pens are. Used to have 'em just outside of town, but the spectators got to be such a problem, they moved them out here."

"Spectators?" inquired Amber. "What do you mean?"

"You'll see."

The spectators were soon very evident – hundreds of them, Indian and white, surrounding the cattle pens. But what for? What were they watching? As they drew closer, Amber stood up in the wagon to get a better view over the crowd. Suddenly, a wild-eyed steer darted out of a chute at one end of the issue pen. There was an ear-splitting yell, and two mounted braves carrying long spears came galloping in pursuit. It was the buffalo hunt of old, all over again! With continuous war whoops and yells from the participants and spectators alike, the terrified animal was pursued, and one by one, both weapons found their grisly mark, and the steer dropped. A roar went up from the crowd, as the two braves jubilantly hoisted on high their bloody spears. It was the first time Amber had seen an Indian smile.

Suddenly, the heat, the excitement, and the gore combined to turn her stomach upside down. She sank to her knees in the wagon box, leaned over the side, and heaved.

"I'm sorry to be such a sissy," Amber apologized, when her uncles returned to the wagon after selling the calf.

"Don't you worry none about it, little gal. It kinda turns my stomach now an' again, too," said Uncle Karl, patting her knee. He clucked to the mules, and they headed for town, an hour's distance away.

For a town scarcely six years old, El Reno was pretty impressive. Amber was not only amazed by the large number of shops and stores, but by their look of permanence, for they were largely of brick and stone. Clearly, here was a town that meant business! Everywhere, there was a carnival-like atmosphere of excitement and progress. The wide, dirt streets were a maze of people, horses, carriages, wagons, and carts. As they passed by the Kerfoot Hotel, Amber stared in awe at the magnificent three-story, sandstone structure, which boasted seventy-five rooms and was acclaimed the finest hotel in the Territory. What fun it would be to stay there! she thought to herself. She knew better than to mention the possibility, however; a fine place such as that was for folks with money.

"See over yonder there?" said Karl, pointing down a side street. "That whole area used to be what they called the 'buffalo boneyard.' When I first came here, back in '91, that whole square block was piled twenty feet deep with buffalo bones waiting for shipment back East."

"What good were they?" asked Amber incredulously.

"They crushed 'em up and made fertilizer out of 'em," replied her uncle.

Carefully, they threaded their way through the crowded streets, past the wagon yard where most travelers stayed, to the livery stable where they would leave the team and wagon, and where, for fifty-cents each, her uncles could also spend the night. Amber, they decided, would take a room in some respectable rooming establishment.

As soon as Karl, Phil, and Wenzel made the arrangements at the livery, the four of them started up the street to find something to eat. "I know a real good place to grab a bite," Uncle Karl told her, as she took his arm. "The Cyclone Restaurant. Yessir, the good ol' Cyclone! We stop there every time we come to town. They serve up the best bowl of chili con carne you ever tasted!"

"What's chili con carne?" asked Amber.

"It's a Mexican dish – beef an' beans, real spicy and good. You'll have to try it."

It sure sounded good to Amber for she was famished! She was even hungrier by the time they reached the tiny restaurant, waited for a table, and ordered. She wasn't too impressed by the appearance of the place, but Uncle Karl kept assuring her the food was excellent. By the time their four bowls of chili were served, Amber was so hungry, she could have eaten the horse she had claimed she never would!

Her first spoonful of chili went down like molten lava. Amber choked and sputtered, and with tears in her eyes, grabbed her glass of water, drinking it down without stopping. "Easy there!" said Uncle Karl, laughing as he patted her on the back. "You'll be all right!"

"Why didn't . . . you warn me . . . it was so spicy?" Amber gasped out the words, embarrassed to discover half the people in the place staring at her in amusement.

"Why, this ain't bad at all!" Karl assured her, wiping the sweat from his balding head. "You should try the chili they fix down in Texas! Now, *that's* hot chili!"

It was several minutes before Amber felt brave enough to sample more, and only then with a fresh glass of water handy. She had to admit the dish was good, if only it weren't so hot!

Her three uncles soon finished eating and were waiting for her. "Say, you know what? You could spend the night here," said Karl, nodding toward a crude, hand-lettered sign he had spied on the wall that read, "Rooms 75 Cents."

Amber was skeptical. "I'd have to see them first," she said, taking her last bite of chili and finishing her third glass of water.

Upon inquiring, they learned there was a room available and, much to Amber's surprise, although tiny, it was neat and clean, with no sign of bedbugs. There were even sheets on the mattress! Grateful for a place to freshen up, she bid her uncles goodbye until tomorrow, and poured some water from the pitcher into the bowl on the washstand. A fine, red sediment had settled to the bottom of the bowl by the time she had finished washing. The wind had torn at her neatly pinned-up hairdo, mischievously pulling loose little wisps here and there, and she made a mental note to purchase several new combs to help keep it in place. After salvaging the hairdo as best she could, she pinned her Sunday hat back on, brushed off her dress, and skipped lightly down the narrow stairs. El Reno was hers for the afternoon!

After a wonderful afternoon of shopping, Amber returned to her quarters above the Cyclone Restaurant, tired but satisfied. It was stiflingly hot in the little room. She unbuttoned her shoes, kicked them off with a sigh of relief and wriggled the cramps out of her toes, then spread her purchases out on the bed to admire them. At Kelso's Dry Goods, she had found some nice blue-and-white-checked gingham for five cents a yard – perfect for the curtains she wanted to make. She had even splurged on a few extra yards for a tablecloth, as well as a sackful of odd remnants to use for braiding a rug. Besides the fabric, she had bought several spools of thread, a package of needles and pins, a small pair of scissors, and a silver thimble. She was all set to sew up a storm! She closed her eyes momentarily, trying to picture how the little house would look when she was finished, and she felt pleased with the image in her mind's eye. Little things made a house a home, she decided, and her uncles had done without long enough.

For herself, Amber had bought a couple of tortoise shell combs for her hair, and splurged on a small luxury – a bottle of lilac toilet water. She felt a little guilty about spending the extra quarter, but she consoled herself with the fact that it was on sale for half-price, and too great a bargain to pass up. She didn't think Uncle Karl would mind; she still had almost half of the ten dollars left which he had given her, so she wasn't doing too badly.

It was too hot to remain in her room for long, so after a brief rest, Amber decided to go downstairs for supper. On impulse, she removed two of her three petticoats, in the hope she would be cooler without them. The result was a shocking feeling of being half-dressed, and she wavered momentarily, unsure whether to risk being so daring. Finally deciding in favor of just the one, she crossed her fingers that no one would notice.

There was even less air in the little restaurant than there was upstairs, and the steam from cooking made it much more humid. As the man behind the counter handed her a greasy, tattered menu, he said, "Our specialty is – "

"Chili!" answered Amber, laughing. "I know. Thanks, but I'll have a bowl of stew instead," she said, fanning herself with the menu. She turned her head away in disgust at the sight of several dead flies floating in a dish of butter that had melted from the heat, at the same time trying to ignore the perspiration dripping from the cook's face.

The stew was slightly rancid, but she ate it anyway, too hungry to be finicky. As soon as she had finished, she hurried outside, where it was slightly cooler, and where the friendly sound of a rinky-tink piano was drifting from the nearest saloon. Amber still had a good two hours until sundown, so she wandered up and down the boardwalks, looking in windows and watching people, wondering what to do until dark, when she would have to return to her stuffy little room. She knew, and Uncle Karl had warned her, that no respectable lady would dare appear on the streets unescorted after dark.

Suddenly, she heard music – band music – coming from up the street. She paused, curious to see what it was all about. It grew louder and louder, and she soon spied three men playing horns and marching down the center of the dirt street, accompanied by two ladies in gray carrying tambourines. As they came closer, Amber was gradually caught up in the beat. "Come! Come! Follow us!" the ladies chanted in time to the music, motioning to all bystanders, as they tapped and shook their silver tambourines. "Come! Come! Come!"

Their enthusiasm was contagious, and several people had fallen in behind the group, with more joining in as they marched along. Her heart pounding with excitement, Amber began tapping her foot, then swaying to the rousing tempo, and soon she found herself joining the group .of followers, men and women, marching down the street, clapping their hands in time to the blaring music. It was great fun!

The boisterous little parade ended up at a large white tent on a vacant lot across the street from the courthouse. A huge sign over the entrance proclaimed, "COME IN AND BE SAVED!" Oh well, Amber chuckled to herself, I've come this far, I may as well go in and hear what they have to say. It can't hurt. And besides, I don't have anything else to do!

She located a seat at the end of one of the wooden benches just inside the doorway, where she hoped it would be cooler. There were printed pamphlets lying on the seats, and she picked one up to use as a fan just as an intoxicated gentleman staggered in and squeezed in beside her on the end of the bench, the smell of liquor strong on his breath. Amber fanned all the harder and tried to ignore him.

Within minutes, a tall gentleman dressed in black approached the podium. Gaunt of face, he stared at them one by one as if he were searching their very souls. A hush fell over the audience. "The wages of sin is death!" he boomed in a voice so loud it caused Amber to jump. She stopped fanning herself and cringed behind the broad shoulders of the man seated in front of her.

For a solid hour the preacher spouted fire and brimstone like a veritable volcano. He had Amber practically convinced she was a lost cause, and she would have gotten up and edged her way out the door, except for the fact that every time she peeked around the person in front of her, the preacher seemed to be staring straight at her. She breathed a sigh of relief when he finally concluded with a solemn "Amen," which was echoed by his constituents and several of the people in the audience, including the drunk sitting beside her.

Now's my chance! thought Amber, but the somber gentleman remained standing in front of them, while the two ladies in gray dresses and bonnets began passing their tambourines up and down the rows for donations. The men with the musical instruments began playing once again, softly and slightly off-key, and Amber decided to wait to make her exit.

When the lady reached Amber's row and handed the tambourine to the drunk on the end, he stopped her momentarily, as he dropped in a dollar bill. "Where shall I meet you?" he asked in a loud, raspy whisper.

"In heaven, brother, in heaven," came the nonchalant reply. Amber almost giggled out loud as she took the tambourine and passed it along the row. After a closing hymn, everyone filed out and went their separate ways into the gathering dusk. Amber hurried back up the street, chuckling to herself over the events of the evening. She was glad when she finally reached the Cyclone Restaurant and climbed the stairs to her room. It was almost dark and she was tired. It had been a long, exciting day.

Amber met her uncles at church the next morning. "I really like your new shirts," she said admiringly, as they walked out to their wagon. "Oh, by the way, don't forget, I want to go by the Caddo Hotel and pick up my trunk on our way out of town," she reminded them.

That's right!" exlaimed Uncle Karl, rubbing his bristle of beard. "I plumb forgot about it!"

"I haven't! It will be so nice to have all my things again."

"First, we've got a surprise for you," said Karl, nodding towards the wagon. Tied next to it was a trim, black mare hitched to a two-wheeled cart and nervously pawing the ground.

"Whose is it?" exclaimed Amber.

"Belongs to a friend of ours," replied Karl, "a fellow by the name of Dave Jenkins. He's going to be doing some traveling and didn't want to leave Black Beauty at the livery stable all that time, so we offered to keep her. Thought you might enjoy driving around in this here sulky."

"Oh, Uncle Karl, you know I would! She's beautiful, just beautiful! I'll take real good care of her. Do I get to drive her home now?

"You bet your boots!" answered Karl. He helped Amber onto the seat and handed her the reins. "Take her easy now. This here's a blooded mare straight out of Ken-tucky. She's bred to be a pacer, and that's the only gait Dave allowed her, so be sure you keep her in it."

Amber frowned. "How will I know when she's pacing? I've never seen a pacer."

"It's like a trot," explained Uncle Karl, motioning with his hands, " 'cept both legs on the same side move together. It's real peculiar – you'll know it once you see her move out. Take her down the street a ways and see."

Nervously, Amber clucked to the mare and gave her her head. Almost immediately, she fell into the rhythmic gait Uncle Karl had described. It was peculiar to watch, too, especially from the rear. "I'll bet that would feel strange if you were riding her," Amber exclaimed, after she had circled and come back. "It would throw you from side to side and really be uncomfortable, I would think. Is she broke to ride, too?"

"She's broke to ride, but you're right – I don't think you'd want to saddle up. That's why these horses are used for driving," said Karl. "Riding one of 'em is like riding a camel!"

"Let's go!" grumbled Wenzel from the back of the wagon, where he and Phil were making themselves comfortable among the cans of coal oil and sacks of flour, sugar, and coffee.

"Okay, okay, we're comin'!" answered Karl, climbing to the wagon seat. "The Caddo's thataway, little gal. Meet you there, and as soon as we pick up your trunk, we'll head for home."

Chapter 19

"How do you like it?" asked Amber proudly. She stood back to allow her three uncles to view the new blue-and-white-checked curtains and tablecloth, and the multi-colored oval braided rug in the center of the floor.

"Well now, it looks great, little gal, just great! Makes it look real homey and nice," said Uncle Karl, surveying her handiwork.

"I like it!' responded Phil. "It reminds me of your Ma's little house back in Ohio."

"Yeah, it sure does," said Wenzel, with a rare smile. "You done a good job."

"Now," said Amber with calculated timing, "I'm going to have a party!" Her uncles looked at her blankly. "I mean, it's all right, isn't it? I've been to everyone else's house at least once, and summer's almost over, and I feel I ought to pay them back . . . "

"Why, of course, little gal," said Uncle Karl finally, "I think that's a fine idea. We ain't got much room here, but we can take the furniture out and – "

"Of course! It's just as big as the Raineys' parlor, or the Campbells' cow shed! I've got it all planned out. I'm going to roast some peanuts and –"

"I have a couple of jugs of blackberry cider," offered Uncle Wenzel, suddenly picking up on Amber's enthusiasm. "And you're welcome to it. I make the best cider in this here country, even if I do say so myself!"

"Oh, yes!" exclaimed Amber, surprised but pleased at his response. "That will be good – roasted peanuts and blackberry cider! And Uncle Karl, would you play your guitar for us? No one else ever has music, and it would be wonderful if we could just once. Would you? Please?" she pleaded.

"Well now, I reckon so," he answered, stroking his beard. "But only if Phil plays his harmonica, too," he added, with a twinkle in his gray eyes.

"Okay, okay," Phil agreed, nodding his head.

"Oh, thank you! We'll have so much fun!" cried Amber, giving them each a quick hug. "Is this Saturday night okay?"

"I guess so," replied Karl, and Phil and Wenzel nodded in agreement.

"I can't wait to invite my friends! In fact, as soon as we eat dinner, and you get back to the plowing, I think I'll just hitch Black Beauty up to the sulky and go around and ask them all."

"Okay, little gal, but remember to make that mare pace," warned Uncle Karl. "I told ol' Dave we would really watch out for her, and not let her pick up any bad habits. He sure sets a lot of store by that there mare."

"Let's eat!" interrupted Wenzel, sitting down at the table.

As soon as she had Black Beauty hitched to the cart, Amber dashed back into the house for the faded pink parasol Mrs. Hardy had given her. On impulse, she also grabbed her Sunday hat. "I might as well go in style!" she murmured to herself, as she peered into her uncles' shaving mirror and pinned the hat in place. Carrying the folded-up parasol under her arm, she walked out to where Black Beauty was nervously pawing the ground and working up a foam around the bit. "You're a restless one, aren't you?" Amber remarked, as she laid the parasol on the seat, took the reins, and climbed into the cart.

The mare moved out in her distinctive, rhythmic gait, and Amber reveled in the beauty of her motion. She was doing what she was trained to do, and apparently knew nothing else. Still, Amber could not help wondering if Black Beauty's nervousness might be an expression of her frustration over the limitations forced upon her. Maybe she would like to run, really run, free and uninhibited, like horses were meant to. Amber knew she couldn't allow her to gallop with the flimsy sulky behind her, but she decided that one of these days, she would borrow the Raineys' sidesaddle, and she and Black Beauty would go for a long gallop by themselves. It would be their secret!

She decided to head for the Pinkston place first, since it was farthest away. She would then swing past the Hardestys' and the Campbells' and end up at the Raineys'. Maybe Will would be free by that time, and they could share some cool cider down in the blackjack grove. She smiled inwardly in eager anticipation.

The sun was getting hotter by the minute. Amber reached for her pink parasol on the seat beside her and quickly opened it. In one terrible instant, Black Beauty shied at the strange object which suddenly appeared behind her. Wild-eyed with panic, she bolted to the side, trying to turn and face the thing that threatened her. The sulky whipped over, and Amber was dumped on the ground before she knew it, hitting hard on her left shoulder. She felt herself being dragged then, for she had somehow managed to retain her grip on the reins, but Black Beauty came to an abrupt halt, and Amber was up in an instant, offering soothing words to the frightened horse. "Whoa, girl. Easy now, easy. It's all right," she said, as calmly as her quavering voice would allow.

The mare stood still, quivering and champing nervously at the bit, while Amber walked up to her head. With a hand that was shaking almost as much as the horse was, she rubbed the mare's neck, talking all the time in quiet tones. She discovered her own left shoulder was scraped and bruised, and the puffed sleeve of her dress was badly torn. But her heart really sank when she viewed the damage to the sulky. The two shafts were twisted so that one wheel was completely off the ground. There was no way she could drive it in that condition!

Quickly, deftly, Amber released the leather straps securing the shafts to the mare's sides and led her free. As she walked the horse the mile or so back to the farm, she was hoping her uncles would still be working in the fields so they wouldn't see her. She didn't want to have to explain what had happened just yet. She breathed a sigh of relief when she found the house and farmyard deserted, except for the white dog, which barked a joyous welcome as though she had been gone forever. After tying Black Beauty in the barn, she hurried back to retrieve the sulky.

A sickening feeling thudded in the pit of Amber's stomach when she surveyed the damage once again. Nothing seemed to be broken, but she wasn't sure if the shafts could be twisted back into their proper position without breaking them. She prayed that it could be done.

The wind had blown her parasol several yards away, and she ran to fetch it. Inspection showed that three of the ribs had been snapped, but outside of that, it was in good shape. She closed it up as she walked back, and then laid it on the floorboards of the cart. Suddenly she spied her Sunday hat lying beside a clump of sagebrush. She hadn't even missed it! The hat pin was gone, so she planted the hat firmly on her head, picked up the shafts of the sulky, one under each arm, and trudged off. This time, she really hoped no one was home to witness the spectacle she must present.

The pesky wind kept blowing her hat off, and it was such a nuisance, she decided to carry it in her mouth, clenched in her teeth. As she trudged into the farmyard, sweaty and dirty, with her hat in her mouth, and her hair falling loose at the sides, she was mortified to discover her three uncles standing there staring at her incredulously.

"Holy catfish!" exclaimed Uncle Karl. "What happened? Where's Black Beauty?"

"She's in the barn," replied Amber, through gritted teeth. "And she's fine. It's the sulky and me that didn't fare too well." She nodded to her torn dress, and then dropped the shafts of the sulky. One rested on the ground, while the other remained suspended in the air. "Do you think it can be fixed?" she asked hopefully. "If it can't, your friend Dave Jenkins is going to hang me from the nearest tree!"

Uncle Karl knelt down and inspected the bases of the wooden shafts. "I think maybe it can," he said finally. "We can take it over to the Hardestys' forge and heat this here metal part where the shafts fasten on, and bend them back into place. If we get it hot enough and work it slow enough, I think it'll be okay. What do you think, Phil?"

"I think you're right."

Amber expelled a huge sigh of relief. "I'm sure glad of that!"

"Now, tell us what happened," said Wenzel.

With their favorable assessment of the damages, Amber felt a little less contrite. "Well, that highfalutin' mare," she said, gesturing toward the barn, "has apparently never seen a parasol! You can sure tell she's only been around men! She threw a fit the minute I opened that thing up, bolted and turned the sulky right over. It's a good thing I kept hold of the reins, or she'd be clear into the next county by now!" Amber paused, her eyes pivoting from face to face searching for sympathy, but she encountered only a reprimanding silence from her uncles. Finally, she bit her lip and looked at the ground. "I. . .I'm sorry," she said dejectedly. "It was my own stupid fault. I should have known better."

"Well now, don't you worry none about it, little gal," Uncle Karl said, putting his arm around her gently. "You go on to the house now and get yourself cleaned up. We'll take care of this here cart. We'll get it fixed up so's ol' Dave will never know the difference."

"Thanks, Uncle Karl."

"This is a swell party, Amber," said Clara, as she poured another cup of blackberry cider and passed it to Luke.

"It sure is," offered Luke, and Matt nodded in agreement.

Marybelle leaned over and whispered to Amber. "Your Uncle Karl is a real character!"

"He can sure tell some tall tales," chimed in Johnny, laughing. "I thought my grandpa in Texas was pretty good, but your uncle's got him beat by a country mile!"

"What happened to your Uncle Wenzel?" asked Will. "He disappeared right after we all got here."

"Oh, he isn't too sociable," replied Amber, fanning herself with a piece of accordion-pleated paper. "He probably retreated to the cellar where it's cool. Poor thing, I don't know how he can sleep with us dancing right above him."

"Do you think your uncles will play another tune for us?" asked Ida Mae, as she reached for more roasted peanuts.

"I think they can be persuaded to," replied Amber. She went to the door and called to the men who were sitting on the steps. "Uncle Karl, Uncle Phil, sing that song you always sing, you know, the one."

"Okay, one more," said Karl, as he and Phil came back inside with their guitar and harmonica, and sat on the bed.

I've got no wife to bother my life,
No love to prove untrue.
I never sit down with a care or a frown,
I paddle my own canoe.

After the second verse, they ended the song with a flamboyant finale that sent the little group into wild applause. "And now, us two old men are goin' to retire and leave you young folks be," said Uncle Karl, as he hung his guitar on the wall next to the cupboard. "I know you've got more interesting things to do than listen to us all night." He winked at them, causing all the girls to blush and giggle. Then he motioned for Phil to follow him out as they bid them all good-night.

It was a beautiful, late summer evening, and Amber envied the other couples their buggy rides home together. She was glad when Will volunteered to stay after everyone had left and help her put things back in order. Not that there was all that much that needed to be done; they both knew it was only an excuse.

"Let's take a walk," he said finally, and hand in hand, they stepped out into the thick, warm darkness. Locusts droned from the trees, lightning bugs flitted through the night, and the smell of the red earth and of growing things was heavy on the air. Neither spoke. There was simply nothing they could say to add to the peaceful perfection of such an evening. Slowly, they walked down the tree-lined lane that led to the barn. Startled all at once by the whoosh of an owl taking flight, Amber found herself in Will's arms. Silently, he held her for a moment, then took her face in his hands and kissed her softly on the lips. Even though it was the first time Will had kissed her, it was so natural and spontaneous that Amber never gave it another thought. She sighed contentedly. She was at peace with her world.

Luke and Clara were married in the middle of September, and by that time, Amber was sure that everyone more or less took it for granted she and Will would be married, too. The idea had crept into the conversations of her friends, and even Uncle Karl had mentioned it a few times. And not just as a possibility, but as fact. This is what disturbed Amber – there was no doubt in anyone's mind. Except her own. She and Will had never even discussed marriage; perhaps he was too shy to bring it up. But she was no more interested in being a wife now than she had been back in Kansas, and she was determined not to get trapped into a similar situation. She simply was not ready to settle down, and if Will ever asked her, she would tell him just that.

With the cooler fall weather, Amber initiated her project to pacify Black Beauty. The more she was around the mare, the more convinced she became that her nervousness was due to her life of constant restriction, and that normal exercise would release at least some of her frustration.

It did not take long to prove her theory correct. Under saddle, Black Beauty responded readily to Amber's offer to let her gallop, and the two of them went for long, glorious rides across the rolling prairie. It was good tonic for them both. The mare settled down appreciably, and Amber returned to her chores refreshed and invigorated, and just a little bit smug in the secret satisfaction of knowing she had been right in diagnosing Black Beauty's problem.

It was a bright, crisp day in October after one of their exhilarating rides that Amber loped Black Beauty into the farmyard and up to the barn. As she reined the mare to a stop, a young stranger dashed out of the barn and grabbed her bridle, shouting angrily, "What do you think you're doing?"

"What do you think *you're* doing?" Amber responded indignantly. "Let go of my horse!"

"I beg your pardon," he countered hotly, "this happens to be *my* horse!"

"Oh." Amber slid off. "You must be Dave Jenkins." He was a lot younger than she had pictured him, short and wiry, with tousled brown hair.

"That's right, and what are you doing galloping my mare? I never let her gallop! She's a pacer, and that's all she's supposed to know. You're going to spoil her for sure!"

Amber's temper flared. "Well, if you want my opinion – "

"I don't!"

"Well, you're going to get it anyway! This mare was so nervous and flighty when we first brought her here – "

"That's because she's a blooded horse – they're all high-strung. Not like the plugs *you're* used to!"

"I don't care! She's a horse, and horses like to run, and I think she should be allowed to once in awhile. It hasn't hurt her one bit, and it's done wonders for her nervousness. She's a lot calmer now when she's driven. She's just a better horse all the way around."

"Don't tell *me* how to handle horses!" replied Dave Jenkins, with a toss of his head. "After all, you're only a girl, and what do they know!" He unfastened the sidesaddle and dropped it to the ground, then led the mare into the barn and put her in her stall.

Incensed, Amber followed, her hands on her hips. "If you know so much about horses, why don't you take better care of her feet? Her hooves were so dry, split, and broken that she was almost lame. I've been greasing them and trimming them, and they're just now beginning to look half-decent."

Dave Jenkins ignored her attack. "Where are your uncles?" he demanded.

"Over at the neighbors'. They should be home by supper time."

"I'll just take this up with them!" he said flatly.

"Hmmph!" Amber snorted. She turned on her heel and stormed out of the barn.

She was still fuming when her uncles came into the house with Dave Jenkins. "I guess you two have already met," said Uncle Karl, warily surveying the situation.

"I'm afraid so!" replied Amber grimly. She purposely avoided Dave's glance. "Are you all ready for some fried mush?"

"You bet your boots we are!" exclaimed Uncle Phil, washing up at the bowl on the washstand. The other three followed his lead, then came over to the table.

"Let's see, we're goin' to be short a chair," remarked Uncle Karl, rubbing his whiskers.

"That's all right, he can have mine. I won't sit down just yet," offered Amber, wanting to keep distance between herself and Dave Jenkins. She sliced more mush and placed the pieces in the skillet to fry, feeling Dave's eyes upon her every move. I wish he'd stop staring at me! she thought to herself. I wonder when he's going to leave? It can't be too soon!

As if in answer to her thoughts, Uncle Karl turned to her and said, "Ol' Dave's gonna be with us for a few days, so you two better make up and be friends."

Amber groaned inwardly. "Oh, swell," she muttered, over the sizzling of the mush.

"What did you say?" asked Karl.

"I said, how nice!" she responded with a wide, fake smile, as she carried another plate of mush over to the table.

"I'm sorry I jumped on you so hard awhile ago," Dave apologized through a mouthful of food. "I realize you're just a girl and don't know any better. Just don't let it ever happen again."

Amber took a deep breath, but silenced what she was about to say. Seething inside, she walked back to the stove, keeping her back to them. "She's cute when she's mad," she heard Dave whisper to the others. "I'll have to bring her around with the old Jenkins charm. Haven't found a lady yet that could resist it!"

Oooooh! thought Amber. That conceited smart-alec! If I were a man, I'd punch him in the nose!

She spent the rest of the evening curled up on her cot in the corner, reading a book by the light of the coal oil lamp, while the four men sat at the table, playing cards, drinking cider and swapping stories. The later the hour, the wilder the stories became. Every once in awhile, she would glance over at Dave Jenkins' profile illuminated by the dim light of the lamp. He wasn't bad-looking, she decided. Too bad he was so stuck on himself! One time, her glance met his, and she quickly dropped her eyes back to her book, embarrassed that he had caught her.

Finally, the foursome broke up, and they all headed for bed – her uncles to the cellar, and Dave Jenkins to the barn. Amber breathed a sigh of relief, blew out the lamp, and snuggled into bed.

She had not been asleep very long when a sound startled her into wakefulness. She sat up in bed, every nerve tense and alert, her heart pounding! Thank goodness, she had turned the key in the lock before retiring! Quietly, she slipped out of bed and tiptoed across the bare floor. Carefully edging toward the window, she peered out at the would-be intruder stealthily attempting to raise it.

Dave Jenkins! she exclaimed silently to herself. That so and so! Without a sound, she reached behind her, groping for the broom she knew was standing in the corner. She found it, and carefully raised it over her head, gripping it hard in both hands. The window slid up as far as it would go, and the dark form of Dave Jenkins slowly eased through the opening. Amber waited until he was half in and half out, then let him have it with the broom.

"Ow! Ow! Ow!" he cried, as she beat him over the head time and again.

"You get out of here, you good-for-nothing scalawag!" Amber shouted in a loud whisper. "Now git, or I'm going to tell my uncles on you!" He backed away, and she watched as he stumbled off in the direction of the barn, rubbing his head and muttering profanities.

Amber closed the window and locked it, checked the others, and crawled back into bed. Judging from the sounds of snoring coming from below, her uncles had not been bothered by the disturbance, and she was glad. There was no need to cause trouble over it. She only hoped that Dave Jenkins would soon be on his way back to wherever he had come from.

Chapter 20

Winter began early one morning with a cold, driving rain that turned to sleet by afternoon. It was a gray, gloomy day that was an omen of things to come. The big white dog wisely sought refuge under the front steps, and the livestock huddled miserably in the barn, while the wind drove stinging pellets of ice through the cracks in the clapboard siding. Amber stared dismally out the window, watching with more than a twinge of sadness as the icy rain battered the lifeless remnants of her flower garden into abject surrender. Inexplicably, she sensed the ending of something else – something besides summer. Desperate to understand it, she ransacked every nook and cranny of her mind for an answer, but to no avail. As she watched a lone surviving fly fighting against the window pane that trapped it inside, her spirits dipped as low as the dark clouds scudding across the prairie, and she shared the frustration of its captivity.

"It's cold in here!" complained Wenzel between coughing fits.

Amber sighed, got up, and added more wood to the fire in the little cookstove. "Here," she said, taking the blanket from her bed, "put this around your shoulders." Wenzel grunted his thanks. She pinned a woolen shawl around her own shoulders, and decided to occupy her time with a useful task.

She would bake bread and some of the cinnnamon rolls Will liked so much. Except that they wouldn't be seeing each other, with the weather the way it was. She changed her mind and decided to write a letter, even though it might be days before she got in to Geary to mail it. Since her three uncles were seated at the table playing Chinese checkers, she curled up on her bed with a writing tablet.

Nov. 13, 1895

Dear Mama,

In the letter I received from Lisa, she said that you were not feeling well again. I'm sorry to hear that, as I thought you were doing better. Please take care, Mama, and do what the doctor says. You are just working too hard, I know. Uncle Wenzel is not well either. He still coughs a lot and is generally unpleasant. I don't look forward to being cooped up with him all winter! I have a feeling it is going to be very trying for all of us.

Will Rainey still comes courting once in awhile. Everyone thinks we are going to be married, and he did finally ask me, but I told him I just wasn't ready. Bless his heart! He is very sweet, but I really don't want to marry him. I guess I'm just not ready to settle down yet!

I love it here in Oklahoma Territory. It's so much nicer than Kansas. I told you about the Indians I've seen from time to time. Well, this fall, I learned all about cotton. It actually grows on a plant as a fluffy, white ball. A lot of our neighbors raise it, as well as peanuts, which grow underground on the roots of the plants. There are so many new things to learn about!

Goodbye for now, Mama. Give my love to the children.

Your daughter,
Amber

As the winter progressed, so did Amber's restlessness at being held captive by the bad weather within the close confines of the little one-room house. With Karl and Phil smoking foul-smelling pipes, and Wenzel's constant, hacking cough, Amber was sure she was on the verge of prairie madness, or as Uncle Karl expressed it, a touch of "cabin fever." By Christmas, she had read a dozen borrowed books, braided another rug, remodeled her torn dress into a skirt, and crocheted more doilies than she could ever use.

But the only thing that kept her from really going mad was the black mare; the two of them were off for a ride or a drive every time the weather permitted. Even though she fervently disliked Dave Jenkins, she was grateful to him for leaving Black Beauty with them when he had left. He'd said he would be back to claim her come spring, a parting that Amber preferred not to contemplate. At least she didn't have to worry about him showing up unexpectedly. That was a relief, because she was still allowing Black Beauty to gallop. After all, she had made no promises one way or another, and she certainly considered the horse more important than what Dave Jenkins thought.

A week after New Year's, 1896, Amber received correspondence from her sister, Lisa. Mama had died the day after Christmas. Amber's grief was compounded by feelings of helplessness and frustration at not having been able to be there. In the weeks that followed, all she could do was wait for letters relating the arrangements Lisa had made for the three younger children. Eventually, she learned that kind neighbors had offered to take them in, and Lisa was satisfied that they were all in good hands. At sixteen, Lisa was old enough to be on her own, and she wrote that she had found a job as a hired girl for a well-to-do family.

With the coming of spring, the men began spending more time in the fields, preparing the rich, red earth for new seed. Amber's cabin fever metamorphosed into spring fever, and she was loathe to stay indoors, devising all manner of excuses to work outside; consequently, theirs was not only the first, but the largest vegetable garden planted in the whole area, and all the neighbors eyed it with envy. The only chore she couldn't transfer to the out-of-doors was the cooking, and she devoted as little time to that task as possible.

Although she was no longer depressed, Amber was still aware of the old restlessness within her, and at times, she felt like Black Beauty champing at the bit. She wondered if Uncle Karl ever felt as she did now. If so, he gave no hint of it. She was surprised that he had taken to the settled life of a farmer so readily. Perhaps all he had really wanted, and had been searching for, was a place of his own, someplace he could belong. Wasn't that what everyone really wanted? She hoped that she, too, would someday find what she was searching for, but right now, it would help if she knew what it was!

"Will told me to give you his apologies," said Ida Mae, as she pulled her lumber wagon and team of horses to a halt in front of Amber. "This will be the first school social he's missed. But that Jersey heifer of his is due to calve any minute and, this bein' her first time and all, he just couldn't leave her. So, it looks like it's just the two of us," she said with a shrug.

"That's all right," replied Amber, hoping to sound unconcerned. "We'll have fun. There should be lots of fellas there. I hear there's a new family just moved in on the old Biswell place, and they have four sons!"

"Four sons!" echoed Ida Mae, her round face beaming. "I wonder how old they are?"

"I don't know, but maybe we'll find out," Amber answered hopefully. "Hold on a minute while I go fetch my Sunday hat!"

Like the creature for which it was named, Buzzard Roost School perched on the top of a hill some two miles from the farm. Hastily thrown up in that first year after the Run, the one-room structure wasn't meant to be permanent, just something to make do until a "real school" could be built. But there were homes to construct, and crops to plant and harvest, and fences to erect, and somehow, the "real school" never appeared. Not that it mattered one way or the other to the children who attended – school was school, and altogether distasteful for the most part.

Amber learned that the social was the annual end-of-school get-together for the students and their families and friends, and people came from miles around. Everyone, it seemed, except the new family with the four sons! All in all, it was a pleasant but uneventful afternoon for the girls, as they sat on top of the storm cellar nestled in the blackjack trees, chatting and giggling with the other young people, and enjoying the cakes and cookies everyone had brought. As Amber was going back for her second piece of chocolate cake, she happened to overhear a couple of men talking.

"Hear you just got back from Bridgeport."

"Yep. Had to go over there to see Gorman. He runs the roadhouse there at the toll bridge, you know. I'm going to supply them with beef and vegetables again this year."

"Does he get much traffic through there?"

"Yep, quite a bit. He has a general store for the Indians, and it's the only place for miles around where you can find a decent meal and a place to sleep, if you're traveling to or from Anadarko. That Indian wife of his – she's an educated Indian – is some cook. Quite a woman, as a matter of fact. I really do admire her. By the way, she's looking for a hired girl to help out for the summer, if you know anyone who'd be interested."

"Can't say as I do. . ."

Amber heard nothing more. Like a tiny seed, an idea began to germinate within the depths of her mind. She walked back to where Ida Mae and the others were sitting. "Where's Bridgeport?" she asked casually, as she took a bite of cake.

"Oh, about ten miles thataway," replied Ida Mae, pointing southwest. "Why?"

"Oh, I just heard someone mention it, and I wondered where it was." Her friends continued their conversation, and Amber sat there eating, lost in thought. Finally she stood up and brushed the crumbs from her red dress. "I'll be right back," she told them.

"Are you going after another piece of chocolate cake?" cried Ida Mae. "You're going to get so fat, Will won't even want you!" she teased.

Amber laughed and went on, dodging the children racing through the crowd, searching for the man whose conversation she had overheard. She found him at last and hesitated a moment, then approached him. "Hello, I'm Amber Lockhardt, and I'm interested in that job you were talking about at that roadhouse. Could you let them know?"

"Why sure," replied the man. "I'm goin' back over there again this week with a couple head of steers. I'll see if the job's still open, and if it is, I'll tell them you want it. Where do you live?"

"With my uncles – you know, the Hagen brothers – over that way about two miles." She pointed in the direction of the Hagen homestead.

"Oh, the Hagen place? Sure, I know where it is, over on the cemetery section. I'll come by there soon as I get back from Bridgeport and let you know what I found out."

Amber thanked the man and turned to find Ida Mae standing behind her. "What was that all about?" inquired her friend, a quizzical look on her round face.

"Oh, I happened to hear that man talking about a job that's available over at the roadhouse at Bridgeport, and he's going to check into it for me." They began walking back to where their friends were. "How would you like to do the wash and clean house for my uncles?"

"You mean you want to. . .leave?" asked Ida Mae, frowning.

"Oh, I guess I'm just too much like Uncle Karl. I just get itchy feet every now and then and – "

Ida Mae's eyes narrowed as she turned to Amber. "Itchy feet or *cold* feet?" she chided. A spring thunderstorm was brewing, and most of the folks were preparing to depart. There was a wild scramble to collect kids and belongings, load up wagons, and head for home. But the two girls took their time, reluctant to end their socializing. They were almost the last to leave, and by that time, the rain was practically upon them.

"If we get drenched, it's all your fault!" Amber teased Ida Mae, as they climbed to the seat of the lumber wagon. "You could have told that fella we had to go."

"I finally did, but you and Johnny were still comparing Texas and Kansas," replied Ida Mae, "and – " A sudden clap of thunder cut her short.

"Head these horses for home!" shouted Amber, as a cool gust of wind showered them with red dust and giant raindrops.

The team of big sorrels needed no urging. They started off at a brisk trot, tossing their heads nervously, their ears flicking back, monitoring the approaching storm. Apprehensive, Ida Mae cast a quick look behind them and tightened her grip on the reins, her round face contorted with fear. All of a sudden, a loud crack of thunder spooked the team into a dead run. "Oooooh! I can't stop them!" she screamed, pulling back with all her strength.

"Here, let me take them!" shouted Amber, above the rising wind and rain. She grabbed the reins from Ida Mae's frozen grasp, and braced her feet against the front of the wagon, while Ida Mae hung on to the seat for dear life.

The wagon careened madly up and down the swells of the rolling hills and across the open prairie, as Amber fought to control the runaways. Desperately, she sawed back and forth on the reins, pulling so hard her arms ached with fatigue. But the powerful horses only bowed their necks and kept running.

"I'll have to try to turn them!" she yelled at last. "Hang on!" With both horses galloping on their left lead, Amber decided to try to turn them to the right in hopes it would be more difficult for them to run, and would ultimately slow them down. She began a steady pull on the two right reins, gradually shifting the horses' heads around to the side, turning the wagon in a wide arc, and then into an ever-tightening circle. The team slowed as one stumbled momentarily, and Amber exerted her last ounce of strength on their mouths, finally bringing them to a lumbering halt. Exhausted, the team stood as though they were planted, sweaty sides heaving and nostrils flaring, both of their mouths foamy and bloody.

The girls breathed huge sighs of relief and sat there, physically and emotionally drained. Ida Mae, who had been sobbing with fright all during their wild ride, sniffed and wiped her eyes on the sleeve of her dress. "Well," she said dryly, "at least we outran the storm."

"I think I'd rather have been caught in it!" Amber retorted.

"Me, too. That was scary."

"I'll drive them on in," offered Amber, clucking cautiously to the horses. They moved out at a fast walk, and she made sure they held that gait the rest of the way home. They'd had enough excitement for one day!

A week later, Amber stood framed in the doorway of the Raineys' barn, hating what she had to do. "I came to tell you goodbye," she began.

Will didn't look at her. He sat in a shaft of sunlight, milking his Jersey cow, his lanky frame sprawled on a three-legged milk stool, his head leaning lightly into the cow's golden flank. "Goodbye," he said.

Amber fumbled for the right words. "I. . . I just wanted to thank you for. . .everything. We've had some good times together. . ." Studying his profile, she could see his jaw muscles working, and she waited for his response, but he said nothing. There was silence except for the droning staccato of.the milk squirting into the metal bucket, emphasizing the seconds that stretched into minutes.

"Goodbye," Amber said again. She turned and walked back to the sulky, pausing for one last look in Will's direction, knowing that she would carry that picture of him in her memory forever.

Chapter 21

Amber lay awake, listening to the far-off beat of tom-toms in the distance. Cheyennes, she told herself, camped over across the South Canadian. She had heard their ceremonies before, but never so distinctly as tonight. They made an eerie sound, one that no doubt had struck fear into the hearts of many, and not so long ago. She was glad the Indians and whites were no longer at war with one another, at least not openly. She knew some folks on both sides still carried hate in their hearts, animosity that could manifest itself in various ways.

Take Mr. Gorman, for instance. She pondered the paradox of the man. Even though he was married to an Indian woman, and relied mostly on the tribes as customers in his general store, he treated them with a great lack of respect; as long as they came in with money, he was more than willing to do business with them, but he had no tolerance or compassion for those without. He waged a continual battle against loafers who congregated in and around the roadhouse, even going so far as to rig his counter with a series of hidden needles, which he could secretly trigger whenever idlers were sitting on the counter. A practical joker at heart, he got a big laugh out of it, but Amber had never found it amusing.

Nevertheless, she was grateful for the new experience she was gaining working at the roadhouse. Her duties consisted of helping with the cooking and serving of meals, as well as maintaining the three sleeping rooms located at one end of the building, and occasionally waiting on customers in the general store and post office. Each day she learned something new about people, about the territory, about life in general. She had to deal with Indians, traveling salesmen and other transients who passed through, as well as Clyde Calhoun, the old bachelor who farmed nearby and came in for dinner every day at noon. She enjoyed her contact with everyone except Mr. Calhoun.

Amber had never met a more repulsive individual. He was smelly and dirty, unshorn and unshaven, and thoroughly unpleasant to be around. And, from the first day Amber had come there, he was in love with her! So far, she had been able to ignore his attentions and pass them off lightly, but Mr. Gorman had picked up on it and was starting to tease her. All this time, she had been trying to recall where she had seen Mr. Calhoun before, and now it suddenly occurred to her – he was the leering old man on the stagecoach that first day she had arrived in El Reno!

"Boy, howdy! I sure attracted a good one this time!" she muttered to herself, as she rolled over on her stomach and put the pillow on her head to mute the sounds of the distant drums. Finally drifting off to sleep, she dreamed she was desperately running from three men who were chasing her through a chaotic maze of dancing Indians.

"May I help you?" inquired Amber, smiling at the young Cheyenne girl standing in front of the counter. She had long, black braids tied with bits of colored ribbon, and was dressed in a cotton skirt and overblouse cinched with a braided cotton belt. Amber recognized her as having been in the store several times before. The girl smiled faintly but said nothing, her dark eyes darting from Amber's to something on the shelf behind the counter. Amber turned around, following the girl's gaze to a small comb, brush, and mirror set on display. "You like?" she asked, and the girl nodded her head up and down, her dark eyes sparkling with desire. Amber placed the set on the counter, and the girl reached out and slowly traced the graceful curvature of the tortoise shell brush handle with a slender, brown finger. "You want?" Amber asked.

The girl looked up, and the twinkle went out of her eyes. "No money," she said sadly.

"Oh," replied Amber sympathetically, not knowing what else to say. The Indian girl sighed and reluctantly pushed the box toward Amber. On impulse, Amber shoved it back. "You take it," she said, nodding her head. "I will buy it for you."

The girl appeared puzzled, and Amber gestured and repeated, "I . . . give . . . to you." When she placed the gift in the girl's hands, her expression of delight was worth a week's salary to Amber. And that was just about what it was going to cost her!

The next day, as Amber was sweeping the floor of the general store, she glanced up to find the Indian girl standing there with both hands behind her back, a shy smile on her angular brown face. "Hello," said Amber.

The girl slowly brought from behind her back a pair of deerskin moccasins, and shyly offered them to Amber. They were creamy white and soft, with blue and red beadwork on the toes and along the sides, and with the seams sewn on the inside in true Cheyenne fashion.

Amber was elated. "Thank you!" she said, beaming with gratitude. "They're beautiful! Did you make them?"

"I help," answered the girl with shy pride.

"I'm going to put them on right now," said Amber. She leaned the broom against the counter, sat down on a stack of horse collars, and removed her high-buttoned shoes. The moccasins were a perfect fit, and more comfortable than anything she had ever known. "I'll never wear real shoes again!" She laughed, not knowing whether or not the Indian girl understood her joke. "My name is Amber," she said. "What is your name?"

"I am called Dawn Star."

"What a beautiful name," said Amber softly. She studied the girl's delicately chiseled face, wishing she could truly know her and understand her culture, but it was as though eons of time stood between them, forming an impenetrable barrier.

"I go now," said the girl. She turned and retreated silently out the door.

"Thank you again," Amber called after her, but she did not look back.

"Amber, I need you to help me shell these blackeyed peas," called Mrs. Gorman from the adjoining room. "I want to cook them with that sowbelly for dinner. Mr. Calhoun informed me he was getting tired of beef and beans every day. The gall that man has!" She snorted in disgust.

"Yes, ma'am," replied Amber, gathering up her shoes and hurrying in to help.

They spent the morning preparing the sowbelly and blackeyed peas, and just before noon, Amber went out to gather some wild lettuce and dandelion greens along the river bank. She came back with her apron full. At the well, she carefully washed the fine river sand from the crisp, green leaves, then tossed them together in a bowl with vinegar and seasonings. Served along with the main dish and the usual bread and butter, it would make a good meal, and the two were satisfied with their efforts.

"I don't know how you do it," said Amber admiringly, "never knowing how many folks to prepare for. The only one you can ever really count on is that obnoxious Mr. Calhoun, and sometimes, I wish he'd forget to show up!"

"Speak of the devil," muttered Mrs. Gorman, with a glance toward the door. "He just walked in."

"Howdy, missy, howdy," said Clyde Calhoun, nodding over and over, as he took off his battered felt hat and proceeded to wash at the washstand beside the door. As usual, he left the dirty water in the bowl when he took his place at the table, and as she always did, Amber tossed it outside and poured fresh water for the next person to use.

A traveling salesman arrived about that time, his light buggy loaded with several big, black valises. He brushed the dust from his fancy clothes and came inside, grateful to find a hot meal and a place to wash up. "Would you like our hired man to see to your team?" asked Mrs. Gorman, her dark eyes sizing the man up in an instant.

"Yes, please," he responded courteously.

Mrs. Gorman disappeared towards the back to summon Jim, the hired man, who soon appeared and led the horses away to feed and water. "I wonder where Stanley is?" said Mrs. Gorman, peering out the door in the direction of the toll bridge. "Uh-oh, I see now – better set some more places, Amber."

Amber hurriedly peeked out the door. A covered wagon pulled by a team of emaciated mules had just crossed the wooden bridge spanning the river, and a family of poor white children were piling out of it like bees out of a hive. Amber counted six, and they were still coming. "Oh, my gosh!" she exclaimed, hurrying to the kitchen.

The wagon, overladen with all kinds of household belongings, soon creaked to a stop out front, and Mr. Gorman accompanied the couple inside, while the children played around the porch.

"This here's Mr. and Mrs. Scruggs," he said, introducing the pair to his wife. "Have a seat, folks, and the missus will fix you up with some vittles."

"What about the children?" asked Amber, setting two more tin plates and cups on the long, wooden table.

"I'm going to fetch them a sack of crackers out of the store," Mr. Gorman quickly replied, "if you'll go out to the cellar and bring in a crock of milk for them."

Amber did as she was instructed, and the eight hungry children were soon gobbling down the crackers and milk. They were a pathetic bunch, in their patched, flour-sack clothing, and Amber wondered how the family had found themselves in such dire straits.

"The drought wiped us out," the man was saying, as she walked back inside. "We had a good farm down in the Chicksaw, but that last dry spell just wiped everything – cotton, wheat, corn – plumb out. And I couldn't see settin' there and starvin' another year – we'd barely made it through the good years, what with the grasshoppers, and the prairie fires, and the thievin' Injuns. You work, work, work, and what do you have to show for it? Nuthin'!"

"Trouble with him is, the grass always looks greener somewhere else," complained the woman, her haggard features lined with toil. "This is the third time we've moved in the past five years. I'm so sick and tired of travelin' from one filthy dugout to another! I want me a true home this time, a wood house, with real glass windows, and board floors."

"We'll have one this time, I promise," said the man. "We're in God's country now – things are gonna be better. You'll see."

"That's what you said last time," mumbled the woman. After a reproachful look from her mate, she fell silent, while her husband entered into a heated debate with Mr. Gorman, Mr. Calhoun, and the traveling salesman about the possibility of another depression like the one in '93. After listening to the man, it seemed to Amber that everyone and everything else was to blame for his misfortune except him! I certainly pity his wife and children, she thought to herself, as she served more bread and shooed the flies away from the table.

As soon as they were finished eating, Mr. Gorman tallied the couple's bill: bridge toll ten cents, two meals at twenty-five cents each, a sack of crackers thirty cents, one crock of milk twenty cents. "That will be a dollar and ten cents," he said. The woman took off her faded, calico sunbonnet, reached inside, and removed the exact amount from a concealed pocket sewn inside.

As they were on their way out the door, Amber touched the woman's sleeve. "There's a real nice place to camp about a quarter of a mile down river. There's wild lettuce and goose-berries all over the place."

"Thank you," replied the woman, with a grateful smile. "We might just stop there." They loaded up their barefoot brood, and slowly rattled their way down the trail east along the river, leaving Amber to wonder if they would ever find a place to call home.

By the end of June, Amber was taking a great deal of good-natured ribbing about her unwanted admirer, the despicable Clyde Calhoun. Mr. Gorman, a true jokester, carried her high, and soon had the hired man Jim teasing her as well. It was all in good fun, and she went along with it laughingly as long as Mr. Calhoun didn't suspect anything. As much as she detested him, Amber would not have hurt the old man's feelings for the world.

"Do you mind if we play a little joke on your friend Calhoun?" asked Mr. Gorman one day after dinner. He looked over at Jim and the two of them giggled like mischievous schoolboys.

"I guess not, as long as no one gets hurt," replied Amber with a shrug of her shoulders. "What are you going to do?"

"We can't tell you, that would spoil it. You'll just have to wait and see." They both chuckled again, and Amber just shook her head and finished clearing the table.

The following day Clyde Calhoun caught the afternoon stagecoach that came through from Anadarko headed for El Reno. Amber was relieved to see him go. At least she would have one day free from his constant staring and unsolicited attentions.

With lots of extra work to do to in preparation for the Fourth of July festivities the next day, she never gave Mr. Calhoun another thought. There was a big shindig planned, and folks were coming from as far away as El Reno to attend. Jim and his employer spent the day erecting a large platform for dancing in a flat, grassy area among the cottonwood trees behind the roadhouse, while Amber and Mrs. Gorman busily prepared extra food for the crowd that was expected.

The Fourth of July dawned clear and hot, with a south wind blowing fine sand up off the river. Before long, people began arriving from all directions in wagons, buggies, and on horseback. They found shady places to camp down along the river, and soon there could be heard the gleeful shouts of children playing tag among the trees. Almost everyone brought a picnic lunch – those without came to the roadhouse and bought one. A huge keg of hard cider appeared next to the dance platform, and all the men readily began to quench their thirsts.

The afternoon stage brought several new arrivals, and one man in particular seemed vaguely familiar to Amber. She studied him curiously out of the corner of her eye, as she slowly pumped water into two metal pitchers one by one. What was it that made her think she knew him? He was nicely dressed in what appeared to be brand new clothing, and his closely-cropped hair was starting to gray, but his pale, sallow complexion gave him a sickly appearance. Whoever it was, he seemed to think he knew Amber, too, for he was staring at her. She looked away, embarrassed. When she raised her eyes again, the man was standing right in front of her, nervously twisting the brim of his new hat. She smiled faintly at him, and he nodded and grinned a crooked grin. Then she knew. "Why, Mr. Calhoun, I didn't even recognize you! You. . .you look very nice."

"Thank you, Miss Amber, so do you," he said with a sort of nervous expectancy. He licked his lips. "I shore do like that red dress you're a wearin'. You look real good in it. Yessir, I shore think it's fine."

"Thank you," replied Amber self-consciously. The way he was leering at her made her skin crawl. "Excuse me, but I have work to do." She took the two full pitchers and brushed on past him and up the back steps.

Clyde Calhoun dogged her steps from that moment on – every time she turned around, there he was. The only thing that kept the holiday from being a total disaster for her was a surprise visit from Uncle Karl, Uncle Phil, and Ida Mae. "Hello, little gal, it's good to see you!" exclaimed Karl, as he jumped down from the wagon and gave her a quick hug. "We decided to come on over and join in the fun."

"I'm so glad," replied Amber happily. "It's so good to see you all. But where's Uncle Wenzel? Why didn't he come?"

"Oh, you know him – he didn't feel like it," answered Karl, then muttered under his breath, "Stubborn cuss!"

"Is that cider?" asked Uncle Phil, spying the large keg.

"It sure is. Help yourself," said Amber. Both men grabbed a tin cup out of their picnic basket and headed for the cider, while Amber and Ida Mae found a shady spot beneath a huge cottonwood to spread their patchwork quilt. As she did so, Amber was reminded of the Fourth of July two years ago when Bryan had taken her to the celebration at the courthouse square in Great Bend. She had worn her red dress then, too, and although it still fit her, she felt that she had grown up a lot in other ways. She wondered how Bryan was doing. The last she had heard from him, he was getting ready to marry a girl named Beth. Amber was happy for him.

"Do you still have to work, or are you free to visit now?" asked Ida Mae, as she took her Sunday hat out of the basket and pinned it on top of her upswept hairdo, in place of the sunbonnet she had left in the wagon.

Amber admired how nice Ida Mae looked in her white smocked blouse and maroon skirt. "Mrs. Gorman said I was free for the rest of the afternoon. She's really nice – stern, but nice. And the most organized person I've ever met! She certainly needs to be, to run a place like this." Amber paused. "You know, I think I'll go in and get my hat, too. I haven't had one occasion to wear it here, and this will probably be my only chance. Be back in a minute!"

The roadhouse itself was quiet and all but deserted, with most of the people outside along the river bank where it was cooler. As Amber reached the doorway of her room, she was startled to discover Clyde Calhoun there. "What are you doing in my room?" she demanded furiously, hands on her hips.

"I. . .I was just lookin' for you, missy. I couldn't find you anywheres, and I wanted to picnic with you, and I thought – " He could see the flush of anger on Amber's face, and nervously edged toward the door. "Can we eat together?" he asked in a small voice.

"No! I have relatives here visiting with me," she said sternly, then added in a voice equally forceful, "Goodbye, Mr. Calhoun!"

He left hurriedly, and when Amber turned to find her hat, she discovered that her room was in total disarray. Her trunk had been rummaged through, as well as the drawers in the washstand, and her comb and brush were lying on top beside the bowl and pitcher, rather than in the drawer, where she always kept them. She frowned at her reflection in the mirror. Why would Clyde Calhoun do such a thing? He was certainly weird – almost frightening. She shrugged, pinned on her Sunday hat with the blue bow and the pink roses, and hurried back outside.

As she rejoined Ida Mae, Uncle Karl and Uncle Phil walked over to them, laughing and shaking their heads. "You should have seen that!" exclaimed Karl. "You know that blind fiddler – I think they call him 'Blind Perdue' – well, his helper that leads him around had hidden a bottle of whiskey out in the bushes yonder, and he couldn't find it when he went to look for it. So that old blind man said, "I'll find it for you. I know where it is! Take me to the back steps of the roadhouse.' So he did. And I'll be durned if that sightless man didn't walk right to it! He must have memorized the direction they went and the number of steps they took when they hid it!"

"Maybe he isn't really blind," offered Ida Mae.

"Oh, yes he is," answered Amber. "I've seen him around here before. I think they said he was wounded in the Civil War."

Phil plopped down on the quilt and wiped his forehead on his shirt sleeve. "When do we eat?" he asked.

"This was my part of the bargain," Ida Mae said to Amber as she removed the checkered cloth from the top of the basket. "They said they'd bring me along, only if I packed a really swell picnic lunch." She laughed. "Help yourself, gentlemen. There's fried chicken, roasting ears, hard-boiled eggs, and tomatoes. And, for dessert, gooseberry pie!"

The two men murmured their appreciation, as they rolled up their sleeves and gratefully dug into the food spread out before them. But neither Amber nor Ida Mae was very hungry, for the July heat had robbed them of their appetites. Men were lucky, thought Amber. In the first place, they didn't have to wear as many clothes as women did, and when it was hot, they could roll up their sleeves or unbutton their shirts or even take them off. But women had to remain covered at all times, from wrist to throat to ankle. As Aunt Grizelda had said time and again, parts of the body were not for public display.

"Tell me everything that's happened since I left," Amber said to Ida Mae eagerly. "Did Marybelle and Johnny get married?"

"Yes, and they bought the old Dietz place over by Coyote Hill. Mrs. Dietz died last winter, you know, and Mr. Dietz just sort of gave up after that. They say he gave away all five kids to anybody who'd take them."

"And how are Clara and Luke and the baby doing?"

"They're fine, just doing great. And, they already have another baby on the way!"

Amber casually pulled several sticktights from the skirt of her red dress. "And how's Will?"

"Oh, he's okay, too." Ida Mae paused and glanced quickly at Amber. "He has a new girl," she said as she daintily stripped the meat from a chicken wing. "I haven't met her yet, but her family just came all the way from Missouri in a covered wagon. They're living in a dugout south of us a ways. I guess she's a real nice girl."

Before Amber could respond, Uncle Karl asked her, "How many beaus have you got on the string here?" He threw a quick wink at Phil.

"Yeah, how many more hearts have you broken?" Phil laughed as he cracked a hard-boiled egg on his knee.

"Only one," replied Amber, shaking her head, "and that one is going to be a problem, I'm afraid." She then proceeded to relate her experience with the obnoxious Clyde Calhoun, all except the part about finding him in her room just now. She didn't wish to worry her uncles unnecessarily. "Anyway," she concluded, "I don't know what kind of trick Jim and Mr. Gorman played on him, but it sure got him to clean up. I didn't even recognize him today when he came back from El Reno! I just wish he'd find someone his own age now and leave me alone! I don't want anything to do with him," she said with a shudder.

They were interrupted by a sudden flurry of excitement, as several small boys had to be pulled from the river. They had not been able to resist the temptation to wade in the shallow water, and had become mired in quicksand. Amber knew that the South Canadian had a reputation as a treacherous river for that very reason, and that was why the wooden toll bridge was erected. The boys were lucky. They were rescued unhurt and were soon playing as though nothing had happened.

The fiddler began playing and the dancing began. Everyone enjoyed themselves immensely as the Fourth of July celebration continued on at a lively pace into the late afternoon. Amber and Ida Mae danced with Karl and Phil until both men pleaded for mercy. "We're gettin' too old for this nonsense," complained Karl, as he rested and tried to catch his breath.

"No, you're not," chided Amber. "Come on, just one more. Please?"

"That's what you told us last time!" quipped Phil, but he took Ida Mae's hand and led her back to the dance platform.

They knew the festivities were over when Mrs. Gorman, concerned over the inebriated condition of most of the men, turned on the spigot in the keg of cider and let the remainder flow out onto the ground. One by one, buggies and wagons were loaded up with tired but happy people, and soon quiet reclaimed the grove of cottonwoods behind the roadhouse.

Amber had just waved goodbye to Ida Mae and her uncles and was on her way inside with a tray full of cups and glasses she had gathered up, when Clyde Calhoun suddenly confronted her. "Howdy, missy, howdy," he said, nodding over and over. "I seen you out there dancin' with them fellers all afternoon. You shore looked purty." He licked his lips and smiled his crooked smile, his breath reeking of alcohol.

"Thank you," said Amber coolly. "Now, if you'll excuse me, these things must be cleared up."

"Now hold on a minute. Don't get uppity with me, missy. I went and done what you asked. Now don't act like you don't care."

"What are you talking about?" asked Amber, dumbfounded.

"You know what I'm talkin' about – the letter."

"What letter?" Amber demanded.

"You know what letter! The letter you wrote me!" Clyde Calhoun's voice became shrill with agitation.

"I didn't write you any letter!"

Clyde Calhoun reached inside his coat pocket. "You did so! I have it right here!" he said defiantly, opening the single, folded sheet.

"Let me see that," said Amber, setting the tray down. *Dear Clyde,* she read, *I might marry you if you would shave and clean up. Amber.* She stared at it in horror. "I didn't write this!" she cried.

"You did so!" he countered. "Don't say you didn't, 'cause I know you did!"

"I didn't! That's not my handwriting – I don't print!"

"This letter is from you!" he insisted, his voice quavering with emotion, his pale features almost ghostly in the fading light of approaching dusk.

Amber drew a deep breath. "Mr. Calhoun, I assure you, I did not send you that letter, but I know who did, and I shall take care of it." She picked up her tray and hurried up the back steps.

"You did so write it!" he shouted after her, shaking the letter angrily in his fist.

Amber confronted Jim and Mr. Gorman early the next day, as they were dismantling the dance platform. "Boy, howdy! You two sure got me into a lot of trouble!" she said.

The men looked up to find her standing with hands on hips, glaring at them. They glanced at one another, then back to Amber. "What do you mean?" asked Mr. Gorman, innocently.

"You know perfectly well what I mean!" exclaimed Amber. "That letter you wrote to Mr. Calhoun and signed my name to – he actually believes I wrote it!"

Jim looked sheepish. "What did you tell him?" he asked.

"I told him I did not, but he won't believe me. He swears up and down that I sent it, and now he thinks I'm just playing hard to get. You've got to tell him the truth!" she insisted.

"Okay, okay, simmer down now," said Mr. Gorman, wiping the sweat from his brow. "He'll probably forget all about it in a couple of days, but if he doesn't, we'll tell him it was all a big joke. Besides, there's no harm done, and look at the improvement in him! He sure must think a lot of you, to go to all that trouble to clean up and everything." He winked at Jim. "Maybe you ought to reconsider. You know, he's really not too bad – "

"Oooooh! You two are impossible!" cried Amber. With a toss of her head, she turned on her heel and walked away.

"Just jokin'," Mr. Gorman called after her. "Don't worry about it though. It'll all blow over in a day or so. You'll see."

The next several days proved that his prophecy was not going to come true, for Clyde Calhoun sought Amber's attentions even more ardently than before. In the evenings, he would ride his pinto stallion back and forth outside her window, and every day at noon, he brought her a bouquet of wild flowers. During dinner he stared at her and smiled his crooked smile until he made her so uncomfortable that she took to eating her meals alone in the kitchen. She pestered Mr. Gorman to confess who actually wrote the letter, but he kept putting it off because he was enjoying Clyde Calhoun's antics. Amber wondered if the man was the kind who tore the wings off flies for the fun of it!

She finally decided to appeal to Mrs. Gorman for help. After dinner one day, she confided to her employer all that was going on.

"I knew those two were up to something, but I didn't know what," Mrs. Gorman responded, after hearing all the details. "This time I think they've gone too far," she added, her dark eyes narrowing. "I'll see that they tell Mr. Calhoun the truth and apologize to him." She turned to Amber, who was frantically scratching her head. "What's the matter?"

"Oh, my head has been itching the past few days," she said miserably. "I couldn't even sleep last night it was so bad. I don't know what it could be. . ."

"Let me see," replied Mrs. Gorman. After close inspection of Amber's hair and scalp, she announced, "My dear, I'm afraid you have lice!"

"Oh, no!" cried Amber. "How could I have gotten lice? You have to get them from someone else who has them, don't you? And I haven't been around anyone – " She stopped short and put her hand to her mouth. "Oh, no! I'll bet Clyde Calhoun used my comb and brush the day I found him in my room!"

"He was in your room?" asked Mrs. Gorman, her eyebrows raised in astonishment.

"Yes," Amber admitted, "on the Fourth of July. He was looking for me to picnic with him and he went to my room. I really got angry with him that day! Anyway, my comb and brush were disturbed, but I never thought any more about it." She scratched her head with both hands. "Another unwanted 'gift' from the lovely Mr. Calhoun! What shall I do?" she moaned.

"There's only one cure – you'll have to soak your head in kerosene! I'll go fetch you some out of the store."

The kerosene treatment was pure torture. Amber's scalp was tender from all the scratching she had been doing, and the kerosene stung something awful. She had never suffered through anything quite as miserable, and she wasn't sure who she was angrier with – Clyde Calhoun, or Mr. Gorman and Jim! But the cure was effective, and she was free of her tormentors.

Before she served dinner the next day, Mrs. Gorman announced to the group that her husband had something to say to Mr. Calhoun. Amber watched from the kitchen door as Mr. Gorman fidgeted and swallowed nervously. "Clyde, uh . . . Jim and I . . . we wrote you that letter as a joke. It wasn't Amber. She didn't know anything about it."

"Yeah, we did it, not Amber, and we're sorry," said Jim, hanging his head.

Clyde Calhoun sat in crestfallen silence, his eyes downcast, a picture of total dejection. Sadly, he rose from his seat and shuffled out the door without a word.

To the regret of all concerned, even Amber, he never returned to the roadhouse for his noon meal, and they heard later that summer that he had taken up with a young Cheyenne girl from the encampment across the river. Amber secretly hoped that girl was not Dawn Star, but it was something she would never know.

With the coming of winter, traffic through the area began to slow, and for Amber there were long days with too little to do. Once again, she grew restless, and just about the time she was about to inform them she was leaving, Mr. and Mrs. Gorman told her she was no longer needed, but assured her they would like to have her back again next summer. Amber thanked them, gathered her belongings, and caught a ride back to Geary with a family headed that way in a lumber wagon.

Eager to catch sight of the homestead, Amber was surprised when they topped the last rise to discover a new house built across the road from the old one. It was larger by far, with a wide veranda across the front. Amber was puzzled as to whose it might be.

The people let her off at the little house and she thanked them and waved goodbye. Her blue and white gingham curtains were still hanging in the windows, and smoke was curling from the smokestack in the roof. Cautiously, Amber opened the door and peeked inside. Uncle Phil was standing at the stove cooking. "Hi!" said Amber.

Phil turned and his face broke into a wide, welcoming grin. "Howdy, little gal, come on in! I was just frying a couple eggs – would you like some?"

"Sure!" replied Amber. She looked around the room. "Where's Uncle Karl and Uncle Wenzel?"

"Well now," Phil began, and Amber was reminded of how much he looked and talked like Karl, "a lot has happened since you left us last spring." He paused long enough to slip the fried eggs onto tin plates. "There's cold biscuits in the bread box." He motioned to Amber and she retrieved them. They sat down at the familiar little table, and Amber grimaced inside at the sight of her nice checkered tablecloth, which was now spotted and soiled from one end to the other. Dying of curiosity, she waited for Uncle Phil to continue.

"Yessiree, a lot has happened," he repeated solemnly. "First of all, Wenz died in August. Consumption finally got him."

"Uncle Wenzel died? Why didn't you let me know?"

"It happened real sudden like. He just didn't wake up one morning. He's up yonder in the cemetery," he said, nodding in that direction.

"And what about Uncle Karl?" Amber was halfway afraid to ask.

"Well now, you aren't going to believe this – I didn't myself – but ol' Karl went and got himself married!"

"Uncle Karl? Married?" Amber was totally flabbergasted.

"Yep! He took the train to Guthrie, to visit some folks he knew from the time he was cookin' for that cow outfit in Texas, and I'll be durned if he didn't come back with a bride!" Phil shook his head slowly, as though he were still having a hard time believing it. "Her name is Mattie and she's a real swell lady. Ol' Karl really lucked out!"

Amber sat there in disbelief as well. "So that must be the reason for the new house across the road," she mused, slowly chewing a bite of cold biscuit.

"Yeah, we been workin' on it for over a month. Just about got 'er finished up now. All we need is the roofing material, and I'm fixin' to go into El Reno tomorrow and get that. Would you like to come?"

"Yes, I would. I guess I'll try to find a job there."

"Still lookin', eh?" Uncle Phil asked her, his brown eyes direct and probing.

"For what?"

"I don't know." He shrugged. "For whatever it is you're lookin' for."

Amber smiled at him. "I guess I am."

He pushed his chair back and stood up. "Come on. We'll go over across the road and I'll introduce you to the new bride."

Chapter 22

El Reno had grown considerably in the year since Amber's last visit, and now some businesses not only boasted the acquisition of telephones, but electricity as well. Amber wondered if folks would ever be fortunate enough to have such conveniences in their homes. She had even heard that someone somewhere had invented a horseless carriage! Just about the time she thought they had dreamed up everything that could possibly be invented, they came up with something new!

One thing that hadn't changed much was the tiny Cyclone Restaurant. Rooms were still seventy-five cents, and the food was still good. As soon as she arrived in town, Amber rented a room upstairs and began her search for employment. She had twenty-five dollars saved up from her summer work at the roadhouse, and to her it represented a small fortune, giving her a tremendous sense of independence which she thoroughly enjoyed.

The results of her first day of job hunting were discouraging, maybe because she was a little more particular now about the job she accepted and the salary she would be paid. She preferred not to work for a large family, nor one with small children. And, she had made up her mind she would not work for less than one dollar-fifty a week. Amber did not consider it an unreasonable sum, although some folks might. "Oh well," she told herself as she got ready for bed that night, "I'm sure I'll find something tomorrow."

It was a warm night for October, and there was a sliver of moon in the cloudless sky. Her little room was stuffy and filled with cooking odors from the restaurant downstairs, so Amber opened the only window. She found the air refreshing as she knelt at the open window and said her nightly prayers. Lingering then, she stared out over the rooftops and the almost deserted streets of the town, contemplating her life up until now.

She pondered Uncle Phil's question. What was she searching for? Happiness? Security? A place to belong? Yes, all those things, she decided, but something more – someone with whom to share them. She was beginning to realize, as Uncle Karl apparently had, that this was the most important thing. She was tired of fleeing, weary of watching her bridges burn behind her. Surely, someplace in the world, the right person was waiting for her. She sighed. She would simply have to trust God for the answer.

Amber awoke with a start shortly before dawn. She lay there momentarily, trying to organize her senses. What was happening? There was a terrible commotion down on the street – people shouting and cursing, horses running, bells clanging. Suddenly the acrid smell of smoke assailed her nostrils, and her heart leaped into her throat. She flew out of bed, dashed to the door, and opened it to discover the stairway in flames. Quickly she slammed the door and rushed to the window, just as a ladder thudded against it and a fireman appeared.

"Quick! Let me help you down!" he shouted.

Frightened, and with nothing but the chemise and knee-length drawers she had on, Amber scrambled across the window sill, and the fireman guided her swiftly and surely down the ladder to safety in the street, where someone quickly wrapped a blanket around her trembling body. "The baby – did you find the people with the baby?" she cried. "I know there's a child in the other room! I heard it crying last night!"

Without a word, the fireman turned and ran back to the burning building, where his comrades had moved the ladder to the other window, and dashed up it. By this time, the figure of a man could be seen at the window, frantically waving his arms and shouting to the fireman. They both disappeared momentarily into the interior of the room, then the fireman reappeared, carrying the limp body of a woman clad in a white nightgown. The man, shoeless and wearing only his trousers, followed him down the ladder clutching a tiny baby in one arm.

"She's only fainted," said the fireman, as he brought the woman over into the crowd.

"Here! Lay her down here!" said Amber. She took the blanket from around her own shoulders and spread it on the ground. The fireman did so, and returned to the fire to help a colleague direct a stream of water through the front window at the inferno inside. The husband knelt down beside his wife, trying to revive her and quiet his crying infant at the same time. "Let me take the baby," Amber offered, reaching out to him. With a quick look of gratitude, he gave her the baby. Amber cradled the terrified infant in her arms, rocking it gently back and forth. "Shhh. . .shhh. . .shhh," she crooned into the tiny ear, so delicate and perfectly formed – like a pink rosebud, she thought, as it caught the glow from the blazing building.

By the time the woman revived, Amber had soothed the baby's fears. She returned him to his grateful parents and reclaimed her blanket, just as part of the upper floor of the restaurant crashed down in a shower of sparks and flame. Another hose cart was pulled up, and several more firemen concentrated their efforts on the blaze. Amber counted ten in all, aided by numerous bystanders. As she watched, she felt her throat tighten and tears begin to sting her eyes. A sob escaped her lips. The lady standing next to her, a large, buxom woman with gray hair, put an arm around Amber and hugged her close to her ample form. "Don't cry, honey, you're safe," she said, consoling Amber just as Amber had comforted the couple's baby.

When it was all over, there was only a smoking pile of rubble where the Cyclone Restaurant had stood. Amber couldn't believe that now there was only a gaping hole between the two brick walls of the adjacent buildings. Everything she had with her was gone – her dress, her petticoats, her shoes, all of her hard-earned money! The only thing she could be thankful for was the fact that her trunk had been left at the livery stable. At least the rest of her belongings were safe.

She was still standing there in shock, wondering what she was going to do, when her rescuer reappeared. He removed his fire hat and wiped the sweat from his brow, and in the first rays of the morning sun, Amber realized he was much younger than she had thought. "Whew! That one had me worried there for awhile," he said. "I was afraid the whole block would go." He turned to Amber then. "And how's this little lady doing?"

"She's going to be just fine," the older woman responded, patting Amber gently.

Amber sniffed and tried to smile. "Yes, I'm all right." She swallowed past the lump in her throat. "Thank you for helping me out of there. I was so scared – "

"Quite all right, miss. It's always a pleasure to rescue a lady in distress, especially a pretty one."

Amber suddenly became self-conscious of her appearance. She must look a sight, with her hair disheveled and her face streaked with tears – and here she stood in her chemise and drawers! This strange man had actually seen her in her underclothes! She blushed at the realization and pulled the blanket around herself more tightly.

The fireman looked around for the couple with the baby, but they were no longer in the crowd. "If you'll excuse me, I have to get back to the men," he said. He donned his fire hat and strode back to the scene, where Amber could hear him shouting orders with brisk authority. In a matter of minutes, they had the hoses gathered up, and the team of nervous, prancing grays hitched to the fire wagon started back to the firehouse.

Amber stared at the smoldering remnants of the Cyclone Restaurant, and a new flood of tears welled up in her eyes and splashed down her cheeks. "What am I going to do?" she cried. "All my money is gone. . ."

"You're going to come home with me," kindly replied the woman beside her. "I just live over here across the alley. I was makin' a trip out to the backhouse when I saw the flames. Bless those fireboys – they sure kept that blaze from spreading, didn't they? Come on, honey," she said, and with her arm still around Amber's shoulders, she began walking her home.

As tragic as the fire was, one good result did come of it – Amber's benefactor, Mrs. Brady, became her employer. The woman and her husband, a retired judge, had been considering hiring a house girl, and Amber filled the bill perfectly. She thanked her lucky stars for finding such nice folks to work for. That same day, her trunk was sent for and money was advanced for necessary purchases to replace what she had lost in the fire.

So, after a dubious beginning, her new venture settled into a pleasant routine. It was good to live in town again where she could shop and attend church regularly. She was sure she could become quite spoiled by the conveniences of city living in no time at all. Why, the Bradys even had a pump right in the kitchen, so she didn't have to go outside for water! Amber was amazed at the number of steps it saved in a day.

"What gorgeous flowers!" exclaimed Amber, as Mrs. Brady carried a big bouquet of vibrant yellow blooms into the kitchen. Amber set her cool flatiron on the stove and picked up a hot one. "They're so huge! What kind are they?" she asked, returning to her ironing board.

"Chrysanthemums," replied Mrs. Brady with pride. "I brought them from Missouri and planted them right after the Run when we built this house, and they've certainly done well. They bloom like crazy every fall. I've got more than I know what to do with," she said with a laugh.

As Amber ironed one of Judge Brady's shirts, she grew thoughtful, pursing her lips. "You know, our church is having a bazaar this weekend, and they asked people to bring items to sell in the various booths. Do you suppose . . . I mean . . . could I take some of your flowers to sell?"

"That's a good idea! You're welcome to take all you want. It will do them good to be picked."

After such a generous offer, Amber could hardly wait for the bazaar. Although she wouldn't be staying for the dance afterward, the bazaar itself sounded like fun!

"FRESH FLOWERS 25 cents" read the hand-lettered sign on the front of her little stand, which was situated between a booth selling popcorn and one featuring a wheel of fortune. Amber had gathered up every vase, bottle, and jar she could find and filled them with the large yellow chrysanthemums. The flowers presented an impressive array, and added a splash of color that was visible from anywhere in the crowded hall. Right away Amber's wares began to sell, mostly to gentlemen buying them for their ladies, and before long Amber had accumulated an apron pocket full of change.

She was thoroughly caught up in the excitement of the bazaar – the noisy crowd mingling in a blue haze of cigar smoke, the tempting aroma of food from the church ladies' kitchen, the shouts from the barkers enticing folks to try their luck on the various games of chance. She finally succumbed to the hot, buttered popcorn next door and treated herself to a huge bag with a nickel from her proceeds. The church would end up with all the money anyway, she rationalized.

Amber was enjoying herself, watching the numbered wheel spinning in the next booth, when she heard a deep voice beside her. "Well, well, look who's here! If it isn't my damsel in distress!"

Amber turned to find the young fireman who had rescued her from the burning building. "Oh, hello!" she said with a warm smile. "Just a minute – I want to see which number wins. I picked number seven." They watched the spinning wheel gradually slow, at last coming to rest exactly on the number seven. "Hooray!" squealed Amber with a clap of her hands. "I picked it right!"

"Think you're pretty good at it, eh? Well, so am I," he said. "Let's just see who can guess the closest on the next turn."

The young fireman was much more handsome than Amber had remembered, with his dark hair and mustache and gray-green eyes, and he was a dapper dresser as well. She felt a strange little tingle inside every time he looked at her. "Okay," said Amber, rising to the challenge.

"Ladies first," he said, with a sweeping motion of his hand.

Amber squinted at the wheel in concentration. "Number three!" she replied decisively.

"Three, eh? I say ten will win this time."

Amber folded her arms and shook her head. "Three."

When the wheel stopped on thirteen, they turned to each other and laughed. "Would you say we won or lost?" Amber asked.

"I'd say we won," the young man replied, his green eyes looking straight into hers. Amber dropped her gaze, her eyelids fluttering nervously. "What's your name?" he asked her.

She looked up then and matched his gaze. "Amber. Amber Lockhardt."

"I'm Sage Harmon."

"Sage? That's an unusual name."

"Yeah, it's a nickname my friends gave me," he explained. "They teased me because when I first came to town in my two-wheeled cart, there was a big piece of sagebrush caught underneath it."

"Aren't you glad it wasn't a piece of loco-weed?" Amber giggled.

They both laughed, and then there was an awkward pause. "It looks like you've sold lots of flowers," Sage remarked, noticing the abundance of empty containers. "Did you grow them?"

"Oh, no, Mrs. Brady did. You know, the lady who lives across the alley from where the fire was. I've been working for them as a hired girl ever since that night. She was nice enough to let me bring the flowers to sell. By the way," Amber added, "did they ever find out how the fire started?"

"Oh, yes. The cook was apparently still half-drunk from the evening before, and he let a pan of grease catch fire. Then, instead of dousing it with flour or something, he panicked, tried to pick it up and run out with it. Of course, it was too hot to carry, and when he dropped it, the fire went everywhere. It's just a good thing those buildings next to it were brick – we might have lost that entire block."

"It's just a good thing El Reno has such a fine fire department," interjected Amber.

"Well, that too," he admitted with pride. "We have a terrific company. Do you know, we made a test run the other day a distance of two hundred and sixty yards, laid one hundred and fifty feet of hose, and threw water in seventy-five seconds – and that included hitching up the horses and everything! It's the best we've ever done."

"That's amazing!" exclaimed Amber. "I'd love to be able to watch the whole procedure sometime – without being involved!" she added with a laugh.

"By the way, I wanted to thank you for your help that night. It's always good to see a female who can keep her wits about her in time of trouble, instead of fainting dead away."

"I didn't do much," replied Amber modestly, and then her voice took on a note of earnestness. "But, you know, Mrs. Brady and I got to talking afterwards, and we think a group of women could be of service during fires or tornadoes or any kind of disaster like that. They could tend to the injured, find homes for the homeless, set up food lines – "

"Quiet crying babies. . ."

"Yes, even that." Amber chuckled. What do you think?"

"Sounds like a fine idea to me, as long as they were properly trained and organized," Sage responded.

"Well," Amber continued, "Mrs. Brady belongs to The Ladies' Aid Society, and she thinks they would be interested in expanding their activities. You have to admit, it's a more worthwhile pastime for us ladies than sitting around crocheting doilies."

"I'll agree there! I think it's a fine idea!"

Before long, a young couple strolled up arm in arm and purchased Amber's last two flowers. "Well," she said, as she pocketed the change, "I guess I'll go turn this money in and go home."

"Aren't you staying for the dance?" Sage inquired.

"Oh, no."

"Well, what's this?" he said. Reaching across the counter, he gently pulled on the red silk cord dangling from the left pocket of Amber's white apron, lifting out a small, folded dance card.

"Oh, it's nothing!" exclaimed Amber, making a quick grab for it and missing. She felt a surge of embarrassment and felt her face flush, as he opened the card and read off the names of her supposed partners which she had jotted in on the lines for each scheduled dance of the evening.

"Waltz: Mr. Somebody; Polka: Mr. So-and-So; Quadrille: Mr. Nobody. . ." He paused and grinned at her. Amber leaned over and made another pass at the dance card, but Sage kept his distance on the other side of the counter and continued reading, while Amber, with arms crossed, sighed and rolled her eyes at the ceiling. "Schottische: Mr. Flyaround; Virginia Reel: Mr. Jumpup; Rye: Mr. Quick Step."

"That's not fair!" she cried. "I was just passing time by filling in those lines with silly names. I really didn't intend to stay for the dance."

"Well, would you stay and dance with me? I know I probably can't dance as well as Mr. Graceful or Mr. Flyaround, but – "

"I'd love to!" Amber heard herself answer.

That evening proved to be the most wonderful of any Amber had ever enjoyed. Sage Harmon was a marvelous dancer and taught her lots of new steps. Oblivious to the other couples, they whirled in a world of their own, as though the two of them were one. Time ceased to be, until the pendulum clock on the wall struck twelve and, much to their mutual dismay, the dance was over.

Sage walked her home then, helping to carry the assortment of vases and jars. "How did you get there with all of these filled with flowers?" he asked incredulously.

"Judge Brady drove me in his surrey. We had the whole rear seat filled, and the floorboards, too. It looked like a hearse going to a funeral!" She laughed. "Anyway, I made almost twelve dollars for the church. That's pretty good, considering the fact that I didn't have anything invested to start with."

"I'll say!" Sage agreed. "I wish I could do as well in my business."

"Your business? I thought you were a fireman," replied Amber, sidestepping a mud puddle which reflected the moonlight in the middle of the dirt street.

"That's only part-time," said Sage, "mostly at night. During the daytime, I run a transfer and storage business."

"Oh, really? That sounds interesting."

"Yes, I started it about a year ago with one horse and one wagon, and now I have two more horses and another wagon. The way folks keep pouring into this territory, there's always lots of freight to be moved. I meet most of the trains and haul stuff here and there. It's a good business, and I'm going to build it into a real profitable venture," he said confidently.

"I don't know how you have time for that and being a fireman, too," said Amber. "You must really be busy."

"That I am," he said. "There just aren't enough hours in the day to do everything I want to do. Why, my head is so full of ideas, sometimes I feel like I'm just goin' to bust! Let me tell you, it's an exciting time to be alive. There's so much happening that I want to be a part of. Do you know some folks.are already talking of statehood for this territory? I think it's a little premature, but it's coming, you can bet on that, it's not far off."

They reached the Brady's house and Sage nudged the front gate open with his elbow. It squeaked in protest and clanged shut behind them. The house was dark, indicating that the Bradys had retired. "How would you like to take a tour of the firehouse tomorrow?" asked Sage softly. "Sunday is a good day for it. The place is fairly quiet then."

"Oh, that would be swell!" exclaimed Amber in a hushed voice. "What time?"

"How about one o'clock?" he whispered, as he set his jars on the porch steps as quietly as he could.

Amber did the same with hers. "Okay, I'll see you then. Thank you for such a nice evening. I really enjoyed it."

"Thank you, so did I." Sage reached out and took both of her hands in his. There was a long pause as he studied her form in the pale moonlight. "Good night, Amber Lockhardt," he said finally.

"Good night."

Chapter 23

Amber spent a restless, sleepless night, her whole consciousness immersed in the personality she had come to know as Sage Harmon. Like a tiny child inspecting a bright, new toy, she examined every aspect of the evening, trying to recall every little thing he had said or done, each special look, the slightest meaning in his most mundane gesture. She wondered if he was as attracted to her as she was to him. Never had she met anyone who so thoroughly captivated her. And why? What was so different about him? she wondered. He was handsome, but not terribly so; he was very nice, but so was Will Rainey. There was something else, a mysterious attribute she could not define. Whatever it was, she found Sage Harmon extremely interesting, to say the least.

Surprisingly enough, she awoke from her short night's sleep feeling rested and refreshed. She hurried to church, then helped with Sunday dinner, all the while aware of a rising tide of excitement within her. Every time she thought of Sage Harmon, which was often, a little thrill shot through her like a ticklish streak of lightning. And, by the time he finally knocked on the door, she was so nervous, her hands were trembling and clammy cold.

"Hello there," said Sage, as Amber met him at the door. "Sorry I'm late. I had to deliver a bunch of freight over to the Kerfoot Hotel, and it took longer than I anticipated."

"That's all right, I hadn't even noticed the time," she lied.

They walked out the front gate and it clanged back into place. "I hope you don't mind riding in a dray wagon," Sage apologized. "I just came on over with it since I was already late."

"I don't mind. It's not much different from the lumber wagon we used on the farm." Amber gathered up her skirts and Sage helped her easily up to the seat. Once up, she adjusted her Sunday hat and waited for him to join her.

"Would you take the lines while I untie these horses?" Sage asked her. "I think this one on the near side is an old fire horse, the way he wants to take off running every time!" Amber held the team in check until he climbed up beside her. He took the reins then and the team started off, with the horse on the left lunging against the harness several times while the other one plodded steadily along. "See? Just like an old fire horse," Sage commented. "All he wants to do is gallop. I think that's why I got him so cheap."

"How do you train a fire horse?" inquired Amber with interest.

"It doesn't take much training – it's called a conditioned reflex. They just love to go, and when they hear the bell, they come a runnin'."

"From where? I mean, how do they – "

"You'll see, as soon as we get to the firehouse," Sage assured her.

From the moment they entered Central Fire Station No. 1, a two-story, red brick building, Amber was fascinated. It was interesting to view the hose wagons and hook and ladder close up, while Sage explained all about them – how they were lightweight but strong, and stripped down for speed and efficiency. He demonstrated every fitting and every tool they carried, proud of the fact that everything was the absolute latest in fire-fighting equipment. "We've won lots of hose contests," he said, motioning toward a small, glass display case filled with medals and ribbons of various colors. "Just got back from the annual tournament in Guthrie, as a matter of fact."

"You mean you actually compete with other firemen in contests?"

"Yep, and we're hard to beat," he said proudly.

"I'm impressed," replied Amber. Then, pointing to a strange contraption suspended from the ceiling, she asked, "What is that?"

"That," replied Sage, "is the harness. It's a special, lightweight one with hinged collars. When the horses," he nodded at the two animals in the small corral just outside, "hear the bell, they run into this aisle here, the harness drops down on them, we snap the collars shut, hitch up the hose wagon, and away we go. That's how we can get out of here so quick."

Amber shook her head in amazement, almost wishing there would be an alarm while she was there so she could watch the exciting procedure.

After looking the horses over, Sage introduced her to Al Murray. "He's our driver," he explained, "and so far, the only paid member of the company, besides the chief, because he lives here in the firehouse and takes care of the horses and all. The rest of us are all unpaid volunteers."

Amber was dumbfounded. "You mean you donate your time and energy, and even risk your life, for nothing? Why?"

"It just sorta gets in your blood, I guess." He smiled and his green eyes sparkled. "Besides, one of these days I'll get paid, because one of these days I'm going to be chief, and a chief gets twenty-five dollars a month!"

Amber smiled, admiring his confidence. "I bet you will be," she agreed.

They spent the rest of that bright fall afternoon seeing the sights of El Reno, and ended up north of town sitting on the bank of the North Canadian River. Water the color of chocolate flowed lazily between the pinkish-white sand of the river banks which were lined with golden willows and cotton-woods, resplendent against the vivid azure sky.

"Where are you from in the States?" Amber asked Sage. In such a new territory, everybody was from someplace else, so she knew she could ask without appearing nosy or forward.

"Indiana. Colfax County, Indiana. I haven't been back since I left, when I was thirteen. I've been on my own, or living with my older sister in Kansas, ever since my folks died."

"Kansas? That's where I lived, in Great Bend."

"Really? I was in Anthony. That's south of there a ways. And now, here we both are, sitting on a river bank in Oklahoma Territory." He smiled and his eyes swept Amber's figure from head to toe. "Your hair is a beautiful color. I love the way it glints red in the sunshine, like spun copper. How long is it?" Amber place one hand at the middle of her back to demonstrate, and he continued. "What is the saying – 'Hair is a woman's crowning glory?' I certainly agree with that. Sometime I would like to have you let it down for me," he said quietly.

Amber thought she would blush at his remarks and was surprised when she didn't. Why did she feel so comfortable with this person?

Sage plucked a long piece of dry grass and absently began to chew on it. "My mother had long, beautiful hair, only hers was much darker. She was a lovely woman, as a matter of fact, in more ways than one. She died when I was thirteen, and Dad died not long after that. That's when I went to live with my married sister so I could finish school. A few years later, I heard about the free land down here in Oklahoma Territory, so I came down to see if I could get some, but it was all gone. So when I got a good deal on that corner lot not far off the main street, I just decided to stay and see what kind of a need I could fill. I really didn't want to be a farmer anyway. I decided on the transfer business because it didn't take a big outlay of money."

Suddenly he turned to Amber. "Here I am doing all the talking – I want to hear about *you*. Tell me all about Amber Lockhardt, and don't leave anything out!" he said, taking her hand in his.

Amber found it hard to believe Sage actually wanted to hear about her own life. "Well, let me see," she began. "I was born in Ohio, and when I was ten, my father was killed in an accident, while he was working for the railroad. Mama was left with six of us kids, all the rest younger than I was, and she didn't know how on earth she would ever manage without Papa. My Uncle John just happened to be back there at the time – he'd been proving up on his homestead in Kansas and had come back to get married – so they got together and decided that I should go to Kansas with John and his new wife and live with them."

"You mean your mother just gave you away?"

"Well, I guess you could say that. She really didn't want to, and I knew that, but we were so poor. . .and I guess I really didn't think it would be permanent. I always thought I would go back home, eventually."

"Did you? Did you ever get to go back and see your mother?"

Amber shook her head. "I never saw her again. She died just last winter, right after Christmas." She paused and looked away momentarily. "Anyway," she continued, "there I was, ten years old, no Mama, no Papa, no brothers or sisters, out in the middle of that awful Kansas prairie. I was so homesick at first, I thought I'd die!"

"I know all about that!" Sage responded sympathetically. "Were your aunt and uncle good to you?"

"Uncle John was – he and I got along fine. He even bought me my own horse, a little mustang I named Kickapoo. But that Grizelda – she was a witch! I used to hate her so much! I even ran away one time, but Uncle John found me and brought me back. That poor man! He was always caught in the middle. He tried to be nice to me and keep peace with her at the same time. I admire him so much. He really put up with a lot."

Amber smiled wryly and shaking her head, she continued. "I couldn't do anything to please Aunt Grizelda, and she would whip me all the time with that leather riding quirt of hers. Of course, she began having babies right away, one after the other, every nine months. She had seven by the time I left. And that didn't improve her disposition any, just made it worse! Poor Aunt Grizelda! Of course, I didn't understand it then, but I think she must have had prairie madness. She had come from a good family back East, and I just don't think she was cut out for that kind of life."

Sage shook his head and whistled softly through his teeth. "You've really been through a lot!" he said. "And I thought I had it bad!"

"Anyway, I stood it as long as I could, and as soon as I turned sixteen, I got a job in town, in Great Bend, working for a druggist's family. They were nice people and I really enjoyed living in the midst of things. There were lots of new experiences and all."

Sage caught the nervous fluttering of her eyelashes. "Like beaus. . .?"

"Well, one," Amber admitted, surprised at how detached she could sound. "He was quite a bit older, and wealthy, and spoiled, and. . ." She glanced sideways at Sage. "He wanted me to marry him. I don't know if he was really in love, or if he just felt sorry for me, you know, like I was some backward little farm girl he had to protect and take care of. He was nice and all, but I decided I just wasn't meant for him. I think I was stuck on his horses more than I was on him! He had the nicest team of matched Hackneys you ever saw! And a maroon buggy with bright yellow wheels!"

Sage grinned at her. "A real dandy, eh? Sounds to me like you turned down a good thing." He chuckled.

Amber laughed and playfully threw a sand plum at him, which he managed to dodge.

"So how did you get out of that little situation?" he asked.

"Well, just about the time I didn't know what I was going to do, I received this letter from my three bachelor uncles down here in the Territory, asking me if I would be interested in keeping house for them, and I jumped at the chance!"

"Three bachelor uncles!" mused Sage.

"They have three farms out west of Geary, and I was so happy there at first. I loved the country, and still do. It's so much greener and cooler than Kansas, don't you think? And for once, I felt like this was where I belonged. But then. . ." Her voice trailed off and she stared into the muddy, brown water flowing past.

"What?"

"Well, a fella out there eventually thought we should get married, too, but I just wasn't ready to settle down yet. I'm afraid he couldn't understand it that way, though. Anyway, I needed to get away, and I took a job for the summer at Bridgeport, at the roadhouse there on the South Canadian. There again, it was just something temporary. I really enjoyed it though. Met lots of different people – my first real Indians, and that was interesting. Then, when the job ended, I went back to Geary to find that one of my uncles had died and one had gotten married, so they didn't need me anymore. So I packed up and came in to El Reno to see what I could find. And you know the rest," she said, turning to Sage. "That was the night the Cyclone Restaurant burned down."

"Hmmm. . .you've really been through a lot," he repeated, looking into her eyes with new appreciation and wonder.

Amber found herself matching the directness of his gaze, wondering why she had divulged her life story to someone she had known for such a short time. At the same time, she was aware of a comfortable inner feeling that told her it was all right. Funny, she never thought anyone would be that interested in her. Bryan had only talked about himself, and Will didn't have much to say about anything. But here was someone who actually wanted to know who she was, what she thought, her hopes, and dreams, and aspirations.

"What would you like to do with your life from here on?" Sage was asking.

Amber grew thoughtful. "I never really tried to put it into words before, but. . .I guess I just want to live life to the fullest. I want to do everything there is to do, and see everything there is to see!"

"That's a tall order!"

"I know, but just think how much fun it will be trying to fill it!"

The slanted rays of the sun were bringing their surroundings into sharper focus and a chill into the air. Sage took her hand and helped her up, then swept her gently into his arms and kissed her, holding her in his embrace for a timeless moment. He was strong but gentle, and smelled of horses and leather, and Amber loved it. Reluctantly, but happily, they headed back to town, with Amber sensing that, somehow, a new dimension had been added to her own being, making her from that day forward, a totally different and more complete person.

As fall deepened into winter, Amber and Sage's friendship deepened into love, an emotion which took root and grew – one day at a time – into something that encompassed them both, an ascending spiral which carried them upward to new heights of awareness and wonder. Whenever they were together, they seemed to experience a unique blending of personalities, a merging of their individual beings. And even in periods of silence, there seemed to be an unspoken communication between them, a gentle, invisible tie that bound one to the other. Amber had to admit, even to Mrs. Brady, that she was head over heels in love with Sage Harmon.

At last, she understood what the lady on the train had tried to convey. When you find the person for you, you know it. There are no nagging doubts, no unanswered questions, no pretending. There was nothing to hide – either from Sage or from herself – and she felt very much at ease and comfortable about their whole relationship.

There was only one problem: Sage Harmon never got around to proposing marriage. After her experiences with Bryan and Will, not to mention Clyde Calhoun, she figured a proposal would soon be forthcoming, but to her surprise, many months passed with no mention of marriage. Amber was glad at first – she still didn't want to rush into anything – but by now she was wondering if he ever would bring it up. Maybe she had scared him off with her stories of Bryan and Will and not being ready to tie herself down.

The closest thing to a commitment she ever got from him was, "One of these days, I'll build you the biggest house in El Reno, right here on this corner!" That was the day he showed her where he lived – a tiny, three-room house, just two blocks east of the main street of town. A friendly winter sun warmed the back porch where they sat that afternoon.

"Thank you," Amber said gratefully, as she admired the delicate floral design etched into the lovely mother-of-pearl cross he had just given her. "You're the first person besides Papa who ever remembered my birthday."

"I'm glad you like it," replied Sage. "Here, let me put it on you." Amber turned around, and he fastened the black velvet ribbon around the high-neck collar of her white smocked blouse. "Crosses at the throat are quite the fashion now, according to the jeweler."

"Oh, yes, haven't you noticed? Everybody's wearing them, and I've been wanting one for ages. Thank you so much," she said, feeling a glow on her face from more than the sun.

Sage looked particularly handsome today, having just returned from the barber shop, and still smelling of shaving soap. He leaned toward her and kissed her on the nose. "Happy birthday," he said. He studied her for a moment, a twinkle in his green eyes. "Tell me the funniest thing you ever did."

"You mean besides our rock-swallowing contests?" Amber giggled. "Well, let me see. . . one time, Uncle John and Aunt Grizelda were going into town, and they told me they would buy me a pair of new shoes, if I would give them a stick the length of my foot, so they'd know what size to get. So I got a stick and put it up against my foot, and just to be safe, I added some to it before I snapped it off. I wanted to make sure the shoes were plenty big so they wouldn't pinch my feet – I was sick and tired of still having to wear shoes that I had outgrown.

"Anyway," she continued, "you should have seen what they brought me! They were at least three sizes too big! I didn't say a word though – I flopped around in them forever. That's the only pair of shoes I never outgrew – they just flat wore out!" Amber laughed again, remembering.

Sage chuckled and shook his head.

"Now, tell me the funniest thing you ever did!" Amber said.

"One time, when I was five years old, I found my father's jug of dandelion wine, and I drank so much, I got drunk and passed out. That's the first, and last, time I ever got drunk!" He laughed again at this childhood antic.

Amber giggled, trying to picture Sage as an inebriated five-year-old.

"Then, there was the time I turned over an outhouse on Halloween – "

"Mischieveous little boys are always doing that," interjected Amber.

"Yes, but this one had a guy in it!"

Amber clapped one hand to her mouth and broke up in laughter. "Shame on you!"

"You can bet I never did that again, either!" Sage exclaimed.

They sat in happy silence for awhile, enjoying the warm sun and just being together. "You know," Amber said finally, surveying the property, "you have enough land here, you ought to build yourself a big building to house your transfer business, one that you could store people's baggage in instead of having to rent space."

"I've already drawn the plans up," Sage responded enthusiastically. "Would you like to see them?"

"Sure."

He brought the plans outside and unrolled them on the porch. The sketches showed a large, square, two-story building of sandstone block. "I'll have enough room downstairs for my teams and wagons and a little office, and then the upstairs will all be for storage," he explained.

"That should be adequate," mused Amber. "And you know what, something else you ought to get someday is a – "

"Telephone!"

"That's right!"

"I'm working on that," said Sage. "They're pretty expensive, you know. Only the largest businesses can afford them. Pretty soon, you'll be telling me I ought to buy one of those funny horseless carriages I've heard about, to haul stuff around."

"Well, someday maybe you will! Have you seen one yet? I haven't."

Sage shook his head. "I've only seen drawings of them so far. It will be an exciting day when one comes to this town, let me tell you. I guess horses are scared to death of them, so they are quite dangerous to have around. Although folks complain about the contraptions because of the disturbance they cause, they say it's the coming thing for the future."

"Well, I'll have to see it to believe it! And frankly, I hope they never replace the horse," stated Amber. "I can't imagine a world without horses."

"Me either," answered Sage. His gaze met and held hers momentarily, then dropped back to the plans spread between them. He rolled the paper up and got to his feet. "I want to show you the new fire department supply catalog that just came in. The chief let me bring it home. You can help me pick out the new uniforms we want to order." He disappeared back inside the little house, where Amber could hear drawers opening and papers rustling.

She sighed. Sage's mind was always occupied with ideas and plans for the future, and she was just as excited about them as he was, but right now, she wished she could become more a part of his present! Time was fleeting. She was nineteen years old and getting older by the minute.

"How far is it to Fort Reno?" Amber inquired, as she settled back into the tufted leather buggy seat.

"About seven miles," replied Sage, slapping the reins against the fat, brown rump of his favorite horse, Pet. "I've been wanting to take you out there for a long time. That Fifth Cavalry Band is really something to hear. They play a lot of Sousa tunes. I think you'll enjoy it."

"Just getting out will be a treat. I thought spring would never come! I hate it when I can't be out of doors," said Amber. For some strange reason, she

361

really didn't feel like going any place, but turning Sage down was out of the question. With his busy schedule, it wasn't often that they had a whole afternoon to themselves.

"You look like you've been out in the sun," he commented. "Your cheeks are really rosy."

"Hmmm, that's funny, I haven't been out of the house at all."

"Do you feel all right?" Sage asked, squeezing her hand gently. "We don't have to go. We can – "

"Oh, yes," she said. "I feel fine, just a little warm. That sun really seems hot for this time of year."

"That's a real smart hat you've got on. I don't believe I've seen you wear that one before," Sage commented.

"It's Mrs. Brady's," explained Amber. "She thought I needed one with a wider brim to keep me shaded, so she let me borrow it. It is stylish, isn't it?" She ran her hand the length of the white ostrich plume along the side. "The blue ribbon on it just happened to match this blue dress of mine perfectly."

The prairie west of town was lush and green, with the smell of loam, and grasses, and wildflowers borne on a gentle wind. Pet pulled the buggy at a brisk trot over the primitive road leading west, and before long, they could see rising in the distance, the cluster of buildings and trees that was Fort Reno. Expecting a high-walled stockade, Amber was surprised to see nothing but a white picket fence surrounding the fort, giving it a peaceful, almost homey, appearance. Only when they entered the grounds did she spy the caissons and cannons stationed in strategic positions.

They found a place to tie Pet, then spread their blanket under the trees at the edge of the grassy parade ground. Other people continued to arrive until there was a good crowd scattered about the area, some with small children and picnic lunches. Amber was glad they hadn't brought food themselves – she didn't feel like eating a thing. Her thirst, however, was insatiable. She drank the small jug of water they had brought along and sent Sage to the pump several times for refills.

"Are you sure you're all right?" he asked again, laying his hand against her forehead. "You look flushed."

"I'm all right," Amber insisted, giving him a wan smile.

Finally, the troopers of the Fifth Cavalry Band filed out and took their places on the makeshift bandstand. Amber was impressed with their snappy, blue uniforms and precision movements. The music began, and for the next hour the audience thrilled to the sounds of Sousa, as well as rousing Army songs such as *She Wore a Yellow Ribbon*, and *Garryowen*. The latter always reminded Amber of General Custer and the 7th Cavalry, the ill-fated troops massacred by the Sioux and Cheyenne a short time before she was born.

Amber thoroughly enjoyed the music, but when it was over, she was quite ready to go home. "I guess I *don't* feel well," she finally admitted to Sage, as he helped her to her feet.

"What do you think it is?" he asked, concern evident in his every feature.

"I don't know. I haven't really felt well for almost a week. I kept thinking it would go away, but it hasn't."

"I knew we shouldn't have come," he said, shaking his head. He took her by the arm, walked her over to the buggy and helped her in.

Amber was silent most of the way home. Sage put his arm around her, and she rested her head against his shoulder, while perspiration dotted her face and soaked through her clothing. When they pulled up in front of the Brady's house, Amber raised her head, struggling to focus her eyes.

"I'm going to have Mrs. Brady put you to bed, and then I'm going to fetch Doc Meyers," said Sage, as he jumped out of the buggy. He reached up and lifted Amber to the ground.

"Thank you," she said weakly. She took one step, and the ground began to reel beneath her feet. Then a deafening roar overwhelmed her senses, and an inky darkness began crowding in on her. "I'm sorry…" she said, as she collapsed in Sage's arms.

She was riding Kickapoo at breakneck speed through total darkness. He was running away with her, racing a frantic race against a long, black train that belched dark smoke and cinders. It had to be a train – what else made such a terrible, deafening noise? Terror seized her, and she desperately tried to rein the horse in, to stop him before he fell and sent her head over heels into disaster. But her attempts were feeble and useless, and Kickapoo continued his uncontrolled, headlong flight. To where? Where was he taking her on this mad dash through nothingness?

Suddenly, the train was gone – swallowed up by the ground – and a stranger appeared, riding beside her. His horse, black as the darkness which surrounded them, matched hers stride for stride, its eyes glowing orange like fire. The grim stranger sat easily in the saddle, staring straight ahead, silent, waiting. For him there was no hurry. He had time. But then, with no warning, he reached for her arm with long, bony fingers.

But he had not reckoned with Amber's stubborn will to live.

"No! No! I won't go with you!" she cried. "I can't! I won't!" She pulled Kickapoo sharply to the left, and without warning, he plunged over a jagged precipice and into the raging river below. She felt the waters closing over her, sucking her into a gigantic whirlpool that went down, down, down, forever it seemed, to the very center of the earth itself. At the very bottom of the maelstrom, she saw little Lucy, floating face down in the water. Amber gasped and tried to turn and run, but she could not. She screamed, and the sound echoed and reverberated in ever-increasing intensity, engulfing her, threatening to smother her. Then, gradually, the sound died away into nothing but an eerie moan.

"Listen! What's that noise?" she asked fearfully, then heard Aunt Grizelda's voice, shrill and evil-sounding, "Wolves! And they're going to get you if you aren't good! Wolves like nothing better than to gobble up bad little girls like you!"

Amber recoiled, then began to struggle, to claw her way back up the steep, rocky sides of the dark, cavernous pit in which she was trapped, keeping her eye on the bright speck of light at the top. Slowly, and with great effort, she drew herself nearer and nearer, the light becoming larger and brighter with every painful step. Finally, she reached the light, a luminescence more brilliant than any she had ever imagined. She paused, absorbing the warmth, and love, and acceptance she felt emanating from it, then passed on through it.

On the other side, she discovered a valley, lush and green, with an iridescent, sparkling lake set like a jewel in the center. All around were birds, flowers, and trees unlike any she had ever seen, in colors of astonishing variety and vividness, each color re-sounding with its own special music. Amber stood there, enraptured with the beauty and tranquility of the scene, feeling a peace and contentment she had never before experienced.

At that moment, she was surrounded by happy, smiling people she had known. Joyfully, she reached out to the faces before her, but always they remained just beyond her reach. "Papa, is that you?" she asked.

"Yes. Your mama's here, too."

Her mother's form appeared before her, and Amber reached out to her as she spoke. "Your grandmas and grandpas are here, too. And Uncle Wenzel and little Lucy."

One by one, Amber gazed upon each shining countenance, all of them radiating such a serene beauty that she wanted nothing more than to stay there with them forever.

But then, it was as though she heard someone calling from a great distance, not that she heard it with her ears, nor even in her mind, but rather with her heart. It filled her with an undeniable urgency, for she realized that a part of her was missing. "I have to go back!" she said, almost frantically, and the scene before her began to dull and then fade, as she felt herself being drawn backwards. "I have something to do. . .I have to go back. . .someone needs me. . ."

Once again, she surfaced from the murky depths of unconsciousness, as she had several times before, only to slip again into the abyss of oblivion. This time, though, she stayed, grasping at fragments of reality like someone drowning, clutching for any floating object. Gradually, she became aware of a hand tenderly caressing her face, of a voice that was little more than an anguished whisper. "Don't die, my darling, don't go! I need you. . .God, I know now just how much I want you, how much I love you!"

Amber's eyelids fluttered momentarily. Slowly, she opened her eyes. It was raining outside. She could hear the gentle splash of the raindrops in the rain barrel outside the window. Sage Harmon was kneeling at her bedside, holding her hand tightly in both of his. She could feel his lips pressed against it, and the tears streaming down his face. "Sage?" Her voice was scarcely audible.

Sage looked at her incredulously, the strain of his long vigil clearly visible in his haggard features. "Amber? Oh, Amber! How do you feel, my darling? I've been so worried. . .I. . .I was afraid I was going to. . .lose you." He swallowed hard and blinked back more tears.

Amber reached up weakly and wiped the dampness from his cheeks. Her own hands appeared strange to her, so thin and white and wax-like. Surely these were not the hands that had plowed and planted, milked cows, and stopped runaway horses! "I'm okay," she whispered, giving him a brave little smile.

Sage caught up both her hands and kissed the palms, then gently caressed her face, brushing back the damp ringlets of her hair. "I think your fever has broken at last. You feel much cooler to me now. The doctor said it should break any day, but. . ." He paused. "I've been here night and day – Mrs. Brady was nice enough to let me stay – because you were out of your head most of the time – delirious. Typhoid fever is like that, you know. That's what the doctor thinks you had." He gazed at her intently. "Do you remember anything? "

Amber shook her head, then stopped abruptly. "Yes, I do think I remember waking up once, and seeing you standing at the window. You had your back to me. I called to you, but you didn't hear me. . . ." She knitted her brows thoughtfully, trying to tear away the cobwebs clinging to her memory, trying to separate fact from dream, reality from illusion.

"Most of the time, you were restless," Sage told her, "tossing and turning and crying out like a child having a nightmare. But then – it was so strange – you suddenly relaxed and became very still, and the expression on your face was. . .I can't even describe it! You were so beautiful at that moment. You were smiling, and. . ." He paused and looked away. "It reminded me of the way my mother looked, when she died in my arms."

"Don't worry any more, please. I'm going to be all right now," Amber tried to assure him.

"Thank God you're so strong-willed and stubborn." Sage paused again and smiled at her. "Amber, I love you so very much, and I need you, darling. I want to marry you, if you'll have me. I know I tend to get too wound up in my business and the fire department, but I want to share my life with you. I think we could build a good life together, I really do." His eyes probed hers, and words were no longer necessary.

Amber lost herself in the depths of his eyes, feeling a sudden surge of overwhelming joy within her. She reached up, encircling his neck with both arms, and they clung together for a timeless moment.

"Will you marry me?" Sage whispered in her ear.

"Oh, yes," Amber murmured. She fell back onto her pillow and smiled up at him happily, her heart singing with joy.

Sage glanced past her for a moment, almost overcome with emotion. "The rain has stopped," he said quietly.

Amber listened carefully. There was stillness, silence, and then a new sound. Through the open window, she heard a meadowlark calling.